-4

12/16

W9-BDI-286

The Butcher Bird

The Butcher Bird

S D Sykes

HODDER &
STOUGHTON

First published in Great Britain in 2015 by Hodder & Stoughton
An Hachette UK company

1

A CIP catalogue record for this title is available from the British Library.

Hardback ISBN 978 1 444 78581 4
eBook ISBN 978 1 444 78580 7

Typeset by HewerText UK Ltd, Edinburgh
Printed and bound by CPI Group (UK) Ltd, Croydon, CR0 4YY

Hodder & Stoughton policy is to use papers that are natural, renewable
and recyclable products and made from wood grown in sustainable forests.
The logging and manufacturing processes are expected to conform to
the environmental regulations of the country of origin.

Hodder & Stoughton Ltd
Carmelite House
50 Victoria Embankment
London EC4Y 0DZ

www.hodder.co.uk

For Natalie and Adam

The Black Death of 1348–50 killed an estimated half of the English population. With so many dead, the poorest people could suddenly demand higher pay rates for their labour. The response of the king was a law to suppress wages:

> 'The King to the Sheriff of Kent, greeting. Since a great part of the population, and especially workers and servants, has now died in this pestilence, many people, seeing the needs of their masters and the shortage of employees, are refusing to work unless they are paid an excessive salary. Others prefer to beg in idleness rather than work for their living. Mindful of the serious inconvenience likely to arise from this shortage, especially of agricultural labourers, we have discussed and considered the matter with our prelates and nobles and the other learned men, and with their unanimous advice, we have ordained that every man or woman in our realm of England, whether free or unfree, who is physically fit and below the age of sixty .... should be paid only the fees, liveries, payments or salaries which were usually paid in the part of the country where they are working in the twentieth year of our reign (1346).'

> 'The Ordinance of Labourers' (letter from King Edward III to the Sheriff of Kent. June 1349)

This ruling was endorsed and strengthened by Parliament in 1351 to form 'The Statute of Labourers'.

THE RED-BACKED SHRIKE
Lanius collurio

Once a common migratory visitor to the British shores, this bird butchers rodents, insects and the nestlings of other small birds, and then impales their corpses on thorns, as a larder. This behaviour has earned the shrike the name 'The Butcher Bird.'

Prologue

Somershill Manor, September 1351

It was the tail end of the morning when the charges were laid before me and I would tell you I was tempted to laugh at first, for the story was nonsense. Or, at least, that is how it sounded to me. Instead I suppressed a smile and carried on. 'Shouldn't Father Luke deal with this?' I said, turning to my reeve, Featherby. 'It seems a more . . . ecclesiastical matter.' This was the first manorial court of 1351 and I had spent the last three hours imposing fines on my villagers for neglecting to plough a field, or for allowing their goats to trespass upon a neighbour's garden. After such triviality, you might expect me to have been pleased for some variety in my caseload. But I have learnt to be wary of excitement. It causes trouble.

Featherby leant towards me and made a show of whispering. 'Father Luke thought you should know about this crime, sire.' He then raised his substantial eyebrows and mouthed a word to me that I think was *affray*, though his lips moved with such exaggeration, it was impossible to know for certain.

'Tell me the story again,' I said loudly, trying to disguise my rumbling stomach. It was late morning and the rich scent of roasting duck drifted across the great hall from the kitchens. We should have finished by now.

Featherby stepped away from me to pull a trembling figure from the crowd. It was John Barrow — a man I recognised immediately, despite his torn clothes and filthy skin. Barrow was often brought before the manorial court, though not because his rents were unpaid, or because he had failed to perform some duty or other about the estate. Instead, the usual complaint against the man concerned his refusal to cease his shrill and piteous grieving. In my opinion his neighbours should have treated him with more sympathy, for he had lost his wife and three children to the Plague — but given the sneers and glowers of those about him, it seemed he had once again tried the village's patience.

Featherby shook the miserable man. 'Tell Lord Somershill what you've done now. Go on. He wants to hear it from your own lips.' Barrow's response was merely the emission of a strange swallowing noise that both began and ended in his throat.

A woman with the sharp face of a weasel pushed her way through the crowd. 'He opened his wife's grave, sire. That's what he did.'

I looked to the man she accused. His skin was pale and moist with sweat. His eyes as veined as a blood orange. 'Is this true?' I said, but he didn't answer. Instead he began to pant like an overheated dog — a condition not assisted by the crowd that drew ever closer about him.

'Stand back,' I told them. The morning was cold, but their bodies exuded a nervous heat that hung in a low fug across the chamber. They drew back with some reluctance.

I leant in close to Barrow's ear, so that the others might not hear me. 'Did you open your wife's grave?' I asked him. 'You must tell me the truth.'

He nodded but didn't speak, only continuing to make the curious gulping sounds in his throat.

'Why?' I said. '*Why* would you do such a thing?'

'It's the second time he's done it,' said the weasel-faced woman.

'We might have forgiven his sins once. But we shouldn't forgive them twice. Oh no.'

I folded my arms and glared in her direction — as fiercely as a boy of nineteen might. 'Are you the judge here?' I asked her.

She looked to the floor. 'No, sire.'

'Then keep your opinions to yourself.'

I turned once again to John Barrow. Now that the surging mob had backed away, he stood alone in the reeds of the floor seeming as unsteady as a newly born calf. 'I ask you again, Master Barrow. Why did you open the grave of your dead wife?'

He wiped a ball of spittle from his mouth. 'I wanted to hold her again.'

'That wasn't all you did,' came a voice from the crowd. I couldn't see its owner, but knew it to be the same busybody as before. At her words the hall erupted with angry calls to punish the sinner.

I shouted for them to be silent, but they ignored me. And then, as I looked upon their agitated faces, I remembered an earlier time, not twelve months before, when I had witnessed another frenzied crowd such as this burn a boy to death.

With this memory soldering my nerve, I raised my voice to a new level. 'Enough,' I bellowed. 'Or I'll fine you for disorder.' For a while they were subdued, allowing me to turn my attentions back to Barrow. I took his hand, hoping that some kindness might calm him. 'Please, Barrow. Just tell me the truth.'

His fingers were hard to the touch and as cold as the icy stream. His voice a thin, rasping trickle. 'I had a dream. There was a fiend. A demon. It told me to return to my wife's grave.'

'And did you?' The faces were once again drawing in about me. He nodded. 'Yes.'

My stomach sank. 'But why?'

'The demon told me I had begot a child upon her.'

I dropped his hand sharply. 'You cannot beget a child upon a corpse, you fool!'

Barrow caught my arm, his fingers now claws. 'But it wasn't a child, sire.' He pulled me closer – close enough for me to catch his sour, feverish stink. 'I heard a scratching from within the coffin.'

'Don't lie,' I said.

'I lifted the lid,' he whispered, digging his nails into my sleeve. 'But I should have left it shut. I should have left the creature in there.'

'What creature?'

'It was a monstrous bird. With great talons and a huge hooked beak.'

'This is nonsense,' I said, pushing the man away.

Barrow covered his face, his words now seeping through tear-stained hands. 'I saw the creature fly away into the night.' He collapsed into the reeds, weeping pitifully. The crowd drew back, calling him both a sinner and a devil. But as I watched Barrow shudder and convulse upon the floor, my disgust at his story slowly turned to sympathy. It was not sin that had spawned this delusion. It was madness.

Featherby coughed. 'What should we do with him, sire?'

I didn't answer.

'Shall I bolt him into the pillory?' he whispered. Loudly. 'I'm sure a night in the cage would sort him out.'

I took a deep breath. 'No.'

Featherby sighed with disappointment. 'Are you sure?'

I looked my reeve squarely in the eye. 'I said so, didn't I?'

'But he sired a monstrous bird,' came weasel-face's voice. 'You can't let such a thing live.'

'I told you to be quiet before,' I said. 'I won't say it again.'

But still she didn't listen. 'You should torture Barrow, sire. Make him tell us where the bird is!' This idea caught hold, and once again the fever erupted. How easily reason is destroyed by fear. They shouted and waved at me, hopping up and down as if the floor were a skillet of boiling resin.

'He wants the bird to take our children, because his own are dead,' came one voice.

'It's a butcher bird,' said another.

'Hang the man,' said a third.

Now I roared with such force they could do nothing but fall silent. 'Go home!' I told them. 'The manorial court is closed.'

Slowly they dispersed, but not Featherby. He sidled up beside me. 'What of John Barrow?'

'Lock him in the gaol house for the night. Let his madness wane.' Then I pointed at weasel-face. 'And put her in there with him.'

Chapter One

Versey Castle is never colder than in March, when the winter winds have frozen its walls since All Hallows and the milky sun is still too weak to disperse the vapours from the river.

It was not an auspicious month in which to give birth, but my older sister Clemence was heavy with child and supposedly in her confinement. Lying in bed, however, did not suit my sister. Instead she wandered the orchards, or even groomed her unpleasant horse in its stable – always in the face of firm opposition from Mother and her physician. Eventually, to provide some relief from this badgering, Clemence had written to me at Somershill and begged for my company at Versey until the child was born. This was a request I had found difficult to refuse, since Clemence's husband was dead and she had nobody to turn to but myself. It was not even that the man had died, which would have been poor fortune enough for a woman expecting a child. Instead he had been murdered only days after their wedding – surviving long enough to assault my sister and conceive the child that she now carried. The wheel of fortune had not turned in Clemence's favour for many months, so I could no longer allow her to face its cruel momenta alone.

And Clemence was glad of my company.

At least I think she was.

*   *   *

Soon after my arrival, I persuaded my sister to walk with me one morning in the hours before Mother usually rose from bed. I needed to speak with her on a delicate subject – on a topic I had been avoiding for months. As we walked through the meadow, Clemence gripped my hand and stepped with care through the grass, the weight of her belly threatening to unbalance her at any moment. 'My ankles have swollen to the size of old Eleanor's,' she told me as we made our way towards a favourite seat beneath the oaks.

'Perhaps you would be better to rest, Clemence? Raise your feet above your head.'

She grimaced. 'Not you as well, Oswald? Mother has done nothing but pester me about resting with my feet in the air.'

'She gave birth to nine children. That must qualify her to have an opinion?'

'She doesn't know everything.' Clemence then held her side and groaned. 'He's kicking his foot into my ribs. Such an energetic boy.'

'He?'

She turned to me sharply. 'Yes. It's a boy. And before you say another word, there's nothing wrong with him. Despite what Mother's been saying.'

I took her small hand again. 'Of course there isn't.' But I wished I had felt more confidence in this statement, for Clemence was carrying a large child that was already two weeks overdue, according to the midwife's calculation. My knowledge of childbirth was poor, but it was sufficient to know that a late birth was more likely to end badly. We sat on the stone bench that looked down the valley towards the castle. Before us the silver catkins perched on the willow like a host of tiny rabbit tails, and the first of the Lent lilies peeked their yellow heads through the grass and nodded in the wind. In the distance, the two young de Caburn sisters, now Clemence's stepdaughters, ran into the woods, pursuing some of their usual mischief. We watched their blonde heads bob through the meadow and then disappear into the trees.

For a moment spring was in the air and I felt all the hope and promise of the turning season, but then I saw Gilbert riding over the drawbridge into the castle. He was my valet from Somershill and there was something unlikely and even ominous in his presence here. I should have returned then to greet him, but as Clemence launched into the next conversation the thought soon slipped from my mind.

She coughed. 'When my son is born, will you keep your promise to me?'

I was tired after a succession of poor nights' sleep, so it took me a few moments to fathom what she was talking about. Unfortunately Clemence read this hesitation as evasion. 'I knew I couldn't trust you,' she said, clapping her hands upon her thighs. 'You mean to keep Versey as well as Somershill.'

'No, I don't,' I said, now understanding her original question. I had once made a rash promise to my sister, just after her husband's murder. Unfortunately I could not be certain that it was now in my power to keep it. 'It's not entirely my decision. Remember? The earl instructed me to take over this estate.' She shrugged, seeming to have forgotten that I had not asked for the wooded hills and poor land of Versey. This castle was cold and grey with only the sky and a wide river for company. She could keep the dreary place as far as I was concerned.

'But what about my son?' she said. 'He's a true de Caburn. Why should he be cheated out of his birthright?'

'I'm not trying to cheat him.'

'Then speak to the earl on his behalf.'

'I promise to try. When the opportunity arises.'

She snorted and pulled a strand of black hair from her face. 'You promise?'

'Yes, Clemence. I do. Even if your child turns out to be a girl.'

She stroked her expansive belly and looked at me with a drop of the malevolence of old. 'It will be a son.'

I touched her shoulder. Feeling the soft fur of her miniver cloak. 'I hope so, Clemence. If that's what matters to you.'

She sighed. 'You think me cruel? That I don't care for my own sex?'

'No. It's just that all of your dead husband's children have been girls. Maybe you should prepare yourself for a daughter?'

She shrugged me away. 'What use is there in being a woman in this world, Oswald? Look how I've fared, compared to you.'

I took her meaning well enough. 'I didn't want any of this, Clemence.'

'But it came to you anyway.'

In the distance we could hear Mother calling for us and suddenly I remembered the reason for persuading my sister to walk with me so far from the castle. 'Listen, Clemence. There's something I want to tell you,' I said. 'Before Mother finds us.'

She turned to look at my face, her eyes suddenly wary. 'Oh yes?'

I took a deep breath, for this was not the easiest of confessions. 'I went to the graveyard to look for Thomas Starvecrow's grave.'

'Who?'

I puffed my lips in frustration. Was she being deliberately dull-witted? 'You know who I'm talking about. *Thomas Starvecrow.*' At the repeat of this singular name, a shadow crossed her face. She knew the name. We both did.

They say that truth can sometimes be stranger than invention, and in this case the adage held true – for the previous summer I had discovered that I was not really Oswald de Lacy at all. That boy had been buried in a grave marked Thomas Starvecrow, after his death in infancy.

So who was I then? If not Oswald de Lacy? Lord Somershill.

Thomas Starvecrow, of course. No grander than the son of a poor girl who had been employed as a wet nurse to the latest de Lacy infant. Her name was Adeline Starvecrow, and though she had managed to feed two infants, there had been a divergence in our fortunes. Whereas I had thrived, this boy had faded – and when he had died at eight weeks, Adeline had substituted me, her own son, for him. I don't believe there was evil or ambition in her act; she had simply feared being blamed for the death of a noble child.

So why, you might ask, when this secret was revealed, had I not been thrown into the streets? My mother (or the woman I had grown up to believe was my mother – Lady Margaret of Somershill) had always known of the deceit. After giving birth to nine children, with only three surviving to adulthood, she had not wanted to risk another confinement – so she had chosen to ignore the slipping of this cuckoo into her nest. In any case, I was the last son. The third spare. Nobody more important than that.

There were only three people now alive who knew this secret. Myself, Clemence, and Mother. It was obvious why I kept quiet – but for Clemence and Mother it was a practical decision. With my older brothers dead, there was no other male heir, and at least I bore the de Lacy name, even if their blood did not flow in my veins. In any case, any revelation about my true beginnings would bring great shame and notoriety to the family. It was expedient for all three of us to say nothing.

Clemence shifted from one buttock to another – the weight of her unborn child causing her some pain. 'Why would you bother looking for Thomas Starvecrow's grave?' she asked.

'I wanted to put the boy's coffin in our family crypt,' I admitted. 'He was a true de Lacy, after all.'

Her face hardened into a scowl. 'You should leave such matters alone,' she said. 'My brother died as a baby and you took his place. You shouldn't be messing around with his coffin.'

Suddenly we saw Mother beating her way through the grass towards us, with all the vigour of a child with an urgent tale to tell. Our time alone was limited.

'But there is more to my story, Clemence,' I said. 'Please listen to me.'

Instead she held out her hand so I might help her from the seat.

When I refused, she heaved a wearied sigh. 'What is it, Oswald? Please be quick. I want to get away from Mother as soon as I can. She's trying to feed me one of de Waart's purgatives to induce labour.'

I felt my stomach roll. 'Don't take anything that man prescribes.'

Clemence waved her hand. 'Just get on with your story.'

I hesitated. The words rested on my tongue, but what an admission they held, and Mother was now within yards of us.

'Be quick, Oswald,' she urged.

'I opened the lid of the coffin.'

My sister screwed up her face in disgust. 'God's nails, Oswald. Why did you do such a thing?'

'I don't know exactly.' Now she rolled her eyes. My sister always thought me so foolish. Lacking the pedigree to be lord. 'I was curious,' I told her boldly.

'Why?'

My tongue felt tied. 'I just was.' She smiled at my discomfort. 'I was right to look.' I insisted, dropping my voice to a whisper. 'There was no body inside the coffin.'

Now Clemence reddened. 'Are you sure?'

'There was nothing inside but a wooden effigy. The small Christ child that had been stolen from St Giles.'

She put her hand to her mouth. 'So where is the body then?'

'I don't know.'

It was too late. Mother fell beside me on the bench, panting and wheezing like a wool dyer beside a tub of steaming mordant. When she recovered her breath, she turned to my sister and scowled. 'What are you doing out here, Clemence? Your humours will be assaulted by this cold air.'

'I'm perfectly well,' said Clemence.

Mother shook her head in despair. 'With this constant insistence on wandering around outside, I shouldn't be surprised if you don't give birth to a little snowball. A child made of ice.'

'Don't be so absurd. I'm wearing a cape. My son is quite warm enough inside me.'

Mother smirked. 'Too warm if you ask me. That child is over-cooked. It should have been born weeks ago.'

My sister's face was beginning to sour. Her small hands tightening into fists. 'Make up your mind Mother,' she said. 'Is my child too hot or too cold?'

I quickly intervened. 'There's no hurry for the child to be born. It's still healthy and moving.'

Mother scoffed. 'What on earth do you know about such matters, Oswald? You were educated in a monastery. Did a monk ever give birth?' I shrugged by way of reply. 'No. Exactly. You are quite unacquainted with the workings of a woman's body.'

'I know more than that fool who claims to be your physician,' I said. 'I hear he's still in the castle.'

'Hush, Oswald. I am a great admirer of Master de Waart. Would you have me suffer without his care?'

'It's his care that's causing your suffering.' I said. 'I don't know why you employ him.'

'To calm my nerves, of course. Versey is a very disquieting place. It doesn't suit my temperament at all.'

Clemence coughed pointedly. 'What is it that you wanted, Mother?'

'You must return to the house. It's time for your purgative.'

Clemence groaned, but Mother ignored this response and turned to me, prodding a finger into my arm. 'And you need to attend to this murder, Oswald.'

'What murder?'

'The murder I've just told you about.'

'You haven't said a word about a murder.'

She wrinkled her nose. 'Are you sure? Gilbert brought the news from Somershill.'

I stood up. 'Where's Gilbert now?'

'In the kitchen, I suppose,' said Mother with a note of

irritation in her voice. 'That's where servants are normally to be found.'

The kitchen at Versey is perhaps the only pleasant room in the castle. The scent from the bread ovens drifts through the air and warms the nostrils. The heat is dry and comforting – a reminder of happier times.

I found Gilbert sitting next to Clemence's servant John Slow in a smoky corner. Gilbert was resting on a wooden stool, whereas Slow, a man who mistrusted furniture, had taken up his usual position on the stone floor. The two servants spoke in a low mumble, on a topic that must have been fascinating, as they failed to look up when I sped into the room.

It was Slow who noticed my presence first. He nudged Gilbert's leg in a panic and struggled to his feet. 'I'm sorry, sire. We didn't see you there.' Then he flinched – crouching and holding his head in his hands, as if I were about to strike him. This was Slow's usual reaction to me, though I had never assaulted the man.

'Please leave us,' I said. 'I need to speak with Gilbert.' Slow backed away from me, bowing as obsequiously as a penitent leaving the presence of the Holy Father, but when the man considered himself out of my sight, he bolted away in his strange gait, rocking from foot to foot like a man upon a hobby horse. On reaching the kitchen door he rested against the door frame and took a deep breath, seemingly under the impression that he had avoided the punishment that Gilbert was now certain to receive.

Gilbert's reaction to me could hardly have been more different. Though I was his master, he took time to wipe the crumbs from his mouth before lethargically getting to his feet. 'Sire?'

I should have reprimanded him in some way, but Mother's story was more pressing. 'I hear you have some news from Somershill? There's been a murder. Is that correct?'

He sighed and nodded, but still did not say a word.

'Come on, Gilbert,' I said. 'I'm a busy man.' This was not

entirely true – since I was neither that occupied and not yet considered a man – but his indolence was provoking.

'A child has been found dead, sire. Murdered.' He clasped his hands together as if he were about to pray.

'Who is it?'

'A newborn girl. Only just baptised.' He then held his nose between his thumb and forefinger, and suddenly I realised that he was trying to suppress a sob. Small tears leaked from the rims of his eyes.

'You say she was murdered?' He nodded. 'Can you tell me her name?'

He composed himself and blew his nose. It was strange to see my valet so affected, as the man was usually no more sentimental than a storm cock smacking a snail against a stone. 'She was the daughter of Thomas Tulley, sire. They named her Catherine.'

'Are you sure she was murdered?'

His shoulders shuddered. 'She was——' But he was unable to finish the sentence. Instead he slumped back down upon the stool and hung his head. A couple of the scullions gathered to look upon him, whispering in wonderment at the man who usually scolded them for a dirty pan or poorly plucked bird. I shooed them away with the command to fetch ale.

The ale was warm and frothy and tasted of bread dough with the bitter aftertaste of dandelion leaves.

Gilbert drank his down promptly. 'I'm sorry, sire.' He blew his nose once again upon his sleeve. 'I don't usually become so affected. It's just what happened to her body.'

'What do you mean?'

'She was left in a bush of blackthorn. Her skin pierced by the spurs and thorns.'

I felt a dismal churning in my stomach. 'Do you know who's responsible?'

'It's not a mystery. That's why you are needed back at Somershill. The whole village is in uproar.'

'Then who is it?'

I'm disappointed to say that a smile began to curl at the corner of his mouth. His tears now washed away by the mug of ale. 'Which creature kills other nestlings and stores them upon the thorns of a tree?'

'I'm in no mood for riddles, Gilbert.'

He put the mug upon a nearby table and stood up. He was no taller than me, but his frame was solid and thick, like a seasoned oak. 'It was a bird, sire. A butcher bird.'

I looked him over. Was he being sincere? It was so difficult to read his weathered face. The sun and wind had worn away its nuances. 'The shrike is a small bird, Gilbert. It couldn't lift an infant from its crib. Not even a newborn infant. It only attacks—' And then I stopped myself, realising what Gilbert had really meant. 'John Barrow did not beget a bird,' I said.

My valet raised his eyebrows, and then wiped away a bead of mucus from his nose. 'But he said he did. I heard it myself only four weeks ago. At the last court.'

'The man is ill.'

'Maybe so. But he'll be dead soon.'

'What do you mean by that?' I snapped.

'They'll hang him, when they find him.'

I groaned. 'Go to the stables and prepare Tempest.'

He straightened his tunic and then bowed to me, though I would say this gesture was no better than half-hearted. 'Very well, sire. Are you riding back to Somershill straight away?' he asked me.

'Of course I am.' He trudged out of the chamber, grumbling under his breath like a starved stomach. 'And be quick about it,' I added.

He pretended not to hear.

Chapter Two

I rode to Somershill at speed, since I would not allow the village to set upon John Barrow like a pack of dogs. For once the forest floor was frozen and a horse moves quickly, if not comfortably, along hard ground. I was thankful for these conditions, since it had rained so often in the last two years that the paths were often quagmires. And I was not alone on these favourable tracks. Bands of people passed me, moving from one place to another, their carts laden with benches and stools. Their livestock trailing alongside them like a troupe of wearied players. More than once, chickens or geese strayed across my path and disturbed Tempest with their squawking and fluttering, before they were rounded up by a child and chased back into their wicker cages.

These travellers were not the ragged fugitives of the Plague years however – those people who had tried to flee its grasping fingers. They were well dressed in the main, with leather boots and fur-lined cloaks. Even the children wore shoes. But beneath these clothes were skeletal bodies that moved with the lethargy and downcast eyes of an overworked donkey. They had inherited or acquired the trappings of wealth, but lacked the food to feed a hungry stomach. Sometimes they asked me for alms, or even a crust of bread. But once I had emptied my purse and given away all of my food, they stopped bothering me and I rode on in haste past their silent faces.

*   *   *

On reaching my home, I found the main street of Somershill village to be deserted – the only sound that met my ears was the shrill call of a robin that disliked my proximity to his tree. I rode on, passing the larger cottages along this street, where those families who had survived the Plague were now taking advantage of the cheaper tenancies on offer. Roofs had been re-thatched. Hedges cut down. Ditches cleared of brambles and dock. And in the fields, where previously a family had toiled to grow a subsistence of barley and turnips, there were now flocks of sheep. Their woollen coats dotted across the grass like the tufted heads of cotton sedge.

My first call was the home of John Barrow, though the likelihood of the man still being behind his own door was small. Sure enough, my knocking was met with silence. I pushed open the flimsy wooden door to find that the chamber had been ransacked. A table lay on its side. The charcoal of the fire pit was kicked about the floor. A straw mattress had even been pulled to pieces, as if somebody had expected to find Barrow hiding in his own bedclothes. There was little else to see in this sad and pathetic place. Barrow was clearly not a man making the most of the new times. From the look of his home, it seemed he was intent upon hiding away in this stinking place until the end of his life.

I left quickly, pleased of the light and air outside, to find a freckle-faced youth staring at my horse.

'Keep away,' I said quickly. 'My horse doesn't like children.' This was true. Their ears were just at the right height for him to bite. They flew further when he kicked them.

I took the boy by his skinny arm and led him out of Tempest's range, for I could now see more of my horse's teeth than I cared to. 'Where's John Barrow?' I asked.

The boy's face lightened. 'He's run away, sire. After his bird killed baby Catherine.'

I was dismayed to discover that this lie was now being repeated by the grubbiest of urchins. 'Is everybody hunting for him?'

He nodded enthusiastically. 'Oh yes, sire. They're going to bring Barrow back to the village and force him to say where his bird is hiding.' A plug of yellow mucus had formed in the boy's nostril and was bubbling in and out of the cavity as he spoke. 'And when he's told them, they're going to hang him.'

I fixed on his eyes and ignored his nose. 'Which direction did they go in?'

The mucus had now escaped the boy's nostril and was descending onto his upper lip like a yellow slug. 'They went in all directions. To every corner of the estate.'

I could almost have growled with frustration. There was no chance I could stop a search party that had scattered so widely. It was better to wait here, and intervene once they had dragged Barrow back to the village. I suddenly felt hungry and exhausted.

The boy looked at me warily. 'Are you unwell, sire?'

'Of course not,' I said. And then, before he could ask after my health again, I dismissed him with the wave I had been practising. The merest flick of my fingers, flavoured with a pinch of ennui. Such behaviour was not in my true nature, but since inheriting this estate I had discovered such condescending gestures were expected of me, and this wave of my hand certainly had the desired effect upon the boy. He bolted away as if I had threatened to stab him with the trident of Poseidon.

Now alone, I stood in the street for a while, but the cold air crept through the weave of my tunic and threatened a full assault upon my skin. I couldn't risk going back to my home in case I missed the returning party, but equally I could not stay here. I dithered for a while, before deciding to call upon my tenant Joan Bath. She, at least, would not be part of this senseless mob.

Joan had taken over the tenancy of her father's cottage the previous July, after the old man had died suddenly. Previously this home had been little more than a dirty hovel, and I had been reluctant to visit. Flies had circled the chamber like winged imps, and it had been difficult to find a clear patch of floor to stand upon, such was the confusion of old boots, broken tools, and animal bones scattered about the place. But, as Joan opened the door and welcomed me inside, I saw an altogether different home. Clear of her father's debris, the cottage could almost be described as comfortable. A polished oak table extended against the length of one wall, and a blackened cauldron hung over the fire, which was lit. Nevertheless, the chamber smelt pleasant, and was not overly choked with smoky fumes.

Joan ushered me to a bench beside the table and set down a cup of ale – her manner as brusque as ever. You might think she was entertaining a friend of her son's or even a passing peddler. 'What are you doing here then?' she asked. 'I don't see you very often these days.'

I sipped the malty ale. 'I'm waiting to stop a hanging.'

'John Barrow?'

I nodded. 'The fools in the village say he's hiding a murderous bird.' I snorted. 'They're calling it a butcher bird.'

Before I could say any more, she put her finger to her mouth. Walking behind the wooden screen that separated the cottage into two chambers, she chased out her two young sons. They dashed through the door, with instructions from their mother to count the family's sheep. Once Joan was certain they were not still hanging around, she drew a stool up beside me, giving me a chance to study her face at close range. It was as severe as when I had first met her, though perhaps there was a little more fat on her cheeks? Her long black hair was no longer loose about her neck – now it was held behind a modest veil that also covered her neck and chin. Some said she only sold sheep these days, though others claimed that sheep were nothing more than a front for her other business. The profession that had kept food on her table for the years before the Plague. For those people a whore would always be a whore, no matter how hard she might work to become somebody else.

For my part, I didn't care what she did to make a living. Joan paid her rent on time, her sons performed their duties on the demesne, and there was never any cause to fine her in the manorial court. She was a successful woman, which was probably the main complaint against her. I noted an embroidered wall hanging in the second chamber, and a crusader chest, carved from oak and wrapped in iron bands. Not an item of furniture owned by most people in this village.

She took a gulp of her own ale. 'You sure Barrow's innocent?'

'Of course I am. How could a man sire a murdering bird with his dead wife?'

She slowly wiped the froth from her top lip. 'I didn't mean that part of the story. You sure he didn't kill the baby himself?'

This possibility hadn't occurred to me. 'Why would he do that?'

'The man struggles with the loss of his wife and children to the Pestilence.' She heaved a sigh and stretched her back. 'But I don't suppose his howling reaches you at the manor house.' I pulled a face. This was the usual accusation thrown at me when I refused to fine Barrow for his nightly caterwauling. 'He keeps the whole village awake with his lamentations,' she said. 'With cries so cold and empty. Who knows what malice lies in his heart?'

'But would he kill another man's child and push her body into a bush? I don't believe so. He might be mad, but not demonic.'

'So who did it then? A demon?'

'Of course not.' I sat up straight to give her the impression that I meant my words. 'I intend to find out.'

She raised an eyebrow. 'Shouldn't the constable investigate?'

I thought of our new constable. A lazy incompetent who didn't care to travel to Somershill from Tonbridge unless the weather was fine and he was served roasted meat at our table. 'No. I'll take care of this. It's too delicate to leave to the constable. I can report the case to the next Hundreds court myself.'

She regarded me for a few moments. 'Are you sure that's wise?'

I felt myself redden. 'Are you doubting my capabilities, Mistress Bath?'

'No. Of course not.' I wasn't convinced. Joan poked a strand of hair back beneath her veil. 'Barrow did open his wife's grave, you know.'

'Which only proves his madness.'

She nodded thoughtfully at this, and then took another long slurp of the beer. 'I expect you're right. I can't see him as a murderer. The man has always been kind enough to me.' I wondered whether she was implying that John Barrow used to be one of her clients, but decided not to ask. 'But he has no friends in this village,' she said. 'If they can find him, they will kill him.'

'That's why I'm waiting here to stop them.'

She laughed into her mug of ale. It made a scornful sound. 'You didn't stop them last time. When they burned my son to death.'

I took a deep breath. 'I know.'

She laid a hand upon mine, with fingers that were long and delicate, and nails that were pink and clean. These were not the usual hands of a peasant woman, and did not match the masculinity of her face. 'At least you tried to stop them.' She squeezed my hand a little. 'Nobody else did.'

I wished she had not said this. I did not want to talk about the burning. I did not even want to think about it. It was the reason I avoided Joan, for her face stoked painful memories – abhorrent recollections that I tried to cast from my mind. Now, as I looked into her eyes, these memories ignited before me like a wall of flames, and would not be extinguished. Suddenly I was running towards the pyre beside the church. I pushed aside the crowd to see a great ox burning upon the fire. The heat was ferocious. There was a stink of burning flesh, and strange noises came from within the neck of the beast. When I asked the gawpers about me to explain what was causing these pitiful wails, they boasted that they had sewn a sinner inside the ox. Alive. They wanted to hear him scream for forgiveness as he burned.

I can never forget what happened next. For this piece of the story is seared into my mind more deeply than any other. Its scar is still raw and will not heal.

I dragged the burning ox from the flames and threw water over its singed flesh. I cut open the carcass to release what they had sewn inside. It was a boy called Leofwin. A disfigured outcast who lived in the forest. I cradled his poor scalded body and tried to squeeze the life back into his lungs. But I failed. For he had died. In my arms. A withered thing. A victim of their pitiless ignorance.

Joan stared into her ale. 'They called Leofwin a sinner, but he was just an innocent boy. My son. And what was his crime?' She laughed once more into her ale. Now it was not a scornful sound. Instead it was melancholy. 'To be born with the wrong face.'

I took a gulp of my ale. I knew not to dwell on this episode for too long, or the nightmares would start again, waking me in the dark hours with their taunts. They had faded a little in their frequency of late, but they still found me, some nights, and the dream was always the same. I reached the pyre earlier. I was more masterful with the crowd. I pulled the ox more rapidly from the flames. But it didn't matter how quickly I acted, or how loudly I shouted, for Leofwin always died.

We sat in silence for a while, and then, just as if we needed a cheering diversion, a butterfly landed upon the table and opened its wings – its red and white markings a flash of colour against the grey of the cottage. 'It's early in the year to see a butterfly,' I remarked, trying to cup it in my hands before it flew away into the gloom of the roof timbers.

'They roost in the eaves over winter. I see them all the time.'

'Better than the flies that used to live here.'

She smiled at this comment and went to the barrel to bring us more ale. We no longer wanted to speak of Leofwin. Neither of us. 'So. How is it to be a lord?' she said as she set the mugs of ale upon the table in front of me. 'Do you like it?'

How easy it would have been to grumble about the role I had

inherited. Had my true mother not passed me off as a de Lacy, then I would have grown up as a Starvecrow – digging fields and droving sheep. If my de Lacy brothers had not died of the Pestilence, then I would be a Benedictine. A nineteen-year-old boy, devoted to a life of prayer and abstinence.

'You will have problems with the men over wages,' Joan suddenly announced. 'I've heard them talking about it.'

I groaned. This was currently a favourite complaint about the village, and I felt no more inclined to discuss the matter with Joan Bath than I did with my reeve – particularly as Featherby brought up the subject at every single one of our meetings. 'What am I supposed to do?' I said, 'Break the law?'

'You could think about it?'

I frowned at such an idea. 'I can't.' I took another gulp of beer. 'There have to be rules.'

'Why?'

'Because . . .' I scratched my head, trying desperately to remember the words of the earl's steward, Hatcher. A man who regularly pored over my accounts to ensure I was paying my dues. 'If the labourers are able to demand their own rates of pay, then there will be chaos.'

Joan raised both eyebrows. 'But you have only half the men you used to have. The Plague killed the other half. Why should your remaining men not charge more? Especially when you expect them to do twice the work.'

'Because . . .' I hesitated. In truth, I could not think how to end this sentence.

Joan gave another of her loud snorts. 'Well you certainly can't expect men to work for the same wages as they did in 1346. This is 1351, and the world has changed.'

'Did I ask for your opinion?'

She whipped my mug away, though I had not finished drinking. 'No. But I gave it to you anyway.' She smiled deviously. 'There's no charge.'

Another piece of advice. Another helpful word in my ear. Did everybody believe that I needed to hear their opinions? Was I so young and foolish that I could not make my own decisions? Joan had annoyed me, so I stood up to leave. 'Good day.'

I strode with some irritation towards the door, but as I reached the threshold she quickly ran from her seat and stood in my way. Her face had changed – more fluid and gentle than I had ever seen it. 'These are dangerous times, Oswald.' Then she took my hand in her own again and pressed it tenderly. 'You must take care.'

She only wanted to help me. I can see that now. At the time, however, I didn't want to listen, for she had pricked at my boyish pride. 'Where do the Tulleys live?' I asked her, shaking her hand from mine.

She stiffened. Her face once again turned to stone. 'They're your villeins. You should know that already.'

She was correct, which only served to needle me further. 'Just tell me.'

'The Tulleys live in the third cottage in the Long Ditch.'

As I mounted Tempest, Joan leant against her doorpost and watched me leave. I felt scrutinised. Judged. I quickly turned from her, but as I cantered away, she shouted after me. 'Don't expect the Tulleys to welcome your interest in their dead daughter. Thomas Tulley speaks the most loudly against you.'

Chapter Three

I headed for St Giles, where a track from the churchyard led along an overgrown hedge towards an area of the village known as the Long Ditch. It was a collection of the poorest buildings on the estate and home to the lowest villeins, since few tenants would choose to rent such inferior plots. Most of these homes were now deserted as their owners, by virtue of living in the close conditions of a rabbit warren, had been easily picked off by the Plague. Many of the dogged survivors had taken the opportunity to move into larger, vacant properties away from the Long Ditch, in return for providing more services on the demesne. But not so Thomas Tulley. He kept to his quarter-virgate of land in a field behind his cottage. At the last manorial court I had been forced to fine him for refusing to plough my fields as is the customary terms of his tenancy. Since the Plague, he had become emboldened to regularly speak his mind, urging others to follow him. He demanded an end to those duties he performed for free, and better wages for those duties he was already paid for. He claimed that God did not create bondsmen nor servitude, so there was no justification for the abomination of fealty to a lord.

That was his actual word. Abomination.

As I reached the Tulley cottage that day, the unmistakeable sound of a woman crying reached me through the thin wattle and daub of the walls. The sobs were low and resigned – not the expressive wailing and weeping that Mother liked to perform, but still passionate enough to make me rethink my visit here. I did not know how to deal with tears at the best of times, but it was too late to retrace my steps. As I crossed a plank of wood over the ditch, avoiding a pile of night soil that had been newly covered with dusty earth, three small and thin faces looked around the Tulleys' door and then disappeared back inside the darkness of the cottage to alert their mother to my presence. While I waited for the woman to appear, I looked down into the ditch, noticing that the stagnant water was still sheeted with thin ice.

Mary Tulley came quickly to the door and curtsied. Her face was as gaunt as a cadaver's, her eyes red from crying. Her ragged children, three boys, hung at her legs like bats in their roost, digging their hands into her gown until she picked up the youngest child and rested him on her hip. He was a boy with blond curls and the defiant eyes of her husband.

I lowered my head to the woman, expressed sorrow at her loss, and then asked if her husband were at home.

'No, sire.' The tallest boy pulled a face at me and she chastised him in a whisper. 'Stop it Robert. This is Lord Somershill.' The boy hid his face behind the folds of her dress, only to peep around her skirts and stick out his tongue when his mother wasn't looking.

Given the circumstances of this interview, I tried to smile at this foolery, though the boy was now opening his mouth so widely to insult me that I could see the lopsided bulge of a swollen quinsy at the back of his throat.

I looked away. 'I'm sorry to intrude Mistress Tulley, but I need to ask you some questions. About Catherine.'

She moved uncomfortably from foot to foot. 'Could it wait, sire? Until Thomas is home.'

'I only need to confirm the simplest of details.' I looked over her shoulder. 'May I come in?' The cold air was dank in this shaded corner of the village and I was anxious to be inside.

'But my home is so dirty.'

I pushed past her to enter. 'It's no worry to me.' She followed me inside, moving as one entity with her children still hanging from her body. The youngest was trying to delve inside her gown and fix himself to her breast. When she dropped him to the floor, he squealed like a piglet.

'Please. Nurse the child,' I said. 'If it comforts him.' She looked uneasy, but settled herself upon a bench and bade the older children to stoke up the fire. As with every other cottage on the estate, this was a shaded and small place. The unpleasant smell of dirty swaddling and wood ash filled the room. I wondered that Thomas Tulley did not swallow his pride and move to one of the larger cottages. There were good terms on offer, if not the free status he was demanding.

I cleared my throat, as the smoke was biting. 'Can you tell me who found the body of your daughter?' I asked the woman.

She took a deep breath. 'It was a boy who lives nearby. Geoffrey Hayward.'

'When did you last see your baby?'

She suddenly sobbed. 'It was yesterday morning, sire. I fed her, put her in her cradle and then left her outside, by the door. A baby needs fresh air.'

She continued to cry, but I felt it was important to persist. 'Were you inside the cottage when she disappeared?'

Mary looked up sharply and wiped a puffy eye. 'No. We were all needed in the fields to weed. Even young Robert here.'

'Would you usually leave a newborn infant alone? I've seen other mothers bind their babies to their backs.'

My implied criticism was met with a further, even more hostile stare. 'We were only in your demesne field near the cottage.' Then she lost her nerve and looked away. 'I've always left my babies at home while I work. I thought she would be safe.'

'You saw nobody come or go to the house?'

'No.'

'And how long were you away?'

'As long as it takes to weed one of your fields, sire.'

I took her meaning well enough. Perhaps there was more than one agitator in this household? 'Where is Catherine's body now?' I said.

Mary took a deep breath. 'What do you mean, sire?'

'Has the infant been buried yet?'

Her bottom lip began to quiver. 'No.'

'Where is her body then?'

Mary Tulley dropped the child that she was nursing to the floor, where he sat on the dirty reeds looking wholly appalled at the interruption to his meal. Sensing the boy was about to roar, I took Mary by the arm and led her to the door of the cottage, where a fresh and cold draught of air blew the oily hair from her head, revealing patches of bare skin across her scalp. 'I would like to see the infant before you bury her,' I said.

I could see she was thinking about shaking me off, but didn't have the nerve. 'But why, sire? I don't want Catherine messed about with. She's with God now.' As her hot tears steamed in the cool of the air, I found myself guessing the age of this woman – if indeed she was a woman, and not still a girl? She might be not much more than twenty. It was difficult to tell if her blue eyes had ever looked out from a pretty face, as she now seemed as exhausted as a breeding bitch.

I would tell you I put my arm about her shoulder and allowed her to cry, but time was short and my compassion was neither expected nor welcome. Instead I demanded to see the child's body with an abrupt voice that was hardly recognisable as my own.

Mary wrapped her thin cloak about her body and led me towards a small shelter on the fringes of the curtilage. It was bitterly cold now in this shadowy vale and the earth was still hard in the vegetable beds about me. A bank of yellow celandine flowered along the ditch, but other than this shock of colour, the Tulleys' garden remained a desolate square of turned soil.

On reaching the shelter, I could see Tulley's selection of tools. He was also a carpenter – though he might have earned more if he hadn't wasted so much of his time giving speeches in the taverns of Somershill and Burrsfield, complaining that he was bound to the estate. We entered the shelter and Mary pulled back a rough blanket to reveal a small wooden box upon a bench.

'Thomas made the coffin himself,' she told me, pulling her hood over her head.

'Is the child inside?'

She nodded.

The box had been nailed shut in three places, and I found myself yet again questioning Thomas's reason. He had used valuable tinned nails, when he might have spared the money to buy his family some bread or better clothes. 'Pass me your husband's chisel,' I said.

She hesitated, then took the tool from a shelf and handed it over to me with a show of reluctance. 'Please don't mark the coffin, sire. Thomas used oak. He'd be angry to see it damaged.'

As the nails lifted gently and the lid began to loosen, my anticipation gave way to fear. The last time I had looked inside a coffin it had been to find the body of Thomas Starvecrow. On that occasion I had found instead a wooden effigy of the Christ child – a baleful object with blank eyes and pointed edges. This time there would be a real infant – a body that was sure to have begun putrefaction. I held my breath, for there is little in this world to exceed the stink of a decaying human body.

As the lid came away from the sides, Mary asked my permission to leave the shelter, clasping her hands tightly about her chest and rocking as if she were comforting an invisible baby. At that moment I was tempted to insist that she stay, as I had the sudden wish to study the woman's reaction to the body. But then I thought better of this scheme. The cadaver was Mary's daughter, and my idea was cruel.

Now alone, I took a deep breath before summoning the courage to look inside the coffin, finding a mass of cloth that had been rolled over and over to create a small mattress for the little girl's dead body. Putting my hands into the folds and pulling them gently apart I uncovered the baby, so tiny she could have been a corn doll. Thankfully, because of the cool winter air, there was little in the way of an unpleasant odour, only a certain staleness.

I lifted her limp body from the coffin and laid her upon the bench, next to the tools that her father had used to make her small and eternal chamber. She was naked beneath the swaddling and I could see scratches upon her skin – probably from the barbs of the blackthorn bush where she had been discovered, but nothing so cruel as the gaping punctures that had been described to me.

Mary called to me from outside. 'Please don't disturb poor Catherine, sire. I couldn't bear it.'

'I've nearly finished,' I told her, in my softest and most re-assuring voice. 'I will not desecrate her in any way.' In the distance some birds that were roosting in the bare trees made their ugly and rasping call, and suddenly I felt as vile and abhorrent as a carrion crow, jabbing at something dead for its supper.

I wrapped the baby up again in the cloth, and for the first time in many months I missed my old tutor, Brother Peter. He had been infirmarer at Kintham Abbey and could have inferred more from this wretched little corpse than I was able. But then the longing for him passed. It turned into a shadow, an unwelcome memory, and I put all thoughts of Peter out of my mind. I could only rely upon my own expertise and powers of deduction to investigate this mystery.

And Catherine's death was a mystery. There was no obvious cause of death on her body, but as I placed her back into the soft folds of cloth inside the coffin, I noticed an odd smell about the corpse. Lifting her as close to my nose as I felt able, I detected a scent. An odour that was not typical of a dead body, with its usual pungent and foul sweetness. It had a sour taint. Both acid and bitter. Both familiar, but difficult to place. But perhaps the smoking fumes of the Tulleys' cottage had ruined my sense of smell? Unable to come to any conclusion, I replaced Catherine in her fine cloth with every care I could bestow upon her small body, before turning to see that Mary Tulley was now sitting on the frosty soil with her back to me.

'I'm about to close the coffin,' I told her. 'Would you like to see your daughter again, Mistress Tulley?' She simply shook her head.

I hammered down the lid with one of Thomas's claw hammers, but missed my stroke and drove a hole into the lid, also catching the end of my finger. The blow was painful, so I cursed and held my finger to my mouth. Mary heard my words and rushed to the door to look at me fiercely, her pale cheeks inflamed with blotches of red. I think she was about to rebuke me for my clumsiness, when we were distracted by noises in the distance. Raised, excited voices, like the tumult of revellers on Lammas Day. There was an edge to their shouting that reminded me of the drunken feasts at Somershill when I was a child – the sort of celebration we would have when my father and his friends returned from the hunt with a stag, or when news reached the village that the king had defeated the French. Whenever I had sensed the imminence of such a celebration, I would lurk in the stables, or even hide under Mother's bed. But I could not hide behind furniture this time. The shouting was too intense.

The tumult came from the direction of the church – so I ran there immediately to find a crowd gathered, with Tulley at its heart. The man held John Barrow by a rope about his neck.

I pushed through. 'Let Barrow go.' But Tulley only pulled the rope tighter, causing the colour of Barrow's face to deepen to a shade of crimson. 'I order you to release him,' I shouted, but the only effect of my command was to silence the crowd. Tulley refused to drop the rope.

I gave the order a third time, but still he ignored me. And then, out of nowhere, a pair of seagulls swooped down upon us, flapping their wings about our heads, and squawking with their yellow, gaping beaks. Barrow now screamed with all the distress his constricted throat could achieve.

Stepping forward, I tried to take the rope from Tulley, but the man withdrew. 'You can't have him, sire.' Tulley pulled at the rope again and now Barrow fell upon the soil. 'His bird killed Catherine.' This elicited a small, but enthusiastic cheer from those behind him.

'Let the man go, Tulley,' I said, 'or it will be all of you on trial.' My tone must have conveyed the level of my anger, for now the crowd shuffled back like a herd of wary cows. The inconstancy of his friends did not deter Tulley, however. Instead it encouraged him to shake Barrow even more vigorously. 'This man set a butcher bird upon us. To steal our children. Because his own are dead.'

I went to reply, when a voice sounded behind me. It was hoarse and tired. 'For the love of Christ, Thomas Tulley. Do as Lord Somershill says.' The crowd parted to reveal Mary Tulley, with her infant children still clinging about her.

Tulley bridled. 'Go home, Mary,' he shouted to his wife.

As the oldest of Mary's boys began to grizzle, she leant down to whisper in his ear. 'Hush child. Let me talk to your daddy.'

'Take them home, Mary,' shouted Tulley again. 'This is no place for children.' Now he cracked his rope like a whip, causing Barrow to cry out once again in pain.

His words did not dissuade his wife, however. Instead they inflated her with a great gust of anger. Thrusting her youngest child at an onlooker in the crowd, she kicked the two small boys at her leg away. She then strode up to her husband and pointed a finger into his face. 'That's right, Thomas Tulley. Get yourself put on trial. Why not get yourself fined again? That would help your wife and starving children.'

Tulley backed away a little, his voice losing some of its force. 'But this man released the bird.'

'Just let him go.'

Tulley was beginning to sweat. I would say he was trembling. 'He knows where the bird is hiding.'

Mary's words were delivered with a spray of spittle. 'Shut up!'

'Don't you care about Catherine?'

This accusation was the final drop of fat upon the fire. Mary ignited. Launching a series of punches at her husband's head, she pulled the rope from within his hands. Tulley was too shocked to do anything but cradle his arms about his face.

With Tulley admitting surrender, Mary passed the rope to me. 'Please don't think badly of Thomas, sire. He is upset by the death of our poor girl.' She spoke through clenched teeth, all the while fighting back the tears that now sped their way down her cheeks. 'He doesn't mean to offend you.'

Then she marched back to her children and baby, shouting for all to hear. 'Hurry up Thomas Tulley. There's a field to sow.'

I noticed that a few men amongst the crowd were amused by this performance. A droopy-eyed man made some taunt about disobedient wives – an insult that Tulley thankfully did not hear, for it might have provoked him to go home and beat Mary for belittling him in front of the village. So I shouted to them all before anybody else could come up with a similar gibe. 'Go home and stay there. All of you.'

Slowly they dispersed, but Thomas Tulley remained. Staring at his feet, he appeared to be daring himself to say something to me, without quite mustering the courage. Sensing his trepidation, I folded my arms and kept my eyes steadfastly upon the man until he thought better of making any further act of defiance.

Wiping his hands through his greasy hair, Tulley eventually sloped away after his angry wife, as awkwardly as a lad who's been thrown out of a brothel.

And then it was just me and John Barrow. A pitiful man with a tear-streaked face and the quailing body of a tormented dog. I tried to speak with him, but instead he whispered words over and over to himself and twitched like a soul in the first seizures of the falling sickness. I untied the rope from his neck, only for him to take my hand – his skin as filthy and scaly as the foot of a chicken.

In truth, he repulsed me.

But I had saved him.

Now I had no choice but to give him sanctuary.

I led Barrow back to my home, Somershill Manor, with the vague intention of finding him somewhere to sleep while the village settled down. We approached the house from the rear side and made our way around the right-hand end of the clogged-up moat, and then past the remaining curtain wall of the old Norman castle that once stood upon this spot. I had avoided walking across the fields to the front of the building, not wishing to announce Barrow's arrival to the whole household.

Barrow followed me obediently to the back porch of the house where I asked one of the scullions if Gilbert had returned yet from Versey Castle. The boy nodded and ran away across the chamber to summon my old servant, who appeared after some time with hands covered in flour. Since Brother Peter had disappeared I had no other trusted man to advise me than Gilbert – but he was often as bad-tempered as a boar pig, with little time for conversation.

Gilbert looked Barrow up and down. 'What's he doing here?' I raised my eyebrows. This was rude, even by Gilbert's standards, and deserved censure – but the episode at the church had been exhausting. I felt a headache brewing.

'I need to keep Barrow away from the village for a while,' I said.

Gilbert straightened up, the bones cracking in his back. 'Why's that then?'

I frowned. 'Because he's in danger, of course.'

'But—'

I held up my hand as imperiously as I was able. 'Find him some-where safe to stay.'

Gilbert wrinkled his nose and then scratched it. 'I don't think your mother would thank me for keeping this flea-ridden fellow about the place.'

'My mother's at Versey.' Then I quickly added, 'And even if she were here, this would be none of her business.'

'He can't sleep in the hall with the servants. He'd spook them with all that shaking and dribbling.'

The pain was building behind my left eye. 'Stop arguing with me, Gilbert.'

Gilbert went to say something, but swallowed the words when he caught sight of my face. 'Very well, sire,' he muttered darkly, grasping Barrow by the arm and roughly pushing him away from the house. 'I'll put him in the north-west tower.'

I rubbed my eye. 'And make sure he's given something to eat. And a bench to sleep upon.'

Gilbert heaved another great sigh and then carried on towards the tower, driving Barrow forward like a man prodding at a stub-born donkey. A set of floury handprints marked Barrow's coarse tunic, where Gilbert had pushed repeatedly at his back. Not that this tactic speeded their journey, for Barrow soon fell to his knees and buried his face in the muddy grass. 'I want to die,' he screamed.

Gilbert looked ready to grant his request, for he pulled at one of Barrow's arms and hissed into his ear, 'Do you?'

My bed was calling. It had been such a long day and the head-ache was now threatening to blind my eye completely. But I could not abandon my charge. 'Be gentle, Gilbert,' I said, running over to them both. 'The man is demented with grief.'

'More like he's demented with . . .' but the remaining words of this sentence were just muttered into his chest so that I could not hear them.

'What did you say?'

'Doesn't matter, sire. It wasn't important.'

'Just take Barrow to the tower,' I said. 'And then bring some pottage and ale to my bedchamber.'

My servant regarded me closely, looking over my face, as if he were sizing up a bull at market. Suddenly his tone was kind. 'Are you unwell, sire?' I didn't dare to nod. Now he whispered. 'Is it the headaches again?'

His kindness unnerved me, and for a moment I wanted to rest my head upon his soft shoulder as I used to when I was a small boy. This short reverie was disturbed when a great shadow fell across our faces. It was large and swooping, and we had not seen its approach.

Once again Barrow shrieked and flapped his arms about his head, but when we turned to look into the sky, our eyes were blinded by a low sun.

'The butcher bird,' said Gilbert as the creature's wings beat a retreat somewhere in the distance.

'Of course it's not,' I said. 'It's just a seagull. There are two of them. Flying about the estate. I saw them by the church.'

I will admit this now, however. Even though I write this from memory, and a mind may warp and inflate an episode until it is hardly more than an imitation of itself. We only saw it for a fleeting moment, but this was no seagull.

Chapter Four

At seven years of age, my family sent me to Kintham Abbey to be educated by the Benedictines. The expectation was that I would become a monk at nineteen and then quickly rise to become abbot, thereby heaping some much-needed ecclesiastical glory upon the de Lacys. I still had two older brothers alive at Somershill, so I could be spared from the estate – there was no reason to believe that these older sons would die. The Plague was just a story from the Bible in those days – a cloud of locusts or a torrent of frogs. It would not turn our rivers to blood, nor our fields to dust. I no more expected to become Lord Somershill than I expected to be King of England.

The first days at the monastery were difficult. I was to sleep in a long dormitory with the other boys, a rabble of noisy, unfriendly creatures who laughed at my affectations and soon stole my satin slippers. As I shivered under my coarse sheet, they made farting noises to incite me. Or they called me such insulting names that I was driven to tears. It would have been bearable if I could have gone to sleep, but I was not used to being sent to bed so early. At Somershill I had slept on Mother's lap as she gossiped at the fire (though, in my last year there, she often complained that my backside was becoming too bony, and was poking into her legs.)

Brother Peter was my only friend at the monastery – often enquiring after my well-being and education – but Brother

Thomas was in charge of the novices, oblates, and students, and would not tolerate any interference, despite Peter's protestations that he had been charged with the supervision of my welfare by Lady de Lacy herself. I remember Brother Thomas's expression at the mention of my mother's name. A grimace spread across his face, as disgusted in attitude as if he had rubbed his upper lip with fish skin, and couldn't wash away the stink.

I understood, even at such a young age, that I would receive no special treatment from Brother Thomas on account of my birth, as he clearly held the de Lacys in as much regard as a family of local cottars. But I was accustomed to favours and privileges due to my position. I was accustomed to being allowed to run about the great hall, making as much noise as I pleased. I was accustomed to being fed sugared violets and minced beef. I could not cope with the coarse rye bread and fatty ends of meat we were served in the refectory. The hours of silence were not con-templative and serene for me. They were a torture.

But worse than the hours of silence in the chapel, were the hours between the prayers of Compline at bedtime and Lauds at daybreak, when we were tucked under our sheets and expected to sleep. I had done nothing the whole day, other than sit at my desk, or rest on my knees at prayer, so I was not in the least bit tired. Instead I lay in my hard bed, missing my mother and lis-tening to the sounds of the monastery at night. The slamming of a distant door. The rhythmic snoring of Brother Thomas in his curtained cell at one end of the dormitory. The creaks and groans of the ceiling trusses, and the scuttling feet of squirrels as they scampered over the stone slates above my head. All these noises served to nail desperation and loneliness to my post, a feeling that was only supplanted by terror.

Some time during that first week, I became aware that a cloaked figure was moving amongst the beds in the dead of night. I raised my head a little, but could not see the face of this mystery person through the thick gloom of the chamber. I went to sit up but a hand grabbed me. It was the boy in the adjacent bed. A boy I had assumed was sleeping.

He squeezed my arm. 'Close your eyes,' he told me in the slightest whisper. 'Pretend to be asleep.'

I wanted to argue. This boy was amongst my greatest tormentors. So why should I listen to him? It was probably yet another of his tricks to belittle me. But his stare was fierce and his grip was tight. This was not a piece of mischief, it was a warning. Even my naivety could not prevent me from seeing that he meant his words. So I closed my eyes and quickly settled beneath the sheets and pretended to sleep as the figure wandered towards our part of the dormitory, his feet treading lightly upon the reeds of the floor, his cloak soon brushing the edge of my bed.

I forgot to breathe as he drew near, such was my fear. I sensed he had passed, but then he returned. I heard his breathing as he leant over my face. It was laboured, erratic and smelt of brandy. A finger touched my cheek and stroked my skin. It was as cold and hard as an icicle and I felt it might burn into my face if it stayed there a moment longer. And then, just as I felt I could hold my breath no longer, he moved away, his cloak creating a small eddy of air in his wake. He left the dormitory and he did not hear me wet the bed – the hot urine stinging my leg and dripping to the floor.

The boy next to me opened his eyes and pulled a face when he realised what I had done. I wanted to talk to the boy. To ask him who this prowler was, and why he had warned me to keep my eyes shut. But my short-lived friend pulled the blanket over his head and turned his back on me. He would not help me again, I knew it.

The next morning I was beaten for wetting the sheets and made to wash them myself in the spring, rather than leave them in the common laundry chest for the women to take. When Brother Peter saw me by the stream, he attempted to intervene and have a lay monk assist me, but instead he was roundly turned upon by Brother Thomas and told to stay in the infirmary where he belonged. Given that Brother Thomas was older and had the ear of the abbot, Brother Peter kept his distance. How well I remember the freezing water of the brook as it chilled my hands and turned them blue. When I had hung the sheets to dry over the cloister wall, I was then punished to a day in silence – though this hardly made a difference to my life, as none of the other boys spoke to me anyway. Particularly now that I was known as a bed soiler. A fool. A laughing stock. They only pointed and giggled, as they made their way from their lessons to prayers.

That night, as I lay in my damp sheets, the prowler came again to the dormitory. This time there was no arm from my neighbour to grip me and warn me of the man's presence. But I was already awake, as I had been for hours – hardly daring to close my eyes, in case sleep found me when it was least required. Once again the soft feet stole through the dormitory door – but these were not the wary, timid toes of an opportunistic thief, this person moved with the quiet, sly confidence of a hunter. A fox. And what were we boys, other than an enclosure of chickens, helpless and weak, with only our ability to feign sleep as protection?

I was only a boy. So young. But I determined that his cold hand would not touch me again. His icy finger would not stroke my skin, and his breath would not puff those fumes onto my face. I knew what this person wanted, and he would not have it.

When the cloak once again stopped by my bed, I could not keep up the pretence of sleep. Instead I leapt out of bed, pushed the man aside with a scream and ran for the door, which had been unlocked by the very prowler who sought me out. Then I skidded through the silent cloister, scaled the crumbling wall of the fruit garden and escaped into the forests that surrounded the monastery. I had some notion to make my way home to Somershill – but this was purely a dream, as I had no idea which direction to take. The night was moonless and dank, and soon I was not able to see ahead in the thick undergrowth. The chestnut, hazel and holly grew into a tangle. I turned back towards an open field, where I could see the monastery in the distance – but even though wolves still called in these woods and unseen creatures sniffed and snuffled in the trees behind me – I would not return to that place. For there were no monsters in this forest as dangerous as the one that crawled about the monastery.

I fell asleep beneath a hawthorn tree, and awoke at first light to see the haw berries hanging above my head in bunches, like small beads of blood. A mist lay across the valley – so low that the turrets and towers of the monastery peeped through its gauze like a city in the clouds. But the mist had not only settled upon the fields, it had also settled upon my chest, and as I coughed it hurt my ribs. I struggled back into the woods, once again intending to reunite myself with my mother. But I did not make good progress and it was only a short while before I was lost. I was cold and hungry, and my coughing had become as dry and sharp as the bark of one of my mother's little dogs.

It did not take long for Brother Peter and his band of men and dogs to find me. I was taken back to the monastery and given a bed in the infirmary. By now the combination of the damp sheets, the damp night, and the fear I had experienced gave way to a fever. I heard Brother Peter arguing in the corner of the infirmary with Brother Thomas, but this time Peter did not concede to Thomas's superiority. The old man shuffled and harrumphed, wobbling the jowls of his florid cheeks at each of Peter's accusations, but Peter kept going. The child in their care was Oswald de Lacy, not some son of a common merchant. If Lord Somershill were to hear that his own son was being treated with such cruelty and that the boy had run away, then the nobleman would withdraw his support for Kintham Abbey. Brother Thomas laughed. What support would that be, he asked? In Thomas's opinion, Lord Somershill was as charitable as a Pharisee. He lent books for the library, of course, argued Peter. Thomas only scowled at this, since he had little regard for manuscripts, despite being responsible for the younger boys' education.

Peter's arguments fell on deaf ears, but he must have found somebody to listen to him, further up the ladder of command – since on recovering from my fever I discovered that I would not return to the dormitory. Instead I would have exceptional treatment and remain under Peter's care in the infirmary. He would educate and care for me. In return I would work with the sick and dying of our community as Peter's apprentice. I would sleep in the warmest corner of the chamber, just outside the curtained wall of Peter's own bedchamber.

The prowler never troubled me again. He didn't visit the infirmary at night. But I saw him often enough in the day, as I walked about the monastery to prayers at Vespers or mass at Compline. It was the abbot himself.

After the rigours and length of the previous day – riding home from Versey and then taking John Barrow into my care – I was relieved when my headache failed to develop into a full assault on my head. Sleep didn't find me that night, but I was pleased of it. I didn't want to dream, as the burning boy would come to me. I knew he would. Instead I used these quiet hours to review the details of Catherine Tulley's murder, remaining certain that John Barrow was innocent. It was too easy to blame the nearest madman or outcast for an unsolved crime. On the other hand, I determined that I should question the man, if only to rule him out completely, and to prove that I was not being dogmatic in my thinking.

At first light I dressed quickly, stepped out onto the frosted grass and headed for the north-west tower, without having my breakfast. Gilbert joined me reluctantly, but on reaching the cell we found that Barrow was crouched in a corner and refused to speak.

Gilbert stood behind me and tutted. 'Would it help if I twisted his arm a little?'

'No!'

Gilbert sighed. 'Very well, sire.'

'Have you fed him yet? As I asked you to?'

'Yes sire. See for yourself.'

I looked into the corner of the room to see a chunk of stale bread and a mug of ale, which remained untouched. A dead fly and a sprinkling of dust floated on its surface. 'Bring the man some pottage.'

Gilbert stiffened. 'Is it wise to give him meat? It might . . .'

'It might . . . what?'

He pulled a face. 'Stir him up. To . . . you know.' Unfortunately I did know. Gilbert thought this man a murderer, and there was nothing I could say to convince him otherwise. Everybody in the village felt the same. I might be able to keep John Barrow under my protection, but this sanctuary would only last as long as I was able to provide it. The last two years had taught me this much, however. Nothing can be counted upon in this world. Nothing at all. You might see the future as a progression of the past, but this is a fool's notion, a delusion – for the future is as mixed up and unpredictable as a stew of leftovers. It could taste of anything.

The only real way to protect Barrow from the same fate as Leofwin was to find the true murderer of the Tulley child. And to be quick about it.

Leaving Gilbert to tend to Barrow, I made for the stables and instructed Piers to saddle up my horse. My plan was to ride straight to the village and continue my investigations without delay. I watched Piers throw a cloth over Tempest's back. The horse was such an elegant creature. The best stallion in my stable. He had taken his time to accept my presence in my father's saddle however, having more than once discharged me in remote spots, or, even more unhappily, in front of an amused audience. Gilbert had advised me to beat the creature into submission, or to sell him to a knight as a warhorse – but I had noticed something about this stallion. He was a haughty creature who could sense fear in a man at twenty paces, but if I approached him with a confident stride and if I spoke calmly into his ear, then he would become amenable and cooperative enough. As long as I backed up my confidence and bravado with a sweet apple or a lump of hard cheese.

I smoothed down the glossy black hair of Tempest's neck and drew myself up into his saddle, trying not to betray the slightest modicum of apprehension, even though I had seen the horse rearing in his stall as I approached. Piers was still a small boy and struggled to hold the creature's reins, so it would have been more convenient for everybody if I had swapped Tempest for an easier horse. But this horse was an invaluable asset in my role as lord. He could be a performer. Even a spectacle. He gave me the last sprinkling of grandeur that was needed in my position.

A low sun shone through the grey of the clouds as I rode towards the village of Somershill. Wood anemones carpeted the forest floor in a sea of white, opening their faces to the sun in a brief dazzle of revelry before the leaves grew above their heads and blocked out their light. But spring kept its distance, and the air still smelt of snow. I pulled my fur cloak about me and made for the home of Geoffrey Hayward, the boy who had found baby Catherine.

It was somewhere to start my investigations at least.

The Haywards had once lived in one of the larger houses along the narrow road leading up to St Giles. An ox horn hung above their door – a crude instrument that his father used to blow if the cattle were invading the hay fields. The Haywards were all dead, apart from Geoffrey – a boy of thirteen who had often badgered me to appoint him to his father's position – though he was far too young to take over such a responsibility. Despite his ambition, Geoffrey would have to wait for the role until he was older, as the hayward in Somershill usually leads the sowing in the demesne fields. I could not rely upon the older villagers to cooperate with such a young boy. Even so, I had given Geoffrey the responsibility of keeping the common pastures free of stray cattle, and of raising the alarm if the land was being used by strangers.

In truth, Geoffrey had taken this role too seriously and liked to come to me with almost daily reports on the state of the commons, until I had been forced to ask the boy not to bother me unless there was an actual problem. After this conversation, Geoffrey had shuffled out of the hall with his head hung low, causing me immediately to regret my rudeness, for I noticed Featherby smirking at the boy's reprimand. The pleasure my reeve took from the boy's disappointment so annoyed me that I made the mistake of telling Featherby to take note of the boy's enthusiasm, for I was tempted to propose Geoffrey as reeve once he was old enough. It had been an imprudent threat, however – for later that day, Geoffrey was thrown into the mud of the cow field and soundly beaten. When I asked the boy to name his attacker, he resolutely maintained that he had not seen the man who had pushed his face into a great pat of cattle dung and then kicked him repeatedly in the ribs. But I knew who was guilty.

Geoffrey Hayward now lived in a cottage with Mary Cadebridge and her daughter Violet – a girl who had given birth to a bastard son following a liaison with a passing flagellant during the months of the Plague. The child was said to be sickly and cursed because of his mother's sin, though whenever I saw the boy, he would be running about the street with legs as thick as small tree trunks and a face as wide as a dinner bowl. Now an orphan, Geoffrey earned his keep by making himself useful to the two Cadebridge women, bringing them firewood, mending the roof and tending the virgate of land they farmed. I'm told that the Cadebridges made more than good use of the boy's labours, but did not always reward him for his efforts. More than once he was forced to beg a meal from other members of the village.

It was Geoffrey's intention to take back his family's house, but he could not afford the rent and I had reluctantly let the tenancy go to the Pavenhams, a family who had moved to our estate in the autumn from Canterbury, having one elderly aunt already in Somershill. They had told me they were in need of a larger home, though they paid only half the rent that I had previously received from the Haywards. And given the behaviour of their youngest son, Felix – a boy constantly held before the manorial court for altering his boundaries and calling his neighbour's wife a whore – I was more than a little sorry to have them as tenants. Still, as Father used to tell me, we must eat bread made of rye when the wheat is exhausted. I had no choice but to allow them residence.

When I knocked at the Cadebridges' door, Geoffrey opened it to me with a smile and a low bow. I was pleased to see that his encounter with a cowpat and the sole of Featherby's boot had not dampened his enthusiasm for life. 'Good morning, sire,' he said eagerly. 'Have you come for a report on the common pastures?'

Mary Cadebridge, seeing that it was my face at the door, pushed past young Geoffrey and curtsied. 'Get away Geoffrey. Lord Somershill doesn't want to hear one of your foolish reports.' Violet's young son now peeped around Mary's legs and, seeing his opportunity for escape, made a dash for freedom into the street.

Mary screamed out loud. 'Lord help us. How did little William get past you Geoffrey? You're supposed to be looking after the child.' By the look on Geoffrey's face, it was obvious he had not realised that guarding William was his responsibility, though he said nothing to defend himself against the charge. I expect he had one mind to the provision of his supper that night. Mary ran into the street after the child, who was now bolting towards the church with impressive speed – his linen napkin trailing behind him in the mud.

Now we were alone, I turned to Geoffrey. 'It's you I wished to speak with. I believe you discovered Catherine Tulley's body.'

He reddened and bowed again. 'It was me. Yes.'

'I would like you to show me where.'

'Well of course, sire.' Then he frowned. 'But it's across the common and the ground is wet.'

'Can you ride with me?'

Geoffrey squinted uncomfortably, and then I remembered that he had sold his father's horses in an attempt to keep the house. 'There's only Mistress Cadebridge's pony,' he said. 'But I'm not allowed to ride Polly.'

By now Mary Cadebridge had returned to the house with the infant struggling and screaming with unbridled fury at his capture. As he yelled, I could see his two small white teeth that poked their way through his bottom gum like a pair of uneven gateposts.

'Geoffrey will be using your pony for a while,' I told the woman, as she launched the boy back inside the cottage.

Mary bridled. 'But he can't ride properly, sire.'

'Of course he can.'

'But last time he mounted Polly he—'

'Enough.'

She opened her mouth to argue, but soon shut it again. 'Geoffrey is most welcome to ride Polly,' she said with a curtsy. 'I'm always pleased to oblige you, sire. You know that.'

I gave my best harrumph at this statement. 'Then you should let the boy ride more often. Particularly as he's sent to the market in Burrsfield.' She went to object, but I held up my hand. 'It's a long way to return with a sack of flour over your shoulder. Wouldn't you agree?'

She squeezed out a smile. 'Indeed, sire.'

I told Geoffrey to saddle the pony, and then turned to leave, but not before the Cadebridge woman had jumped in front of me. 'May I ask where you're going, my lord?' Once again she curtsied.

I regarded her for a moment. So unremittingly devout, and yet so staunchly unkind. 'No,' I said. 'You may not.'

Chapter Five

March is not my favourite month, but I will say this, it is preferable to October and November when the world is decaying in front of your eyes. Autumn is the season of wet leaves and woodsmoke, when a bleakness takes hold of the land and squashes out the memory of summer. There are some people who claim to like the cold months, but I will never count myself among their sombre numbers. I wish, instead, that I were a hedgehog, able to sleep in a mound of dry leaves until the next spring – only waking when the new year grows some skin upon its bones.

As I rode beside Geoffrey this particular March morning, there was no promise of spring, only the shadow of the previous winter with its melancholy chill still hanging around like a beggar at the city gate. As Tempest ambled along, displaying a modicum of hostility to the smaller pony beside him, I turned my mind to the murder and tried to imagine who could have killed a small and innocent newborn child such as Catherine Tulley. What would be the point of such an act? She had hardly breathed a scrap of air, nor eaten a morsel of food. She could have formed no enemies nor made any friends. Her coming and going had been as brief and unnoticed as the mayfly's.

A sadness washed through me and settled in my stomach.

Geoffrey trotted forwards to advise me that we would be

taking a side path along the edge of the common, rather than the track that led diagonally across this higher land. In the distance a man with a stooped back herded his sheep away from us. A flock of peewits climbed into the sky and then tumbled towards the earth with their acrobatic dives. Cowslips waved their heads in the patches of soil where cattle had trodden the grass into muddy wounds.

Geoffrey stopped his pony beside a length of hedge and dismounted. 'It was here, sire. That I found the baby.' I had to forgive his youthful naivety, but he beamed with pride, as if he were announcing the location of a hidden chest of treasure.

'Why were you on this side of the common?' I asked. His face froze, so I attempted to smile at the boy and put him at his ease. 'I only ask because the villagers tend to keep to the other side. I can see ragwort and thistles grow here.'

Geoffrey relaxed a little and wiped his face with a small gloved hand. The glove was made of soft leather and betrayed the former wealth of the boy's family. 'I was looking for a stray calf, sire,' he said. 'John Moore offered to pay me a penny if I could find the creature.' And then his face returned to its usual level of eagerness. 'I thought to check along the hedges to see if the beast had fallen into one of the ditches. Or perhaps it was caught in the blackthorn. Sometimes they do that.' Then he bit his bottom lip and looked away. 'I didn't expect to find a baby, sire. Oh no, not at all. It was a horrible thing to find. I ran straight back to the village with her. I didn't waste a moment.'

I threw my leg over my horse and dismounted. 'Just show me exactly where you found her.' Geoffrey scanned the hedge and then pointed to a blackthorn bush, dotted with small buds that were on the verge of breaking into white blossom.

'Are you sure it was here?' I asked. 'There are so many other blackthorn bushes along this hedge.'

Geoffrey nodded nervously. 'Oh yes, sire. It was here. I'm sure of it.' But I was not so convinced. This hedgerow ran for many yards along this edge of the common, and one stretch looked exactly like another, being a patchwork of beech, hawthorn, and blackthorn.

I decided to change tack. 'Describe what Catherine looked like when you found her.'

I would say Geoffrey grimaced at this question. But then who likes to recall such a discovery? 'Her body was pushed onto the thorns,' he told me.

'And she was definitely dead?'

'Oh yes, sire. The butcher bird never skewers a living thing onto a spike. I've seen them do it before. They kill the young of other birds, while they are newly hatched and naked.'

I groaned. 'There is no giant butcher bird, Geoffrey. And you know it.'

He bit his lip again and looked to the grass, his cheeks as coloured as the petals of a dog rose. 'But I've seen it, sire. Soaring over the meadows.'

'Of course you haven't.'

'It's taken lambs. Ask Silas.'

'Lambs? Are you sure?'

Now he backtracked. 'Well. They've gone missing.'

'And a fox is not suspected?'

He shook his head, but not with conviction.

I put my arm upon his. 'You've learnt to read, haven't you Geoffrey?'

He looked up at me. 'Oh yes sire. I was to attend the Grey Friars school in Maidstone. If—' Then he took a deep breath and appeared to be holding back a tear.

I chose not to answer this. What was I to say? Nobody could have predicted this present from the recent past. If the Plague had not warped the world, then I would be a monk and Geoffrey would be at school with a prosperous family to support his studies. Instead he was an orphan, and I was a lord. But his situation did not excuse his ignorance. He was spending too much time around the fools in the village and needed to recommence his education. 'Come up to the manor house Geoffrey. I can let you read some of my books.'

'Thank you, sire. Thank you.' His gratitude was almost over-whelming, and now faced with such desperate fawning, I almost regretted having made the offer.

I put my hand upon his shoulder in the hope of calming his spirits. 'Now tell me about finding the child. I want to know every detail.'

Geoffrey looked into the sky. 'It was morning. Two days ago. I had been up since dawn, as Mistress Cadebridge asks me to sweep out the fire and to roll up my straw mattress before she rises from bed. She doesn't like me to come up to the common, as she thinks I'm doing it to get out of minding little William. But I have to remind her that you yourself, sire, Lord Somershill, have requested that I supervise the pastures.'

I have met many windbags in my time, though few have been as young as Geoffrey. Expanding a story to the point of boredom seems to be a learnt quality, and none are better at it than the elderly. But Geoffrey was proving my theory wrong. 'Please keep to the facts,' I said.

He coloured again. 'Oh yes. Of course. It was just after dawn. The moon was still visible in the sky. And there was a hoar frost on the branches. I was looking for the calf, but something caught my eye in the bushes. It was a red woollen shawl. But something was wrapped inside.' He hesitated. 'It was the baby.'

'I thought you said she was skewered onto the thorns of a bush?'

He bit his nails. 'She was in a shawl . . . but pushed into the thorns.'

'Hardly the work of a butcher bird, then?' The boy blinked nervously. 'And this shawl. Was it red with blood?'

'No sire. The cloth had been coloured with madder root. It was as bright as a newly dyed cape.' Then Geoffrey leant into the bush and pulled a small fragment of fluff from one of the thorns. I had noticed it earlier, but had dismissed it as the wrinkled skin of an old rosehip. 'This is from the shawl,' he told me. 'It must have got stuck in the bush when I pulled her from it. You can see how red it is.'

I held the fragile skein between my fingers and took a deep breath. 'Tell me, Geoffrey. When you opened the shawl, was Catherine's body rigid or slack?'

He grimaced and for once remained silent.

'It's important. Please. Try to remember.'

He wiped his eye. 'Her poor little body felt stiff, sire.'

So Catherine had not been murdered immediately before Geoffrey's discovery of her body. I knew this must be true, since I had often dealt with corpses at the infirmary. It took a couple of hours for stiffness to set in after death. Sometimes a dead body could then remain rigid for another day, making it difficult for me to prepare them for the grave. I turned back to Geoffrey. 'Did her body smell at all?'

Another unpleasant question. The boy shook his head. 'Only of babies. The way little William can smell. Sort of sickly.'

'And you took her body straight back to Somershill?' He nodded. 'And when you passed the dead child to her mother, what happened?'

'Mary Tulley cried, sire. She was very sad.'

'And Thomas Tulley?'

'He raised the hue and cry at once.'

'And they were looking for John Barrow?'

'Yes.'

'Nobody else?'

Geoffrey began to pick at the stitching to his glove. 'John Barrow went missing before Catherine was taken. And he had begot the . . .' Geoffrey's words trailed away to silence.

'And what time did Catherine go missing?'

'The night before, I think.'

'Mistress Tulley told me that the infant had been taken while she was helping with the ploughing. That would have been during the day.'

Geoffrey stepped nervously from foot to foot. 'I must be mistaken then, sire. Perhaps it's only when I heard the news.'

'Perhaps?'

I had only a couple more questions for the boy, which was fortunate since Tempest was beginning to paw at the soil. 'Did you see anybody else around here?' I said.

'When, sire?'

'When you found the baby in the bushes, of course?' My patience was being strained. Why was answering a few simple questions so difficult?

Geoffrey ran his fingers across his forehead. 'There was something, sire. I didn't want to tell anybody at the time. I thought perhaps I was dreaming.'

'Please tell me, Geoffrey.'

The boy had removed one of his gloves and was now picking at the fine stitching in the other. I wondered that Mistress Cadebridge had not taken these garments from the boy, as she had appropriated most of his other possessions in the name of Christian charity. 'I thought I heard wailing,' he said.

'The wailing of a man or a woman?'

'I don't know.' Then he looked up sharply. 'I'm not lying, sire.'

'I'm not saying you are. But it's normally easy to tell the sex of a voice.' Geoffrey was continuing to frustrate me. I didn't believe him to be a liar, but he was an exaggerator. An actor, happy to have some currency to trade, if only a few crumbs of evidence.

He reddened. 'Perhaps it was just the call of the peewits? They are singing now for their mates.' And just as he said this, a pair of the birds fell from the sky in their spectacular rolling dive. The calls not unlike the lament of a person.

'But you saw nobody?'

He put his thumb to his lips and bit at the fingernail. 'That's right, sire. I didn't.'

The library at Somershill is always a cold room, having a large north-facing window and no fire. I only usually frequent the room in the spring and summer when I'm able to breathe out and not create my own personal miasma. This last winter the tapestry of the three-headed dragon had grown a whitish mould. I touched the cloth to find it damp, giving off an odour that smelt like rotten fruit and the must of a mushroom. I would have strayed back into the great hall, but today the chamber was full of servants as they gathered about the fire, sewing up the loose seams in their tunics and patching up the holes in their leather shoes. I had given permission for them to remain indoors as a late frost had made little else possible on the farm. I noticed Piers the stableboy huddling up towards Ada as if she were his own mother. As she tenderly showed the boy how to thread a latten needle and then draw it through a piece of cloth, his face blushed and broke into a smile.

I closed the door of the library on this scene of contentment as it made me feel lonely and unloved. Sitting at Brother Peter's old stool, I took out a book that I had asked Ada to sew me that morning from a selection of parchment squares. It was a rough and primitive thing, but sufficient for my purposes. I would write down what I had discovered thus far regarding the death of Catherine Tulley, to see if the information made any sense. I was reviewing my findings – with no particular conclusions being drawn – when Featherby knocked at the door and walked straight in without my permission.

'What is it?' I asked. He had disturbed my train of thought.

He stalked over towards me, his hat held in his hands. I quickly stood up.

'We need to discuss the wages, sire. I'm having such problems with the men.' He looked embarrassed for once. 'You see—'

And then, before he had the chance to continue, we were interrupted by a second intruder. This time it was Piers. Featherby turned on the boy. 'What is it? We're having an important discussion here.'

Piers trembled. 'I thought Lord Somershill would want to know this.'

'What is it?' I asked, irritated both by these disruptions, and Featherby's assumption that it was his role to chastise the boy.

Piers gave a short bow. 'Sire. There's news from Versey Castle.'

'What is it?'

'There's a messenger in the hall. He will only speak to you personally.'

As I went to leave the library, Featherby had the audacity to stand in my path. 'But what about the wages, my lord?'

I swerved around him. 'We'll discuss this another time.'

Following Piers out of the library, I found the messenger from Versey to be none other than Clemence's stooped and dirty servant, John Slow. He was gathered with the others about the fire and was giving his strongly held opinions on how to darn a heel in a woollen hose. As I approached, he performed his customary flinch.

I cleared my throat and waited for him to drop his hands from his face. 'I understand that you have come with news from Versey?'

'Yes, sire.'

I waited, hoping that the man would have the sense to continue the story, but he only looked at me with a stare so vacant that I wondered if he were having a dream. 'And? What is your news?' I said at last. 'Does it concern Lady Clemence?'

The man focussed his gaze and juddered into reality. 'Ah yes, sire. She has given birth to a boy.' The other servants exclaimed their delight at this news, though not one of them cared in the least for my sister.

'When was the baby born?' I asked.

Now Slow screwed up his face. Was this such a difficult question to answer? 'Come on Slow. When was the child born?'

An expression of enlightenment flickered across his face. 'It was yesterday morning, sire. I was sent immediately to tell you.'

'It's taken you over a day to get here?'

He nodded vigorously. 'Yes. I had to walk.'

'Why didn't they give you a pony to ride?'

'I can't ride.' He then smiled. A toothy and lopsided expression that was entirely disconcerting. 'My legs are too wide apart,' he said, pointing to his groin. 'See. I can't grip the barrel of the beast. I keep sliding off.'

Some of my servants began to laugh, so I held up my hand to prevent Slow offering any further insights into the deficiency of his anatomy. 'Why didn't my mother send a messenger who could ride a horse?'

He shrugged.

'Is there anything else you need to tell me?'

He opened his mouth in astonishment, but if I was expecting a further piece of news to follow, I was to be disappointed, for the fool simply pointed to the mitten that lay in Piers's lap. 'You can't sew a glove like that.'

Now I did grab Slow. And I will admit to shaking him. But it was only the once, and it was gentle – though anybody would think, given the way he flung himself onto the floor, that I had assaulted him with a horsewhip. When he stopped shaking, I offered him my hand, and pulled him up. 'I'm sorry, sire. I'm sorry. I won't do it again, sire. I won't do it again.'

To stop his shaking, I rested my hand very gently upon his arm, making sure not to move too quickly and alarm the man's sensitive nerves. I even contemplated an apology, but remembered the disquiet that such acts of deference could cause in my servants. Instead I spoke calmly. 'Please, Slow. Is there any other news that you have been asked to give me?'

He scratched his head. 'Well, yes. There is, sire.'

'And?'

He paused. 'Lady Clemence is dangerously ill.'

'She is?'

'Yes. The infant was very large. They say she will die.'

Chapter Six

Irode with all haste to Versey, angry that Mother had sent such a deficient messenger as John Slow to tell me the news. If my sister were already dead by the time I reached the castle, I would take great issue with her mistake.

Versey loomed through the fog as I galloped out of the forest and down into the valley where the de Caburn family had built their home centuries ago. The grass was still frosted, and the air smelt of wood ash and the pine tar of the small boats that were moored by the moat. The old-fashioned drawbridge was raised as if my mother and sister were expecting an attack, so I had to call for it to be lowered so that I might gain entry to the inner bailey, where I left my horse with a servant and made straight for Clemence's bedchamber. I was told that she clung onto life by the frailest of threads.

I found Mother sitting outside the door to the ladies' bed-chamber, on the high-backed chair that her dead son-in-law Walter de Caburn had used at the dining table. She looked up on seeing me, but did not stand. 'At last, Oswald. We thought you were never coming.'

'If you had sent a messenger who could ride a horse, then I might have been here sooner.'

She waved her hand in front of her face and slumped further back into the chair with a sigh. 'That's a silly excuse, Oswald.' I went to argue, but she seemed so despondent that there was no point.

I went to open the door to the ladies' bedchamber, but now Mother leapt out of her chair and stood in the way. 'I wouldn't go in there, Oswald. The place smells like a latrine.'

'I want to see Clemence.'

Mother bit her bottom lip. 'Just remember your sister as she was.' I went to push her away, but she stood her ground, placing an arm across my path. 'A foul miasma infects that chamber, Oswald. If you enter, your lungs will harden. The air is poisoned.'

This description was enough to prompt a moment's hesitation. 'Is Clemence alone in there?'

She shook her head. 'No, no. That dunderhead Humbert is in there, of course. Though the fool does nothing but sob by her feet. And there's—' Then she hesitated, wrung her hands and looked to the ceiling. I would say she seemed embarrassed.

I suddenly felt suspicious. 'Who else is in there, Mother?'

'Nobody. Well not really—'

'Who is it?'

She licked her thin lips. 'Actually, it's my physician.'

I gasped. 'Not Roger de Waart?'

She sat up stiffly. 'There's nothing wrong with Master de Waart, Oswald. He's—'

I pushed past Mother's arm and opened the door to find a chamber just as stinking and foul as she had described. Thick tapestries had been hung at the window to block out the light, while a pungent steam rose from a pan on the fire. Mother slammed the door behind me, and for a moment it was difficult to discern exactly who was in the chamber. Then a figure emerged from the shadows. A tall and thin man with the pointed beak-like nose of a seagull.

'Who's there?' he said. 'You will agitate Lady Versey with such a loud entrance.' It was de Waart, wagging his skeletal finger in my direction. His accent was from the Low Countries, though I had always suspected a certain affectation to its lisp, as if this might justify the extra penny he added onto his charges. This man had ministered to me as a child, feeding me purgatives with excessive regularity. I had escaped his eye at seven, but had frequently taken over the care of de Waart's patients at the abbey infirmary – poor souls who had been nearly poisoned to death by his experimental methods. Mother knew my opinion of him, which now explained why she had chosen the slowest messenger to bring me news of the birth.

I pulled back a corner of the tapestry to let some light into the chamber. De Waart covered his eyes with his hands and cowered as if he had never seen the sun. His skin was still as sickly and pale as I remembered, as if his whole head had been moulded out of hoof jelly. I couldn't help but think, in my boyishly stupid way, that de Waart was such an appropriate name for the man, for he had a face full of raised moles that clustered like ticks about the crevices of his nostrils.

'Pull that back,' he said. 'The light will damage my lady's skin.'

'Of course it won't.'

His hands remained in front of his eyes. 'Who are you?'

I pulled the tapestry from the window in a dramatic gesture. In fact, it was spectacular enough for de Waart to let out a gasp. How I thanked Providence for allowing this performance to go so well, as I would have looked very foolish if the cloth had remained fixed to the window.

De Waart bowed obsequiously. 'Lord Somershill. I do apologise. I did not realise it was you.'

I ignored this insincere act of contrition and looked about the room to see Clemence lying silently in the bed with her eyes closed, while her faithful servant Humbert held her hand in his own. The large boy turned neither to look at the light, nor me. Instead he maintained his unerring gaze upon my sister's face – a face that was as pinched and drawn as a corpse's. As I reached the bed, the unpleasant scent from the boiling pan gave way to the acrid, smacking stink of a pissing alley.

I turned to de Waart. 'Why does Lady Clemence smell so bad? Have you allowed her to wet the bed?'

'My lady must stay perfectly still.'

'Why?'

'She must not move. It will allow the birth fever to settle and dissipate.' He then made a great show of pointing out how he had raised the bed below Clemence's head with a square of wood, so that the frame might be inclined by a shallow angle. 'See how the heat will descend towards her feet, leaving her lungs and heart to cool.'

I leant over my sister, only to find the smell was even more pungent at close quarters, except now the reek of urine was mixed with the unmistakeable odour of night soil.

'Have you allowed Lady Versey to shit in the bed, as well?' I said.

'Of course not, sire. She was administered a purgative before she took to her rest.'

'Then what is that stink?'

De Waart clasped his hands together unctuously and bowed his head with a smile. I could see he was proud of the answer. 'It is a remedy I have prepared especially.' He moved over to my sister's side, pushed Humbert's hand away and then pulled back the blanket to reveal Clemence's linen nightgown, a garment that was stained with a large and watery brown circle.

I reeled back, for this stink was stinging to the nostrils. 'By God, what is that?' I asked, now holding my nose as I attempted once again to approach my sister.

De Waart gave another of his self-satisfied smiles, revealing a front tooth, which was grey. 'It is a tincture mixed with vinegar.'

'What sort of tincture?'

'I prefer badger droppings. But I was somewhat short of that ingredient, so I have mixed it with horse dung. It will have the same efficacy.'

I dropped my hand from my nose. 'Efficacy to do what, exactly?'

'It will draw the fever from my lady's chest.'

'I thought you were draining the fever into her feet?'

As we spoke Clemence stirred for the first time, emitting the faintest of moans and then opening her eyes to regard me desperately. I went to touch her, but Humbert blundered past and grabbed her hand before I was able. She asked feebly for something to drink, but Humbert only dabbed a small sponge into a mug of ale and then held it to her dried lips.

I turned to de Waart, who was now stirring the foul and astringent-smelling concoction of herbs and pieces of bark in the pan. 'I will relieve you of Lady Versey's care,' I told him.

De Waart looked up. 'But sire. Your sister's care is only in the remedial stage of treatment. To interrupt it now would risk a full recovery.'

'I'll take that risk, thank you.'

He stopped stirring. 'I must object most strongly to this decision.'

At this very moment the door was flung open as Mother made her entrance. As usual, she had been listening closely to proceedings from the other side of the wall. She went to speak, but the steam from the boiling pan caused her to cough, and she was forced to retreat towards the fresh air of the passage.

De Waart ran to her aid. 'Dear lady. You should not have come into this chamber. The miasma is poisonous to your lungs.'

I picked up the steaming pan by its long handle and removed it to a corner. 'The miasma in this room is poisonous to everybody's lungs. Particularly my sister's.'

Mother stopped by the door and cleared her throat. 'Listen to me, Oswald. I insist upon Master de Waart staying to complete Clemence's treatment.'

'And I insist that he leaves.'

'But—'

I clapped my hands. 'I am Lord of Somershill and Versey. And I say de Waart goes.'

Mother dropped her hand from her mouth and stared at me, and I had the impression she was tempted to say what we were both thinking. That I was neither truly Lord of Somershill nor of Versey. That I was no more the true Oswald de Lacy than the blundering boy servant who held Clemence's hand. She shook her head haughtily and turned her back on me. 'Come Master de Waart. I have a malady of the foot which I would like you to examine.'

De Waart stood his ground. 'But madam. What of Lady Versey? The fever is still in her chest.'

Mother crossed her arms and peered over at him. 'My son has spoken. You are relieved of your duties in this chamber.'

'But—'

'Please, sir. Do as you are bid.'

De Waart performed a fawning bow. 'But of course, my lady. May I just collect my remedies and equipment?'

'Very well. But be quick about it.'

As de Waart busied himself about the room, picking up bottles of potions and small bags of dried this and that, I took Mother to one side. 'Where is the infant?' She looked confused. 'Clemence's son, Mother. Where is he?'

A scowl formed across her face. 'With his wet nurse, of course.'

'Is he well?'

'Yes. Fat as a piglet. And howls like a hound. I'm surprised you didn't hear him as you approached Versey.'

'Don't let de Waart near the child. Do you understand me?'

She shrugged a little. 'There's no need. He's a healthy child.' Then she smirked. 'A vigorous de Lacy boy.'

The words hung in the air provocatively, and I could not let them pass. 'No, Mother. This boy is a de Caburn.'

She turned on her heel, swept up de Waart in her wake, and vacated the room, leaving me alone with Humbert, who would not look up from my sister's face.

I approached the boy with some trepidation. 'We need to lift Clemence from the bed,' I told him. 'She needs to be washed.' The stink was so fetid on this side of the room that I had to hold my nose again.

Humbert coloured a little, but didn't say a word.

'Do you want my sister to die?' I asked.

Now his eyes jerked quickly from side to side. His huge fingers twitched. 'No,' he said warily, as if my question might be a trap.

'Then help me to move Clemence from this stench-ridden bed.'

Humbert regarded me for a moment longer, and then made the decision to cooperate. He fetched the chair from the passage that Mother had previously been sitting upon, and held Clemence's hand as she staggered inelegantly across the room. She was sweating at the forehead, and moved as clumsily as a lame heifer.

I called another servant into the chamber and told the man to remove Clemence's filthy feather mattress, and to replace it with another – although he soon returned with the news that the only spare mattress available was one made of straw. But no matter, at least it was clean and did not smell like the bedding of a beggar. And then I decided that Mother should donate her feather mattress to Clemence. After all, the woman was responsible for appointing de Waart to my sister's care. So I told the servant to take the straw mattress into Mother's bedchamber and swap it with hers. I did not hear a subsequent commotion, so could only assume that Mother was not in the chamber when the exchange took place.

Humbert was persuaded to leave his mistress momentarily in the chair, and to lift the wooden bathtub into the room. Then water for a hot bath was warmed over the fire in the great hall before being hauled up the stairs and deposited into the tub along with three bottles of Madeira wine and a cup full of salt. When the bath was ready, I left the room, dragging Humbert with me, as the boy was reluctant to quit. With our male eyes removed, my sister was washed by three of the female house servants, before being dressed in a linen nightgown and put back into a clean bed. We then lit another fire in the chamber, though this time it warmed a pan of lavender and sage. If Clemence were to die, then she would pass away without the perfume of a latrine to accompany her passage from this life.

I remained at one side of her bed with Humbert at the other. Her fever was still high, and I could see, even though she wore a loose gown, that her breasts were hard with milk. So hard that she groaned if she touched them, or even if she turned her body to one side. Looking at Clemence, I thanked the stars that I was not a woman.

Mother tiptoed into the chamber every so often to prod at Clemence's breast, but I refused to let the foolish woman apply a hot poultice. She claimed it would draw the milk and relieve Clemence's pain, but I suspected this sharp-smelling porridge had been prepared by de Waart and would doubtless contain a whole collection of foul, if not poisonous, ingredients. The man was still in the castle. I was sure of it, though I had told Mother to make him leave.

Mother harrumphed her way around the room, finding any excuse to linger now that the tapestry had been taken from the window and the pot of bitter herbs and bark had been removed from the fire. When she began to complain about the loss of her feather mattress, I banned her from the chamber completely, for I couldn't listen to her idle conversation and grumbles any further.

Our only disturbance during those hours came from the young de Caburn sisters, Mary and Rebecca, who liked to run up and down the passage outside the apartments, teasing Mother's little dog Hector by poking at his face with a stick and making him squeal with fury. More than once I left the room to ask for them to be quiet, whereupon the sisters would skid down the spiral stairs, only for the noise to reoccur in the courtyard below. Thankfully Clemence was too ill to be disturbed by their exuberance, for it was only childish joy and nothing that deserved to be stamped out by my sister's usual crabbiness.

When I left the room for a little air, I would watch the girls playing with their leather balls, sometimes brawling and then chasing each other about the inner courtyard. Sometimes merely stroking Mary's large grey cat and then dangling a length of yarn for the creature to paw. Their games were full of spirit and verve, as if the wave of their wooden swords might save England from an invasion of Saracens; or as if their make-believe spells would turn Medusa herself to stone. I looked upon these games with some envy and thought back to my own staid and stifled childhood – when I had sat upon my mother's knee having my blond hair combed as I was fed sugared violets. I had no playmates, since my sister and brothers had been so much older than me, and Mother had so thoroughly convinced everybody of my delicate constitution that I was barely allowed to place my feet upon the floor, let alone chase a dog or fight an imaginary foe.

I requested that Mary and Becky join me at supper on two occasions, hoping to enjoy their noisy company after the sombre silence of Clemence's bedchamber. On both occasions, however, a servant informed me that the girls had disappeared into the forest, with food they had stolen from the kitchen. They then returned, late at night, with mud on their boots and scratches on their hands, and without a proper explanation of where they had been, or what they had been doing. I was too tired and preoccupied with Clemence's care to press them for answers. But I should have.

On the third night, Clemence seemed a little stiller. I would say she remained hot to the touch, but a corner had been turned in this path and it appeared she might be recovering. I was falling asleep on the chair beside her bed, when I heard her say my name. It was so softly spoken that it did not even wake Humbert, though he slept at the end of her bed like a faithful dog.

I leant over her. 'Clemence. Is that you? Are you awake?'

Her sharp black eyes opened. 'Where's Henry?'

At first the name meant nothing to me, as I had more or less forgotten about her son. He now resided in the anteroom to the great hall, where a village girl sat with him attached to her breast, while she consumed as much food as the cook would provide.

'My son, Henry,' she repeated. 'Where is he?'

'He's well, Clemence. He's sleeping at the moment.' I knew this to be true, since Henry's screaming was not reverberating about the walls of Versey like the screech of a vixen, as it had been for most of the day.

'Would you bring him to me, please,' she said.

'Now?'

Her sharpness was still blunted by the birth fever. 'Yes,' she said feebly. 'I wish to see him.'

I took her limp hand, which was cold and sweaty to the touch. And so small, with tiny, childish fingers. 'Let me bring Henry to you tomorrow. Rest a little longer.'

She withdrew her hand with all the affronted belligerence of old, and I was pleased of it. It meant she was recovering. 'I just want to see my own son,' she demanded. 'Why won't you bring him to me?' Then her anger subsided and she looked at me with eyes that were both scared and tearful. 'Please Oswald.'

The passageways of Versey Castle were eerie and dark at this time of night, with only a prowling kitchen cat or a scampering rat happy to venture along their stony surfaces. After crossing the inner keep, I reached the great hall, where a blazing fire warmed the whole household, though I had not expected to see the face of Henry's wet nurse glowing in the light of these flames. She had seated herself amongst a group of the younger men, and was keeping them entertained with a gaping tunic. Before the group noticed my presence, one of the men tried to put his hand inside her gown, at which affront she only laughed and took another gulp of ale.

I coughed loudly, and at the sight of my face the laughter came to an abrupt end. The wet nurse rearranged her tunic and quickly scuttled back to the anteroom where she should have been caring for Clemence's child. I told the others to settle down for the night and then followed the girl into the chamber, noting that her gait was unsteady. She stood by Henry's wooden cradle and attempted to focus her eyes upon me. 'I only left the boy for a minute, sire,' she said. 'He's been suckling all day and was happy to sleep.'

'Are you drunk?'

'No, sire,' she assured me. 'Not at all.'

I regarded her for a moment. Such a pretty face. Without warning, I felt the desire to look inside her gaping tunic myself – just as the men about the fire had been doing. Her breasts were full and rounded, even through the unflattering looseness of her woollen gown. I took a deep breath and quelled such a crude and debased thought. 'I'm taking the infant to his mother.'

She didn't seem to understand what I had just said. 'I'm not drunk, sire.'

'I know. You just told me so.'

'I'm just sad.' So, the girl had drunk enough ale to loosen her tongue.

I should have taken Henry and left, but her face was pretty. So very pretty. 'Why are you sad?'

'I was thinking of my own boy, sire. It makes me sad to think about him.' Now she wiped her face. 'My sister feeds him cow's milk. Though it makes him sick.'

'I didn't realise you had a baby.'

It was such a foolish comment to make, for the existence of a second baby had not occurred to me – though it was an obvious and essential part of this arrangement. The girl now snorted and suddenly focussed upon me. Her words were as sober as those of an anchoress. 'How else would I be full of milk, sire?' Then she laughed, a bitter cackle that caused her to double up before she collapsed onto a stool. As I looked upon her face, I suddenly thought of my own mother. My real mother, Adeline Starvecrow. She had been a young village girl such as this, but until last year I had never even heard her name.

The girl's laughter stopped. 'I'm not allowed to see him. Though I have enough milk to feed them both. And then I worry about him, being left alone. They say the butcher bird is flying. Looking for the young and weak.'

I sighed. 'That isn't true.'

'But it took a baby from Somershill. I heard that.'

'No it didn't. That's just a foolish tale. How could there be a bird big enough to take a baby? Have you ever seen such a beast?'

'So who killed the child then?'

'A man. Not a bird. Your baby is safe,' I insisted.

She shrugged. 'If he doesn't die of hunger.'

'Where's your husband then? Can't he care for the child?'

The girl sighed. 'Poor Hugh. He's had to move away to Canters Cross.'

'Why?' I suddenly felt suspicious. I didn't remember giving anybody with the name of Hugh permission to leave Versey.

Now she seemed awkward, 'He's a free man, sire. He can go, if he wants to.'

'And he's being paid more at Canters Cross, I suppose?' She wouldn't answer this question, claiming that she knew nothing of such matters. But I knew she was lying. And then I felt a sudden wave of sympathy for the girl. As I looked at her closely, she was more pale and sickly than I had first supposed. The firelight had conferred a beauty upon her that was lessened without its flattering glow. Was it a cruelty to separate her from her own baby? If my mother had been prevented from feeding me as well as the de Lacy boy, then I would probably have died.

'You have my permission to bring your son here,' I said.

I didn't receive the gratitude I might have expected for this gesture. Instead she looked up at me with the edge of suspicion in her eye. 'Are you sure?'

'Yes,' I said and then almost immediately regretted my decision. What if the girl was unable to feed both infants? 'Though you must take care of both boys,' I added. 'I will be watching you closely.'

'But what about my Lady? Your mother.'

'What about her?'

'She'll object to this arrangement.'

'Let her.'

I lifted baby Henry from his cradle and found him to be heavier than I had expected. He was cocooned in his swaddling as tightly as a fly in a spider's web, but he did not wake as I clumsily gripped him. He only blew a milky bubble from his lips and then screwed up a face that was as wrinkled and flaky as the crust on a beef and bacon pie. A shock of thick black hair poked out from beneath his lace bonnet and stuck unctuously to his forehead. He was not a handsome child, but then I do not find any newborn infant easy to admire. Most look as if they have been squashed inside a bottle and then steeped in vinegar.

It was bitingly cold outside as I hurried across the inner keep to the family's private apartment, but the chill in the air did not stir Henry. He merely turned his head towards my chest and smacked his lips, as if a nipple might drop into his mouth. I now lamented bringing the child to Clemence, afraid that he might wake up and renew his screaming when milk did not appear. There is little in this world as terrifying as a hungry baby. They can shift from gentle disciple to ferocious tyrant in the blink of an eye.

I opened the door to the ladies' bedchamber to find the room in darkness, except for the embers that still glowed in the hearth. Humbert had pulled the thick curtains about Clemence's bed, and now he sat by the fire, trying to stoke it back into life. The chamber had a peaceful calmness to it, reminding me of the infirmary at the monastery, once all of our troublesome patients were asleep.

'Is Clemence awake?' I asked Humbert.

The boy went over to the bed and peeped through the curtains. He shook his head.

I hesitated now. Should I leave Clemence to sleep, or try to wake her before the baby needed feeding again? While I deliberated over this mild but perplexing dilemma, Humbert sidled over to me and peered cautiously into the swaddling. As Henry blew another of his milky bubbles, Humbert frowned and quickly withdrew.

'It's nothing to worry about,' I said. 'It just proves the child is breathing.'

Humbert bit his lip and returned cautiously to look again at Henry – his face then breaking out into the widest of smiles, for the baby in my arms was now pulling the most amusing of expressions. His soft eyebrows were raised and his tiny lips pursed, as if he were experiencing a wave of ecstasy. And then, suddenly, his skin became a violent shade of crimson before he wriggled and squirmed inside the swaddling, as if he were in excruciating pain. Humbert and I now regarded each other in alarm, before the child emitted the longest fart I have ever heard.

When the long coil of wind had finally exhausted itself, the baby gave a little sigh of satisfaction, but not so Humbert – for now the foolish boy had retreated to the other side of the room, as if the fart might attack him. He really was the most foolish of servants, and I often wondered why Clemence was so tolerant of his peculiarities.

'Go and find the wet nurse,' I said. 'Tell her to come here immediately.' Humbert sidled about the very edge of the chamber before fleeing through the door. 'Don't be long about it!' I shouted after him.

Once he had closed the door, I awkwardly lit a candle with one arm and then sat upon the chair, cradling the baby upon my lap. Henry had not woken throughout this episode, but his head was still turning towards my chest with increasing regularity, meaning that we only had a few minutes before he would wake and demand to be fed. His legs started to kick inside the swaddling with surprising strength, and the sweet and sickly perfume of rotting vegetables wafted up towards me.

'Please hurry up, Humbert,' I said aloud.

'Is that you, Oswald?' It was Clemence's voice, from behind the curtains of her bed.

'I'm sorry. I didn't mean to wake you, Clemence. Go back to sleep.'

'Do you have my son with you?' Her voice was weak.

I hesitated to answer.

'Oswald. Do you have my son with you?' she repeated.

'Yes, Clemence. But he is about to wake, and he smells very bad.'

'Bring him to me,' she said. 'Please.'

I lifted back the curtain and looked down upon my sister. She had somehow managed to prop herself up against the bedstead with a bolster, and as I held Henry before her, her eyes filled with tears. She held out her hands to take him from me, and I noticed her nightgown was stained, though a maidservant had bound her breasts with linen. Once again I thanked the stars that I was not a woman. 'I'm not sure you should hold him, Clemence. You're still too weak.'

'Just pass him to me.'

'But Clemence—'

'Oswald!' She leant forward and groaned these words, only to collapse back against the bolster. It was obvious she had exhausted herself. 'He is my son,' she said. 'Please let me hold him once before I die.'

How could I deny such a request? I passed Henry to my sister gently, so he might sit upon her stomach and rest in her arms, but the contrary little creature chose this exact moment to open his eyes and begin to bawl. Perhaps it was the motion of moving from my arms, or perhaps it was because he could smell his own mother's milk, but he changed from a restful, if odorous angel into a roaring and kicking monster. I tried to take him back from Clemence, as this exertion would not aid her recovery, but she held on to her child with an obstinate strength.

'Leave him where he is,' she said. 'I'm not concerned by his crying. Bring the candle over, so I can look at him properly.' I did as she asked, holding the flame aloft so she might see her son's face. 'Isn't he perfect?'

I found it impossible to agree that this squashed-up, red-faced monster was anything near perfection, so instead I changed the subject sharply and informed Clemence that Humbert would soon return with the wet nurse. Humbert did not return, however, and just as I was about to run to the great hall myself to retrieve him, Clemence called me back to her.

'Help me to remove the bindings upon my chest,' she said.

'What?'

She threw me the fiercest stare. 'I want to feed my own child, Oswald. He's hungry.' The boy was now squirming and struggling against his swaddling, with his head fixed upon Clemence's chest and his mouth sucking at the air like a surfacing fish. In truth, the child now revolted me, reminding me of a leech with its pulsating sucker.

Clemence took my arm. 'Help me.'

I placed the candle back by the fire and then returned to lift her nightgown, before gently pulling at the bindings to release both of her swollen breasts. Now free of the sour and cheesy-smelling compress, Clemence was able to hold the whining baby to her body, whereupon he latched on to her breast, and did not make another sound, other than the occasional slurp and burble.

Clemence sighed in pain, but with an edge of relief, even pleasure.

'Don't worry. The wet nurse will be here shortly,' I told her. 'She can take over.'

'I don't want her to take over.'

'But this will tire you, Clemence.'

'Oh be quiet.'

I removed myself to a stool and looked at my feet, trying not to listen to the farmyard noises coming from the bed.

Clemence looked up at me after a while. 'Do you find this disgusting, Oswald?'

'No,' I lied.

She gave a feeble laugh. 'Yes you do. Foolish boy. How did you imagine a baby is fed?'

I turned to the fire, in the pretence of needing to stoke up the flames. 'Are you warm enough, Clemence?' I asked.

Her voice was softer now. 'Yes. Thank you.'

'Is there anything you need?'

'Only that you keep your promise to Henry when I'm dead.'

'You're not going to die, Clemence.'

She ignored this comment. 'I want you to promise that Henry will have Versey when he comes of age.'

I raised the candle and returned to Clemence's side. The air around the curtained bed was fusty and cloying, and I was tempted to hold my nose. 'I've told you before, Clemence. Whether Henry becomes Lord Versey is not entirely my decision. The earl may object.'

'Isn't Somershill enough for you?' The baby fell away from her breast, sated. 'Though, by rights that estate should be Henry's as well.'

'I didn't ask for any of this Clemence. You know that. I was prepared to return to the monastery and take my vows.'

She snorted, with as much vigour as she was able, but did not answer.

'I can only promise to try,' I said.

'But is that good enough, Oswald?' I grimaced and shrugged,

which only infuriated her further. 'How do you think it feels?' she asked me. 'To be dying. Leaving a child.'

'I don't know,' I said with a sigh.

She closed her eyes and took a shallow breath. Feeding the baby had exhausted her, just as I had feared would happen. When I tried to take Henry from her, however, Clemence clasped him to her breast. 'Leave him with me Oswald.' Tears now streaked her cheeks.

I placed the candle on a shelf inside the bedstead and then wiped Clemence's face with a square of clean linen. She drank a little ale to quench her thirst, but still she would not release her child. 'Do you promise to give Versey to Henry?' she asked me again, when I had removed the cup and dabbed her dry lips.

I sighed. She had worn me down. 'Yes, Clemence. I promise.'

'And you will not renege on that promise?'

What an oath to make. How foolish to set myself against the fates. 'No. I will not.'

She raised her small hand and held it to mine. 'Thank you. You are a good brother.' It was rare for Clemence to speak to me with tenderness, and I will admit to enjoying those warming, if fleeting rays of affection.

At that moment, Humbert returned, accompanied by the wet nurse. Seeing Clemence propped up in the bedstead with the baby in her lap, Humbert appeared to freeze, until my sister raised a finger and beckoned for him to look upon Henry's face. The baby now slept soundly, but as he gave a little burp Humbert once again recoiled.

'He's only a baby,' said Clemence. The colour had returned a little to her cheeks since our last conversation. A rash of pink to match the rashness of my promise. 'Come and hold him.'

Humbert mumbled something at his feet, before shuffling reluctantly to the bedstead, unable to resist the urge to be at my sister's side. Now she held Henry up for him to view, angling his still and sleeping face towards the light. The infant was peaceful, but as Humbert drew near, the little boy hiccupped. This time Humbert only smiled, however. And then a look passed between he and Clemence.

What manner of glance, I cannot say.

But nonetheless it troubled me.

Chapter Seven

I stayed at Versey Castle for another three days and Clemence didn't die. In fact, with Henry's cradle now set up in her own chamber, my sister's spirits seemed to revive by the hour. The wet nurse remained, although Clemence, much to Mother's disgust, was continuing to feed the child herself. On the morning of my last day, I met the pretty girl leaving Versey with a smile across her face. In her arms she held a small bundle that contained her own miniature son.

'Where are you going Alice?' I knew her name, having spent some time conversing with the girl over the last few days, while we were both confined to the family's apartment.

Alice curtsied to me. 'I've been dismissed, sire.'

'By whom?'

'Your sister, Lady Clemence.' I must have frowned, since she followed up her statement with an explanation. 'The boy only likes his mother's milk. He won't take from me any longer.'

'Is that true?' I asked, since I had witnessed Alice feeding the boy with little trouble the day before.

She reddened a little. 'Lady Clemence says my milk makes the child choleric.' And now I guessed what was truly happening. Clemence was jealous of the girl's ability to feed the child.

I gave Alice a penny and wished her well, before hurrying to Clemence's chamber to find my sister sitting in the chair. Once again Henry was at her breast, but he was no longer swaddled. Instead he wore a lace gown, and it was possible to see the size of him. I had rarely encountered such a large newborn child. It was no wonder that his birth had nearly killed his mother.

'You shouldn't have dismissed the wet nurse, Clemence,' I said. 'You will wear yourself out.'

'Nonsense. Henry is curing me with his suckling. I could barely leave my bed a couple of days ago. But now he is feeding from me, my fever is gone.'

There is something about the word *suckling*. It makes my stomach turn.

Clemence noticed the look upon my face and rolled her eyes. 'What is wrong with you, Oswald?' she said with some exasperation. 'Feeding your own baby is the most natural act for a mother. Why did God give me breasts? They are not simply for a man to squeeze on his wedding night.'

I tried to defend myself. 'It's just that a lady in your position usually uses a wet nurse.'

Now she laughed at me. 'And then she takes the risk that the wet nurse will swap the lady's baby for her own.' An uncomfortable silence followed, with only the baby's muffled slurping audible. Clemence heaved a sigh. 'I'm sorry, Oswald. I shouldn't have said that.'

I cleared my throat. 'No matter, Clemence.'

She held out a hand to me. 'Please, Oswald. Accept my apology. There was no need for me to mention your mother.'

I wasn't sure how to read this. On one side it was an apology. On the other it was yet another reference to my true beginnings. A secret that Clemence would never let me forget, no matter how many apologies and pleasantries passed between us.

So I declined the hand and simply bowed to her. 'Now that you're making a good recovery, Clemence, I shall return to Somershill. Mother can stay here with you.'

She dropped her hand and groaned. 'If she must.'

'I need to attend to the murder. Find who's responsible, before the village calls again for Barrow's head.'

Clemence wasn't listening. Her eyes were closing, so I decided to leave her in peace. Just as I reached the door, however, she woke with a start. 'Oswald!' I stopped in my tracks. 'Oswald. Don't forget the promise you made to me about Henry.'

I didn't turn around. 'You don't need to keep reminding me, Clemence.'

'Don't I?'

'No.'

I was packing away my belongings into a saddlebag when my peace was disturbed by a great scream. Realising that it came from Clemence's chamber, I ran to the room to see what was causing such a fuss, only to find my sister clutching baby Henry to her chest, while Humbert held a grey cat aloft by the scruff of its neck. It was the creature that Mary and Rebecca de Caburn often played with.

Mother pushed past me as I stood in the doorway. 'What is the matter, Clemence? Such a noise. At that pitch, you will attract every tomcat in the castle.'

Clemence waved Mother away. 'Bring Mary de Caburn to me, this instant. And that spiteful little sister of hers.'

'Why?' I asked. 'What have they done?'

Clemence turned on me. 'They've tried to kill my son. That's what.' Her teeth were clenched.

This was such an outlandish suggestion that I couldn't help but laugh.

'Do you think this is funny?' said Clemence, pointing a finger into my face.

I stumbled over my words. 'No. But I think it's a stupid accusation.'

Her face was beginning to ferment. 'Oh do you? Humbert and I left baby Henry for just a minute in his cradle, so I might walk about the courtyard. When I returned, those two little demons had dumped their flea-ridden cat upon Henry's face. He might have suffocated.'

'But cats will sit upon infants, Clemence. It's merely warmth the creature was looking for.'

I tried to put my arm around her, but she elbowed me away. 'The door was closed, Oswald,' she said, 'so the cat was let in deliberately.'

I looked to the cat, who was now hissing and clawing at the air. 'Mary and her sister wouldn't do such a thing. Henry is their own half-brother.'

Clemence backed away from me. 'Oh but they would, Oswald. I let Mary hold Henry yesterday and she nearly dropped him. On purpose.'

Mother interrupted, though, as usual, it was neither a helpful nor welcome intervention. 'The de Caburn girls would have much to gain by this boy's death. It can't be denied. And using their cat to do the deed is a devilish plan.'

I was astounded by this statement. 'What nonsense! As if two small girls would try to murder a baby.'

Mother folded her arms and joined Clemence – the two of them opposing me like a pair of wrestlers at a Lammas day match. 'So, who do you think is responsible then?' Mother said. 'Did your butcher bird fly in and drop the cat upon the baby's face?'

I ignored this stupid provocation. 'It was an accident, Mother. Clemence or Humbert must have left the door open. Or the cat was already in here and they didn't realise. You know how silent they can be. Slinking through doors and hiding in corners.' With this the cat gave a last frantic wriggle and succeeded in releasing itself from Humbert's grip. And though the enormous servant tried to catch the creature again, it shot out of the door at speed with a spitting howl.

Clemence began to cry. 'Henry must be guarded, every hour

of every day. I shall have no peace with those two little goblins and their wicked cat running about the house.'

Mother smoothed my sister's brow. 'Don't fret Clemence. I shall have the two girls locked in their father's dungeon. That will teach them to behave.'

'No, you won't, Mother,' I said, but the silly woman wasn't listening.

'And as for the cat,' she said. 'We shall hunt it down and roast it upon the fire. I may even use its coat to make a pair of mittens.'

I grasped Mother roughly by the arm. 'You are to leave the sisters and their cat alone. Do you understand me?'

She ignored me and whispered into Clemence's ear. 'Or I could have Master de Waart prepare a sedative for the two girls. That would temper their spite.'

So de Waart was still on the premises. Just as I had suspected. Now I shook Mother. 'You're not to let that fraud anywhere near the girls.'

She bridled. 'He's skilled at dealing with such maleficence. Last year he cured a madman with a tincture of mugwort.'

'The man died.'

'Yes. But not before he was cured.'

'He wasn't cured, Mother. He was poisoned!'

She snorted and turned her back on me, as Clemence continued to cry. 'I have a suggestion,' I said, trying to cool the heat of all this raging sentiment. 'I'll take Mary and Rebecca back to Somershill. They can stay with me until Henry is a little older.'

Mother frowned. 'No, no. You can't do that. What a foolish idea.'

Annoyed that my proposal was so soundly disregarded, I will admit to losing my temper. 'I don't suppose you do, Mother. But then you would lock the sisters in a dungeon their father used for torture. Then you would kill their favourite cat. And if that were not enough, you would then let your useless physician poison them.'

Mother affected the first swoons of a faint at my words, but on receiving no sympathy or even comment from my sister, she trimmed down the drama to a mere fanning.

It was Clemence who spoke first, after blowing her nose into a square of linen. 'Do stop play-acting, Mother.' Mother went to protest, but stumbled over her words. My sister continued. 'I think it's a good idea. Let Oswald take them.'

Mother's fanning ceased. 'But Clemence. The sisters are your stepdaughters. They should be in your care. You should be seen to punish them.'

Clemence's teeth began to clench. 'I don't want them near my son.'

'But you are responsible for them,' said Mother.

'I don't want to be.'

'Really, Clemence. If you excuse this behaviour, then who knows what trouble they will cause you in the future?'

Clemence's knuckles were now white against the skin of her bony hands, and she continued to hold Henry in a vice-like embrace. She turned to me. 'Thank you for your offer, Oswald. It would be of great service to me if you would take those two she-devils with you to Somershill.'

Mother went to object, but Clemence and I stared her into silence. A feat that was rarely achieved.

I bowed my head. 'Very well. We will leave this afternoon.'

Chapter Eight

O ur party returned to Somershill from Versey along the
drover's road. It was not the most direct route through the
forest, but there were three of us on horseback, and a wagon
following. We needed to follow a road, rather than taking our
chances on the forest trails where beard lichen often drooped in
great curtains from the trees, concealing the path ahead. As we
travelled, I found myself wondering if wolves still roamed these
dappled glades? I hadn't heard their melancholic calls, nor seen
their tracks in the mud for many months – but wolves are secretive
creatures that keep to the shadows and hide far away from the
footsteps of man. If their dwindling number still lurked in this
forest, then we were most unlikely to meet them.

The sisters rode behind me on their ponies, followed by a
servant and the wagon that carried all their belongings, including
a battered wooden box containing the troublesome cat. Mary had
made holes in this box, so that the creature could breathe, but
even so, it seemed disturbed – for a strange rustling noise came
repeatedly from within the chest. When I attempted to look
closer, Mary pulled me back sharply with the warning that the
cat would spit.

As we rode towards Somershill, Mary was full of false bluster,
hitting out at every low-hanging branch with her sword, and
shouting regularly that she was pleased to have left *that bitch*

Clemence behind at Versey. And no matter how many times I told her to be quiet, she only repeated the insult until I began to wish I had indeed left the sisters in the care of my mother. Rebecca, on the other hand, was withdrawn, this being the furthest she had ever travelled from the castle of her birth. She kept lagging behind us, as if we might change our minds and return to Versey.

When our small party arrived back at Somershill I passed Tempest's reins over to Piers and was looking forward to my own feather mattress and a bath – a luxury I had avoided at Versey, as it was Mother's insistent opinion that sitting for too long in a bathtub of warm water only invited the Devil to soak into your skin.

On reaching my bedchamber I removed my heavy riding gown, pulled off my leather boots, and flopped onto the woollen blanket across the bed. I was so pleased to be back in my own bed that I reached quickly under the mattress to pull out one of my indecent manuscripts. It was the first time I had been alone for many days and I'm ashamed to say that I needed to purge myself of a certain longing.

I was in the middle of such a purging when Gilbert blew into the room like a blast of cold air. 'Sire. I cannot tend to that lunatic you are keeping in the tower any longer,' he announced.

I quickly pulled up the sheets. 'Can't you knock, Gilbert!'

The old man pulled a face. 'Didn't know you were in bed, sire.'

'I've had a long journey. And I'm tired.'

Gilbert merely raised an eyebrow.

'What do you want?'

Gilbert cleared his throat as if he were about to make a much-practised speech. 'Barrow has to go, sire. He dirties himself like a ewe. And he wails like a banshee. All of the day and all of the night. I can hear it all over the house. It's a good job your mother isn't at Somershill. Her humours would be stirred up into a soup.'

I heaved myself wearily onto my elbows, the low sun catching my eyes. 'What would you have me do, Gilbert? Send Barrow back to the village and wait until they've torn him into pieces?'

He shrugged.

I flopped back onto the mattress with my hands above my head. 'Perhaps you would prefer it if they burned him?'

Gilbert heaved a sigh and then bustled about the room, picking up my riding gown and boots and grumbling into his chest. 'And it's not just Barrow, you know. Now it seems I'm to look after those two wayward de Caburn girls as well. As if I didn't have enough to do.'

'Just hire a maid for them,' I said. 'You don't need to trouble yourself.'

My suggestion was ignored. 'And there's been a village boy hanging around here, at your request apparently. Getting in my way.'

'Which village boy?'

'That Hayward boy.' He gave one of his scornful laughs. 'Claims you promised to help him with his reading.'

'I did.'

He laughed again. 'What? With one of those books you keep under the mattress?'

This was one impertinence too far. I swung my tired feet off the bed and stood over him – my frame now seeming larger than his stout and square-shaped body. Was Gilbert getting shorter, or was I getting taller? 'I'm planning to offer Geoffrey some employ-ment,' I said sharply. 'In fact, he could become my new valet.'

Gilbert reddened a little at my threat, though only a little.

I relented. 'Come on, Gilbert. Geoffrey might be of some help to you. And the boy could do with some luck.'

He pulled another face. 'It will just be more work for me, sire. I'll have to waste my time training the boy.'

I looked him in the eye. 'You'll do as you're instructed.'

We faced each other for a moment, until Gilbert gave in. 'Very well.' He cleared his throat. 'I'm sorry to speak so plainly. I won't do it again.' He bowed solemnly and went to leave — with my folded cape over his shoulder and my dirty leather boots under his arm. At the door he stopped and turned to speak to me, however. His expression now conciliatory. 'You've got John Barrow, the de Caburn sisters and now this Hayward boy under your care. But you can't save everybody, sire. That's all I'm saying.' Then he trudged into the darkness before I had an opportunity to answer.

I first regretted not listening to Gilbert that very same night, for John Barrow howled from his cell within the north-west tower as loudly as the wicked priests of Baal. If only Elijah himself were here to stop him, for Barrow's calling was an unpleasant and sporadic noise that woke a person at the very moment of sleep. Right then I wanted the man to leave, but where would he go? I had made a commitment to protect him. A tired mind is neither rational nor sympathetic, so each time Barrow disturbed me with his wailing, I imagined stuffing a length of linen into his mouth and keeping it in place with a firm binding. He made more noise than baby Henry.

Eventually I placed a bolster over my head to block Barrow's calling from my ears, though now, when sleep found me, I fell into a bad dream. It was not the burning boy, nor the great ox. Instead I was crawling through a strange forest, where the beard lichen hung in ribbons from the trees. When I looked up, however, it was not lichen, but hair that blocked my path. Human hair — falling from a head hidden amongst the branches above me. I dared not look for this face however, for I knew exactly whose it would be: Catherine Tulley's.

I woke with a start. I was sweating and cold. I had neglected my investigation too long.

With this purpose, the following morning I rode to the village to ask more questions regarding the murder. So far I knew the child had disappeared while her mother, Mary Tulley, had left the cottage to work in the fields. It still seemed slightly odd to me that Mary hadn't taken the infant with her, as so many other women do, but she already had three children hanging from her skirts, so it was possibly no wonder that she had left her smallest child behind. Deciding to call at the neighbouring cottages along the Long Ditch, I wanted to ask if anybody else had seen anything suspicious on the day of the infant's disappearance.

The cottages were lined up along the edge of a narrow waterway, which was full of mud and leaves, as well as the raw sewage that should have been dumped in the woodland, rather than emptied into this gulley right outside these homes. Since the Plague, I had fined people at the manorial court for just flinging their filth into the street, but in truth it had done little to stop the practice, as my argument that foul miasmas would only speed the spread of the contagion did little to convince anybody. Most of the villagers still maintained that the Plague was a punishment from God, and though I wanted to ask them what sort of Father would inflict such cruel punishment upon his own children, I knew such talk would be regarded as blasphemy. So I kept my mouth shut.

I made for the cottage next door to the Tulleys', though my presence had already been noticed. The Tulley children had scampered indoors at my crossing of the rickety bridge, to alert their mother, for I soon saw the wan face of Mary Tulley at her door. 'Did you want to speak to me, sire?' she asked with a weary curtsy.

I bowed. 'No. Thank you, Mistress Tulley. Not today.' I thought about telling her my purpose, but then decided against it. She didn't need to know each step of my investigation. The woman looked relieved that she was not about to be questioned a second time, quickly pulling her eldest son into the shadows in the hope that I had not seen the child once again poke his tongue out at me. I should have boxed the child's ears for such gall, but the scene was so melancholic that his impertinence hardly mattered.

There was thatch now missing from the Tulleys' roof, which I can only assume had been burned on the fire, and the three children were as thin and filthy as city beggars. The smell of boiling cabbage filled the air. Most probably the meal for breakfast, lunch, and supper.

I felt for a halfpenny in my pocket and held it out to the boy, but he only buried his head into his mother's leg. So, instead I offered it to Mary. 'Here, Mistress Tulley. Please take this and buy the children a little meat to accompany that cabbage.'

She held out her hand and then withdrew it. 'I can't, sire.'

'Why not?'

She looked to her feet. 'Because, Thomas—' Then she clammed up and tried to shuffle back inside the cottage. 'I have to go. I'm sorry.'

'Take the halfpenny, Mistress Tulley. Thomas won't know.' I held the small silver coin out to her, the relief of King Edward's head catching the morning light, with the curls of his hair sprouting out from either side of his head like a pair of unravelling scrolls.

Mary looked over my shoulder in case her husband should jump out from the shadows, and then quickly she seized the coin from my hand. 'Thank you, sire,' she said, before firmly shutting the door upon me.

A strange, but not unpleasant perfume drifted through an open window as I made my way across the muddy gap towards the cottage next door. It was the scent of camphor and rosemary and reminded me perversely of both the almond comfits that I'd eaten at wedding feasts, and the ointment we used at the monastery to dab upon the gums of a brother with toothache. I knocked at the door, which unlike Mary Tulley's was neatly boarded without any holes for the cold air to creep through. I knew the owner of this cottage – a widow named Agnes Salt – a woman the village often visited in place of a physician. Though, given that the only person in this part of Kent to qualify as a doctor was my old friend Roger de Waart, who could blame them? Especially as Agnes charged little more than the cost of her ingredients.

There were some, however, who were wary of Agnes and her cures, calling her a meddler and a pest. A woman who should leave the study of medicine to men. Agnes spoke against the teachings of Galen. That was well known. But there were some who said she also spoke against God.

Agnes opened the door to me, her face red and sweating, and I wasn't quite sure where to look, for the woman was dressed only in a tight-fitting chemise, with a breast band across her scrawny chest. A pan steamed away on a trivet over the fire, and the heat of the chamber quickly escaped into the street. I would tell you she looked flustered to be opening her door to her lord in nothing but her undergarments, but she simply wiped her brow with a square of linen and curtsied as if this were the most ordinary of occasions. I looked past her to see that the room was completely bare, other than the fire pit, a rolled mattress and a single stool.

'Good morning to you, sire,' she said, with a smile revealing most of her upper gums. 'I'm sorry that you find me busy, but I'm brewing this morning.'

Agnes wasn't known as an ale-wife and the smell that billowed out of the cottage was certainly not that of beer. 'What are you brewing, Mistress Salt?'

Her smile waned a little. 'It is a special kind of ale.' Then she opened her eyes widely and fixed me with such an unnerving gaze that I didn't feel inclined to enquire any further.

I looked away and cleared my throat. 'I would like to ask you some questions regarding the disappearance of Catherine Tulley.' I then waited for Agnes to invite me into the cottage, but she remained in the doorway, still smiling at me with a set of gums that would shame a horse. After clearing my throat a second time and nodding towards the fire, the woman still did not take my hint, so I had no option but to push past without waiting for an invitation.

Agnes took the pan from the fire, so that the steam would abate and we might see each other properly. She then disappeared into a dark corner of the room and returned with a mug of mead, which I accepted in the hope it was not flavoured with the same herbs as the *special kind of* ale that had been heating on the fire. Agnes offered me the stool, before perching on the rolled-up mattress.

From her position beside me, she stoked the fire and then looked at me expectantly, and for a moment I felt as tongue-tied as a child asked to recite a rhyme at the supper table. Her eyes were large, and whereas I was sure they had been blue when we stood by the door, they suddenly appeared as dark and peculiar as two great blood blisters.

I shook myself. 'Mistress Salt.'

She answered slowly and softly, which only made me feel more heavy-eyed. 'Yes, sire.'

I stood up quickly, in the hope of becoming more alert. 'Please. Take my place on this stool.'

'As you like.'

She shifted her lithe body onto the stool, and I now made sure to stand behind her, so that she couldn't look into my eyes. Feeling unsettled, I sipped too eagerly at the mead, but only succeeded in choking myself.

'Are you unwell, sire?' she asked me.

I coughed and wiped my running nose upon my sleeve. 'No. I'm perfectly well.'

'Let me fetch you a posy.' She went to stand up, but I put my hands upon her shoulders. 'Stay where you are, please.' She tensed. Her body as bony as a carcass stripped of meat.

I released my hands quickly and she remained on the stool. 'Were you at home the morning baby Catherine was taken?' I asked her.

She nodded. 'I was, sire.'

'Did you see anybody approach the Tulleys' cottage?'

'I saw only Thomas leaving at dawn, followed by his wife and sons soon after.'

'Did you see Mary Tulley leave her child outside their cottage, before she left?'

She shrugged. 'I can't remember.'

'And you didn't go to the fields yourself?'

'No, sire. I stayed behind all morning.'

'Doing what?'

'Brewing ale.'

I looked over at the pan she had taken from the fire, noting that a dried plant was now floating on its surface. Having been soaked in water, this plant, a summer flower, had taken on something of its previous shape, with a spray of feathery leaves and a cluster of small-headed blooms that might once have been yellow.

I turned back to Mistress Salt. 'So you heard or saw nothing that morning?' I said.

'I heard only the beat of a bird's wing.'

An anger welled inside me. 'What sort of bird?'

'The butcher bird, of course.'

Now I walked around to look directly upon Agnes's face, taking my chances. 'Don't lie to me.'

Her chin tilted forwards, obstinately. 'I'm not.'

'So you would have me believe that a bird took Catherine Tulley from her cradle?'

She nodded, but the gesture was curious. Ambivalent. 'It's certainly true that a butcher bird haunts this parish.'

'It does not.'

She pulled some of her greasy hair behind her ear. 'As you say, sire.' Then she smiled with such a gum-filled grin that I quickly withdrew my gaze to the edge of the room, where my eyes once again fell upon the pan of ale. 'Is it Tansy in that brew?' I asked.

'That's correct,' she said.

'But there's another herb in there, I think. I can smell mint, perhaps?'

Her voice returned to its soft slowness. 'It's only pudding grass.'

I'd never heard of such a plant. 'It seems a strange combination for flavouring ale,' I said, nonetheless.

Agnes stretched a hand towards the pan and stirred the ale with a long pole that moved slowly through the mixture, like a washing bat in a tub of soaking fleeces. 'As I said before, sire. This is a *special* brew,' she told me. 'I call it dull ale.'

'Dull ale?'

She nodded and fixed me with her eyes. Now they had returned to a shade of blue. 'A glass of this brew and you won't notice that you haven't eaten for a whole day.' She leant her head to one side, but did not break her stare. 'It dulls the appetite.'

I tried to look away, but it was impossible. 'I've not heard of such a thing,' I said, but suddenly my words sounded distant, as if they were the voice of another person on the other side of the room.

Agnes laughed. 'No. I don't suppose you have. I doubt there is any call for such ale in your castle.'

I suddenly felt faint, with the consuming desire to sit down again upon the stool. Even to flop onto the floor. I bit my teeth into my tongue in the hope some pain would wake me from this stupor, but could not shake myself fully from the trance. Whether Agnes had enchanted me with her eyes, or whether there had been some noxious sedative in the mead, I could not say. And had I not argued so vociferously on so many occasions against the existence of witches, I might have accused this woman of sorcery. But what is sorcery, other than deception? And I had been tricked in some way – of that I am in no doubt.

'Why do you think the poorest people of this village drink my dull ale?' she asked me. Her face loomed in and out of focus and she did not wait for an answer. 'Then I'll tell you. They're starving, sire. They might have survived the Plague, but what for? Not everybody has profited from this new world. Not everybody has been lucky enough to inherit a larger field, or been able to buy up their dead neighbours' flock of sheep. What about those people? There's plenty of them who continue to suffer. Two years of rain. Two bad harvests. It might not matter, if they could earn a decent wage. But instead you insist upon paying them the same as you did five years ago. What good is that? When the price of grain rises daily?'

'It's not my doing,' I said. 'It's the king's law.'

'Then break the law.'

'I can't.'

She leant in closer. Her words now undulating like a mother's song, lulling me to sleep. 'It would be just a small transgression. Nobody would find out.'

I felt dazed and unsteady. 'I don't know.'

'Or why not grant your villeins their freedom? So they might find an estate where the lord will pay more.'

I bit my tongue a second time to stop myself from falling against the wall. 'What was in your mead, Mistress Salt?'

'Nothing, sire. Apart from honey and water.'

'I feel sick.'

'Let me take your hand.' She held out a pair of pale, skeletal hands, while her fawning eyes and distorted grin continued to nail me to the spot.

'Stop looking at me,' I said, now using every drop of my remaining strength to refuse her hands before stumbling towards the door.

'Don't go, sire,' she said, trotting after me. 'We could talk a little further.'

'Get away from me.'

She followed me outside, and now the cold air stabbed at my chest, sharp as a claw. I struggled back over the small bridge, and before the woman could say another word to me, I had mounted Tempest and ridden away at speed.

I didn't dare to look back.

*　　*　　*

I woke later that day, staring at the canopy that drooped from my bed frame like the jowls of a mastiff. I had no recollection of riding home, and clearly I had just fallen into bed, since I still wore a riding gown and muddy leather boots.

And what was I contemplating, as I lay upon this bed? It was not poor Catherine's murder. Instead it was the king's law. The Statute of Labourers. Mistress Salt's plan had worked. She had so riddled my head with her argument that I was not even tempted to reach under the mattress for my favourite manuscript.

As I ran my eyes along each dusty wrinkle in the canopy, I now questioned my strict and determined adherence to the Statute. Perhaps Agnes Salt was right? Who would know if I were to add a few pence here and there to the wages? The villagers were hardly likely to confess such a matter. But it would only take one gossip or blabbermouth to give me away. And then how would I stand with the earl, as it had been his specific order to restrict wages. In fact, he regularly sent his steward, an odious man named Edward Hatcher, to check over my accounts, just to see if I was behaving myself. I might want to help my tenants. I might even be tempted to free my villeins. They were struggling for survival. I could see that. But what was I to do? My hands were tied.

Chapter Nine

I never returned to the boys' dormitory at the monastery. Instead I slept every night in the infirmary. To begin with, I had a small bed at the foot of Brother Peter's, but as I grew older, Peter secured me a chamber of my own. It was a small and private cell that was kept for the care of any rich and influential benefactor who might wish to be tended to by monks in their later years. But it was rarely in use, as these benefactors either died soon after their entrance to the monastery, or they tired of our strict, monastic life and decided to return to society and take their chances on Heaven.

I was educated by Peter. I assisted Peter in the infirmary. I ate with Peter. My life centred around the man, and his life centred around me. I even felt able to speak with him concerning my unbelief, though I knew it troubled him greatly. Sometimes he even blamed my blasphemy for driving him to drink – but this was not the case. The man was already a drinker, long before I bothered him with my arguments and questions.

I would tell you that it was the Plague that had finally deadened my heart to the Church and its teachings. That God did nothing to save his own people from its greedy tongue, so how could there even be a God? Many of the most saintly were taken, and many of the most sinful were spared. But my unbelief went further than this easy equation. It was a furrow that had grown

deeper with every year I spent at the monastery, and though I had
tried repeatedly to cover it with the soil of prayer and reflection,
it eventually became a chasm that could not be filled. Peter
warned me against such thoughts. He tried to turn my mind back
to the Church, but I could not be convinced that there was anything other than the earth and the sky in the universe. Where was
the evidence? My one promise to Brother Peter was this: if I could
not believe in his God, then I would, at least, keep my feelings to
myself.

For many years I did. I obeyed Peter. But when I was around
thirteen years of age, I began to notice another boy about the
monastery who seemed to share my lack of enthusiasm for mass.
His name was Edmund, and years before, he had been the boy
who advised me to feign sleep when the abbot came prowling.
We had not communicated in the meantime. In fact, I did not
communicate at all with any of the boys. If they saw me, they
laughed. If I saw them, I cast my eyes to the floor and walked
more quickly. I was like a rare bird, kept in a cage by Peter, away
from the sparrows of the yard.

A couple of times, at vespers, or even in the early dawn at
lauds, Edmund caught my eye. I looked away on the first few
occasions, afraid that he might be trying to mock me, or catch
me in some sort of mischief to amuse the other boys. But after a
while, I relented. Edmund was worth looking at, I will say that
much. He was a tall boy, with broad shoulders and the handsome,
even features of a Roman statue. I was both pleased and embarrassed that he had noticed me.

After a few weeks of passing secret glances, Edmund came to
speak to me in the herb garden. There was nobody else around,
and it was early evening. We should have been at vespers, but we
were both playing truant. I remember our conversation began
shyly. Why was he there? Why was I there? But soon we put aside
such talk and we were laughing – about the warts on Brother
Thomas's chin, the poor food in the refectory, or the boredom of

mass. We met often after that occasion, usually in the herb garden in the evenings. I was able to shirk vespers by pretending that I needed to care for an elderly monk. I don't know how Edmund came to miss the prayers, as he wouldn't say. But nevertheless, we kept our meetings a secret. A joyful secret.

I will admit this. I began to look forward to those meetings more than any other part of my daily life – a life that celebrated nothing other than routine and silence. We discussed our thoughts and ideas. Edmund felt the same way as I did regarding our religion, but we both had had nobody else to confide in for all these years. Can you imagine how welcome it was to find a confidant, after so long?

Peter noticed a change in me, complaining that I was becoming withdrawn and secretive. Then he complained that I had become opinionated and vain. He even caught me looking at myself in the polished silver of the chalices, to see if my face had become any more handsome. I was never pleased with my reflection, for it did not match the beauty and perfection of Edmund's face. Peter asked me repeatedly to confide in him, to tell him what was happening to me. Why my openness had suddenly frozen over. But Peter would not stick his nose into every crevice of my being. My friendship with Edmund was my secret. Not his.

Not long after, Peter caught Edmund and me together in the garden. We were trying to throw a stone through a hole in the wall that led out into the orchard. At the time I thought it had been our excitement at hitting the tree on the other side that gave us away. We cheered each time the stone passed through the hole. But now I think about it, Peter had probably been following me. Spying was entirely in his nature. He sent Edmund back to vespers with a clip around the ear, but I was punished more harshly. I was not allowed to leave the infirmary for three weeks. I was more miserable than it is possible to be, during my confinement. I would neither speak to Peter, nor even look in his direction. I knew my behaviour was driving him to drink more, since he was hard to rouse from his bed in the mornings, and more bad-tempered than ever. But I could not forgive his interference.

When the three weeks were over and my punishment was complete, I looked about for Edmund at every mass, but his fine head was nowhere to be seen. I even grasped the courage to speak to one of the other boys – choosing a studious, unpopular boy who was more likely to answer my questions. His reply caused me to run to the infirmary in tears, for Edmund had been moved to another monastery, and I knew I would never see him again.

Peter tried to comfort me, but I pushed him away. I even threw a candlestick at the man. Peter was behind Edmund's removal – I knew that much. Of course he denied it at first, but I would not believe his stories. Even then I knew him to be a consummate liar. Eventually he confessed that he had been instrumental in moving the boy, but then had the affront to argue that it had been for my own good. How could that be – I wanted to know? Edmund was my friend. My only friend. Peter tried to stroke my head to comfort me, but when I still rejected him, he told me the vilest of lies.

Edmund was not my friend at all, he said. Instead he was the abbot's boy – responsible for recruiting the other pupils and oblates that the abbot had his eye upon. If Peter had not stepped in at this early point, then he would not have been able to protect me later, once Edmund had lured me into the abbot's trap. I did not believe this story then. I do not believe it now. It stank, but, in retrospect, it did not deserve my response – for I accused Peter of removing Edmund because he wanted me for himself.

He was disgusted by my words. He denied the charge vociferously. He was only concerned for my welfare, and one day I would discover the truth about his affection for me. What truth was this, I demanded to know. Tell me now. He tried to speak, but the words would not come out, and then he seemed to lose all courage. At the time I took this to be nothing more than a lie, but, of course, I know now what he was tempted to tell me. The secret that both bound us together and threw us apart.

Perhaps he should have told me then?

Instead he kept his silence, and as the months went by, I slowly forgot Edmund. But a distance grew between Peter and me. A distance that Peter filled with drink.

I slept in my clothes all night, feeling uncomfortable and stiff when I woke at first light, as I had neither closed the curtains about the bed, nor even pulled the counterpane over my head. The air in the room was chilled, with condensation forming a dank gauze over the tapestry on the wall. I went to sit up, but my head felt heavy and my mouth dry, as if I had drunk a gallon of best ale the night before. Except that I hadn't. It had been nothing more than a mug of Agnes Salt's mead. I rubbed my head, in an attempt to wake myself up, but only succeeded instead in pro- voking memories of my visit to the strange woman.

I changed my shirt and braies, wiped some mist from the window and looked out over the fields to a line of bare trees on the distant ridge, their dark branches feeling upwards at a cold, white sky. A thin veil of mist hung over the fields, and then, though it pains me to admit this, I felt as lonely without Brother Peter as I had felt since his disappearance. I had a murder to solve and unhappy villagers to appease. I had nobody to talk to.

It was then that the idea came to me. I would visit Joan Bath. She could be blunt and uncompromising – but I trusted her more than any other person on the estate. I was tying my boots when a shouting and commotion from outside distracted me. From the window, I could see that Gilbert was chasing the two de Caburn sisters across the dewy grass towards the forest. He held a wooden club aloft and was waving it as fiercely as Orion hunting with Artemis. They disturbed a great flock of starlings that flew into the air in a cloud of beating wings. The girls were too fast for

Gilbert, and easily outpaced his tired old legs, forcing him to slump down upon a stack of logs, with only the energy to shout and wave his stick, while the girls disappeared into the trees.

I wondered then whether I should venture outside to discover what crime the girls had committed, but decided against such an enquiry. I was bored of Gilbert's complaints about Mary and Rebecca. Only the previous afternoon he had moaned to me that they wouldn't brush their hair or wear their shoes, and that they were stealing meat from the kitchen.

I finished dressing and then crept down the steps, but found my servant at the bottom of the stairwell, standing in my path. I groaned. 'What is it Gilbert? I'm in a hurry.'

He tried to catch his breath. 'I don't know what to do with them, sire.'

I was tempted to push past, but the man seemed genuinely upset. 'Is it Lady Mary and Lady Rebecca?'

He nodded. His chest was heaving up and down like a ship at sea. 'I was grafting some pear whips onto the dwarf apple stocks. And those little devils pulled them up and threw them into the barrels.'

This was bad behaviour indeed – but something about this latest piece of mischief made me want to smile.

Gilbert noticed the curl of amusement upon my lips and scowled. 'I'd taken months to graft those maiden pears, sire. Now they're sticking out of a barrel of night soil like a pair of battle flags.'

'Can't the trees be saved?'

'No. They're poisoned.'

I thought of the large wooden barrels that stood at the bottom of the chute beneath the garderobe. 'But don't you spread the contents of the barrel onto the vegetable garden?'

Gilbert now swapped his frown for a look of bemusement. 'Only after it's been dried and mixed. And I *spread* it sire. I don't stick a load of shit in a pot and try to plant seeds in it.'

I felt a fool, so tried once again to circumvent the man. 'I'll sort out a suitable punishment for the girls.'

Gilbert cheered up at this suggestion. 'I'll lock them in the cellar.'

'No. Don't do that.'

He frowned again. 'But they deserve it, sire. This isn't their first transgression. Oh no. Not in the least. They are thieves, the pair of them. Always stealing the best meat from the kitchen and then disappearing into the woods with it.'

I will admit to sighing at this point. 'They have a cat. I've told you that before.'

'Well I've never seen it.'

'It's big and grey.' Gilbert went to answer, but this time I did push past. I was thoroughly tired of this conversation. 'Why don't you lock them into the ladies' bedchamber? That might cool their spirits.'

'That's if I can find them, sire.'

'They'll come back when they get hungry.'

'Or when their imaginary cat is,' he shouted after me, as I finally made my exit.

I knocked at Joan's door to find that she was not quite as pleased to see me as I had hoped she might be. In fact I would say she was a little flustered, and suddenly I had the impression she was about to go out somewhere. She was wearing a black gown and a silk veil that was arranged modestly about her face. Looking at the woman, nobody would have guessed Joan's previous profession, for these days she looked every bit as demure as a minoress. I will say this, however. Her gown bore none of the coarseness of a nun's simple scapular, for the wool was of the finest quality.

I took a seat at her long table while she lit a tall wax candle and stoked the fire in the centre of the room. Her boys were sent outside as ever – this time to clip the ewes' hooves, for she wouldn't discuss one single matter in front of them.

'So what brings you back here so soon, my young lord?' she asked, as she settled herself onto the bench beside me. 'I thought I had offended you the last time you visited.'

'I wanted some advice.' Then I coughed, for this was an awkward admission. 'I needed to speak to somebody.'

She remained impassive at my entreaty. 'What about your mother? Why don't you talk to her?' I pulled a face. I didn't need to say more.

She folded her arms. 'So what's the problem? Are you in love again?'

'Of course not!' Then I hesitated, suddenly lacking the courage to say the next words out loud.

'Is it about wages? Or the murder?' she prompted.

I sighed. 'Both.'

Joan regarded me for a few moments, as if sizing up a ram. Did I deserve any of her time and effort? I passed the examination, for she got up from the bench, walked over to her crusader's chest and pulled out a wicker-covered bottle of wine. It was dusty and looked as if it had come back from the Levant, along with the chest itself. She pulled at the cork and poured me a good measure into one of her pewter cups.

'I thought you might be going out somewhere,' I said, letting the warm liquid roll down my throat. I still felt unwell from Agnes Salt's mead, but this wine was soothing and welcome.

Joan shrugged. 'I was. But it's nowhere important.' She shuffled a little closer to me on the bench. So close that I could catch her perfume. Cinnamon, and the sweetness of newly-gathered hay.

She took my hand. 'So, Oswald. Have you changed your mind about the men's wages? Is that why you want to talk to me?'

'I don't know.'

She withdrew her hand immediately. 'That's no good, is it? As a lord, you have to know.'

'Very well. I'm thinking about it.'

She poured me some more wine. 'Don't think too long. Delay

will mean you lose your men. Some to other estates. Some to starvation.'

I took another gulp of the wine. 'It's not easy, you know. I would be breaking the law. And the earl sends that thug Edward Hatcher to check through my accounts.'

She stroked my arm lightly. It felt maternal and reassuring. 'If the man is a thug, then you can beat him with cunning,' she whispered. 'Pay your men more, but swear your reeve to secrecy. This Edward Hatcher will never know.'

I stifled a groan and looked about Joan's room to see a new crucifix hanging on the wall. It was of the most delicate and intricate copper enamelling. Joan seemed to read my mind. 'The sales of my fleeces are going well.' Though I doubted this, since her sheep would not be sheared until the summer.

She quickly turned the subject back to wages. 'So you'll do it? You'll raise wages.'

This time I did let the groan surface fully. 'Yes. Very well. When the time is right.'

Joan stood up. 'Well done to you, Oswald,' she said as she disappeared into the curtained end of the cottage and returned with a salted knuckle of ham and a great slice of seed cake. I was starving, as I had not had breakfast, and this was the most welcome of feasts.

As I devoured the contents of my plate, she watched me, but did not eat herself. 'So what about the child's murder?' she asked. 'You're no closer to finding the culprit?'

'No. I seem to be going in circles.'

'But you still have Barrow under your protection?'

I nodded. 'He's locked in one of my towers. For his own safety.'

'And there have been no further murders since you locked him away?'

I turned to her sharply. 'I thought you, of all people, would resist jumping to the easiest conclusions.'

She bowed her head to me and cleared the plates from the

table. When she returned to sit next to me, there was a larger gap between us than before. 'Tell me what you've discovered so far,' she said. 'Perhaps I can help?'

I wiped some crumbs from my chin, and took a last slurp of wine. 'I know so little. Only that Catherine disappeared while her mother Mary Tulley was working in the field. The poor child was not seen again until Geoffrey Hayward found her dead body the next morning in a blackthorn bush.'

'Nothing else?'

I puffed out my lips and looked to the rafters. The butterfly that I had seen at my last visit was once again fluttering its wings against the crude thatch of the roof. 'Nobody saw anything. Or knows anything. Or so they say.' Then I gave a wry laugh. 'Other than one neighbour who heard the beating of bird wings.'

'Which neighbour was that?'

'Agnes Salt. But she's a liar.'

Joan raised an eyebrow. 'She makes a good potion. Most use her.'

'That's only because she's cheap.'

'No. It's because her methods work.' Joan then threw me a sideways look. 'There has been something flying over the fields, Oswald. My boys have seen it circling. High over the priest's glebe.'

'It must be a buzzard.'

She laughed. 'A very big one. My boys wouldn't lie.'

'Have you seen it yourself?'

She hesitated. 'No. I haven't.'

'And have you asked the priest if he's seen it?'

Now she laughed. 'That skulking jack snipe? He never leaves his house.' And then she sighed. 'And I'm still not welcome in his church, so our paths don't cross.' She looked up. 'Perhaps you should ask him yourself? He may be able to shed some light upon this murder.' Then she laughed, a little bitterly. 'A priest hears all sorts of secrets.'

'Are you suggesting I ask Father Luke to break his vows and tell me what somebody has said in Confession?'

She frowned. 'Of course not. But he might give something away. You never know.'

I shrugged at this suggestion.

'Do you have any better ideas?' Joan asked me.

I puffed out my lips. 'No. I don't.'

Father Luke had only joined the parish of Somershill recently, as we had been without a priest for many months since the departure of our last incumbent – Father John of Cornwall. While I was pleased to see the back of Cornwall, a man who had led the baying mob to Leofwin and stoked the fire about the boy's feet, his departure had left an obvious gap. Without even a chaplain in Somershill, my remaining villagers had been forced to travel to Burrsfield or even Tonbridge to take communion. The journey was long and difficult however, and over the winter the churches had noticed a decline in attendance.

When rumours spread of the return of the Plague in the east of the county, nobody would leave the village at all. And though I received letters from the bishop threatening to try the whole village for non-attendance at mass, I could not persuade them to travel. In the end I wrote back to the bishop and demanded a new priest be provided or I would appoint a travelling Franciscan to take Sunday services. The Bishop, having no time for the Franciscans and their supposed vows of poverty and abstinence, promptly sent Father Luke – a boy so young and hairless about the chin that he made me look like an old boar. Installed at St Giles, Father Luke mumbled his way quickly through the Sunday services and made sure to collect his tithes. Other than that, the village saw little, if anything, of him.

Crossing the glebe field to reach Father Luke's cottage, I thought back to my last visit here, when I had thrown John of Cornwall from the parish. When searching his home we had found a collection of fine ermines and embroidered capes, the type of clothing no priest could afford, or would even be allowed to wear. Clothes that had been financed by the selling of relics and indulgences during the months of the Pestilence, during which time the people of Somershill clung to his bits of bone and slips of paper in the desperate hope of some divine deliverance.

When Father Luke first came to Somershill I had forbidden him to sell anything to anybody – for I would not countenance a resurgence in this trade. Father Luke had simply looked bewildered at this order, seemingly with no plans, not even an inclination to start trading with his parishioners. For, unlike the ambitious and bullish John of Cornwall, our new priest was a timid rabbit, happy to scuttle back to his burrow at the slightest opportunity. He would no more sell a relic than he would make an impassioned popular sermon.

I came to a halt in front of the priest's cottage to find Father Luke peeping around the door nervously, as if I might be a freebooter about to raid his tithe barn and take all his grain.

Screwing up his eyes to focus, Father Luke's poor sight finally informed him that it was his lord at the door and not an invader. He stepped gingerly onto the wet grass. 'Good morning to you Lord Somershill.' His voice quavered a little. 'I apologise. Did you send a message that you were making a visit? I haven't prepared for you.'

I dismounted. 'Good morning to you, Father Luke. This isn't a formal visit. I simply wanted to talk with you.'

His lip trembled a little. 'But of course, sire.' He stepped forward to take Tempest's reins from me, but the horse sensed the man's trepidation and began to shy, so I quickly produced an apple from my pocket. These days I rarely left the house without a treat for my horse.

Father Luke gave a small gasp as Tempest settled. 'You have a gift with horses, sire.'

'Not really.'

'Oh, but you do. You have calmed the beast. As Saint Francis tamed the wolf of Gubbio.'

I would tell you that such praise was flattering, but the compliment had been delivered with such toadying awkwardness that I felt more inclined to groan. 'Are you an admirer of Saint Francis then, Father Luke?' I asked, knowing this would send the silly priest into a cataplexy of nerves, since our bishop's opposition to the Franciscan movement and its egalitarian aims was common knowledge.

Luke stuttered a couple of words before managing to get his mouth to work. I noticed scabs about his chin where he had scratched some spots. 'No, no my lord. I was simply reminded of the wolf when I saw you calm the horse. Francis is said to have ventured into the woods above the town and faced a wolf, which—'

'Thank you. I know the story.' This interruption was rude in retrospect, but I will admit to a fault, if only on these pages. I was uncomfortable with the gift of power and authority when it first fell into my lap. My villagers were slow to show me respect, and certain of my servants, namely Gilbert, still denied me the honour. But when I met a soul such as Father Luke, a man who was clearly as spineless as a lace of thong-weed – I couldn't help but behave like a braggart. But it is weakness to browbeat the weak, I know that in my heart. What marks out a man is his ability to influence the strong – and not with bullying and threats, but by the weight and truth of his words and deeds. Strangely enough it was Brother Peter who taught me this, and, though he failed to live up to his own dictum, the words have stayed with me.

Father Luke hurried to open the door to his cottage, which was a building of medium proportions, with glass at one solitary window. I followed him inside, and once the door was shut behind us, the nervous priest fussed about the chamber, calling in an old, toothless servant who set a mug of ale in front of me. When the priest saw it was a wooden mug, he chastised the man profusely, and demanded he replace it with a pewter cup.

Once the cup mistake was rectified, Father Luke settled himself opposite me — the light that strained through the window
only serving to highlight his youth. His face was blessed with a
pallid complexion, and only a few blond whiskers grew from his
chin to betray his sex. 'How can I help you, sire?' he asked. His
eye twitched.

'I wanted to ask you about Catherine Tulley.'

Father Luke now blinked anxiously, a reaction that might have
raised my suspicions, until it became clear that the priest simply
didn't know whom I was talking about.

'The murdered baby.'

The relief was palpable across his features. 'Of course, sire. I'm
sorry. I am still to learn the names of all my communicants.'

I was tempted to suggest this might never happen, if he holed
himself up in this cottage and refrained from visiting the village.
'Are you familiar with the Tulley family?'

Father Luke now nodded, though it was accompanied by a
frown. 'Yes, sire. They are known to me.' He hesitated for a
moment. 'Thomas Tulley can be a little . . . difficult.'

'About what?'

'His tithes, mainly. He resents giving one tenth of his harvest
to the church.'

'Maybe that's because his children are hungry?'

Father Luke stiffened. 'The tithe shows his commitment to
God. It would be a poor service to his family if he refused his
contribution to the church.' These words were said with a conviction that he immediately seemed to regret. 'Of course I can
see that a tithe is a sacrifice, sire. And times are hard for some
villagers.'

'Indeed.' I then heaved a sigh, for I knew I must ask the next
question, no matter how foolish I felt it to be. 'Have you seen a
large bird flying over your glebe field?'

Red patches formed on his white face. 'No. I've seen nothing
like that. Why do you ask?'

'No matter.'

A cat mewed in the distance, causing Luke to jump from his chair and open the door to call for it to come in. A sizeable grey cat then slunk into the cottage and let itself be fussed and stroked by the priest.

'Is that your cat?' I asked, as Luke picked up the creature.

He smiled and shook his head. 'No, sire. He just turned up.' Then he tickled the cat under its chin. 'But he's very welcome, as he catches the mice in the barn. Don't you, Sir Tom?'

A knighted cat indeed? At least I had solved the mystery of why Gilbert had not yet seen Mary and Rebecca's animal about Somershill. It had taken to living in the priest's barn.

'Can you tell me anything else about the Tulley family?' I asked, as Father Luke returned to his seat. The cat was now planted in his lap.

He shook his head. 'I don't think so.'

'But you conducted the funeral of the dead child?'

He looked at the ceiling as if struggling to remember something as rare as the burial of a murdered infant. The cat purred loudly. 'Yes.'

'And her baptism?'

He nodded now, with more energy. 'Though that ceremony was a little rushed.'

'What do you mean by that?'

He let the cat fall to the floor and then ran his fingers through his hair, which was soft, blond and already threatening to recede at his temples, giving him the look of a balding baby. 'Thomas Tulley sent a boy to rouse me in the middle of the night, only a day before the child disappeared. The Tulleys were anxious the child should be baptised quickly.'

'What was the hurry?'

He frowned. 'The boy told me to come immediately because the child was mortally ill. He was insistent.'

'And was she?'

'No. Not really. Once I reached the Tulleys' cottage, the infant was screaming, it's true. But wailing is in an infant's nature. She looked hale and hearty enough to me.'

This was a curious turn of events. 'Did you ask Thomas Tulley why he had summoned you so urgently, when his daughter was healthy?'

Father Luke smiled a little awkwardly. 'I didn't really need to, sire. I've fallen for this same trick on previous occasions.'

'And what trick is that?'

'It is commonly played, I'm afraid. I am often called out in the dark hours for a quick baptism. It is usually with newly born infants such as Catherine Tulley.' He hesitated for a moment, and once again drew his hands through his thinning hair. 'The parent hopes to avoid my fee.'

'And did you waive it?'

'No, sire. I did not. I'd been woken in the dead of night to baptise a child who was perfectly healthy. The Tulleys were attempting to fool me.'

'Did you not suspect something when the boy roused you?'

He shook his head. 'Not initially. The boy they sent was very convincing. He had an answer for everything.'

'Who was it?'

'I don't know his name, my lord. But he's often here, offering to write up the church rolls, or make the additions on the ledgers.' He coughed. 'He wants paying of course.'

'Is it Geoffrey Hayward?'

'As I said, my lord. I don't know his name.'

Then why didn't you ask, I thought to myself. 'Have the Tulleys paid you?'

The priest wrung his hands, his confidence gone. 'No sire. They have not.' Then he let out a kind of sigh. 'I felt it was unsavoury to demand the fee. Since their child was then murdered.'

'Yes. She was murdered.' Then I leant forward. 'Some are saying she was taken by a butcher bird. What do you say to that story?'

'I say it stands against reason.'

'Will you say so. At mass?'

'Indeed I will, sire. I have no time for such tales. They are dreamt up by pagans.'

This comment encouraged me, and suddenly I wondered if Father Luke and I might become friends? We were roughly the same age, and he was an educated boy.

'How do you like living here alone?' I asked. I thought the question a harmless gambit to open a conversation, but I might as well have asked if he worshipped the Devil.

His cheeks coloured. 'Yes. I am always on my own, sire. Indeed I am. There is nobody here but me. Save my servant, Simon, who sleeps in the kitchen. And he is an old man with a crooked back and teeth so rotten I steer clear of his breath, lest its vapours should poison me. There is nobody else but me and this man in the house. I can swear to it.'

I was quite lost for a response, so I moved on to some topics of conversation that Father Luke might not find so alarming. He would have read Bacon and Aquinas at the cathedral. Perhaps he was a lover of the antiquities or even the science of Galen and Archimedes.

I missed conversation, but if I had hoped to find it here, I was mistaken.

Father Luke sat opposite me and answered my questions on geometry and mathematics with the minimum of enthusiasm. Always he kept his head to the floor, and after a while I found myself damning his humility and servitude. He had been well educated, that much was obvious, even from the paucity of his responses. But he seemed not to think himself worthy of discussing these matters with me.

I stood to leave with something of a frustrated sigh, which only served to make the priest wring his soft hands and tremble even more violently. 'I'm sorry, sire. I don't possess the skills to debate these matters. I'm afraid I have bored you.'

I slapped my gloves petulantly against my leg before putting them onto my hands. 'A man may still have opinions. Even if he doesn't possess experience at debating.'

'I'm sorry, sire,' he muttered again. Such grovelling was unbecoming. 'You must miss Brother Peter and his disputations.'

I nearly dropped my gloves upon the floor. What did this parish priest know of Peter? The old monk had disappeared the previous July, long before this spotty sycophant had taken up his post.

'Why do you say that?' I snapped.

Now the priest held his hands to his mouth. 'I'm sorry, sire. I didn't mean to trouble you. Please don't be angry with me.'

'Do you know Brother Peter?' I asked him. The priest didn't respond. 'Do you know him?' I repeated forcefully.

'I met Brother Peter at Rochester,' he told me. 'Though I can't claim to know him well. He was a respected monk and I was nothing but a simple student.'

'So why do you think I would miss him?'

'The villagers talk of him, sire. They told me you were close.'

This explanation was rational, and yet I couldn't imagine this shy priest having such a conversation with his parishioners, particularly regarding such a matter. The chamber suddenly felt cold and unwelcoming, and the talk of Peter ignited an uncomfortable churn in my stomach.

Despite Joan's good advice it seemed I had learnt little to assist in my murder investigation by visiting this priest. I said my goodbyes, but as Tempest slugged away from the house, I heard my name being called. I halted my horse and turned to see a man running towards me with a blanket wrapped about his shoulders. It was the priest's toothless servant, Simon. 'May I speak with you a moment, sire?' he said, squinting up at me with some difficulty.

It was cold and I was anxious to be away. 'Yes. What is it?'

'I overheard you talking with Father Luke.'

Tempest's ears flicked. He did not like the man. 'And?'

'Father Luke hasn't seen the bird over the glebe field, but I have.' He pointed upwards. 'It soars very high. But I've seen it. A monster so large that it scares the other birds away.'

I looked down at this man. His eyes were rheumy and his back was crooked. I doubted he could even turn his head to the sky. 'But your master hasn't seen a thing.'

'That's because he don't ever go outside.'

I kicked my horse and galloped for home.

Chapter Ten

My return to Somershill that afternoon coincided with the unexpected sight of a carriage and three horses, trotting in the direction of my home. A single groom rode the first mount, with his long whip flicking at the head of the lead horse. Heavy chests hung from the rings beneath the frame and were being splashed with the thick mud that the wheels churned up on its slow progress along the track. I rode alongside and pushed at a fabric flap that had been tied down, so as not to gape open in the wind.

A face soon appeared in a small gap, poking out with a beaky nose and a pair of sharp, suspicious eyes. 'Who's there? Is it a bandit?'

'No Mother. It's your son. Oswald.'

Her face relaxed, and she untied a bow in the flap so it might open a little further. Looking inside the carriage I saw Clemence sleeping against Humbert's arm, her mouth drooping open and her hair loose from its veil.

'What are you doing here?' I asked.

Mother huffed. 'We're coming to Somershill, of course.'

'But why?'

'The vapours. Versey is no place to raise a child. How many times have I said so? The castle should be rebuilt upon the hill. But no, it remains in the bottom of the valley, like a stone sucker swimming in the mud of the river.'

I looked over Mother's shoulder to see a wooden cradle being shaken about the carriage like a ship at sea. 'Is Henry in there?' I asked.

'Where else would he be, Oswald? Riding the second horse with a whip in his hand?'

'You should have warned me that you were returning,' I said.

She shook her head and began to retie the bow, in order to mark the end of our conversation, but I stuck my hand against the flap before she had a chance to fasten it completely. 'How long are you staying, Mother?'

'As long as we please, Oswald. As long as we please.'

I galloped back to the house to break the unwelcome news to Gilbert that Somershill would soon become filled with even more guests – a piece of information he greeted with the same enthusiasm as a boy being sent to vespers. Gilbert would round up some women from the village who we used occasionally for serving at table. I also suggested that this might be a good time to bring young Geoffrey into the house, though this proposal was greeted with a loud puff. Gilbert shuffled away into the great hall, muttering curses under his breath and twisting his finger into his ear.

I waited for the arrival of the carriage by the main door, and when Clemence stepped down, I offered her my hand. 'Welcome back to Somershill, Clemence,' I said, but she only smiled thinly in return.

Mother held out her hand to me. 'Clemence has been sick all the way here, Oswald. The jolting and jarring of this carriage is enough to shake the bones of a bull.' As I helped Mother put her feet to the ground, she leant against me and whispered in my ear. 'And your sister will insist upon feeding the child herself, though she is making herself quite the drab donkey. She needn't think about taking another husband. Nobody would look at her.'

Clemence wrapped her coat about her neck. 'Be quiet Mother. I can hear everything you're saying.'

Mother threw up her hands. 'For goodness sake, Clemence. Why don't you let Oswald find a wet nurse?'

Clemence ran her hands across her face and pushed the hair from her eyes. 'I'm feeding Henry myself, Mother. How many times must I tell you?'

'But there must be a nursing mother in this village.' She turned to me. 'Isn't there, Oswald?'

'I've no idea.'

'What about that woman?'

'Which woman?'

Now she scowled. 'You know. The one whose child was murdered by that bird thing.'

I grimaced. 'God's nails, Mother. What a suggestion!'

'Oh tush, Oswald! Don't be so sentimental. Her milk won't have dried up yet. And the woman might welcome the money.'

Clemence swept her cloak about her and strode towards the door. 'I am not using the mother of a dead baby to feed my child. Do you understand?'

Mother raised her eyes to the sky and once again spoke in one of her perfectly audible whispers. 'You see what I have had to contend with, Oswald? My nerves are spun to a thread.' Then she grasped my arm. 'Have you found that bird yet? I know how you like to investigate.'

I led her towards the door. 'No, Mother. Because I'm not looking for a bird.'

Her face fell a little, and she poked a bony finger into my side. 'Then I think you'd better get on with it, Oswald. Before it steals baby Henry from under our noses.'

Mother and Clemence climbed the spiral staircase from the great hall to the solar, closely followed by Humbert, who held the wooden cradle in his arms. I stopped Humbert in order to look upon baby Henry. The child's cheeks were as round and red as two old pearmain apples, and a shock of black hair poked out from his knitted bonnet like a tuft of badger fur. As we watched Henry, the baby began to stir a little, so Humbert stroked his great paw of a hand against the boy's head and tucked in his blanket, with a tenderness that was touching to watch.

'Has he slept all the way here?' I asked.

Humbert nodded and then lifted the cradle away, just as we heard Clemence's voice at the top of the stairs. 'Why is the ladies' bedchamber locked, Oswald?'

'I don't know,' I shouted back up to her, and then immediately remembered why. Gilbert must have bolted Mary and Rebecca into the room, just as I had suggested.

'Wait a moment,' I called to Clemence. 'I'll find Gilbert and get him to open the door.' But Gilbert was nowhere to be found.

In the end I climbed the stone steps to find my sister pulling at the door of her chamber. 'Is there somebody in there, Oswald?' she asked me, curtly.

'Yes. Mary and Becky.' Clemence's face fell.

'Where else do you expect them to sleep?' I asked. 'They're ladies. And this is the ladies' bedchamber.'

She frowned. 'Why are they locked in?'

I was reluctant to answer this, but it was pointless to lie. 'They were misbehaving this morning, so I asked Gilbert to shut them in their room for a while.'

Her eyes flashed. 'You should have locked them in the cellar.'

'That's what I said, my lady.' We turned to see Gilbert standing behind us. I had not heard his approach and his words nearly made me jump.

'Well I didn't want to do that,' I said. 'It's cruel.'

'You're too soft, Oswald,' said my sister. We moved aside for Gilbert to open the door with a large iron key, but Clemence suddenly placed her hand upon his. 'What's that I can hear? They're saying something.'

I would say Gilbert seemed a little awkward. He even gave a rare laugh. 'You don't want to listen to their cursing and calling, my lady. Nasty little things, they are. No better than a pair of screeching jackdaws.'

Clemence didn't take this advice. Instead she shouldered the servant aside and put her ear to the door, although she hardly needed to, since we could all now hear exactly what the young girls were shouting. For the purposes of this account I will not repeat the exact wording of their foul language and uncouth insults. It should only be known that they were naming intimate parts of Clemence's person and claiming that they smelt as bad as a stall at Rye fish market.

Clemence screwed her face in rage before she grasped the key from Gilbert's hand and opened the door herself. But if we were expecting the girls to be cowering in the corner and waiting for their punishment, we were to be disappointed. As soon as the door was flung open, the two imps sprang past us at speed, raced down the stairs, and shot out through the back porch, bounding across the grass like a pair of startled rabbits.

Once again I turned to find Gilbert at my shoulder. He held his favourite club in his hands. 'Would you like me to take some men and hunt them down?'

I shook my head.

'You sure, sire?'

'Just leave them. They'll come back when they're hungry.'

Mary and Rebecca de Caburn did not return, however. And by nightfall I was becoming increasingly worried by their absence. The sisters had not eaten anything since breakfast, having been locked in the ladies' bedchamber from late morning. Gilbert admitted, a little shamefacedly, that he had not thought to take them a piece of bread and a mug of ale during their imprisonment. It was, at least, comforting to be informed that two loaves and a dried sausage were missing from the kitchen – a crime that was soundly blamed upon the sisters.

That evening I left the house with three servants, and we walked the fields and the nearby purlieu calling repeatedly for the girls to return. But if they heard us, they did nothing to come forward, though I repeatedly promised, at the top of my voice, that they would not be punished for their mischief. The night was brutally cold and a sharp frost was already settling upon the naked branches of the trees. As my feet crunched across the frozen grass of the meadow, I tried to imagine the two girls, holed up somewhere warm and safe, laughing at their own daring – but instead the fear that they were cold and hungry came repeatedly to my mind. It didn't matter how naughty and insolent the sisters had been, Mary and Becky were still the daughters of a nobleman, and should not be living in the forest like two little pucks. And then a darker thought crossed my mind. There was a child murderer on my estate, at just the moment I had managed to lose two children.

I made my way home as we gave up on the search for the night, taking my place beside the fire in the solar. At least there was one small mercy to be grateful for. John Barrow had ceased his wailing. In fact there had been no sound from the north-west tower for most of the day. When I asked Gilbert the reason behind this silence, my servant revealed, somewhat sheepishly, that he had given the man one of Agnes Salt's sleeping potions. While I didn't openly approve of this scheme, it had allowed a welcome peace to descend upon the house. A peace that was soon ruined, however, by the screaming bellows of Clemence's baby son.

I stared into the fire and listened to the conversation from the ladies' bedchamber next door, where Mother, Clemence and Humbert tried to settle Henry. The low mumble of Mother's words of advice seeped easily through the thin wooden wall, accompanied by Clemence's continual rebuffs to any of her suggestions. No, she wouldn't stuff a brandy-soaked rag into Henry's mouth. No, she wouldn't bind Henry in furs and let him sleep outside. And no, not under any circumstances, would she allow Mother to send for her physician Roger de Waart.

As I began to close my eyes, there was a nervous knock at the door and young Geoffrey Hayward entered, holding a tankard of ale. He walked over to me with such care that he might have been carrying a vial of the virgin's milk.

'So Gilbert has found you some employment?' I said.

He carefully placed the ale down on the table beside me and then bowed. 'Thank you, sire. I am so grateful for this opportunity.'

I held up my hand, in case the boy was about to launch into one of his long speeches. 'Do exactly as Gilbert tells you, Geoffrey. Keep on his good side and don't get in his way.'

'I will do, sire. Thank you for your wise advice.' He bowed again. 'Is there anything else I might do for you?'

'No. Go to bed now. You will have an early start in the morning.' He had nearly reached the door when I called him. A thought had just occurred to me. 'Geoffrey. Come back a moment.'

'Yes, sire.'

'Was it you who raised Father Luke in the middle of the night? So that Catherine Tulley might be baptised?'

Even in this light I could see that the colour drained from his face. 'Yes. That was me.'

'You're not in trouble,' I said, in an attempt to reassure him. 'I'm just curious. Why did you go to the priest's house? You're not part of the Tulley family.'

He relaxed a little. 'I run errands for people about the village, sire. They give me a farthing, or even a half-penny, if they're pleased with me. I wasn't doing anything wrong.'

I took a sip of ale and studied the boy's face. 'Tell me the exact message you were given.'

He scratched his head. 'I was to tell Father Luke that he must come straight away. To baptise baby Catherine. As she was near death.'

'Did you see the child yourself?'

'No. Thomas Tulley called me over from the street, and we spoke at their door. I didn't go inside their cottage.'

Geoffrey shifted from foot to foot, as I took another long sip of ale. 'What were you doing outside the Tulleys' cottage in the middle of the night? You don't live on the Long Ditch.'

He froze. 'I can't remember.'

I cocked my head. 'That's a feeble excuse, isn't it?'

He was beginning to shake. 'No. It's the truth sire.'

I put down the ale and stared at his young face. 'I think you'd better remember. Don't you Geoffrey?'

Now he trembled from the knees. 'It wasn't my idea, sire. Felix Pavenham made me do it.'

'Made you do what?'

He wiped an anxious tear from his cheek. 'He wanted me to write some words on their neighbour's door.'

'What words?'

He blubbered something inaudible, so I made him repeat it. 'He wanted me to write that Abigail Wolfenden is a whore.'

I rolled my eyes, for no doubt this transgression would be brought before the next manorial court, accompanied by an abundance of emotional recriminations. 'Why did Felix want you to do that?'

'He can't write himself.'

This story made me want to laugh, but I repressed a smile. 'It's not a good use of your education, is it Geoffrey?'

Now he sobbed. 'I know, sire. I shouldn't have done it.' His tears flowed liberally.

'But he paid you, I suppose?'

He nodded and continued to cry, so I let this outburst blow itself out, before continuing my questioning. There were elements of Geoffrey's story that still were not clear in my mind. 'I need you to think back to the moment that Tulley called you over, Geoffrey.' He stiffened again. 'Was it definitely Thomas who asked you to raise the priest? Not his wife?'

'I could see Mistress Tulley,' the snivelling boy told me. 'She was calling from behind Thomas. She said to make sure the priest knew how ill Catherine was.'

'Why didn't you tell me about this before?'

Geoffrey only bit his lip and threatened to recommence his sobbing.

'You should have mentioned it, Geoffrey.'

He looked to his feet and let his shoulders drop. 'I'm sorry, sire. I just didn't think it was important.'

With the boy gone, I was finally alone in the solar, watching the flames as they crackled and spat in the hearth. The light of a wax candle made shadows dance upon the wall, while a draught picked at the corners of a tapestry, forcing its way behind the cloth and causing it to billow out occasionally into the room, like a bed sheet in the wind. I pulled my cloak about me, since it was too cold to remove the garment, and leant back against the stone of the wall. The ale that Geoffrey had delivered was flavoured with cinnamon and mace and was pleasant on this miserable evening. Whilst I sipped at its warmth, I only hoped Mary and Rebecca were somewhere that was safe and dry, with their stolen sausage and pieces of stale bread.

I dozed for a while, and then woke to find Clemence had come into the room. 'Where's Mother?' I asked when she had settled down on another chair.

Clemence closed her eyes and heaved the weariest of sighs. 'Mother won't leave Humbert alone with Henry, as she doesn't think we should allow a servant to sleep in the ladies' bedchamber.'

'It is unusual, Clemence. Does he stay in there all night?'

She opened one eye. 'He can stay there, if I want him to. Henry likes to sleep in his arms.'

'And you allow that?'

Now both eyes opened and she sat forward. 'If it means that my son is contented, then I don't object.' When I didn't answer, she leant against the back of her chair and stared at the ceiling. 'I feel safer with Humbert in the room. We don't want any more children to disappear, do we, Oswald? Another two lost today.'

I ignored her sarcasm. 'I just hope the girls are safe.'

Clemence sighed. 'They will be fine, Oswald. Mary and Becky are as feral as wildcats.' She looked over to me and attempted a smile. 'Tomorrow they will run back here, with ripped gowns and muddy feet.'

I wished Clemence's confidence could have reassured me, but it didn't. Instead we sat in silence for many minutes while I tried to forget about the girls – but the stillness of the room only served to shake another shadow from the corner of my mind. Something that had been lurking there since my visit to the priest that morning.

My legs must have been fidgeting, since Clemence let out the sort of groan she used to emit when we had shared a bed as children. If I had been sitting any closer, she might even have thumped me. 'What's troubling you, Oswald?' She held out her hand for my mug of ale.

I passed her the ale. 'I had an odd conversation today. That's all. It disturbed me a little.'

'What sort of conversation?' she asked.

'I was visiting Father Luke, to ask him some questions about the murder.' I hesitated. 'The priest suddenly mentioned Brother Peter to me. For no reason.'

Clemence cocked her head slightly. 'Why would Father Luke say such a thing?'

I coughed to clear my throat and tried to settle my unfaithful voice. 'He claims to have known Peter from years ago. At Rochester. He even asked me if I missed the man.'

'And do you?'

I wiped my face and rubbed my eyes. 'Of course I don't.'

Clemence yawned. 'As it happens I've also been asking around about Brother Peter.' Her nonchalant delivery did not soften the blow of this disclosure.

I sat up in my chair. 'You have? Why?'

She hesitated. 'To see if he still lives.'

This was unwelcome news. 'Peter died, Clemence. You threw a pan of boiling water over his face.'

'Where is his body then?'

'Probably in the forest. He could not have survived such injuries.'

Clemence stared at me for a few moments. I felt the weight of her eyes upon my cheeks. 'But you wish he was alive. Don't you?'

I turned away so that she could not see my face. 'Of course not. Don't say such things. I hate him.'

Clemence touched my arm. 'I know you have inconstant feelings about the man, Oswald.'

'Well I don't wish he was alive,' I said, pushing her away. 'You're wrong about that.'

Clemence tried again, but this time she caught my hand in a firm grip that I could not throw off. 'I think he still lives, Oswald.'

'You're wrong.'

'Perhaps so. Perhaps not.'

'And what if he is alive? What would you do if you found him? Try to kill him again?'

'I was acting to defend myself. He would have killed me, given the chance.'

'I'm not so sure.'

She dropped my hand abruptly. 'Don't be foolish, Oswald. Peter had already killed three people, including my own husband. Of course he would have murdered me. He believed that I would reveal your secret.'

I folded my arms and turned away from her.

She leant forward. 'I would just like to ask Peter some questions, that's all.'

'About what?' I said, petulantly.

She looked into my face. Her expression was conciliatory. Even gentle. 'I'd ask why there was no body in Thomas Starvecrow's coffin. Only an effigy of the Christ child. Then I'd ask what happened to my true brother, the real Oswald de Lacy. Peter is the one who supposedly buried the boy. Doesn't that interest you?'

I bristled. 'Yes. It does. But—'

She looked away. 'Your position's not in danger, Oswald. Nobody is going to remove you as Lord Somershill. We've discussed this enough times. I just want to find out the truth. And Brother Peter is the only person who knows.'

'But he's dead.'

She went to answer, just as her baby began to cry in the next chamber. His calls began softly, but soon grew in volume. Clemence got to her feet and tramped wearily towards the door, turning to address me just before she left. 'You would tell me if you heard any news of Peter, wouldn't you Oswald?'

'He's dead, Clemence.'

Chapter Eleven

There are few things in life more trying to a nineteen-year-old boy than his own parents. They are an embarrassment, a hindrance, sometimes even a disgrace. The boy can scarcely believe that he was created by the union of these same two people. Indeed, the very idea that two such ancient and hopeless persons ever possessed the wherewithal to make love completely stupefies him. When he can bear to think on such matters (and this does not happen often, since the suggestion appals him,) he suspects they only performed the act once, which resulted in his own conception. He does not stretch his imagination to wonder how his siblings came into being, as this would lead into even darker realms of disgust – signifying that his parents might have continuously enjoyed each other's company on a carnal level.

I grew up thinking just the same of my own parents, Lord and Lady Somershill. My father, Henry de Lacy, was a tyrant, a pinchpenny, and a bore. My mother was, and remains, a woman who continually affects silliness in order to achieve her own ends. Of course, only half of her eccentricity is genuine – but gauging which half is where the problem lies. But Lord and Lady Somershill were not my parents. Not my true flesh and blood.

I have already said in this account that my true mother was a young village girl, Adeline Starvecrow. A girl who had been employed as a wet nurse to the de Lacy family. I never knew her, so she remains a perfect angel in my mind. Her behaviour, her appearance, and her personality do not cause me a moment of mortification, because the poor woman is dead. And so we come to the identity of my true father. Was he a man who could be exhorted in the same way as my mother? Was he a saint, an exemplar, a man of good deeds and heroic action? No. He was not. For my true father, the man whose blood runs in my own, was a liar, a drunkard, and a murderer. He was also a priest.

Since our argument in the monastery, after the departure of Edmund, I had accused Peter of showing too much of an interest in my welfare. I had suggested that his motives were not altogether moral – even that he shared the same corrupt tastes as the abbot. But I had been both wrong and blind. I had not seen that the attention and watchfulness Peter afforded me was the love and care that a father gives to his only son.

Peter had finally confessed the truth to me last year, when I was eighteen – but with great reluctance, for this story was wretched and shameful. As a young man, Peter had fallen in love with the pretty and poor Adeline. Their love had been so intense that he had abandoned his vows of celibacy, and soon Adeline was expecting an inconvenient child. I suppose Peter could have disappeared at this point – plenty of errant fathers do. Instead, he arranged a speedy marriage for the girl to a villager, William Starvecrow, and left Adeline to explain away an early birth. When the true Oswald de Lacy died in Adeline's care however, it was not her new husband that she turned to – it was Peter. In a panic Peter had taken the young de Lacy boy's body away to be buried, swearing to me that he had laid this child to rest in the churchyard. In a grave marked Thomas Starvecrow.

Peter confessed his sins to God. He kept away from Adeline, and he paid his penance. But Peter could not keep away from me, his own son.

I shall never know with absolute certainty whether fortune or stealth placed me in the cradle of Oswald de Lacy, but that is

where I grew. Peter had watched over me, always making excuses
to visit Somershill in order to check upon my progress. It had
even been his suggestion that I be sent to the monastery to be
educated and prepared for holy orders. His reasoned appeal to
Mother, that the de Lacy family should have a priest in their ranks,
was a successful one – though Peter had been forced to promise
my father that I would become an abbot. At seven years of age I
left Somershill. At eighteen I returned. Peter accompanied me.

If Peter's love for me did not begin as a corrupted emotion, it
soon became so. Now that his own son was Lord Somershill, he
was ambitious for me. His watchfulness turned to suspicion, his
care to obsession. He saw danger and enemies at every turn,
fearing somebody would reveal my true identity and snatch away
my fortune and position. He even murdered three people in
order to protect me – two young girls and Clemence's husband
Walter de Caburn. He committed these crimes to keep our secret
hidden – a secret that I did not yet know.

I did not discover that Peter was my father until I had investi-
gated the murders, and the trail had led me back to the old monk
in the midst of my own family. Now that he was cornered, Peter
had no choice but to confess the whole sordid story. That he was
a murderer. That his motivation was a desire to protect me, his
son. I didn't want to believe it, of course – who chooses to discover such a thing? Though, in my heart, I knew it to be true.

I had not been the only person listening to this confession,
however. My sister Clemence, a seasoned eavesdropper, had
been hiding in the room and had heard the whole tale. When
she revealed herself and threatened to tell our secret to the
whole world, Peter held a knife to her throat and went to stab
her. I begged for my sister's life, but Peter refused to spare her.
She would destroy me, he argued. She hated me. Why would I
want to save this viper, when she would not extend the same
favour to me, if the tables were turned? I tried to reason with
the old fool, but when this failed, I managed to pull Clemence

from his clutches. As Peter berated me for my foolishness, Clemence threw a great pan of boiling water over his face, burning the skin from his bones. He lay upon the floor, convulsing in pain. He panted and struggled for breath. It seemed his heart would stop.

We only left Peter for a few moments. I went to fetch some brandy to ease his journey into the next life. He was my father, after all. Despite his sins, I wanted to lessen his suffering. When I returned however, he was gone. He had completely disappeared.

We searched for Peter for days, but found nothing. In the end I was convinced he had taken himself to a quiet corner of the forest and died. His injuries were too severe, and his body was too old and abused to allow his survival.

But if he was dead, then where was his body?

The next morning I organised a wider search of the estate for the de Caburn sisters, feeling sure that Mary and Rebecca must be hiding somewhere in an abandoned cottage or a dry hay barn. They knew how to look after themselves, having been raised by their father without the education and attention he would have lavished on a son, but even so, it was time they came home. It was too cold to be outside for long. The sky was leaden, and the sporadic rain was threatening to thicken into icy rods of sleet. There was also another important and more practical reason for finding the girls as soon as possible. The rumour that they had been taken by the butcher bird was now running through the village like a flooded stream, and though I had ordered such talk to stop, it was impossible to close the mouth of every gossip, or the ears of every gullible fool.

I split the men into groups and then sent them into the different sections of land that radiated in all directions from the house. I stopped short of calling this a hue and cry, knowing the effect such words would have upon the village. Instead I described our search as a hunt for two lost girls, and when I offered a five-penny reward to the person who could find the sisters, there was less grumbling from the men about having to leave their own fields for the day.

I would tell you that my authority over these men had grown in the months since my last tale, that they respected my dominion and obeyed me without argument or resentment. But I found they still gathered into surly groups at my approach and folded their arms with guarded hostility to my commands. In the weeks before the girls' disappearance I had given up trying to win their respect and favour and now shouted my commands as noisily and arrogantly as any other nobleman in Kent. When my reeve Featherby tried to intervene with unsolicited advice, I would tell him to keep his peace, even if I found, upon reflection, that his suggestion was better than mine. I thought it was a weakness to change my mind. But I was wrong, for it turns out that intransigence is weakness. Holding blindly to your first utterance in the hope that it will appear more commanding is, in fact, one of the best ways to fail.

None of the various search parties appeared to need my assistance, so I chose instead to check once more about Somershill. There was always the possibility that the two girls were hidden under our very noses in some nook or cranny. I wandered the house, searching in the corners where I had hidden as a child, when my brothers were in the mood to taunt me with their sticks, or to incite one of their dogs to chase me about the courtyard. I looked in the cellar, behind the barrels in the buttery, and at the end of the stables where we used to keep the smallest ponies. The smell of my childhood filled my nostrils and induced a sudden melancholia that I struggled to shake off.

Wandering across the wet grass between the rear of the house and the curtain wall, I decided to look around the back of the north-west tower. Brambles grew in a tangle about the base of the walls and had only recently been cut away into a path so that food could be taken to and from my ward, John Barrow. The man was still in there, though we no longer heard his wailing – thanks to Agnes Salt's sleeping draught.

Pulling aside some stray brambles that were determined to stick their barbs into the wool of my new hose, I made for the door – only to stop in my tracks as a crow landed above me on the narrow sill of an arrow slit. Its eye was bright and black. Its feathers were lustrous and shimmered in the weak winter sunlight. But any beauty possessed by this creature was short-lived, for when it began to call, it made a crabby, grating noise that filled the air with its ugliness. I shooed it away, but as its rasping call diminished into the distance, it left a more subtle sound in its wake. It was a whisper, not of one voice but of two.

I crept closer to the door of the tower, not wanting to disturb the originators of this low murmuring, for there is nothing more provoking to an investigator than a whispered conversation. I placed my ear at the crack in the door and then pressed it against this small sliver of space in the hope that some words would leak through. But ears are an unreliable friend. At times they will let you hear the most disagreeable of noises, or even some cruel words of criticism. At other times, when you need them most, their powers will desert you.

I poked a finger into my ear and twisted it in the hope that I might hear better, but unfortunately this did little to help. All I could tell for certain was that there were two people conversing. One had to be John Barrow, since he was imprisoned behind this door. The other voice I did not recognise.

I noticed the key had been removed, so either both of them were locked into the tower, or the owner of the second voice had turned the lock and now had the key in his possession. Realising that there was little to be gained from trying to eavesdrop any further on this conversation, I decided instead to push at the door. As I then entered the chamber and adjusted my eyes to the darkness, two faces looked up at me. It was John Barrow and the priest, Father Luke. Both were crouched in the corner of the room, and looked as guilty as two boys caught drinking the best port in the cellar.

Father Luke jumped to his feet. 'Lord Somershill. We didn't hear you approach.' Now he bowed and then forced Barrow to stand and do the same. I noted that Barrow's clothes were covered in pieces of food, suggesting that the man had been sick in recent hours. I will admit, at this point, to wanting to vomit myself, since nothing is as contagious as the stink of another person's bile. Instead I held my hand to my nose.

Father Luke bowed again. 'Perhaps you should leave this chamber, sire? Barrow has been sickened by some sort of sleeping tonic. The fumes could be noxious.'

The priest sounded like my mother and I was not about to be ordered about by somebody who was barely a year older than me. 'What are you doing here, Father?' I asked.

The fool bowed a third time, and I wondered if such excessive servility would accompany each of his responses. 'I came to visit John Barrow, sire. The man is in need of spiritual guidance.' It seemed to me that Barrow was more in need of a clean tunic.

'What were you whispering about?' I asked.

Father Luke's face fell, and I would tell you that the colour drained from his features, but the priest was a pale and bloodless creature anyway. He mumbled some answer or other, but then our attention was drawn away from the chamber entirely, and I'm sorry to say that I did not press my nose any further into this nook.

Somewhere outside the tower my name was being shouted repeatedly. The voice was shrill and insistent, and at first I assumed it belonged to a woman. When I ran outside, I found that it was our new servant Geoffrey, trying to summon me. He bounded across the grass like a deerhound. 'You must come quickly to the great hall, sire.'

'What's the matter?'

He hesitated. 'Master Featherby says I'm not to tell you.'

I crossed my arms. 'Geoffrey?'

The boy winced. 'It's the missing sisters, sire. Something's been found.'

I quickly returned to the tower, telling the priest to lock the door and then to join me immediately in the house.

The great hall at Somershill is my least favourite part of the house. Perhaps this antipathy to grand dimensions and high ceilings is distilled from my true essence, as the child of a peasant. I prefer the warmth and intimacy of the upper chambers, where I am not on show to every member of the household – for the great hall is a stage where I must perform as a lord.

As I strode into the hall that morning, I was confronted by a small group of men who were gathered in a circle, staring intently at something on the floor. Their backs were to me, but my reeve Featherby was immediately recognisable by his height and the tight curls upon his head. It was with great trepidation that I pushed my way through the crowd to look upon the object of their inspection.

They parted to allow me to look down at the floor, where two pairs of shoes lay in the reeds. Both made of green satin. One pair a little larger than the other. Both unmistakeably belonging to Mary and Rebecca de Caburn.

'Where did you find these?' I asked the man standing next to me.

He went to answer, but Featherby shoved him away. 'They were hidden inside the tithe barn, sire.'

'The priest's tithe barn?'

Featherby frowned. 'There are no other tithe barns in Somershill.' Now he crossed his arms and seemed poised to revert to his habit of leaning over me, so I stepped back hastily, standing upon another man's foot.

'Where's Father Luke?' I asked, looking around to see the

priest hanging back behind the group, his sickly face now blotched with patches of colour.

'Yes, sire?' He was trying to behave as if he hadn't heard the conversation.

'Mary and Becky's shoes have been found on your property. Do you know anything about this?'

He shook his head vigorously. 'No, sire. I am as surprised as you.'

'You didn't see the girls before they disappeared?'

'No, no. I've been at church most of the last few days, preparing for Holy Week. I've hardly been at my house at all.' He bowed again, with such deepness that he nearly fell over. 'I really don't know why such items might be lying around in my barn.'

Picking up one of the delicate shoes, I found it to be undamaged but muddy. Looking for Featherby's face again amongst the host of men who now bore down upon me, I asked, 'You say these shoes were hidden?' Featherby nodded. 'Were they tucked away behind something, or just abandoned?'

'The shoes were behind some sacks of flour, sire.' At the mention of flour, some of the men began to grumble beneath their breath, repeating their perennial complaint that one tenth of their harvest might sit in a tithe barn, whilst their own children went hungry.

'So the shoes were found easily?' I asked.

'I don't know what you mean, sire,' said Featherby.

The man was beginning to irritate me. 'I imagine an attacker might have made an effort to conceal these items?'

'So you think the girls were attacked, sire?'

I went to answer this, but could hardly make my voice heard above the chattering that suddenly erupted.

A man known locally as Roger the Toad pushed his droopy face forward and bowed to me. 'Have the sisters been murdered, sire? Like poor little Catherine Tulley?'

Once again I tried to answer, but the clamour amongst the men was now deafening, and they had stopped paying any attention to my words. It was not long before the name of John Barrow was mentioned, and his accursed butcher bird.

'John Barrow has nothing to do with this,' I said. 'He's been locked in the north-west tower for nearly two weeks.' I spoke as loudly as possible, though nobody listened – their ears blocked by their own stupidity. I made my way quickly to the dais at one end of the hall, so that I might stand above them and fully gain their small-minded attention.

Once I had established myself upon the platform, I will admit to shouting and waving my arms like a farmhand trying to communicate across a field. 'Listen to me!' I shouted. 'Quieten down.'

I was angry by this time and must have looked a foolish sight upon my small stage, beside the long supper table and the disarray of stools and benches. On the other hand, my display of temper had succeeded in gaining their attention. The room fell silent, with only the distant echoes of baby Henry screaming for his feed.

'Thank you,' I told them as they settled down and finally stopped talking. 'Now listen carefully. The de Caburn sisters have not been murdered.'

'But what about their shoes, sire?' asked Roger again. 'Why are they in the barn?'

I stumbled over my words slightly. 'I expect Mary and Rebecca hid them.'

'But why would they have done that, sire?'

Their faces looked at me blankly. There was some logic to Roger's question, but it was hardly the place of a man with the face of a toad to interrogate me. It didn't help that I noticed a wry smile creeping across Featherby's face.

'That's what we need to establish.' Roger went to answer this assertion, but I raised a hand to signify that I would not welcome any further interjections. Thankfully he chose not to argue and merely shook his head, swaying his toad-like jowls like the cheeks of a wet dog.

'I applaud you for discovering the shoes, Featherby,' I said. 'I'm not sure what they tell us as yet, but I'm sure they will help with my investigation.'

'Wasn't me that found them, sire,' he said. 'It was young Alfred here.' Featherby pointed to a boy in the crowd whose mournful face often caught my attention about the village. I had rarely seen a living person appear so disappointed with life.

'Did you find anything else?' I asked. The boy shook his head and cast his eyes to the floor, as if looking up might blind him.

I took a deep breath. 'And there was no sign of a struggle? No blood, for example.' I once again held my hand up before the mention of blood caused another uproar. 'Please let the boy answer.'

Alfred muttered some more words to his feet, only raising his voice to an audible level when he was shoved in the side by Featherby. 'I didn't see nothing like that, sire,' he said. 'Just the shoes. Stuffed behind a sack of flour. With some old bones. And some feathers.'

How I wished he had not mentioned bones and feathers. 'It's the butcher bird,' they shouted. 'It killed the sisters.'

Now I bellowed to be heard. 'There is no butcher bird I tell you!'

'What about them feathers then?' said a voice from the crowd. I couldn't see who said this, or they would have regretted it.

'The feathers came from the kills of a cat,' I said. The voices fell silent. I cleared my throat. 'Mary and Rebecca have a large grey cat who hunts in the priest's barn.' I looked across the crowd. 'Where has Father Luke gone?'

His small white hand was feebly raised. 'I'm here, sire.'

'You see a large grey cat about the glebe, don't you? You told me yourself that it hunts in your barn.'

He nodded nervously. 'Yes. That's true.'

I looked about me. 'You see,' I told the men roughly. 'The feathers mean nothing. Now go home.' Some of them went to argue, but I shouted them down. 'I said. Go home!'

The crowd broke up slowly, but not silently, and though I tried not to listen to their grumbling, it seemed I had convinced them regarding neither the feathers, nor the cat. There was, at least, one aspect of this whole episode to be thankful for. Thomas Tulley was nowhere to be seen.

Chapter Twelve

W e continued to search for the missing sisters, but found no further clues to their whereabouts. Clemence had her own theory, and when she cared to speak to me on the subject, she argued that Mary and Rebecca had run away just to cause her trouble. If this was the case however, then where had they gone, and who was caring for them? It was true that the girls were resourceful, but I still found it difficult to believe that they were fending for themselves somewhere deep in the forest. Rain still fell relentlessly, as it had done for the last two years, and yet again the spring was late in breathing its warmth across the land. Dirty snowdrops still thrust their dying heads from the mud and the frost fastened the buds to the branches. I doubted that even these two quick-witted girls could survive a winter that would not retreat.

As the days wore on they reappeared, but only in my dreams. My nights were no longer haunted by the scalded boy within the carcass of the burning bull; instead I met three strange children in a dark, empty forest. They were wretched, shrivelled creatures with scratched and naked bodies. Dried blood hung in their tangled hair. I often woke and then tried to sleep again, in an effort to forget their faces. But what is a nightmare, other than a distorted mirror – throwing back reality in a twisted reflection? I knew who these children were. How could I forget them? They were Mary and Rebecca de Caburn and poor Catherine Tulley. Come to taunt me. For what had my investigations discovered? Nothing.

One afternoon, during Holy Week, I walked in the gardens behind the house after a night of broken sleep and bad dreams. The weather was still cold, so the moat was not yet stinking, but the sun was shining at last. A blackbird sang in the coppiced hazel, and a slow-worm wriggled feverishly across my path. I picked the creature up, cupping its silken body in my hands, and went to sit on a favourite wall that overlooked the herb garden. My idea was to study the small snake-like animal, but my attentions soon turned to another subject when I heard a noise on the other side of the wall. As I peeped over, I saw it was Clemence's servant Humbert. He was singing a lullaby to baby Henry. His voice was sweet and his words were clear.

> *'Sweet child, don't let the cold air bite,*
> *Don't sleep at day and not at night,*
> *Eat your fill and do not cry,*
> *May foulest Pestilence pass you by.'*

Then he held the baby to his lips and kissed him tenderly upon the head.

> *'Be strong, grow fast and marry well.*
> *And prosper where the others fell.'*

I dropped the slow-worm and stood up, giving Humbert every reason to jump back in shock. 'What do you want?' he said rudely.

I smiled, in an attempt to reassure him. 'I was just admiring your song, Humbert. I don't know that lullaby. Did your mother teach it to you?'

'No,' he said. 'I made it up myself.'

I must have let the surprise show on my face, for this was a complex and melancholy tune. I can remember its unusual melody, even now. My reaction alarmed Humbert however, for now he denied composing the tune himself. He even muttered something about a mother, and I realised then that my comment had been thoughtless. He had been dumped on our doorstep as a young boy, and had Clemence not decided to keep him, then his chances would have been poor. For nobody claimed him.

As Humbert quickly took his leave of me, I watched his great frame plod back across the grass to the house. The boy was a puzzle. A contradiction. If he had composed the song himself, why did he deny it?

Apart from my failing investigations into Catherine's murder and the sisters' disappearance, there was another matter that needed my attention. I had made a promise to Joan that I would improve the wages, but my nerve was beginning to wane. When I saw Joan about the village over Holy Week, she made a point of reminding me of our conversation, and I swore to attend to the issue as soon as the girls were found and Easter was over. But, in truth, I was finding excuses to delay a difficult issue.

I was in the library the Monday after Easter Sunday, claiming the space at the one and only table before Clemence installed herself in the room. My sister liked to use the library after break-fast, while Humbert carried baby Henry about the garden to bring up his wind. Once Clemence was at the table, it took a great force to remove her to the bench, since she did not think it suited her posture to read with a book in her lap. I, however, had to read my ledgers, and needed a flat area to roll out the parchment.

As I scanned the documents, it was impossible to not stifle a yawn, for these accounts were boring enough to induce pain. I carried on until Featherby knocked at the door and then entered without waiting for my acknowledgement. I groaned inwardly to see his face – even though I had requested this meeting myself.

Since resolving to increase wages, I had done some rough calcu-
lations and estimated what the estate could afford to pay. But the
plan depended greatly upon Featherby's agreement to keep his
mouth shut.

'Please take a seat,' I said, gesturing towards the bench, which
sat against the wall. I did not want the man leaning over me.

Featherby straightened up a little. 'I'm happy to stand, thank
you sire.'

'No, no. Please sit down.'

'My back is stiff,' he said with a sudden stretch. 'The physician
told me to sit as little as possible.'

I felt a small defeat approaching, so I stood up to join him, but
as I did so the rolled ledger sprang away from me as if it were
possessed by a devil. Once I had tamed the wilful manuscript, I
turned back to my reeve, but did not find a man with a smile
across his face. Instead he looked as awkward as I had ever have
seen him.

'What's the matter?' I asked. He was cautious enough not to
answer. This was not like Featherby at all.

He cleared his throat. 'I have to report that three of our best
tenants are planning to move their families to a different estate.
They say they've been offered better land, and a penny more per
day.'

This took me by surprise. 'Is it true?'

He blew his lips and looked to the ceiling. 'Hard to say. They
could just be pretending of course. As a ruse. But we wouldn't
want to lose them. Not seeing as they're our best labourers.'

As Featherby went to take another step forward, I held up
my hand to prevent his further encroachment. 'Stay where you
are.' The man froze on his feet, amazed at the sudden force of
my command. In fact, I surprised myself. 'Thank you.' I took a
deep breath and tried to loosen my voice. 'Well, you'll be
pleased to hear this then. I've come to a decision regarding the
issue of wages.'

Featherby looked at me oddly. 'Indeed?'

'Yes, Featherby. I'm going to—' My hands felt sweaty.

He paused, scrutinising my face hopefully. 'Sire?'

I cleared my throat. 'So. You see, the thing is—' At this very moment Clemence opened the door, and I found it difficult to disguise my annoyance at her entry. 'We're discussing important matters here, Clemence,' I said. 'You can read your books later.'

Clemence bristled. 'I've come with some news, brother.' She pursed her lips. 'But if you're too busy, I'll send a servant later.'

'What news?'

'No, no. Don't let me trouble you.' She stepped back and bowed with exaggerated sarcasm. 'I wouldn't want to interrupt.'

Noting the curling smile across Featherby's face, I ran to the door to block her exit with my arm. 'Just tell me, Clemence.'

She felt slowly and deliberately at both cuffs of her dress. 'Very well, Oswald. You may wish to know that Earl Stephen's steward is here.'

I dropped my arm from the door post. 'Edward Hatcher? Here?'

'That's what I just told you.'

My heart began to bang in my chest. 'What's he doing here? He isn't due until next month.'

She shrugged. 'How would I know?' Then she gave the slightest of laughs. 'Such matters are too *important* for a woman.'

I might have replied to her sarcasm, but the news of Hatcher's arrival was so unwelcome that it subdued my usual urge to argue with my sister. Instead I peered around the door to look into the great hall, but did not see the object of our conversation. 'Where is the man then?'

'Mother has invited him to sit with her in the solar.'

'What?'

Clemence frowned, turning what beauty she still possessed into an ugly grimace. 'Edward Hatcher's an honoured guest,

Oswald. And you'd do well to follow Mother's lead in your treatment of him. He is the ears and eyes of the earl on this estate.' She then exchanged a glance with Featherby, which expressed their shared frustration at having to deal with such an idiot as myself.

I turned with my own frustration to Featherby. 'Were you expecting Hatcher?'

Featherby shrugged. 'No, sire.' He then approached the door with the pretence of also looking into the great hall, though his true aim was to lean over me. 'But then again, Edward Hatcher likes to just turn up.'

I left Featherby with instructions to stay at the house in case he was needed to answer specific questions about the running of the estate. Despite having been lord for around a year and a half, I will admit that my understanding of the accounts, and particularly those pertaining to the farm itself, was still woefully poor. I ran up the stairs to the solar to find the earl's steward sitting next to my mother in the window seat, their heads drawn together in scheming secrecy.

Hatcher took his time to rise when I entered the room. He was a man of middle age, tall and weather-worn. The low sun glinted from the shininess of his bald pate. He wore the hooded tunic of a ploughman, with a pair of gloves hung from his belt, but his clothes were of the best cloth, and his gloves of the softest leather. This was a man who no more ploughed the fields than I did.

He bowed to me. 'Lord Somershill.'

'Master Hatcher.' I tried to suppress my panting from having run up the stairs. 'I didn't know you were visiting this week?' I then forced a smile. 'But it's good to see you.'

Hatcher looked to Mother and laughed. 'I was just saying to Lady Somershill that I was passing and thought I might take a small diversion. I do hope this is not inconvenient?'

This was an obvious lie, since the man did nothing without

purpose, but I played along. 'Of course not. You are always welcome here.' More lies. I did not want my accounts and records pored over by this man any more times than was absolutely necessary. I had scraped together enough funds to pay the rent the earl now required from both the Somershill and Versey estates. Of course we did not call it *rent*, as that would be far too demeaning and commonplace, and would debase the nobility of our arrangement. Instead we laughably called it a contribution. There had been a time of course when the promise of the de Lacy family to provide men for the king's wars had been enough to secure our family's tenure of this estate. But these terms no longer satisfied the earl, and now he required me to pay him money like any other tenant on the land. What made this worse was that he sent a man, whose family used to tend sheep and mend the gates in the hunting forests, to check my records to see if he could exact any more money from us.

Our conversation was interrupted by Humbert, who strolled through the solar, with baby Henry resting upon his broad shoulder. For once the squawking infant was fast asleep.

Mother let out a gasp at the sight of our large servant and then shooed Humbert down the stairs with hurried embarrassment. 'Whatever next,' she hissed at the boy. 'Will your mistress come in and start nursing the child in front of our guest? Take Henry to the chapel and make sure he does not catch a chill.'

Hatcher smiled with slight bewilderment, as if such domesticity was completely alien to him.

I held out my hand. 'Please, sit down. Finish your ale.' He bowed his head to me, revealing the tanned skin of a skull that was pitted with whitened scars.

'How long are you planning to stay?' I asked, as nonchalantly as possible. As if to emphasise how little his answer might concern me, I then stoked up the fire – but only caused the logs to roll apart.

Hatcher watched this episode with some amusement. 'This is

just a social visit,' he assured me, with a grin he might dish out to a simple child. 'I shall be leaving before nightfall.' I noted his accent was still soft and Kentish in its burr, though he had sharpened its edges with more acute pronunciation.

I went to answer, but Mother interrupted. 'No, no. Edward. You must stay the night.' She turned to me. 'Mustn't he, Oswald? He may stay with you in the men's bedchamber.'

I was silenced on two fronts by this last statement. Not only was Mother on Christian-name terms with this man, but secondly she was making the odious suggestion that we might sleep under the same sheets.

Thankfully Hatcher was equally disconcerted by this idea. 'Thank you, my lady. But I've come with some of the earl's men,' he protested. 'And we are not a small party.' I looked from the window of the solar into the courtyard to see four men on horseback in the livery of the earl. If the steward were accommodated at the house, then we would be forced to offer the same hospitality to these men. At least they were only squires and not knights, so they might sleep beside the fire in the great hall.

Mother clapped her hands. 'I'll have Gilbert slaughter another lamb and we shall have a banquet.' She then took Hatcher's arm. 'You can tell me all of the news, Edward. I am terribly isolated out here with just my children for company. Not a whisper of the outside world reaches me.'

Mother ended this ridiculous statement by pretending to wipe a tear from the corner of her eye. Hatcher then did the most extraordinary thing. He took Mother's hands in his own and bowed his head slowly. 'My lady. You are so gracious, with your kind invitation. But we must return this evening.'

Mother's pale cheeks reddened to a girlish blush. 'Must you? Really?'

Hatcher continued to cup her hands in his own – her fragile boniness now clasped in his tanned and calloused fingers. Even Mother's little dog Hector looked up at the man in awed silence.

I let my mouth hang open at this hideous display, which only became more revolting when Mother began to flutter her eye-lashes. 'Never mind, Mother,' I said. 'I'm sure Master Hatcher will be able to stay another time.'

Mother threw me the stoniest of stares, before turning back to Hatcher. 'Will you at least stay for some more ale and cheese, Edward?'

Hatcher nodded. 'Is there any pottage, my lady? I'm sure the men would appreciate some warm food on this cold day.'

Once again Mother blushed like a girl. 'Of course, Edward. And I bet you would prefer something warm yourself?' And then I believe she winked at the man. What was she thinking of? A woman of her age! Most of her contemporaries were either dead or propping up the corner of a fireplace, and yet it seemed that my mother was making crude insinuations to a steward. Thankfully she left the solar to make arrangements with the kitchen.

'What a woman,' said Hatcher, as Mother made her exit. He smiled to reveal a set of stained teeth. Unable to say anything to this comment, I merely pulled a face, but my response went unnoticed, for the man now appeared to be mining his ear for something with his little finger.

Finding this distasteful, I distracted myself by poking again at the logs on the fire. 'I think we need a little more wood,' I said. 'I'll just summon a servant.' In truth this was an excuse to leave the room, since I found it awkward to be alone with Hatcher. What would I speak to the man about? I doubt he read books, ever thought about geometry, or cared the slightest bit about the trajectory of Venus. It was more likely that we would have to discuss the breeding lines of our bulls, or the quality of our wheat harvest – both of which subjects held no interest for me. And then I had the idea of inviting Featherby to join us. The two men were of the same station in life and would doubtless find endless interests in common. I must have said as much, for Hatcher stopped me. He put his hand upon my arm – very firmly. He saw no impropriety in such an action, but I did.

'No, my lord,' he said. 'I think it's better that we have a private conversation. Let your reeve stay in the hall.'

I stepped away from him and dusted down my sleeve, as if his touch had somehow dirtied my arm. 'I thought this was a social visit, Hatcher?'

He laughed jovially. 'I was only passing nearby. I thought it rude not to pay Somershill a visit. And I do enjoy my lady's company. There are few such lively women in this county.'

'She is nearly sixty you know.'

He only laughed at this comment. 'Well, I would have thought her half that age.' Was the man blind as well as bald?

He cleared his throat and patted his large hands upon the tops of his legs, drumming his fingers rhythmically upon the hard muscles of his thighs. If ever a man were displaying his strength to a minor, this was it. If Hatcher had been a bull he might have snorted and dropped his head to display the points of his horns, before pawing at the ground with his hoof and despatching me with a charge. Instead he continued to look at me with his eyebrows raised.

'The earl has requested that I visit all his tenanted estates,' he said, 'to ask certain questions.' He savoured the word *tenanted*. He and I were not so different after all. The name of the de Lacy family was carved over the door, but we did not own this land, we only held it from the earl, who in turn held it from the king. In some parts of the country there were yeoman farmers who rented nearly as much land as I did. In truth the de Lacys were no more noble than pigherds with a pot of money.

'What questions are they?' I said.

He broke his stare and began to scratch at his ear a second time, now as urgently as a dog with fleas.

'Are you unwell?' I asked.

'I think there is something inside my ear,' he said. 'Would you take a look, my lord? I can feel it itching and wriggling.'

I hesitated, but now he knelt down in front of me and cocked his head so I might inspect the cavity of his ear. 'I'm not qualified for such a diagnosis,' I protested. 'My near sight is not always good.'

Now he banged the side of his head with his fist. 'Please, my lord. There is something inside. I can feel it wriggling.' He appeared to be panicking.

I had treated men with madness at the infirmary. Under Brother Peter's guidance, I had learnt to indulge the fantasies of lunatics in order to appease them – since a flat denial of their claims often led to a violent outcome. I had assured one patient that I could see the Minotaur that was hiding in the room, though when I looked beneath the table the beast was listless and tired. Another poor demented priest had claimed to be the Pope. Whereas the other brothers would inflame the man's anger by calling him a heretic, I managed to keep him calm by calling him Your Holiness, and bowing upon entering the room.

Of course, I didn't believe that Hatcher was mad, though this sudden episode with his ear was troubling. 'Have you put a maggot inside?' I asked, as this was common practice amongst some of the villagers, in the hope the small grub would devour the person's ear wax and thereby relieve their deafness.

Hatcher shook his head. 'No. Please. Look further inside.'

His voice was now urgent, so with great reluctance I leant further towards his head, seeing only a small black hole fringed with hair.

'Can you see anything?' he asked.

'No.'

'Look closer.'

'But I cannot see inside your head Master Hatcher.'

'Put your finger in and feel about.'

I recoiled. 'What? No. I don't think that would help at all.'

His voice sharpened. 'I said put your finger in.'

'But—'

'Do it!'

I put my hand in the small opening to his earhole, but no further. 'There's nothing there,' I said, quickly removing my finger.

'Press in further. Feel about.'

I felt sick, but also terrified. Hatcher was as cross as a baited bear, ready to strike out his paw at any moment. 'This won't do any good,' I protested.

He took my hand and pressed it against his ear, squeezing it firmly until I had no option but to obey his instruction. The interior of his ear felt greasy, but clear of any obstructions or indeed any small, crawling intruders.

'Anything there?' he asked.

'No.'

He let my hand go and quickly got to his feet. 'That's good,' he said, his tone now rational. 'Thank you, my lord. I just needed to make sure I could hear properly.'

I shrank away from him, for it was clear that he had been playing a game with me and I felt feeble for having surrendered so easily. 'Perhaps next time you should ask to see a physician to inspect your ear,' I said, making a point of wiping my finger on the edge of a tapestry.

He only laughed at this suggestion. 'I cannot afford to travel with a physician, my lord. I'm just a lowly steward.'

'I'm sure the occasional consultation would suffice.'

'But I have such problems with my ears. So many people tell me lies, you see. Then they deny what they've said.' He leant towards me in an attitude not dissimilar to Featherby's. But whereas Featherby's posturing was an irritation, this man's bearing exuded menace. 'I must make sure to hear their answers clearly. Then I can tell the earl exactly what has been said. You see, he hates lies as much as I do.'

'You won't hear lies here, Hatcher.'

He threw up his hands in sham alarm. 'God bless you, my lord.

I was simply talking about some of the other estates I visit. The earl has the greatest faith in you. He often says how well he can trust the young lord of Somershill and Versey. He doesn't expect to hear lies here.' Then he straightened up and moved to the window. 'The spring is late, don't you think?'

Was this another trick? I answered ambiguously. Something about a mixture of rain and sun.

'Have you started to sow yet?' he said.

'In some fields.'

'And how are you paying your men this spring?'

'In the same way as before.'

'Have they asked for higher wages?'

I hesitated. 'No. They are being paid according to the Statute.'

Hatcher put his finger to his ear and twisted it about again. 'Would you mind repeating that?' he asked.

I took a deep breath. 'Do I need to?'

He threw me a look. 'I believe you do, my lord.'

It was difficult to stop my voice from shaking. 'I am paying my men according to the Statute of Labourers,' I said. 'They receive the same day rates as they did in 1346.'

'And you will continue to do so?'

'Yes.'

He bowed his head. 'Thank you, my lord. This will certainly please the earl.' He looked out of the window again, appearing to focus on something in the distance. 'You see, my master has become very concerned that some of his estates are breaking the law. And once one lord gives in, then others will. You do understand that, don't you?'

'I'm not breaking the law,' I said.

'Of course not. But others try.' Then he turned back to me. His voice now the cruel hiss of an adder. 'They are foolish enough to think that they may hide what they're doing. But you see, the truth is this. I always find out.'

I let my mouth fall open. 'And then what happens to them?'

'Don't worry yourself about that, my lord. The earl trusts you.' He smiled, revealing his yellowed teeth. Like a row of tiny wax tablets – tarnished and flecked by years inside this man's noxious mouth. 'He would not throw your family from this estate. The earl is your friend.' I took his meaning well enough.

He broke his gaze and suddenly clasped his hands together, as if we had just concluded the arrangements for a forthcoming marriage, or the sale of a piece of land. 'I can smell the pottage, my lord. Shall we join the others in the great hall?'

'You go ahead Hatcher,' I said, with all the churlishness I could muster. 'I need to wash my hands.'

Mother had invited the four squires and Hatcher to join her at the family table on the dais. Seeing this was the arrangement, I deliberately seated myself at the other end of the long table, to be as far away as possible from this unpleasant group. Clemence was my only company.

We ate our meal in silence, though we were disturbed every few minutes by the peal of raucous laughter and the stamping of feet. 'Look at Mother,' I whispered to Clemence. 'Anybody would think this was her wedding feast.'

Clemence scraped the spoon about her empty bowl. 'Are you going to eat all of that?' she asked, looking at my own bowl, which was still half filled with pottage. The kitchen had struggled to stretch our midday meal to suddenly accommodate another five guests, and the pottage delivered to our end of the table was decidedly watery and bulked out with bread.

I pushed the bowl to my sister. 'You have it. Mother is ruining my appetite.'

Clemence greedily spooned the pottage into her mouth. 'She's enjoying herself, Oswald. Why don't you just ignore her?'

'But she's an old woman,' I whispered. 'Those young men don't find her company amusing.'

'I wouldn't say that.' At that exact moment one of the squires jumped from his seat to perform a dance like a flapping chicken, which nearly caused Mother to fall from her seat in laughter.

Clemence licked her spoon. 'You see, Oswald. Older women still enjoy the company of men. Their bodies are not yet dead beneath their gowns.'

I pulled a face.

'Does that disgust you?'

'No,' I lied.

She exhaled with a sudden weariness. 'You are still such a stupid little boy.' With that she stood, bowed indistinctly – possibly to me or to Mother, or perhaps it was merely to the hall itself – and then she left us. The raucous crowd at the other end of the table didn't notice her departure. I thought to leave myself, but knew this would be shirking my duty. Instead I fiddled with my fingernails and attempted to ignore Mother's continual mirth until a sudden commotion disturbed the hall. We heard shouting from outside, and the door was banged heavily. Somebody threw a stone against one of my grandfather's beloved windows, though thankfully it did not break the precious glass.

As I looked along the table I saw an alley of faces looking back at me. 'I'll go and see what's going on,' I said, getting to my feet.

'Is it the Danes?' asked Mother.

I quickly wiped my mouth on my sleeve. 'No. Mother. Not today.'

Gilbert opened the cumbersome door of the hall to a great horde of faces with Thomas Tulley at their head. In his hands he held a pile of wrinkled green cloth that was torn and muddy.

'What do you want?' I said, though I might have predicted Tulley's answer.

He stepped forward. 'John Barrow.'

The others repeated his words – now swaying with rhythmic menace. 'Barrow. Barrow.'

I was tempted to step back inside the house, but suddenly

found Gilbert behind me. I would almost say he was blocking my retreat. 'I've told you before,' I shouted. 'You can't have Barrow. Go home!'

Thomas thrust the pile of cloth at me. 'Recognise this, do you, sire?

The cloth fell onto the soil at my feet, leaving me dumbfounded for a few moments. 'No,' I said. 'What is it?'

Tulley knelt down to pick up one of the items, and then held it aloft for me to view. It was the gown of a child. The cloth was cut asunder and stamped with mud. 'These are the dresses of the de Caburn sisters.'

The garment was now familiar. Horribly so. 'Where did you find them?'

'In the nest of the butcher bird.'

'That's not true,' I said, but my voice was disobligingly small.

Another man now pushed his way through the crowd to join Tulley. He was small and wiry with clouded blue eyes, which were striking against the dark tan of his skin. I recognised him as Silas Beck, though I rarely saw his face about the village, since he kept to the furthest meadows with his sheep. 'We found this in its nest, sire.' Silas held a skull aloft, whitened and free of any flesh. 'The bird has been taking my lambs.'

'When it isn't taking children,' said Tulley. These words caused a shrieking from the crowd that was almost deafening.

'Where is this nest?' I shouted above the cacophony.

They didn't listen to me until Tulley turned to them and put his finger to his lips. When he had achieved the silence that I had failed to impose, he had the impudence to serve me an ultimatum. 'Give us Barrow, and then we'll show you.'

I made my answer plain. They would no more have Barrow than I would organise a search for their foolish bird. When I told them all to go home again, they began to advance upon the door, all the while shouting Barrow's name. I commanded them to leave, but my voice was once again lost in the tumult, and I was about to bolt back behind the door when I felt a tap upon my shoulder. Quickly turning, I expected to find Gilbert's dour face looking into mine. Instead it was the hard jaw and bald head of Edward Hatcher.

'What's going on here, de Lacy?' he said.

Once again my voice was not cooperating. I wanted to tell Hatcher to go back to the table, as the disturbance was under control, but only managed a dithering mumble.

Hatcher pushed me to one side and then stepped forward. He said nothing to begin with, but merely the fold of his arms was enough to halt their progress. 'How dare you approach this house?' he said, hardly raising his voice. 'Get back to your fields.'

Most people withdrew, but Tulley remained rooted to the spot. 'We want the sinner.'

Hatcher tipped his chin upwards and regarded the man with light, cold-blooded eyes. 'I told you to go home.'

Tulley was now sweating, despite his bluster. 'The sinner's name is John Barrow. Lord Somershill keeps him under his protection.'

Hatcher shrugged. 'Then that's where he'll stay.' He pointed his short, calloused finger at Tulley. 'If Lord Somershill wants to protect this John Barrow, then that's his business. It has nothing to do with you.' The crowd looked to me, and I have rarely felt smaller and more utterly feeble. Hatcher was standing the ground that I should have been standing myself.

But Tulley would still not concede. 'Barrow released a great bird on this village. A monster that stole my infant daughter from her cradle and left her dead body in a bush.'

Another shrug from Hatcher.

Anger flared in Tulley's eyes. 'If you don't care about my daughter, then you'll care enough about the two noble children the bird has killed.'

'Which noble children?' said Hatcher.

'Mary and Rebecca de Caburn.' Tulley pointed to the heap of

discarded clothes. 'These were their dresses. Torn from their bodies.'

This time Hatcher did not shrug. Instead he laughed. 'What nonsense is this?'

'Don't laugh at me!' said Tulley.

'I'll laugh at who I like. And I'll tell you this. The de Caburn sisters haven't been murdered by a bird. They were certainly wearing dresses when I saw them last week. In London.'

Tulley dropped the gowns. He looked askance. 'You're lying.'

Hatcher pointed his finger at Tulley a second time. 'Watch your tongue, churl. Or I will cut it out.'

I tugged at Hatcher's sleeve. 'Are you sure you saw them? Mary and Rebecca de Caburn?'

Hatcher swivelled his head to regard me, his amusement now completely extinguished. 'I don't have a problem with my eyesight. They are the daughters of Walter de Caburn, are they not?'

'Yes.'

'Then I saw them. They are guests of Eloise Cooper.'

'Eloise Cooper?'

Hatcher folded his arms. 'She is their aunt. She lives in London.'

'London?'

'Yes, de Lacy. London. It is a city on the River Thames.'

A few bystanders smirked, but soon stopped when Hatcher turned to stare at them. 'Is something amusing you?' To which nobody answered.

I quickly dusted down my tunic and straightened my back. 'The girls ran away and we thought they were dead. I'm very relieved to hear they are safe.'

Hatcher hesitated. 'Safe enough.'

'What do you mean?'

Hatcher shifted his body to speak more privately. 'Let's go inside and discuss this, shall we?' Then he turned once more upon my unruly subjects. 'Get your ugly faces out of here.'

At first the crowd didn't move.

'Go on. Get back to your fields. And if Lord Somershill reports another such disturbance, I will have each one of you flogged!' Then he pointed for the last time at Tulley. 'And you. You will be hanged.'

We closed the door and returned to the dais, where Mother was waiting for us. 'What did those people want, Oswald?' she asked me. In truth, I was surprised that she hadn't involved herself in the commotion at the door. Instead she had preferred to remain at the table and enjoy the company of the young squires. Their pewter cups were once again full of wine.

'They wanted John Barrow,' I told her.

'Who?'

I sat down with a sigh. 'Never mind. Master Hatcher has just informed me that he's seen Mary and Rebecca de Caburn.'

Mother turned her attention to the earl's steward, who was continuing his meal, as if the affray by the door had never happened. 'Really? Is this true Edward?'

He bowed his head to Mother. 'They're in London, my lady. At the household of Eloise Cooper.'

Mother flung up her arms at this news. 'With Walter de Caburn's sister? And how did they get there? We've been searching for that wicked pair for days.'

Hatcher shrugged and said nothing. Instead one of his squires answered the question. It was the boy who had previously performed the chicken dance. 'The story is the talk of London, my lady. How two young girls were mistreated by the de Lacys and had to run away to their aunt.'

'You might have mentioned this earlier,' I said.

He scratched his stupid head. 'We thought you knew, my lord.' He then smiled to my mother. 'Of course I didn't believe a word of such a tale, my lady. I'm sure they were treated with the utmost kindness by you.'

Mother was no longer charmed by this boy. 'What ungrateful

little devils those girls are. Spreading such stories about the de Lacy family. I do hope such lies have not reached the king's ears.'

Hatcher put his hands upon the table and thereby wrested all attention back to himself. 'I would doubt so, my lady. I'm sure he has more pressing concerns.'

'Well let them stay in London,' said Mother with a flourish. 'If that's what the two little hobgoblins want. Their behaviour was quite atrocious, Edward.' She wiped a false tear from her cheek. 'Their feral habits quite blackened my bile.'

Hatcher spoke with a mouth full of bread. 'I understand, my lady. Children can be trying.' Then he sucked his teeth for a moment. 'I would say only this. Is it wise to let them remain with such a woman as Mistress Cooper?'

'What's wrong with her?' I asked. 'Are the girls in some sort of danger?'

Hatcher rotated his head slowly to look at me. Like an owl, his body remained perfectly still. 'It's only rumours and gossip. Perhaps nothing more.' He then rotated his head back and returned to pulling apart a hunk of bread. 'I wouldn't want my own daughters living there.'

'I think you should explain yourself,' I said, now irritated. There was no need to draw out this explanation in such a frustrating manner, other than to rile me deliberately. I would tell you that my displeasure provoked an immediate response from the man, but he only gestured towards the chicken-dancing squire, indicating that his own mouth was now too full of food to speak.

The boy adopted the faux solemnity of a saint. 'They say Eloise Cooper practises sorcery.'

Mother's mouth fell open. 'A witch?'

The squire nodded. 'Indeed, my lady.' He turned to the other squires. 'We've all heard that story, haven't we?' The other boys nodded silently, suddenly mute and seemingly not willing even to speak aloud on the subject.

'I don't believe in witches,' I told them, unable to hold my tongue.

I might as well have announced that I didn't believe in God. The squire looked uneasy. 'But what about Eloise Cooper's daughter then, my lord? She was poisoned by her own mother. Only a witch would do such a thing.'

I let out a small laugh. What mother poisons her own child? 'And this is a widely held opinion, is it? That Mistress Cooper is a witch?'

The squire scratched his chin. 'Well yes, sire. It is.'

'I think even witches baulk at killing their own children.'

'It was when Master Cooper died. She didn't want to be bothered with the child, did she?' He once again looked to his fellow squires for a flurry of corroborating nods. 'And Master Cooper's death was strange enough.'

'In what way?'

'He died so quickly, sire. One day he was well, and the next he was dead. They say his body was covered in boils.'

I huffed. 'Sounds exactly like the Plague to me.'

He shook his head. 'No, no. More like witch blight.'

Now I groaned. 'Has Eloise Cooper been charged with witchcraft?'

The boy scratched his neck. 'Well, no, sire. She hasn't.'

'Then this is just idle talk.'

Hatcher stood up, dusting the breadcrumbs from his lap and letting out a belch. 'My lord. It's up to you whether or not to believe the story. The de Caburn sisters are wards of this family, after all. So if you are happy to leave them with such a woman, then that is your decision.' He looked to his men and bade them rise with his hands.

As the party left Somershill, he took me to one side. 'Thank you for cleaning my ear, my lord.'

My skin prickled.

He tapped his ear and smiled. 'Now that I can hear so well, I shall make sure to report your exact words to the earl.'

The departing group cantered about the courtyard in a great salute, causing Mother to squeal with delight at the speed of their horses and the spectacle of their billowing capes. The foolish woman then stared at them until they disappeared into the woods, and sighed as sadly as a child who is waving goodbye to a travelling fair. 'Edward Hatcher does so remind me of your father.' Then she broke her distant gaze and looked to me. 'Well. The man you thought was your father.'

I took her arm. 'Come with me, Mother. We need to talk to Clemence.'

'Why's that, Oswald?'

'We need to discuss the de Caburn sisters.'

She screwed up her eyes. 'Why?'

'They've run away to London, and we need to get them back.'

'Oh,' she said vaguely. 'Have they?'

Chapter Thirteen

Clemence refused to come into the solar to speak with us, as she was nursing baby Henry.

'But it's urgent,' I said, standing by the door to the ladies' bed-chamber and making sure not to look inside.

'Nothing is more urgent than feeding a hungry infant, Oswald,' she said. 'If it's so important, come in.'

'But—'

'For goodness sake, Oswald. My breasts are covered.'

'Very well,' I said, and then sidled into the room, pressing Mother to enter before me. When Clemence saw Mother was my companion, she let out a groan. 'You didn't tell me that *she* would be here as well.'

Mother shielded her eyes, as if hiding from a leper. 'Thank goodness nobody knows about this. A de Lacy child sucking at the breast of his own mother.'

'Be quiet,' hissed Clemence. 'You'll upset Henry.'

Mother shook her head again in disgust. 'Your breasts should have been bound weeks ago to stop your milk. Then you could be looking for a new husband.'

Now Clemence laughed. Bitterly. 'What makes you think I want a husband, Mother?'

Mother pointed to Humbert, who stood in the shadows like a sentinel. 'Well you can't spend the rest of your life with this clod in your bedchamber, can you? While you're sitting around Somershill, like an old maid.'

'Why not? You do.'

Mother inhaled loudly and Clemence clenched her teeth. A hostile silence seethed, so I quickly took a seat and tugged at Mother's sleeve to force her sit down next to me.

'Will you stop pushing and pulling me about, Oswald?' she whispered. 'I'm not a dog on a lead.'

Clemence made a point of finishing feeding her baby before she would speak to us. She passed Henry to Humbert and re-arranged her gown. 'So what's this urgent matter then?'

As Humbert rocked Henry, the baby looked ready to posset his latest feed onto the floor, so I spoke quickly, and kept clear of any likely trajectory. 'We know where Mary and Becky are. Edward Hatcher told us.'

'They're alive then?' I wasn't able to decipher any sentiment from this statement. Her voice was flat.

'Yes. They ran away to London.'

Clemence now dropped her indifference. 'London? Goodness me. How did they get so far?'

'We don't know.'

'And where are they living?'

'With their aunt, Eloise.'

Clemence's face whitened and she was about to answer, when Mother decided to butt in. 'And everybody in London is saying you abused the girls, Clemence. That's why they ran away. I'm told your name is as black as tar.'

I once again shoved the foolish woman, despite her previous protests at being treated like a dog. 'That's not true, Mother. If they're saying anything, then they are blaming all of us.'

'Yes. But it's mainly Clemence,' she whispered hoarsely.

I expected Clemence to erupt, but instead my sister stood up and marched to the window, where she appeared to be counting to ten. When her shoulders dropped and her breathing finally slowed, she turned to Humbert. 'Take Henry into the garden, please. But keep away from the moat. The air there is too damp for his chest.'

Humbert wrapped the small child in a woollen shawl and descended the staircase, though we soon heard Henry open his lungs in fury at being separated from his mother. Thankfully Humbert carried on into the garden and did not return.

When Henry's pitiful wails had receded far into the distance, Clemence addressed me, making a concerted effort not to look in Mother's direction. 'How do you know Mary and Rebecca are really in London?' she said. Mother tried to answer, but Clemence held her hand up to Mother's face and continued to stare at me. 'Can we trust the story?'

I shrugged. 'I think so. It seems an odd story for somebody to make up.'

Mother peeped around Clemence's hand. 'But people will say anything to cause trouble for the de Lacy family. They like to demean us in front of the king.'

Clemence's hand tightened to a fist. 'Oh be quiet Mother. Nobody cares about the de Lacy family. Especially not the king.'

Mother pushed the fist away. 'Your grandfather built this house so the king would visit. To hunt in our forests.'

Clemence laughed. 'But he never has, has he?'

I stood up in an attempt to end their squabbling. 'I'll go to London,' I said. 'I'll check on the girls' welfare and then try to bring them home.'

My announcement silenced them. But only for a moment. 'Thank you Oswald,' said Clemence. 'That's a good idea.' I will admit this enthusiasm surprised me, since I thought my sister might happily let the girls remain with their aunt.

Mother flared her nostrils and threw Clemence a vicious glare. 'Very good Oswald. *You*, at least, will protect the good name of this family.'

Sensing the embers of this squabble would reignite into flames at any moment, I quickly asked, 'What do we know about Eloise Cooper?'

Clemence shifted awkwardly on her seat. 'I've not met her.' Then she hesitated. 'Though I've heard certain things.'

'What sort of things?'

'That the woman is a witch of course,' said Mother. 'A sorceress.'

Clemence frowned. 'No. That wasn't the story. And I'd thank you not to speak for me, Mother.'

'Then what did you hear?' I asked.

Clemence began to chew a nail. 'That she's . . . cruel, I suppose.'

'Do you believe that?'

Clemence blushed and looked towards the window. In the distance we could still hear Henry's thin wails as his large protector carried him about the garden. 'She was my husband's sister,' said Clemence. Her voice was now soft and wearied. 'So, yes. I do.'

'Do you know where she lives?'

'Her husband was a rich merchant, so I expect they lived near Saint Paul's.'

Mother flapped her hands. 'No, no. The Coopers don't live near Saint Paul's. They could afford it of course, but William Cooper wouldn't part with the money to buy in such a street. Not even when his new wife demanded it.'

This was an unexpected revelation on Mother's part. 'How do you know this?' I asked.

'Everybody knows that William Cooper was one of the richest free men in London.' Then she gave one of her contemptuous laughs. 'No wonder the de Caburn family arranged for their daughter to marry him. Though he was no more highly born than a hayward.' She held out her pale fingers and then pinched at the loose skin on the back of one of her hands. 'Mind you, Eloise Cooper deserved no better. She was a very cunning girl.'

Before I could ask more, Mother stood up and began to bustle about the room. 'Now. We should prepare for our visit to London, Oswald. Where's Ada? I need her to pack my trunk.'

Clemence and I exchanged looks of dismay. 'You can't go to London, Mother,' I said. 'You're too . . .'

'Too . . . What?' said Mother, distractedly, as she searched for something beneath the bed.

'You're too old for such a journey,' said Clemence.

Mother lay on the floor and began to burrow under the bed-stead. 'Nonsense. I'm stronger than many women half my age. And you might come yourself, Clemence, if you hadn't saddled yourself with a nursing infant.'

'I've no desire to go to London,' said Clemence. 'The place is a stinking latrine. I've heard the dead of the Pestilence still float in the Thames.'

Mother reappeared with a shoe. It was old, with a wooden sole, and clearly not what she had been looking for at all, since she threw it back under the bed. 'Nonsense. The Plague is over.'

Clemence sneezed from all the dust Mother had dislodged. 'You hope it is.'

Mother waved away this warning, grabbed a stool and then stood on it to see if the object of her search was hiding on top of the bed canopy. 'We don't need your company, Clemence. Oswald and I shall go alone.'

'There's no need for you to accompany me to London, Mother,' I said, holding out my hand to steady her, since she was now wobbling on her stool.

She waved away my concern. 'Of course there is. I know where the Coopers live. And how else will you find your way about the city?'

'I can easily hire a guide.'

'No, no. Those men are all thieves and fraudsters.' Then she leaned out, even further across the canopy, nearly falling onto the mattress. 'Ah here it is.' She passed me a small leather pouch. 'Guides should never be trusted, Oswald. They will lead you up an alley and then their associates will assault you. Everybody knows that.'

I helped Mother down from the stool, whereupon she emptied the contents of the leather pouch onto the bed. I would tell you that something useful fell out, such as a handful of golden coins. Instead it was three ancient ivory dice – yellowed and lined with dirt.

Mother clasped them up in her hand. 'These will keep us entertained on the journey.'

I looked once again to Clemence in despair. 'But it's a long way, Mother. You can't ride that far.'

'No. Of course I can't. But we will use Clemence's carriage.'

I was cornered. One by one my excuses cut away. 'But it's very difficult to navigate the streets of London with a carriage,' I said, trying to dampen the desperation in my voice.

Mother pulled a face. 'Don't be so silly, Oswald. We'll leave the carriage at an inn in Southwark, and then we can walk over London Bridge. Or take a wherry boat across the river.'

Clemence did nothing to assist me. I suspected that the ordeal of my visit to London with Mother was amusing her. 'You see, little brother,' she said. 'You will not persuade Mother to change her mind.'

It was the first time in many months that Clemence had called me her *little brother*, and the slight stung like a nettle rash. 'Mother is welcome to travel with me, thank you, Clemence,' I lied. 'I was merely concerned for her welfare.'

My sister smirked. 'If you say so.'

'I do.'

We departed for London the following morning at daybreak. Thankfully the days were becoming longer, with a weak sun now drying the damp grass. Our party was large. I hired Edwin Stoves from the village as our groom, since Piers was too young to drive the carriage on the busy roads up to the city. Edwin was a quiet and strong young man, who could also wield a sword and fire a longbow, should we need protection from thieves and beggars. He had lost his wife and baby to the Pestilence, but unlike John Barrow, the man who was still locked up in my tower, Edwin bore his grief stoically, telling me that he was planning to remarry on our return from London. He made this arrangement sound as romantic as a trade at the horse fair, not naming the girl in question, and leading me to speculate that he didn't, as yet, have a candidate in mind.

Mother insisted that she couldn't travel without a lady's maid, so Ada was nominated for the task. Ada was to sit next to Mother under the hood of the carriage, though by the sourness of Ada's face she was as excited by the prospect of this journey as were the three horses we had harnessed ahead of us in single file. And there was nothing I could do to prevent Mother from bringing her small dog Hector. She could not travel without her *dearest friend*, and that was the end of it. She even packed him a small blanket and a selection of pewter bowls.

Edwin had spent the early part of the morning trying to attach Mother's trunk to a hook beneath the carriage. This was an unnecessary affectation, since there was room for this luggage inside the carriage itself – but Mother had once seen a royal carriage with such an arrangement, and insisted on imitating the fashion. I had some difficulty in arguing that her trunk would soon catch on the ruts of the road, necessitating frequent stops whilst Edwin freed the obstruction. Eventually we persuaded Mother to allow the trunk to sit behind her and Ada, with the promise that it would be reattached to its hook when we neared London.

Mother had also requested that we travel with a priest, as this was the custom for a lady of her status. But here I did make my feelings clear. I would no more travel with that custard pudding of a priest, Father Luke, than I would invite the kitchen cat to join us.

For my own servant I chose young Geoffrey Hayward, causing him nearly to faint with excitement.

'Will we see the king?' he asked, his eyes widening.

'I doubt it,' I told him.

'And will we see the white tower?'

'I hope not.'

Undeterred by my pessimistic answers, he scurried away to pack his few belongings before getting a cuff on the ear from Piers for being a braggart.

Before I left for London there were two conversations I had to conduct – both with some reluctance. The first was with Featherby. I found the man in the bakehouse, cornering one of the younger servants by the bread oven as she kneaded a ball of beery dough.

It took a few moments for him to notice that I'd entered the room, and it was only the nod of the girl that alerted him to my presence.

'Can you please join me in the library,' I told him, making my best efforts to sound authoritative. He gave the girl a sly smile. The sort of smile that says, 'What does this fool want now?' But I noted the girl kept her eyes fixed upon the dough, not wanting to be drawn into any form of covert alliance with this overbearing man.

Once we were in the library, I insisted Featherby sit down, which he did with the greatest reluctance, only hovering above the stool, ready to leap up again at a moment's notice.

I cleared my throat and spoke loudly, so that Featherby could not mishear me. 'When we discussed wages yesterday, I might have given the impression that I was considering a raise in the day rates.'

His face brightened. 'Indeed, sire.'

I took a deep breath. The feel of Edward Hatcher's ear wax was still fresh on my fingertips. 'Yes. Well . . . after a lot of thought, I've decided that they must remain exactly as before.'

He stood up with some indignation, but I waved for him to sit back down again. I was wearied of his arguments and in no mind to discuss this matter further. Edward Hatcher had been very clear on the subject, though I chose not to share this with Featherby. My reeve should see this as my ruling, and not a decision that had been forced upon me.

'The Statute is the law, Featherby. I won't break it.'

He sighed with some dejection. 'Very well, sire.' He stood up again. 'When will you return from London?'

'Within the week.'

Then he shrugged and turned for the door. 'Well don't expect the sowing to be done by the time you get back. At this rate I'll be hiring the village dogs and cats to do it.'

I went to speak, but he slammed the door on me. He actually slammed it.

My next visit threatened to end just as unpleasantly. I crossed the ditch that ran in front of the Tulleys' decrepit cottage and knocked loudly at their battered door, noticing eyes upon me from every occupied window along the street.

Thomas Tulley opened the door with typical surliness. 'Sire?' Behind him, in the shadows of the room, sat his wife Mary. As ever the poor woman was nursing the younger boy, while the older boys clung to her skirts. In this light she looked no more substantial than a ghost.

'I'm travelling to London for a few days. Perhaps as long as a week.' Tulley merely raised an eyebrow and pulled a face. I continued nonetheless. 'I wanted you to know that I'm still searching for Catherine's murderer. She's not been forgotten.' This, I'm ashamed to say was not entirely true. I had not forgotten Catherine's murder, but I had placed it momentarily to one side.

The man crossed his arms, and didn't answer.

I drew myself up and leant towards Tulley. 'If any harm comes to John Barrow while I'm away, I will hold you responsible.' I looked into his blue eyes, which were clear and defiant, but then something else caught my attention. It was Mary Tulley's small face. She had crept forward to join this conversation without our noticing.

She curtsied to me. 'Thomas understands that, sire.' She turned to her husband. 'Don't you, Thomas?'

The man didn't answer her. His face glowered.

'Don't you, Thomas?' she said again, speaking as sharply as she might to a naughty child. Thomas gave the most desultory of nods before withdrawing into the shadows.

'You won't have any problems from us, sire,' Mary assured me. 'And we thank you for your interest in our daughter.' She then curtsied and closed the door. I wouldn't say she slammed it, as Featherby had done. But I will say this. It was shut with energy.

The village was busy as I rode back to Somershill. I passed a group of men digging marl from a pit, heaving great clods of grey clay into a wagon, before they spread it thinly over their fields. In the distance, I noticed Joan Bath. She was waving to get my attention – as if she had something urgent to tell me. But I knew what she wanted to discuss – it could be nothing else. My progress on improving wages. How could I tell her that I had changed my mind? How could I admit that Hatcher had intimidated me with his threats? I kicked Tempest's flanks and he broke obligingly into a canter.

I am not proud to admit this, but I pretended not to have seen her.

Chapter Fourteen

Our journey to London began with an argument. My own preference was to take the route from Sevenoaks towards Bromley Saint Peter and Paul, then approach Southwark from the east at Greenwich. Mother preferred to go west to Hever and then follow the road north to Caterham, pass Croydon and then approach Southwark from the south. Unfortunately it was Mother who won this argument, since she had the backing of Edwin, our groom – though their choice of route would involve climbing the North Downs after the Eden Valley, where the carriage was sure to struggle on the steep tracks.

There was another reason for my opposition to this route, which I did not share with Mother, since it would have hurled her humours into a somersault. The route from Hever towards Caterham was heavily wooded, and therefore more likely to harbour the group of people that Mother feared more than anybody else – bandits. I gave young Geoffrey a sword and told him to let it hang obviously at his side. I also dressed both him and Edwin in the livery of the de Lacy family, in some tunics and surcoats that Gilbert had searched out from the chest in the gatehouse. The outfit didn't fit Geoffrey well, as the arms of the tunic needed to be turned over at his wrists, and the surcoat was belted with great difficulty at his waist. Nevertheless, these uniforms gave our party the air of nobility, which would either profit or harm our progress. Either we would appear a more attractive target to a band of robbers, or they would leave us alone, in fear of some high-ranking retribution.

The sun was thin as we headed west along the drover's track to Burrsfield, before we turned north-west and followed the Eden Valley towards Hever Castle. The winter had been long and wet, and the soil was often heavy and grey where the clay had worked its sticky way to the surface. At times the mud threatened to fix our carriage as firmly to the road as if the wheels had been smeared with the glue that Gilbert often brewed up from rabbit skins.

Winter still reigned in these forests and valleys, where the paths were carpeted in the fallen saw-edged leaves of the sweet chestnut. As we ventured deeper into the woodland, through the hatches that allowed entrance to the hunting forests, we passed fallen trees that had not been cleared from the tracks after the storms of the previous month. They were often the tallest ash trees, snapped at their waists by the wind and now lying across our path like dying soldiers. Once or twice we had to work our way around these obstacles by taking long diversions, and it was then that I truly cursed Mother and her insistence upon accompanying me on this journey.

Had I travelled on horseback alone with just one companion, then I would have been in Caterham by now. At this pace, I worried we would not even make Hever by nightfall.

We were rarely alone on the road, for yet again it seemed that England was on the move. We often met small groups — young men mainly. They were on foot, but looked well-enough dressed, making their way silently and steadfastly from one place to another. When our carriage became stuck yet again in a forest mire, a group of such youths helped Edwin and Geoffrey to pull the wheels from the stinking marsh, after the promise of a half-penny reward. When I asked their destination, they were reticent to say, and only mumbled some responses. When I asked them where they had come from, they quickly made their excuses and left without waiting for their money.

Mother expressed the opinion that these same men would be waiting for us a little further up the track, ready to leap out from behind a rock and rob us, but Edwin told me later that they had confided their plans to him, at least. They were mostly from the farms of Kent. Frustrated by the wage restrictions, they had deserted their estates and were travelling to London to make their fortunes. Now it was obvious why they wouldn't answer my questions, for no doubt they had left behind such a lord as me – a man who was unwilling to break the law. I thought back to Featherby and his predictions that I would lose all my best men, and a sense of dread settled in my stomach.

We reached Hever by nightfall and were begrudgingly given a place to sleep in the solar – though Lord de Hevere regarded me suspiciously, as if I might be an impersonator. If only he had known the truth about my identity, for I am no temporary sham. No player upon an evening stage. I have an enduring role. For I am a permanent imposter, forever playing my part.

It is the custom among families of our status that we will entertain and accommodate each other as we travel about England, but following our second day of slow progress over the hills of the North Downs, we were unable to reach the local manor house by nightfall. Instead we installed ourselves at an inn, and given that I was prepared to pay a good price for a decent bed by this point – a reaction to the frustration I felt at our lack of progress – we were given the best bedchamber in the house.

The innkeeper's wife, Mistress Nash, was a talkative sort, happy to repeatedly appear with mugs of ale so she might have the opportunity to ask her many questions. I avoided her prying by reading my book, but Mother was delighted to reveal our business to a woman who would coo and curtsy at every disclosure.

'Are you fleeing the child murderer?' Mistress Nash asked,

upon returning to the chamber with a wax candle, after I had refused to read any longer by the glow of a stinking rushlight.

'Which child murderer would that be?' I said, without raising my eyes.

'The butcher bird, sire.'

Mother butted in, before I had the chance to say anything. 'Goodness me, dear woman. There is no butcher bird. My son here is investigating the murder, and he is certain of it.' Mother spoke with the rational air of a woman who had never uttered a foolish story in her life. Of course, this transformation could never last. 'I shall have to tell everyone at court not to believe such a silly tale.'

Mistress Nash gasped. 'You're going to court, my lady?'

Mother picked up Hector from the floor and stroked his bristly head. 'Oh yes. Once the king hears that the de Lacy family is in London, we shall be sent for.' Now she whispered. 'My son has become a famous investigator you know. His name has reached the king's ears.'

I put down my book. 'Mother. I don't think that—'

But Mother silenced me with blustering arms. 'See how un-assuming and modest he is. Though he is quite celebrated in cer-tain circles.'

The innkeeper's wife studied me. With my head in a book and my lack of interest in gossiping, I hardly seemed the inquiring type – but somehow I knew that everybody to pass this inn in the next few weeks, maybe even years, would hear of the great inves-tigator Oswald de Lacy, and how he had spent the night in this room before he journeyed to London to visit the king.

'How did you hear the butcher bird story?' I asked the woman.

Her face wrinkled in delight at this chance to discuss the story further. 'We have so many travellers now, coming and going along this road.'

'From Somershill?'

She nodded. 'From all over. But yes. Many are from the Somershill estate.'

A thought suddenly came to me. 'Have any children passed this way recently?'

'Oh yes. Plenty of children.'

'What about two girls? They would have been travelling alone?'

She stroked her lips, as if trying to tempt the answer from her tongue. 'Boys I've seen in pairs. Yes. But never girls. They always stay with the groups. It's safer for them, you see. What with this butcher bird flying about.' I went to object, but she didn't give me the opportunity. 'It's been taking lambs, sire. And rabbits from the warren. Everyone's been talking about it. And then it tried to snatch poor Cissie's baby. Even when she had him wrapped across her back.'

I wanted to ignore this story, but knew I couldn't. 'Who is Cissie?' I asked, wearily.

'She works in the kitchen.'

'And did she see this bird?'

Mistress Nash nodded proudly. 'Oh yes. It scratched her head with its talons when she fought it off. Made a set of scabs to be proud of. Would you like to see them?'

'The scabs?'

She looked at me strangely. 'No, no, sire. I meant Cissie and her baby. The scabs on her head have healed now.'

Suspecting this story to be a foolish performance for the sake of getting my attention, I didn't show the enthusiasm that the innkeeper's wife had hoped for. Nonetheless Cissie was summoned from somewhere in the tavern.

A sullen, hostile girl was then presented to me, with a face that wore the gaunt mask of unrelenting hunger. I noted that she looked continually at the plate of bread and cheese that was laid on our table.

Mother withdrew into the corner, for the girl exuded the

pungent, spicy body odour of a labouring cottar in the summer heat. Hector let out a slow growl at the girl, but couldn't be bothered to jump down from Mother's arms to bite her, since he was now being fed the leftovers of our supper. I took a deep breath and attempted to ignore the girl's biting perfume by asking a flurry of questions. What had she seen? Where and when had this encounter happened? How could she be certain it was a bird that had attacked her baby? Each of my questions was met with very unsatisfactory answers that no more convinced me of the existence of this giant bird than I believed in the miracle of Lazarus.

I then duly inspected some scars upon her head, though they were covered in her thick and sticky hair that did not make my task any easier. There were a few dots of pink-fleshed scarring on her scalp, but these could easily be attributed to the enthusiastic scratching of flea bites. It was not until I asked after the health of Cissie's baby boy that our conversation took an unexpected turn.

'My boy's dead, sire,' she told me.

I was taken aback by this announcement. 'Dead? How did he die?'

She shrugged. 'I don't know.'

'You must have some idea.'

She shrugged again. 'They always die.'

'What do you mean by that?'

Now she became maddened. 'My children always die!'

At these words, the innkeeper's wife interrupted. 'Come on, Cissie. Don't be foolish. Your baby is still alive, isn't he? You know that. He's in the kitchen now. Lord Somershill only wants to hear about the bird.' She began to push the girl out of the room. 'I think you'd better get back to work, my girl.'

'No, wait,' I said. 'Why does she say that her baby is dead when he's alive.'

'Because he's as good as dead,' the girl said.

Mistress Nash pulled a face. 'Of course he isn't, Cissie. You just fed him. Remember?'

'Bring me the child,' I said. 'I want to see him.' Mistress Nash hesitated, so I raised my voice. 'Just bring him to me.'

The two women shuffled quickly from the chamber and soon reappeared with a swaddled infant, whose face was as thin and sickly as his mother's. A deep scratch scored his hairless head.

'You didn't say the child had also been attacked.' I ran my finger along the baby's scab – a wound that ran along the soft spot in the child's skull. A yellow mucus oozed lightly as I pressed, but the child neither cried, nor even flinched at my touch, leading me to believe that he had already lost his will to live. He was limp and his head rolled in my hand.

'Tell me exactly what happened,' I said. When the innkeeper's wife went to answer, I held up my hand. 'I want to hear Cissie's account.'

The girl pulled her ragged tunic about her body and heaved a sigh. 'I was by the chickens. My baby was on my back.'

'What time of day was it?'

'I can't remember.'

'Try.'

The innkeeper's wife interjected before I had the chance to stop her. 'It would have been first thing in the morning, wouldn't it? You'd just fed the little one. I asked you to fetch some eggs.'

The girl shrugged. 'I suppose so.'

'And the bird?'

'It swooped down from the trees and tried to take William.'

'What exactly did it look like?'

At last Cissie began to show some life. 'It was big. With great talons and a hooked beak.' She had given me the description of any hawk or merlin, but then she added an unusual detail. 'It had a great crest of feathers on its head. Like a crown.'

Mistress Nash could not keep silent. 'You fought it off, didn't you, Cissie? After it had taken two of my chickens. They were my best layers too.'

'I see.' Now a faint odour was rising from this story. 'And nobody else saw this attack?'

Both women shook their heads.

'Where is your husband?' I asked Cissie.

Cissie reddened a little. But only a little. 'I don't have one.'

'Who is the father of your baby?' She wouldn't answer. 'So how do you feed yourself and the child?'

'I give her food and a bed,' said Mistress Nash. 'For doing the washing.'

'But perhaps not enough food?'

Mistress Nash opened her mouth to say something, but I sent her away before she had the opportunity to protest. I insisted Cissie stay in the room, however. The girl retreated towards the wall and regarded me with unfriendly eyes.

'You caused this wound on your son's head, didn't you?' I said, pointing to her small bundle of a baby. 'Then you pretended he had been attacked by a bird.'

The girl mustered an indignant snort. 'No, sire. The bird did it.'

I strode over to her and caught her by the arm. 'Don't lie to me. You took the chickens, didn't you?'

'No! That's not true!' She wriggled free, before bolting through the door and disappearing down the steep steps. 'It was the bird,' she yelled. 'The bird, you clotpole!'

As the girl's voice receded into the distance with her curses still ringing about the room, Mother reappeared from the shadows. 'That girl should be flogged for such insolence.'

I shook my head. 'She wouldn't survive such a punishment.'

Mother put her hands on her hips. 'Well. Sometimes I don't know why you bother with such questioning, Oswald. I really don't.'

I fell upon the bed. 'Because I am a celebrated investigator, Mother. Remember?'

*   *   *

That night my nightmares began again. This time it was not the burning boy, nor even the three scratched and shrivelled children. Instead I was running through a valley where there were no trees. The ground was bare earth. The sky was dark, though it was not night. I was escaping from something, but was unable to move any faster. Now the soil became a swamp, and though I tried with all my might, it was impossible to pull my feet from the mire. Then I heard a piercing screech from the air. The shadow of a great bird spread across the ground in front of me. I could hear the flap of its broad wings. I was trapped. As the bird swooped down to attack me, I woke in a sweat.

The next morning, before we left the inn, I took Mistress Nash to one side. I gave her some coins, with the express instructions that this money was to be used to feed Cissie and her child. I warned her that our party would visit the inn again on my return to Somershill. If I found the child had died in the meantime, then I would alert the nearest constable. This was a lie, as I had no intention of using these roads for our return journey, but the woman took me seriously. At least I hoped she did.

Chapter Fifteen

Once we had passed the hills of the North Downs, we travelled along the dry valleys towards London, where the rivers only peeped their heads above the chalk during the wettest of years. And then across the fields of Croydon and past the archbishop's summer palace towards the great north wood, where the road would take us up to Lambeth and then finally Southwark.

Our small band no longer cut an exceptional sight. We had passed only people on foot during the early part of our journey, but now we met many other carriages. To begin with, Mother liked to wave them down to discover the destination and identity of the family within. But, once or twice, the somewhat forlorn look of the cloth across the frame of our carriage, or the worn-out condition of our servants' livery, was enough to cause the other party to ride on quickly, after the most cursory of acknowledgements.

In the end, Mother retreated under the hood whenever we saw another carriage, and then knotted the flaps of the canopy together so that nobody might look in. She claimed to be sleeping, but we heard a long series of complaints every time we negotiated a small bump in the road, or even had to change direction. Yet again I cursed my decision in allowing Mother to join our journey, and even more for letting her choose our route. We would be returning to Somershill through Bromley and Sevenoaks, and there would be no negotiation.

As we finally reached Southwark, we found the place thronging with a multitude of people who were heading to or from the city. On the opposite bank of the River Thames, the great spire of Saint Paul's dwarfed all other buildings on the skyline. Before us, the many arches of London Bridge dug their fingers into the riverbed, forcing the water to rush through their grip in furious torrents. I noted immediately a capsized boat, whose captain had not successfully navigated his path under the bridge. We stopped to watch for a while, as other wherries came to the boat's aid, and then, because nightfall was approaching, I hurried our party along, for we needed to find somewhere to sleep.

Finding an inn should have been an easy task, given that there was a bushel on a pole hung above every second door on this street. But Southwark was brimming to its lip with people. Not only the pilgrims, as they gathered into groups before making their way towards Canterbury, but also a far more unholy crowd – men here to take their pleasures at the Southwark stews, where they might eat, drink and soak themselves in the company of women. As we passed one of these bawdy establishments, I will admit to feeling a shameful twinge of excitement. Especially when a pretty girl called out to me. Her accent was Flemish. Her breasts were large.

We moved on quickly and eventually found a place to stay further away from the priory, towards the flat and marshy lands of Lambeth moor. It was a poor and ramshackle inn, owned by a miserable widow who brewed watery ale that equalled her enthusiasm for life. The widow agreed to stable our horses, but would not tend to them – no matter what I offered to pay her. This inconvenience meant I would have to leave Geoffrey behind to feed and care for the animals, while we crossed the river the next morning to retrieve the sisters.

Geoffrey could not hide his disappointment at this arrangement, so I offered to walk with him to Southwark before sunset, while the widow fed the rest of the party with a frumenty of wheat and sultanas. Given the resemblance of this meal to something that might have been thrown up on the street outside one of the stews, I was pleased to excuse myself from the table and find a pie seller near the priory instead. Geoffrey sloped along behind me, kicking at the stones in the road. If he hoped this display of umbrage would somehow change my mind about him staying to look after the horses, then he was completely mistaken. I had more important matters on my mind than hurting the feelings of a boy.

They say the light in London is different, and I would agree. Standing that evening on the south bank and looking over the leaden Thames towards the city, it was the sky that made the greatest spectacle. So vast and wide. Streaked in pink and gold against a clouded backcloth. Seagulls wheeled and soared, making their sad, screeching calls, while the silent cormorants skimmed the surface of the river, their feathers as black and gleaming as Whitby jet. While I marvelled at the clouds and the birds, however, it was the sight of the city itself that most thrilled my young companion.

Geoffrey pointed into the distance, where the white walls of the Tower of London stood out against the muddy banks of the Thames. 'Is it true that traitors are pulled apart on the rack in there?'

I shrugged, uncomfortable at the boy's interest in such a story. 'I'm not sure,' I lied. 'But listen. They say the walls are built with French stone. Shipped over from Caen.'

Geoffrey's mouth closed and his face fell. He was not at all interested in the construction of the tower. 'But is it true the king keeps lions and leopards inside the tower?' he now asked. 'And that they sometimes eat their keepers?'

I was beginning to feel irritated by his prurience, but then remembered my own gruesome obsessions as a young boy. At that age I probably would have been just as interested in the tower and its macabre reputation.

The boy tugged lightly at my tunic. 'While you're away, may I cross London Bridge, sire?'

I quickly shook my head. 'No, Geoffrey. You must stay on this side of the river.'

Now he bobbed from foot to foot, as if he needed to visit a latrine. 'But sire. The bridge is full of shops and houses. I'm sure I would be safe.'

'It is also full of thieves and outlaws. You must stay at the inn.'

'May I not go as far as Saint Thomas's chapel?' he said plaintively. 'It's only halfway across the bridge. Then I could hear mass.'

'This isn't a pilgrimage, Geoffrey. You are here to work.' A dark cloud suddenly crept across his face. He might even have been on the point of stamping his foot, before thinking better of it. 'But I told Piers I would walk across London Bridge, and he didn't believe me. Now he will call me a liar.'

'That's no concern of mine.'

'But—'

I took the boy by the arm and marched him back to the inn, warning Geoffrey to stay with the horses or be sent back to live with Mary Cadebridge.

The next morning, after the poorest of night's sleep, Mother, her lady's maid Ada, and Edwin joined me in crossing the Thames at first light. I hoped Edwin might be of some use in scaring away the many beggars who continually approached us in search of alms. The day before, as we had reached Southwark, I had seen a poor woman wheel her crippled son along in a barrow – his song was so sweet and mournful that it moved me to give him a farthing. I do not believe that such afflictions are a punishment from God. Instead I see the fickleness of life being wheeled before me – for what decides our place in this world, other than chance?

My farthing was supposed to be a quiet act of charity, but word of my generosity soon went around, and then I was besieged by beggars – blind men, starving orphans, women with withered arms and no hair. And though I asked them politely to leave me alone, it seemed they would not listen to my respectful entreaties. It was only Edwin, armed with a horsewhip and a barrage of foul language, who was able to get their full attention. I soon learnt that charity in London must be either discreet, or not entered into at all.

Our destination that morning was an area of the city near to the Guildhall. A place called Milk Street, where Mother claimed the Coopers lived. Personally I would have taken one of the many wherry boats that bobbed on the river, waiting to take their passengers from the south bank to the city. But once again Mother was instrumental in twisting my plans to suit her own ends, insisting she would not put foot on one of the boats, as it would induce sickness. Instead we were to find, at no little expense, a covered litter, so Mother might be carried across London Bridge without having to place her shoes onto the filth of the streets. She insisted that her little dog Hector join her inside the litter, as his delicate stomach might be affected by nibbling at the piles of discarded food that lay everywhere about the city. The addition of a dog added a halfpenny to the fare.

Following the fuss over the litter, we set off much later than I had intended, now joining the tide of people walking towards the city. It was said that London had lost nearly forty thousand souls in the Great Plague, but if that were true, then this gap had been quickly filled, for this was not a halved city. Now it heaved with a new population of migrants from the farms of England, or escapees from the continent. There could be no doubt, the wounds of the Plague had healed fast in London.

As we made our way under the southern gatehouse, I looked upwards to see the famous array of heads, impaled upon spikes. These heads had been dipped in tar to preserve the skin and hair against the elements, and now they appeared as evil as a clutch of demons in a doom painting. I wondered what crimes these men had committed – for I guessed they were mostly men. Ada crossed herself and looked to the floor, but I noticed Mother peeping out through the curtains of the litter.

'It will give you nightmares, Mother,' I warned. She quickly closed the cloth and didn't answer.

We made slow progress across the bridge, and I found time to wonder at the profusion of life that clung to this long and thin strip of stone. The desire to trade on London Bridge was strong and had resulted in a street of buildings that hung so far over the river, it seemed they might collapse into the water at any moment. On either side of the narrow street – a track not much more than twenty feet wide – tall buildings towered above us, blocking out any chance of sunlight.

Worse than the lack of light and the profusion of people, how- ever, was the smell of London. I have lived in the country for all of my life, and the farmyards of Kent may smell bad enough, but this was a stench of wholly new proportions – an evil mixture of dung, sewage, rotting fish and meat. I wanted to purchase a bag of lavender to crush in my hand, but was afraid to open my money pouch, in case a cut-purse should see me.

We tried instead to push forward through the stinking throng, but our progress was not assisted by Mother's litter chair, which frequently banged into the backs of fellow travellers, causing them to turn and curse at us. And it was not only people in our way, it was also chickens, pigs and goats. Dogs ran about our feet, weaving in and out of the crowd, sniffing at the ground. They were scrawny, loping creatures of no particular breed, and though a man was employed to walk up and down the bridge and chase them away with a whip, they only fled as far as a dark corner, before soon reappearing when his back was turned.

Hawkers and pedlars jumped in front of us at every opportun- ity – selling shrivelled apples, flapping geese, or small pieces of bone that were absolutely and incontrovertibly certified as the finger of a true saint. A man with the colouring of a boiling beetroot stood in my way and thrust a bowl of cloves under my nose. In his other hand he rattled a glass jar that contained a handful of small brown nuts. He called out repeatedly, 'Mace for sale. Direct from the Orient.' When he shoved the bottle into my face, I replied politely that I wasn't interested. But once again, my error was to engage with the man at all, when I should simply have ignored him – for, the result of my politeness was to give the impression that a sale was imminent. It then fell to Edwin to chase him away, whereupon the man called me a stinking idler who had wasted his time. He even shouted to other hawkers to avoid our party, though none paid any attention to his warning, and soon he returned to his calls. 'Mace for sale. Direct from the Orient.'

There was little in life that a person could want, that could not be bought upon London Bridge. In fact you might never have the need to leave this short and populous edifice – for there were shops, inns, latrines, and even a church built above its stone arches. I was pleased to leave, however. The bridge was nothing more than the congested throat of London and it had taken us nearly an hour to cross.

Mother once again lifted the curtain of her litter. 'Did the cutpurses get you, Oswald?'

'No, Mother.'

She let the curtain fall with a disdainful flick, almost disappointed.

On several occasions I had felt the small and grasping hands of children about my body, as they had searched for my purse within my tunic. I shooed them away, but then felt another kind of scrutiny. It was not the starving urchins, or even the older cutpurses who watched me from the shadows. I turned quickly on many occasions to catch out my examiner, only to be confronted by a sea of faces. Some met my gaze, but most ignored me and carried on with their journey, as if I were nothing more

interesting than a feral pigeon. This feeling was disquieting, however – no matter how often I tried to convince myself that it was
merely my imagination.

Once leaving the bridge, we moved northward. The street was
wide enough at first, but soon it narrowed into yet another
stinking alley, where the projecting jetties of the houses on either
side of us trapped the stale air in the street. The air was thick with
the fumes of woodsmoke, tanneries, and the rotting food and
ordure that should have been pushed down the gullies towards
the Thames by a street raker.

When we finally reached our destination near the Guildhall,
we were to discover that the Coopers no longer lived in Milk
Street, as Mother had firmly asserted. Instead Eloise had moved
outside of the city to a grander residence on the Strand, after the
death of her husband and daughter. A servant informed us, with
something of a shrug, that Eloise had prospered from the Plague
by purchasing the largest empty house she could lay her hands
upon. We were all tired and irritable, and it was a great disappointment to discover that we were not already at our destination.
To compound our troubles, the litter carriers refused to trans-
port Mother any further than Ludgate, as they argued that nobody
outside of the city walls would pay their return fare.

We stopped at the gatehouse of Ludgate so that Mother and
Hector might be deposited onto the street they had so assiduously
been avoiding. The air was chill by now, and a fog had risen from
the River Fleet – its smell betraying the river's evil cargo of
entrails and carcasses from the slaughterhouses of Smithfield further upstream. Now we had left the city walls, Mother clasped
Hector under one arm and held onto me with the other, as we
made our way along Fleet Street. We tried to stay together as a
group, but soon we lost Ada and Edwin in the crowds and the fog,
and though we called for them, they didn't answer. And then,
though the road is straight, we became disorientated and found
ourselves in a narrow, twisting street that soon became a dead

end among broken carts and worse. Our only company was a wild pig that snuffled through the bones and onion skins of a rubbish tip. Hector struggled from Mother's grip and chased the pig into the warren of alleys.

Mother panicked. 'Hector!' she called. 'Hector! Come back immediately.'

'He won't go far,' I argued. Though the dog had the sense of a cock pheasant.

We turned to retrace our steps, but found our path to be blocked by two men. They wore long tunics and their hoods were pulled low over their faces.

Mother squeezed my hand and whispered, 'I told you not to come up this street, Oswald. They'll cut our necks.'

'Shut up Mother.' I turned to address the men, who had moved closer. 'Good day to you.' There came no reply.

Mother squeezed my hand again. 'Tell them to be gone, Oswald. We are known to the king. They should stand aside.'

The men sniggered at this remark. I cleared my throat. 'Is this the way to Fleet Street?'

The man on the right thrust his hand forward. He was missing the ends of three fingers. 'Your purse. Hand it over.'

Mother clung to my arm. 'Don't let them have it, Oswald.'

The second man drew a knife from within his tunic. 'Shut up, you old goat.' He waved it towards Mother, causing her to scream with such drama and volume that he drew back momentarily. His hood fell slightly to the side, revealing a face that was as potholed as an apple with bitter pit. 'Your purse. Or we'll cut you.'

I swerved to avoid the knife, but in doing so slipped on one of the many rotting leaves that littered the ground. And then the man was upon me, with his hands inside my cloak, desperately searching for my purse. His knife was ready to cut the leather bag from my belt. I fought back, kicking and punching, but he was as strong as a stubborn ox and my attempts to fight him off were in vain. I only managed to squirm and wriggle so he might not easily find the purse, but then his companion held my arms down, giving me no opportunity to defend myself. Mother stood behind, doing nothing more helpful than waving her arms and wailing.

And then, suddenly, the two men jumped away from me and fled. With no explanation. I had not suddenly found the strength to fight them off. Mother had not helpfully seized a length of wood and walloped them about their heads. It was a mystery.

I staggered back to my feet. 'What happened? Why did they just run away?'

Mother held a hand to her mouth. 'There was something in the shadows, Oswald. It scared them.'

'What do you mean?'

'It was hideous.' Now she fanned herself, as if she were about to faint. 'I think it was a leper.'

I dusted myself down and checked that my purse still hung from my belt. 'Let's get back to Fleet Street. Quickly.'

We retraced our steps through the warren of alleys and eventually found ourselves back in Fleet Street. Thankfully Edwin and Ada were sitting on a bench outside the New Inn with a mug of ale, looking only partially relieved to see our faces. Hector sat at their feet, panting. I noted that Edwin was looking down at Ada's large bosom as he spoke. By her position on the bench next to him, she was comfortable with this arrangement. In fact, I would say she was allowing him to look.

We carried on with some haste, as the clouds were threatening rain – passing Whitefriars, Temple and then the many grand mansions and palaces that lined the Strand, as the city bled away into the fields of the abbey and convent gardens. We reached the house said to belong to Eloise Cooper just as the weather turned, and were relieved to find a large projecting jetty above the door that afforded some protection from the rain. We stood beneath this shelter and looked upwards to see an ostentatious building with blackened beams and an abundance of glass at the windows. This residence might have drawn all this attention to itself, but it was still on the inner side of the Strand and did not look down upon the river. For all its finery, it could not compete with the grander palaces that it faced.

Mother looked up at the elaborate house and sniffed. 'Merchants. Always building their homes out of wood. A nobleman lives in stone.'

'It looks grand enough to me.'

'You cannot make a castle from a cabin.' Then she whispered, 'It's a person's birth that signifies nobility. And the de Caburn family polluted their daughter's stock. By marrying her off to a man who farmed customs at Southampton.'

'Well. He clearly made more money than we do, farming wheat in Kent.'

Mother turned her back on me and knocked loudly at the door. 'What does that matter? His father was a true cooper, Oswald.' She sniffed disdainfully. 'He made buckets.'

Chapter Sixteen

A servant opened the heavily oiled door of the Cooper residence, but would not admit us straight away, despite Mother's protests. The haughty-looking fellow returned after quite a while and opened the door – allowing Mother and myself into the main hall, whereas Edwin and Ada were sent down a side alley, and told to call in at the kitchen porch. The servant then suggested that Hector should also proceed to the kitchen, but Mother would not release the dog from her grasp, not under any circumstances.

As we walked through the Coopers' hall, I looked about with wonder at its opulence. Tapestries of vivid red and purple hung at every wall. These were not the blanched and moth-eaten cloths that covered our own cold and supposedly *noble* stone. I had rarely seen such quality, not even in the archbishop's palace at Gillingham. These tapestries were of the very finest designs, depicting Arthur and the Knights of the Round Table, or the doomed love of Tristan and Isolde. If we had hoped to stumble upon the obvious signs of Eloise's devilry and love of witchcraft, then we were to be disappointed, for there was nothing other than respectable decoration on show.

We even passed a small reliquary shrine upon an oak table, a gilded triptych at its centre, decorated with an array of delicate paintings of the virgin and a host of angels. It was probably French, given its design and the quality of its workmanship, and though I was unmoved by its message, I could not help but admire its shiny ostentation. I took a moment to look into the face of the virgin. The artist had portrayed the tones of her skin with great skill – but then I noticed something peeping out from beneath her gown. It was a small winged creature, with a hooked beak and clawed feet. Its eyes looked at me strangely, and I immediately felt uncomfortable.

Moving quickly away, I was then nudged by Mother. 'See how the Cooper family try to pass themselves off as noble,' she whispered. She pointed at an embroidered wall hanging depicting the battle of St George against the dragon. 'This house scales the very heights of affectation, if you ask me.' At these words the haughty servant spun on his heels to stare at Mother, clearly having heard every word. Mother's response was to tilt her nose in the air. 'I hope you made it clear to your mistress that Lady Somershill was visiting.'

The servant bowed his head. 'Please excuse me, my lady. I didn't catch your name properly before. So I merely told my mistress that a group of travellers were at the door.'

This man might first have thought us a group of wayfarers, with our tired faces and dirty clothes, but I had no doubt he now knew our true identity – otherwise, we would never have been allowed past the two men who guarded the house with pikes in their hands.

After working our way down a long passage, we came to a door that led out onto an unexpected garden, where a woman was playing ball with two small girls. The girls I recognised immediately. They were Mary and Rebecca de Caburn – their slight and boyish frames now dressed in heavy gowns. Their blonde hair covered in linen veils, and their hands warm inside white gloves. There should have been a touching quality to this scene, but instead it left a strange impression, as if the whole tableau were staged. The woman in the distance waved to us and then passed the ball to Mary, to end their game.

Mother leant towards me once again to whisper, 'Look at her

gown. It's far too narrow in the waist and low at the shoulder. She might as well be touting for business at the stews.'

'Be quiet, Mother,' I said. 'I'm not interested in her gown.'

This was not true, however, for I had noticed Eloise Cooper's gown from the moment she had turned around to acknowledge us. Or perhaps I should say, I had noticed the body within it, which was as lithe and sleek as a black cat's. As she made her way towards us, I was immediately charmed by her appearance – though Eloise was not beautiful in the manner I had previously admired. There was nothing of the pretty kitten about her – instead her face was angular and almost masculine. A large nose was softened by a pair of striking eyes that were as green and lustrous as the scales of a perch.

Eloise curtsied to me, ignoring Mother. 'Lord Somershill. I welcome you to London.'

I could feel Mother stiffen beside me, as I bowed and kissed the hand Eloise extended to me. 'Mistress Cooper.' Her fingers were long and delicate, with nails that lightly stroked my skin as she removed her hand.

Eloise now bowed her head to Mother, and then curtsied with an exaggeration that I suspected was mocking and discourteous. Mother did not read it this way, however. I would say she was impressed by such an act of servitude. 'Lady Somershill,' said Eloise, letting her eyes rest upon Mother's dusty gown. 'I'm honoured that you have come to this humble house.'

Mother raised her nose to the sky. 'We had to come, Mistress Cooper. After we heard you were harbouring the girls.' Now Mother pointed a finger. 'They're wards of the de Lacy family, you know. You should have informed us they were here. We thought they'd been murdered.' Mary and Rebecca hung back and would not meet my stare.

Eloise bowed her head once again to Mother. 'But I've written to you. Did you not receive my letter? I assumed that's why you're here.'

Mother frowned. 'No. We only heard the news of the girls' whereabouts from Earl Stephen's steward. You should have written sooner.'

Eloise stiffened, but almost indiscernibly. 'You're right, Lady Somershill. It's just that my nieces were so disturbed when they arrived, that I promised not to tell a soul. This went against my own judgement, of course. Which is why I wrote after a week or so.' Her eyes flashed. 'With their permission, of course.'

'How did the girls get here?' I asked quickly, before Mother had the chance to respond.

Eloise turned to me, though I'm not sure how well I listened to her answer. 'They dressed themselves as boys and followed the crowds to London.'

Mother frowned. 'Boys?'

'Yes,' said Eloise. 'They even cut their hair to look the part.' Mother went to answer, but Eloise interrupted. 'But please. Let's not talk about this now. You must be hungry and thirsty after your journey?'

'We'll just take the girls and go, thank you,' said Mother.

Eloise raised an eyebrow, but remained unprovoked. 'But I was hoping you might stay for a night. You have come such a long way.'

Mother touched her cheek. 'We don't wish to stay in London. The place is a den of thieves. We were attacked by two cutpurses. Not half a mile from this very house.'

Eloise frowned. 'Did they take your money?'

'Indeed they did not. They were scared away by a leper.'

'A leper?' A cloud suddenly passed across Eloise's countenance. 'Did you see his face?'

'Only his vile lesions.' Mother shuddered. 'I looked away.'

Now Eloise smiled. I would say she seemed relieved. 'There's a lepers' hospital at St James's. I expect he came from there.'

Eloise took Mother's arm in a show of bonhomie that even Mother was unable to resist. 'Do stay, please. After such a shock. And I would value your company. In London people will only talk of the king and politics. It's so dull.' She then nestled in towards Mother. 'I long to hear about the country again,' she paused. 'To talk about such matters as sheep shearing and the rotation of crops.'

I nearly laughed out loud, but Mother was completely taken in by this mockery. Nobody, not even the most avid and dreary of ploughmen, wants to talk about crop rotation. Nevertheless, I had had my fill of Mother in the last few days, so was without compunction when it came to laughing at her expense.

Eloise led us into a chamber to the side of the central hall. I would call it a solar, except it was on the ground floor, with large glass windows that faced the street. I noted a wing-backed chair by this window, positioned at an angle behind a shutter so that a person might look out, but passers-by might not look in.

Mother surveyed the room, which was small compared to our own solar. Then she sighed. 'You are so very crammed in here, aren't you Mistress Cooper. I fear I could never live in London.'

Eloise smiled again. 'Indeed, Lady Somershill. I fear London would not suit you at all.' Then she led us to the table. 'Please. Sit down. Take the best chairs and I will arrange for some refreshments.'

'Will Mary and Rebecca join us?' I asked. The girls had been spirited away during our journey from the garden to this chamber.

Eloise drew close. Close enough for me to catch her woody perfume. 'Let's talk without the girls first. They can join us later.'

Over the next hour a team of liveried servants brought a series of edible fancies to the table. Served on silver plates, we were offered dates pressed into small squares, dried sausage flavoured with cardamom, and balls of marzipan rolled in powdered sugar. All were delicious and exotic, but I was so hungry that a simple portion of bread and a square of cheese would have sufficed. When Mother made a comment to this effect, Eloise arranged for more substantial pastries and cold meats to be served. Though, once again, most of this food was highly flavoured and completely impossible to identify, even after the haughty servant had announced the name of each offering in his most flourishing French. I ate each *Delice de Lille* or *Morceau de Savoyard* in haste. I was hungry and didn't care to know too plainly what I was eating.

Mother found this act harder to maintain. 'A pottage would have been adequate,' she grumbled, as she fed another unidentifiable morsel to Hector.

Eloise licked the sugar from her fingers. 'Goodness no. I wouldn't serve you such fare. Pottage is for servants.'

Mother pulled a face. 'I like it well enough,' she said, before realising her mistake.

Eloise smiled. 'Indeed.'

The supper continued in such a bad mood, with both women jabbing at each other with increasing momentum – acid, venomous bites that were thinly hidden behind honeyed smiles. Whenever I tried to turn the conversation to the future of Mary and Becky, it was thwarted by an irrelevant condemnation of the immodesty of London fashion by Mother, only to be followed up by a gibe about the foulness of country air from Eloise. In the end, I ate my food in silence and looked to the door, where every so often Mary peeped around the panelling to look at me – though as soon as I acknowledged her with a smile, the girl vanished back into the shadows. Mary's presence went unnoticed by my supper companions, who were now arguing about the worth of garlic in a diet, and were only distracted from this topic when a new guest joined us. As this man walked into the room and saw our faces, I had the distinct impression he was disappointed to find other company at Eloise's table.

His name was Thomas Dukinfield, the partner of Eloise's dead husband, and easily the most tedious bore I have ever met. As ever, London exaggerates and amplifies the ordinary – so this man was not only a braggart, he was an outright liar and self-confessed cheat. As he poured himself Madeira from the silver decanter and offered it to nobody but Eloise, he explained, in some detail, how he and Eloise's dead husband had made their money.

I did not ask to know about their business, but nonetheless he told me, very proudly, that their dishonest dealings and countless swindles had allowed them to amass so sizeable a fortune that they had been able to lend funds to the king himself. In return for these loans, the king had allowed the pair to farm customs on imported goods at Southampton and Portsmouth, taking a small proportion of each duty payment for themselves. It seemed they were more efficient at collecting these taxes than the king's authorities, so the arrangement had suited all parties.

I had watched Dukinfield over the supper, trying to brush his hand against Eloise's when she leant forward to pick up one of the delicacies on offer. I had seen his greedy eyes drinking in her strange beauty. Who could help but notice the way in which he hung upon her words, was amused by her wit, and was awed by her wisdom to a much greater extent than any of her utterances warranted. He dropped his shoulder and laid his handsomely dressed arm upon the table to exclude me from the conversation, but I noted every flirtatious smile and every over-played compliment he gave her.

Mother coughed to get my attention, when pulling at my arm hadn't worked. She had been sitting in peeved silence since Dukinfield's appearance, since the man showed no interest in her at all. Her interjection was particularly unwelcome, as I had just managed to turn the conversation to the trajectory of Venus, and was on the cusp of saying something that was certain to impress Eloise.

'I'm going to vomit,' Mother whispered, loudly. 'I've been poisoned by all this appalling French food.'

Eloise and Dukinfield stopped talking immediately. So the ploy had worked. 'Are you unwell, Lady Somershill?' asked Eloise. Mother nodded, dropped Hector to the floor and began to rock, with her hands clenched to her stomach. When nobody moved, she then heaved. A little too theatrically.

Dukinfield clasped his hand to his nose. 'God's nails. The woman is going to be sick.' He then ran from the room, towards the garden, clutching his hand to his mouth.

At Dukinfield's departure, Mother seemed to settle a little, having succeeded in disrupting the party and re-establishing her- self as centre of attention. Unlike Dukinfield, Eloise was not appalled by this display, instead she swept to my mother's side and laid a hand upon her cheek, pronouncing that Mother was indeed pale and sweaty.

Eloise spoke softly. 'Would you care to rest, my lady?'

Mother nodded silently.

'There's a chamber up the stairs where you may sleep.'

I looked out of the window. 'I think we should return to our inn, thank you Mistress Cooper.'

Eloise stretched her neck and turned to look at me. 'But your mother is ailing, Lord Somershill. You must stay the night.'

She called for the haughty servant before I had a chance to reply, and as the man stepped reluctantly into the room – no doubt aware that he was about to deal with a vomiting woman – Eloise took my arm and led me to one side. 'You must not rush away, Lord Somershill. We are yet to discuss my nieces.' She gazed into my eyes a little longer than was necessary, and I felt the bones in my legs give way at the knees.

The moment ended abruptly when Mother emptied her stomach onto the shoes of the servant, causing the man to utter the vilest of obscenities and stamp his feet about the floor, as if he had just trodden upon a wasps' nest. Incensed by his rudeness to my mother, I stepped away from Eloise and told the servant to drop his conceit. With a sharp intake of breath, he looked to his mistress for support, appearing to have every expectation that he would receive it. To his obvious surprise, Eloise repeated my threat, demanding that the puffed-up fool apologise to Lady

Somershill, or she would call for the constable and have him stuck in the pillory on Fleet Street, where he might be pelted with buckets of water from the River Fleet.

Mother was tucked into the largest bed I have ever seen, seemingly lost between the linen sheets – not unlike a small child who has crept into her parents' bed. Hector settled down beside her, splaying his squat legs out behind him like a pair of oars. As I held Mother's trembling hand, I noticed that the four posts of the bedstead were carved with cardoon and acanthus leaves, though on closer inspection I also saw snakes amid the twisting boughs. And though the light was poor, I could discern small faces peeping through the tangle of foliage. They were puckish and grinning.

Eloise observed my interest in the carvings. 'This was my marriage bed,' she said. Then she flexed her long fingers and admired her nails. 'Such a gift to a young wife,' she sighed, 'from an old man.' A silence fell and I was unable to think of any response to this melancholy statement. Eloise must have sensed my unease, for she then laughed and bade me join her downstairs in the solar, where we might continue our conversation.

I left my mother's bedside feeling awkward, as if I were walking up a dark corridor. Is it childish and cowardly to admit that part of me wanted to creep into bed with Mother and curl up beside her in the sheets?

I fear it is.

Chapter Seventeen

The downstairs chamber was empty upon my return. It was late afternoon and the candles had been lit already. Shadows played upon the walls, and though the fire remained low, the room was warm and stuffy. This was a pleasant and unusual experience for me, since it was always cold and draughty in our own grand house. Mother often berated me for complaining about the lack of heat at Somershill, saying that a true nobleman hardly noticed a cold home. It was a sign of his breeding. His noble blood was warm enough to heat his body. In that case, my blood was showing its modest colours – for I was as contented in this hot and airless room as a cat upon a sunny step.

Waiting for Eloise to join me, I sat myself in the chair that faced the window to the street and rested my head against its high-backed wings. As I stared through the window at the gathering dusk, I suddenly had the impression that somebody was looking back at me. Their face only just the other side of the bevelled glass. I caught their outline, but not their features and when I jumped from my chair to look closer, they quickly walked away.

'Have you seen something?' I turned to find that Eloise had come into the room.

She had surprised me by her silent entrance. 'I don't know.' My heart was beating soundly against my chest. 'I think somebody was looking in.'

'Should I ask the guards to go out and check the street?'

I shook my head. 'No, no. They've gone now. Probably just an inquisitive passer-by.'

She swept towards me, her gown brushing the floor. 'We are so very close to the road here, that people will sometimes look in.' Then she gave a wry laugh. 'I expect you find it strange that I live next to a street?'

I didn't know quite how to answer this, so muttered something meaningless.

She smiled again. 'I know how you feel. I was raised at Versey Castle. I was accustomed to a moat about my home. Not a street outside the window.'

'But the Strand is hardly a usual street, is it? We passed a whole host of bishops' inns.'

'Yes. And here I am amongst them. A mere merchant's wife.' She lifted a pewter goblet from the table and took a long sip. 'Not that such people would ever associate themselves with me.' She placed the goblet back onto the table, though I might say she even banged it down. Petulantly.

'But you don't seem in want of company,' I said.

She smiled. 'If you mean Thomas Dukinfield, then the man is a horrible bore. Don't you agree?'

How to answer this question? I decided to be honest. 'Well . . . yes, I do.' I coughed. 'Is he coming back?'

She shook her head. 'No, no. He has a terror of any sickness. Your mother has done us quite a favour.' Then she sat down upon the bench and stretched her long and beautiful neck from side to side. 'But his company and my husband's are still linked, so I must humour the man to be sure of my fortune.'

The awkward silence returned, until she smiled at me. It was both a sweet and an odd smile. Unguarded for once. 'Oh listen to me,' she said. 'I'm sorry to burden you.'

She motioned for me to sit down near her on the bench, and as I did so, I had the chance to admire her closely. She had changed her dress to a red kirtle, which once again was tailored to fit very tightly to her waist and breasts. A gown edged with miniver provided the dress some level of propriety, though I was still able to see the shape of her body beneath the cloth. The candlelight sat softly on her face, showing a fine grid of lines across her forehead, which made me realise that she was older than I first supposed. But it didn't matter. She was so very handsome.

She asked me to call her Eloise, and I asked her to call me Oswald. Then I felt a warm stirring in my braies – which only became worse when she let her fur-edged gown fall back to reveal the skin of her breastbone. This skin was white and lightly freckled and I wanted more than anything to touch it.

'We should discuss Mary and Rebecca,' she said. I nodded, though my mind was not fully on the subject.

'I think they should return with you to Somershill,' she said.

This woke me from my trance. 'You do?' I said, sitting up.

'Yes. The Pestilence will return to London in the summer. They say there are already some new cases in Greenwich. This city is not a place to raise children.' Then she gave an unexpected sigh and closed her gown about her. 'You've heard I had a daughter, no doubt.'

I reverted to mumbling.

She gave a scornful laugh. 'I know what people say about me, Oswald. That I killed my own daughter.' She fixed me with a glare. 'Do you believe such a story?'

'Of course not,' I answered.

'Good.' Her face relaxed into a smile. 'Because it matters to me what you think.'

'It does?'

She lowered her brow and looked up at me. 'Of course it does. You're an intelligent man. Not one of these fools who will lap up any drip of bilge water that spills at their feet.'

She had called me a man. 'I don't like gossip,' I announced, as if the sweet smell of hearsay had never tempted me.

She nodded in agreement. 'My daughter died of the pox. I merely kept others from the room. I did not murder her in some darkened solitude as they say. I was trying to stop further contagion.'

'Then you were lucky to have survived yourself.'

'There was no luck involved. I had suffered the pox already.'

This surprised me, since no pockmarks had burrowed their ugly potholes into her beautiful skin. My face must have betrayed my scepticism, since she answered me immediately. 'In truth, what I suffered was more similar to a cow pox. I caught it as a child, after being sent to work in the dairy.'

'Really?'

'My father held daughters in poor regard. We were often made to work with the servants.'

'I meant how does cow pox offer protection?'

Now she laughed. 'You must have heard such stories. From the village healers.'

I shook my head. 'No.'

She smiled. 'You should listen to these women, Oswald. They often know more about medicine than any monk.' I went to answer, but she interrupted. 'And don't tell me you've never noticed the unblemished complexion of a dairymaid?'

I blushed a little. 'No. I haven't.'

She giggled and put her hand on mine. 'You're such a sweet boy, Oswald.'

I coughed, both excited by the hand, whilst at the same time disappointed to be called a boy. Only moments ago, I had been a man.

Eloise suddenly withdrew her hand, stood up and began to pace the room, and the genial mood of our conversation turned. 'Will you give me your assurances that the girls will be better treated when they return to Somershill?' she said, as she strolled behind the bench on which I was still sitting. 'They've told me some alarming stories.'

I turned my head to try to look at her. 'Clemence can speak harshly to the girls, but she didn't mistreat them. It's just that she has a new baby. And she has been in poor health since his birth.'

Eloise stopped by an elegant tapestry and began to roll her fingers over the stitching, tracing the image of a white horse as it charged into battle. She did not turn to face me. 'Ah yes. Lady Clemence and her new son. How is my brother's child?' she asked. 'Is he a healthy boy?'

'Oh yes. Very.'

She began to pick at the stitching. 'I believe Clemence has called him Henry.'

'That's right.'

A snort. 'Named after my father.'

'No. I believe he is named after mine.'

Another silence followed. Stiff and pointed. Somewhere in the distance the bells of Saint Bride's rang for the evening curfew. The gates to the city would soon be locked. As I listened to their plaintive chimes, Eloise swept her gown about her, floated across the floor, and fell to her knees in front of me. It was both an unexpected and vaguely alarming act, and in truth, it felt a little like one of Mother's performances. Even so, and I am ashamed to admit this, it gave me the perfect opportunity to look down her gown.

She took my hand. 'I love the girls, Oswald. Very much. So I must be sure they will be safe and well cared for.' She paused. 'If I am to allow them to return with you.'

Her eyes were wide and pleading. Her hand trembled touchingly in my own.

'Mary and Rebecca will stay with me, Eloise,' I said. 'They won't return to Versey with Clemence. That way I will ensure their care and happiness.'

She squeezed my hand a little tighter, and leant forward so far that I was able to look right down the neckline of her dress. 'What about their education? They can barely read.'

'I will attend to it, immediately.' I spoke softly. 'Though you should know it was your brother who is to blame for neglecting their lessons.' She stiffened at this remark, but I carried on, for it was important that this particular criticism was not laid at our family's door. 'When Clemence married your brother last year, I discovered the girls running about Versey like a pair of savages.'

She gave a short, mocking laugh. 'Then nothing had improved by the time they arrived here,' she said. 'In fact, I barely knew them. With their butchered hair and filthy clothes I nearly turned them away as beggars. The poor creatures must have been very unhappy to degrade themselves in such a way.'

'It won't happen again. I give you my word. I will keep the girls safe.'

She withdrew her hand and leant back, so that I was no longer able to spy upon her breasts. 'And what about this murderer I hear of. This butcher bird.'

This question took me by surprise. 'There is no butcher bird. It's been dreamt up by the villagers.'

'But a child has been murdered on the estate. And Mary tells me you have a man under your protection. A madman.'

'I do. But only because I refuse to let the village mob set upon him.'

'And you are certain he's innocent?'

'Yes.'

Eloise raised an eyebrow. 'I hope so. As I hear he is kept in Somershill itself. And I would hate to think he posed a danger to Mary and Becky.' She then got to her feet, before slipping gracefully into the comfort of the wing-backed her chair by the window. 'Very well, Oswald. The girls will return to Somershill with you and your mother.'

'Thank you, Eloise. We can set off tomorrow.'

She smiled, a little distantly. 'If Lady Somershill has recovered.'

I bowed to her. 'Of course.'

The remainder of our evening was spent in more pleasant conversation, as we discussed philosophy and astronomy. Eloise was more interested in the trajectory of Venus and the writings of Pope Pius than any other woman I had ever met, though when I expressed this opinion, she scolded me for dismissing the mental capabilities of her sex far too easily. At last I was unable to stifle a yawn, and she bid me retire to a bedchamber on one of the upper floors. I had rarely been to a house with the advantage of so many separate bedchambers. It was a modern design, which allowed for such privacy – not at all like most manor houses, where the servants slept in the great hall, and the family kept to the solar.

It was a welcome luxury after the long day to wilt upon a feather mattress, and to be given a basin of hot water to wash the scum and stink of London from my hands. From outside I could hear the screams and shouts of drunkards and vagrants as they wandered along the Strand. The calls of the men on the river, as they delivered wine to the waterside cellars of the palaces. The occasional squawk of seagulls as they fought over scraps of food on the many rubbish pits that lined the streets. London was a dangerous and hostile place – but no less thrilling for it. I pulled open the wood of the shutter to look out through the latticed frame to the street below, and saw people moving along in the darkness. Some carried horn lanterns with the soft glow of the candle flickering through the translucent bone, but most scuttled along in the dark like beetles – hooded and anonymous.

Then, once again, I had the impression that somebody was standing perfectly still and looking up at me from beneath the jetty of the house opposite. Quickly drawing back, I extinguished my own candle so I might better see their form, but there was no moon that night, and the sky was as dark as a vat of treacle. All I could make out were the wagons parked at the side of the road, and the struts and the fancy herringboned work in the frame of the house.

I closed my shutters and retired to bed, but sleep failed me. My eyes scanned the room, running along the beams and panelling, until they were drawn to a small sliver of light in the wall. It came from the neighbouring room. I turned on my side and pulled the sheet over my head in an attempt to ignore the light, as I prefer to sleep in complete darkness, but soon heard the sound of water being poured into a tub.

At first this sound prompted a desire to visit the garderobe. But then I heard a woman singing – a soft, melodic sound – and suddenly I was tempted to look through the hole. I ignored this ignoble thought for a while. I buried my head back under the sheets, but could not ignore the arousing images that were now running through my mind. I had once secretly watched a girl washing in a river – the whiteness of her skin and the rounded shape of her naked body had both shocked and excited me. It was a memory that I called upon regularly – particularly on the nights when I was unable to look at my book of obscenities. Now, it seemed, I had the opportunity to spy again.

But it was wrong. I would not do it. I kept my head beneath the sheets.

Then the singing became slightly louder. The splashing of the water became more vigorous. I could ignore this temptation no longer. Now I crept from my bed, as stealthily as a thief, and peeked through the hole, to see it was Eloise sitting in a small tub of steaming water – her body naked, her dark hair tied into a knot on top of her head. I should have looked away. But I could not. Instead I watched with greedy fascination as Eloise dipped a large jug into the water and then poured it over her shoulder, letting its steaming warmth run down her long and graceful back. Then she looked to the ceiling and this time she arched her spine as she poured the soapy water over her naked body. Her breasts small and firm. Her nipples hard and stiff to the air.

I was transfixed by the sight – an image I had only ever imagined in the privacy of my bedchamber, or seen crudely drawn in a manuscript – so when Eloise looked to the wall and blew me a kiss, I did not flinch from staring at her. I was neither embarrassed nor guilty, instead I was drunk – not with wine, but with lust. When she called my name, I went to her chamber without the slightest hesitation.

I will not write on this subject for long, but I will say this much. Our nights together while Mother recovered from her sickness were the most enjoyable I have spent in my life. If it were a sin, then I do not repent. How could I? It was joyful. Pleasurable. It offended nobody. So why should I feel any shame? At a dark time in my life, Eloise offered light. Something that was good at last. I can never regret it. Not even given the way it ended.

During these days I attempted, when not otherwise occupied with Eloise, to speak to Mary and Rebecca, but the girls had adopted a regime of dogged silence in my presence – an act that they tried to pass off as bashful obedience. They had, no doubt, been informed that they were to return to Somershill, but they would not discuss the matter with me, other than to nod their heads sullenly and then find the quickest excuse to disappear.

Eventually I asked Eloise to organise a discussion between the three of us at an appointed time and place, so that the sisters could not avoid speaking with me. I only wanted to assure them of my good intentions for their continued education, future happiness, and provision of good marriage offers.

The girls were waiting for me in the chamber that overlooked the street, but as I walked into the room they were both staring out of the window, so did not notice my entrance. This gave me the opportunity to overhear a conversation that was neither harmonious nor genteel. Mary had Becky by the ear and was twisting it enough to cause her younger sister to wince. 'Don't you dare tell him,' she said. Her teeth were gritted.

Becky was shaking. 'But I don't want him any more, Mary. Please.'

Mary twisted her ear again, causing the girl to squeal. 'I'll kill you, if you tell. You promised to keep him a secret.'

I coughed, noting how admirably each girl now dropped the disagreement and presented themselves as two loving and devoted sisters. Becky held Mary's hand as if she had never had her earlobe pinched in her life, and Mary smiled at me with angelic innocence. What a pair of seasoned performers these girls were.

I wanted to confront them about this *secret* they spoke of, and why they felt it necessary to whisper their conversations, when a more thoughtful plan occurred to me. To bide my time. The girls had made stubbornness and secrecy their coat of armour, and I might never be able to pierce the thick metal of their lies. Especially in this place, where they enjoyed some protection from their aunt.

So I will not report here on our conversation in the parlour that morning, since the girls dutifully nodded and curtsied to each of my suggestions and assurances about their life back in Somershill, whilst promising upon the Virgin's heart to wash their faces, comb their hair and show respect to their stepmother Clemence upon their return.

After this, I kept an eye on them both – sometimes following them, sometimes listening at their door. They mentioned the *secret* again on a few occasions, but I was never able to glean any further information. I was still deciding whether or not to confront them openly, when another lead weight was added to the net that was closing about them.

On the fourth morning of our stay in London, Mother called me from her bedchamber with screaming that was so desperate and penetrating, it had disturbed the whole house. As I ran to discover the problem, I passed the haughty servant on the stairs. He was descending from Mother's room with his hands over his ears and made no attempt to stand out of my way. I pushed past him to open the door to the bedchamber, finding Mother searching about the floor in her nightdress. Her hair was loose about her shoulders, and she had hitched up the skirts of her gown to reveal legs so luminously white they might almost have belonged to a corpse.

'What's the matter, Mother?' I could see she was genuinely agitated, so I took one of her hands and tried to grab the other, though she struggled against me like a feral cat. The shutters were wide open, and a cruel wind blew into the room.

She squinted and focussed her eyes, before my face made sense to her. Then she fell against my chest. 'Oh Oswald. Thank the Lord. I thought it was that awful servant again.'

I patted her head, which was hot. Her hair was damp. 'Mother? What is it? What's the matter?'

She was shaking. 'I had the most horrible vision, Oswald. A vile bird was sitting on the windowsill. So enormous it cut out the light.'

'You just had a bad dream, Mother.'

I spoke calmly, but she was not reassured. 'No, no, Oswald. It was there, on the windowsill. It was the butcher bird, Oswald. And it was hungry.' Then she began her frantic search once more. 'Where is Hector? Where's my little boy?' Then she stood up straight and pointed her finger at me. 'You see. He's gone. The butcher bird has eaten him.'

I let go of her hand and went to close the shutters, but when I turned around Mother was lifting the mattress from her bed, as if her small dog might be hiding amongst the feathers.

It was the most unfortunate timing, but Eloise's pompous servant chose this exact moment to reappear at the door. His hands were now removed from his ears and held politely at his side. 'Does the mattress need turning, my lady?'

'No it doesn't,' I told him.

He looked at Mother and then at me. 'Very well, my lord. If you are sure.'

'Yes I am.' I pushed him from the room and then slammed the

door so hard in his face that the wooden panelling of the wall shook with the impact.

Mother didn't seem to notice. 'Where is Hector?' she cried. 'Where is my little dog?'

'Don't worry. I'm sure he is safe.'

Helping Mother back into bed, I covered her gently with the sheet. 'I'll look for him now. He's sure to be somewhere about the house.'

'Do you think so?' Her eyes were shutting.

'He's probably in the kitchen, begging for some food.'

A small tear trickled down her cheek. 'Will you find him, Oswald? Bring him back to me.'

I stroked the hair away from her forehead. 'I will, Mother. Of course.'

The kitchen at the Cooper household was smaller and yet more frenzied than our own in Somershill. Low beams criss-crossed the chamber, lengths of oak that often caused the cook, and his many assistants, to hit their heads as they moved about the room. As I entered the chamber they were boiling a set of hooves in two vast cauldrons. The smell was peculiar and tangy. Steam hung in the air.

'Have you seen a small dog in here?' I said, to nobody in particular. 'It belongs to Lady Somershill.'

The haughty servant appeared through the haze. 'No, my lord. We do not allow dogs in *our* kitchen.'

I ignored his insinuation. 'Have you seen the dog anywhere else?'

Now he pretended to be thinking, though I knew it was an act. He stroked his chin in the most provocative fashion. 'No, my lord. The last time I saw the dog, he was in your mother's bed.' At this comment he raised his eyebrows to display his contempt at such a practice. Some of the others in the room looked ready to laugh.

'I want you to organise a search of the house,' I said.

The man sighed.

'Immediately!'

He bowed. The weight of his large, superior nose pulling his face forward to the floor. 'Very well.'

While servants peered under benches, or lifted back cabinets from the wall, I decided to question the de Caburn sisters, to see if they had hidden Mother's dog, or even just commissioned him into a game. The dog was fond of the girls, despite the teasing he endured at their hands, and it was possible he had run after them into the fields at the back of the house. God knows, it must have been boring enough for Mother's dog, just sitting on his mistress's lap all day and waiting for the rare chance to lick her face.

The morning was damp, and as I tramped through the long grass of the field, the dew stained my hose with its watery and unwelcome paint. Apple blossom coated the trees in white papery stars, and soft green lichen wrapped itself about the trunks and branches. These trees were unpruned, with stems grown too long for easy harvesting – but it was too late in the season to attend to this problem. In fact, the whole orchard was a neglected, forgotten place, despite belonging to Westminster Abbey. In one corner was a large pile of timber, freshly sawn and stacked. And then I knew the future for this square of land was not as a garden, but rather as a building site. It was no wonder that the trees had been left to grow, untamed.

Somewhere in the distance, a group of birds were making their alarm call. A constant and tuneless refrain, which caused me to wonder if a cat or even a fox might be prowling this same field. I stepped forward silently – a tumbledown byre by the far hedge was my destination. It was an obvious hidey-hole and, surely enough, when I reached its rotting beams and peeped through a hole in the boards, I saw the sisters, huddled into a corner of the barn. About them were broken stalls, lengths of sawn wood and an old grinding wheel – its great circular stone leaning from its frame at an awkward angle.

I watched a while, as Mary and Rebecca sat there in silence. It was an odd and unnerving stillness. Why didn't they speak to each other? I shifted my position slightly, to see that Becky clasped a tiny rabbit in her hands. She lifted its grey and silky head to her lips and kissed it between the ears. The rabbit struggled a little, but could not free itself from the girl's tight and zealous grip.

Becky turned to her older sister Mary. 'Please let me keep him,' she pleaded, kissing the rabbit's head a second time. 'Please.' Was this the secret they spoke of?

Mary refused to look at her. 'We can't keep him. I told you that before.'

A tear was welling in Becky's eye. 'But I can hide him in a box when we go back to Somershill. He'll be a good boy. You can find something else.' She clasped the rabbit even tighter, causing the terrified creature to thump its legs against her chest. 'Please.'

'No I can't, Becky. They're too watchful in this kitchen. Just give him to me.'

Becky clambered up onto her feet. 'No. You can't have him.' She attempted to dodge Mary, but almost immediately lost her footing and dropped the rabbit onto the muddy floor. Both sisters gave chase, as the creature tried to escape the byre, but it was Mary's superior strength and speed that soon cornered the rabbit by a dilapidated stall. With the speed of a sparrowhawk, Mary grasped the animal by its leg and then held it up by its ears.

Becky squealed. 'Give him back. Give Baby back.' But Mary was not moved in the least by the tears of her little sister. Instead she swung the rabbit behind her head and then cast it soundly against the stone of the grinding wheel. The creature was stunned, if not dead, following this assault, but Mary had not finished. Now she took a knife from her belt and then stabbed the rabbit at the neck. As blood spurted profusely, Mary continued to cut at its limp body, until her hands were bathed in a crimson rinse.

I've seen a rabbit killed before, of course I have. But never by an eleven-year-old girl. It was a vile, horrific sight. But worse than this slaughter, was the expression upon Mary's face. Or should I say, the lack of one.

I broke my silence and sped into the byre. 'What are you doing?' Mary looked up – her stupor broken by my unexpected appearance. Now released from her cold and murderous trance, she regarded her bloody hands and screamed. I tried to calm the girl, but she was frantic. Soon her sister joined in, as if the emotion were contagious.

It was only when Eloise appeared at the door that the girls ceased their shrieking. 'What's going on? Why all this shouting?' Then Eloise saw my face. 'Oswald?' she said tentatively. 'You're here?'

'Mary has just killed a rabbit,' I said. 'I saw the whole episode.'

Eloise frowned. 'A rabbit?'

'It was Becky's pet rabbit,' I said. 'I saw Mary stab it to death with her knife. I don't know why she did it.'

Mary spoke up. 'It wasn't Becky's pet rabbit. That's not true.'

Becky wailed at this. 'But I loved him. Why did you have to kill Baby? Why?'

By way of answer, Mary went to slap her sister about the face, so I grasped the girl by her arm. 'How could you do something so cruel, Mary? What's the matter with you?'

'He had to die,' was her answer.

'No he didn't. You just did it for your own enjoyment.'

She struggled and tried to punch at me with her other arm. 'I had to kill the rabbit because . . .' Then she stopped still. Her mouth was firmly and absolutely shut, and she wouldn't say another word.

'Because what?' I asked. 'Come on. Tell us why. Let us understand your reasons.' Mary only stared at the floor with a dose of her most sullen and belligerent hostility.

Eloise laid a hand on my shoulder and spoke softly into my ear. 'Don't be too hard on Mary. It's just a rabbit. There are hundreds of them about this field. We can find another for Becky.'

'You didn't see it happen.' I let go of the girl's arm. 'You didn't see Mary's face when she killed the animal.'

Eloise only sighed. 'But it was just a rabbit.'

It wasn't just a rabbit. That much was obvious. Becky now held the dead creature to her chest, though its blood was seeping into her gown. 'Mary wanted to feed Baby to Rab.' She turned to her sister. 'Didn't you?' she said, bitterly.

I looked to Eloise, but she merely shrugged her shoulders.

Mary hissed, 'Shut up, Becky!'

'Who's Rab?' I asked. Again silence. 'God's nails, Mary. Who, or what, is Rab?'

Mary waited a few moments and then tramped over to a dark corner of the byre, where some lengths of timber were stacked against the bowing walls. We followed the girl to find a fishy, sawdusty smell. But there was something more stinking than wood shavings here. It was the meaty stench of death. And though it was still early spring, a solitary fly circled the area, buzzing about the chamber like a winged devil. When it landed upon my arm, I smacked the filthy thing away.

Mary turned to me. 'Sure you want to see Rab?'

I nodded.

She removed the planks from their organised formation, revealing their true function – as a rudimentary cage. With three planks gone, Mary stood to one side and pointed into the darkness. 'Rab.' The smell had increased to such a strength that my eyes watered.

I looked to Eloise, took a deep breath, and then peered into this strange, black hollow to see something lurking below. I don't know what I expected to see, but it was not this. A creature held its head up to the light. A giant, decrepit thing with scaly yellow claws and a breast pecked clear of feathers. A leather hood covered its head and eyes, and jesses hung from its feathered legs. The floor beneath its perch was littered with bones and a small mountain of its own feathers and droppings.

I quickly stepped back, with my hand over my nose. 'Where did you get this bird?' I asked.

Mary poked out her chin with defiance. 'Father.'

'He gave such a bird to you?'

She looked away. Awkwardly. 'No. We saved Rab.' She turned to her sister. 'Didn't we Becky?' Rebecca nodded.

My heartbeat quickened. 'What sort of bird is it? I've never seen such a large beast.'

'Father bought him from the best hawk dealer in London,' said Mary. 'He said Rab came from the land of the Berbers.' She seemed sadder now. 'But he was no good for hunting. That's what Father said, anyway. He was going to kill him. So we hid Rab in the forest.'

Becky tugged at my cape. 'I wanted to tell you about Rab, Uncle. I did. I did. But Mary wouldn't let me.'

I dropped my fingers from my nose, as a dread descended. 'You brought this bird to Somershill, didn't you? It was in the box you said contained the cat.'

Becky nodded.

'And how did you get such a bird to London?'

Mary smiled. I would say slyly. 'He sat upon my arm, of course.'

I looked back into the hole, where the tattered and squalid bird sat upon its nibbled perch. 'He's far too heavy for you to carry.'

She shook her head, but I didn't believe her.

Eloise clasped her hands together. 'I think we should drop this matter now, Oswald. The mystery is solved. Let's go back to the house.'

I looked at Eloise with some surprise. 'I need to ask the girls some more questions.'

She raised an eyebrow, somewhat petulantly. 'If you think that's really necessary.'

'I do.' I turned back to Mary, to catch the girl exchanging worried glances with her sister. 'Why did you kill Becky's rabbit, Mary? You could have fed this bird scraps from the kitchen.'

Mary paused a little. The sly smile returned. 'He won't eat anything from this kitchen.'

'Why not? A bird won't starve himself.'

'He doesn't like French food.'

I rolled my eyes at this stupidity. 'He ate enough food from my kitchen, didn't he?' Now she wouldn't answer.

'Do you fly him?' I asked. 'He has jesses on his legs?'

'They've been there since Father kept him,' she said sullenly.

Becky interrupted. 'Sometimes we fly him, don't we Mary. But he catches things.'

Mary turned on her sister. 'Shut up Becky!'

I turned to Becky myself. 'What sort of things?' The girl only chewed her lip, so I raised my voice. 'Tell me what this creature catches.'

Becky trembled. 'I don't know.'

'Is it lambs?'

Patches of red coloured her cheeks. 'Yes. Sometimes.'

'Did it take my mother's dog?'

'I don't know.'

'Or did it steal a newborn baby from its crib? And leave her in a bush of thorns?'

The girl began to cry. 'No. No. Rab would never do that.'

'How do you know, Becky? See the size of him.' I pointed into the dark corner where this enormous, evil-smelling bird sat upon his perch, looking like a great stone lectern.

I will admit this. I went to shake the girl. Suddenly a hand was on my arm, digging its hard nails into my flesh. But they were not Mary's fingers, instead they were Eloise's. 'That's enough,' she said.

'No, it isn't,' I said. 'I need to know if this bird has been attacking children.'

Eloise dug her nails in harder. 'How dare you accuse my nieces of having anything to do with such a crime? They were simply caring for an injured bird.'

I dropped Becky's arm and turned to Eloise. 'Look at it. This is no poor injured sparrow.' The bird cocked its head obligingly as if it were listening to our conversation, before letting out a loud whistle. It was no wonder that the girls had kept it away from the house.

Eloise released her fingers and patted her face. 'It's just a large falcon, which used to belong to my brother. I can't see what all the fuss is about.'

I put my hands over my eyes. 'I'll tell you what the fuss is about. All this time I've discounted the possibility of an actual butcher bird. But now I find the creature exists. In the midst of my very own family.'

'Nonsense.'

I removed my hands. 'People have seen it, Eloise.'

'What people?'

'In my village. I kept hearing reports of a bird taking livestock. I dismissed such stories, since no normal bird can take something as large as a lamb. But I was wrong.'

She pushed a strand of hair from her face. 'The bird might have taken the odd lamb or rabbit. But that doesn't mean it attacked an infant.'

I turned to Becky. 'You travelled past Hever, didn't you? And then through Caterham.'

Mary pressed herself between us. 'Don't say anything to him, Becky.'

But Becky was still too angry with her sister to be obedient. 'I don't know which way we came, Uncle. I just followed them.'

'Them? Who is *them*?'

Mary's eye twitched. 'She means me and Rab.' She turned to her sister. 'Don't you, Becky!' Becky was losing her nerve. I could see that. I needed to act quickly, if I were to get to the truth.

'I stopped at an inn in the hills above Caterham, where your bird had attacked a child,' I said. 'Did you know that?' Becky trembled. 'The victim was a small, sickly baby who was being carried on his mother's back.'

'We came through Bromley,' said Mary, adamantly.

'Don't lie to me, Mary. I saw the scars upon the infant's head.'

'It wasn't Rab,' she insisted.

I pointed to the bird. 'Take off its hood.' Mary didn't move, so I shouted again. 'Take off its hood!' She approached the bird with some reluctance, and untied the small leather cap that covered the creature's skull. Sure enough, a fierce eagle looked back at me, with a great crest of feathers upon his head. 'It's just as the child's mother described,' I said. 'A bird with a crown.'

Eloise gave a huff. 'Enough, Oswald. The girls have told you they didn't go to this inn.'

'The bird must be destroyed,' I said.

Eloise repeated the huff. This time with even greater consternation. 'Absolutely not. I will not allow it.' The girls ran to her side. 'The bird is precious to Mary and Rebecca. A keepsake from Versey.' Then she placed her arms round her nieces' shoulders. 'Heaven knows, they have nothing else left to inherit from their father.'

'Their bird has killed one child, Eloise. I cannot allow it to strike again.'

'You will not harm their bird.'

An unexpected feeling of hatred rose in my chest. 'It's a murderer. Trained to kill its prey.'

She folded her arms. 'What would you know about falconry?' she said mockingly. 'Did they teach you about such sport at the monastery?' Then she cocked her head and looked at me with her green eyes. Her pupils large in the poor light. 'Perhaps you should have stayed at the abbey. Because you are still a novice, aren't you,' she scoffed. 'In so many ways.'

I took her meaning well enough. I had been an inexperienced lover, it's true. But I had made a good enough attempt at the job – and our lovemaking had seemed a success – from my point of view anyway. The girls couldn't possibly have understood the sarcasm of her remark, but now all three of them laughed, and to my shame, my response to this ribbing was a greater desire to kill the bird, right there and then.

I stopped still. Emulating my sister Clemence's trick, I counted to ten silently and then swung my cloak about my shoulder. 'The bird cannot live.'

'You have no evidence against it,' said Eloise, as I brushed past her to make my exit. 'You're stupid,' she called after me. 'Just a stupid little boy.'

The words smarted in my ears as I marched towards the house. Mary caught up with me. No longer laughing, she tried to curtsy in front of me as I strode ahead. 'Please Uncle. Don't kill Rab. He's caught lambs before, but he would never attack a baby.'

I walked on, but she pursued me.

'I nursed poor Rab back from death. Father starved him and pulled out his feathers.'

'The bird is a killer, Mary. I cannot let it live.'

'Please, Uncle. Don't kill him.'

I pushed her away.

It was easy enough to find an axe, near the kitchens. I returned to the byre immediately. My heart beat strongly and my legs did not feel entirely my own, but I knew what I had to do.

Eloise watched my approach from the door and tried to stand in my way. When I pushed through, she grasped my arm. 'Not now, Oswald.'

'Don't make this difficult.' Did she believe that I was enjoying the prospect of killing this bird? Mary and Rebecca were lying in front of its perch, sobbing like mourners at a grave. This was the most unpleasant of tasks.

Eloise would not release my arm. 'I'm sorry for what I said before. But please, don't do it now,' she whispered. 'Not in front of the girls. It's too cruel.'

I shoved her away. 'Then when?'

'I'll instruct a servant to kill the bird. Tonight. When the girls are in bed.'

I dropped the axe a little. 'I don't know.'

'If you don't trust me, then you may see the bird's body in the morning.' I hesitated. Could I trust her? 'This is my house, Oswald,' she said, her face hardening. 'You must respect my decision.'

I looked at Mary and Rebecca's sobbing bodies. Their wailing rang about the byre. Eloise was right in one respect. It was cruel to kill this bird in front of two such young girls. I would respect Eloise's decision. But only for their sake, not hers.

As I sat in my bedchamber, my own bedchamber, I made the decision that our party had stayed in this place long enough. It had been lust, rather than love that had drawn me to Eloise, and at that very moment I determined never to speak to the woman again. Her words still stung like the bite of a hornet. I would inspect the bird's dead body the next morning, and then we would leave.

I didn't see Eloise or the girls for the rest of the day, though she knocked three times at my door and begged to speak with me. Each time she knocked, I hid my head beneath the bedclothes and tried not to think about her breasts, or the soft skin between her legs. Instead I remained silent, and dwelled upon the feathered killer that she and her nieces harboured in the byre. To think I had discounted the possibility that an actual bird existed. I had been foolish and slack in my investigations. I had not listened properly to my witnesses, too easily dismissing their sightings as delusions. I could only be thankful for one mercy. At least I had discovered the bird before it killed again.

Eventually I fell asleep, and at dawn, there was another knock at my door. At first I thought it might be Eloise with a further apology, so I shouted for her to go away. Another voice answered however, and when I opened the door I found my visitor to be the haughty servant, regarding me like a piece of dried dung that needed scooping up and taking to the tanners.

'Yes?' I said, in as condescending a manner as was possible. 'What do you want?'

'There is a message for you, my lord.'

This seemed unlikely at this time of day. 'From where?'

'The country, I believe.' He coughed. 'Simple Hill, is it?'

'Do you mean Somershill?'

He smiled. 'Of course, sire. Somershill. The messenger arrived last night.'

'So why didn't you rouse me?'

The servant bowed his head. 'We didn't know where to find you, sire. You are not usually in your own bedchamber.'

I dressed quickly and followed the servant to the kitchens, finding the messenger in question to be my stableboy, Piers. He was perched on a shelf in a corner, where he had spent the night sleeping against the wall. In the opposite corner were Edwin and Ada, sleeping together in an awkward embrace. I noted immediately that Edwin's hand was resting inside Ada's kirtle. It seemed I had not been the only person to experience an affair of the heart this past week.

Piers was dirtier than ever. His hair was ruffled and sticking up like the tufted ears of a squirrel. I will admit to being embarrassed that this boy was associated with the de Lacy household, given the wildness of his appearance. It was clear the haughty servant felt likewise, as he woke the boy with a kick before quickly leaving, as if the boy might give him fleas.

Piers burst into life, his enthusiasm irrepressible. 'Sire. I saw London Bridge! I even stopped to pray at the chapel. And the tower is as white as they say, though I could not hear the lions roar.'

'What?' I still hadn't fully woken up, and the words had fallen out of the boy's mouth in a tumble.

'Geoffrey said I would never see London Bridge. But I did, sire.'

I put my hand on his shoulder. 'Enough, Piers. What is this message you have for me?'

Piers fumbled about in his belt pouch and produced a roll of parchment bound with a red ribbon, and fastened with my sister's seal.

I held it to my nose before unravelling it, noting the smell of Somershill, the slightly musty and sweet scent of hay and horses. Suddenly I felt sad and homesick. I settled myself in a corner and broke the seal.

Somershill Manor
3rd May 1351

Dear Brother,

I hope this letter finds you at the correct house. We received a letter from Eloise Cooper just after you had left Somershill, informing us that Mary and Rebecca de Caburn were in her care and giving directions to her house in London. I am assuming you have found her, since we have received no news from your party.

My news is this. You must cut your visit to London and return to Somershill without the slightest delay. Another infant from the village has been discovered in the bushes of a blackthorn and is assumed murdered. She was a baby girl — only a few days old. I don't know her name, but her mother is the widow Christina Beard.

I would not trouble you with this matter, but it has caused a great disturbance on the estate. John Barrow — the man to whom you insisted upon giving sanctuary — escaped from the north-west tower only hours before the child's disappearance. There is uproar amongst our tenants and you are blamed entirely for protecting this man, who was clearly always a murdering lunatic. I still cannot imagine why you did such a thing — though you will no doubt argue that it was kindness that motivated such a foolish act. You harboured a child murderer in our house, when there was a child in our own family. Or perhaps you do not care for the safety of my own child, Henry? Sometimes I wonder at your mental capacities.

But you should not think me your biggest critic. That person is Thomas Tulley, the father of the first murdered infant, and he rallies the men about him and they storm through the village on their horses like the four riders of the Apocalypse. While they search for John Barrow, there is not a fragment of work being done on their farms, not a penny of rent is being paid and the demesne might as well be the wilderness of Judea. I half expect to find a wandering penitent whenever I leave the house and walk into the fields. Your reeve Featherby is unable to discipline or quell their rebellion, and now I hear nothing but mention of the butcher bird about the house. The servants are in a frenzy of fear and will shoot an arrow at anything with feathers. It is an intolerable situation. I may not walk about my own meadow for fear of being shot by my own staff.

By now her writing was becoming smaller and smaller, so she might include as many rebukes and warnings as possible onto this square of parchment.

I do not know what delays you in London Brother, but you must return to solve this problem. If you do not arrive within the week, I shall be forced to appeal to the earl.

Your loving sister Clemence

Addendum. I should also tell you that I have prevented the murdered infant from being buried. Given that you are now the family's great investigator, I assumed you would want to inspect her dead body? She is currently kept in the cool of the cellar at Somershill. But if you do not return with haste, then I shall release her to the priest before her poor decaying body releases its foul miasma.

I read the letter again. And then again. As if hoping the words might change. But, of course, they didn't. I felt sick and put my head between my knees.

When I sat up again, I saw my groom Edwin standing in front of me. 'Are you unwell, sire? You look very pale.'

Of course I was pale. I was ready to heave the contents of my stomach upon the floor. The killer of Catherine Tulley was not some ragged eagle that my nieces kept in an outhouse. It was a madman. A monster. A man I had protected in my own home.

Clemence was right to chastise me. I was no great investigator, or I would have smelt the poison beneath this man's skin. Instead my skills had proved no more effective at drawing out this abscess than a poultice made of cold butter.

Edwin asked again after my health.

'I need to get back to Somershill,' I told him.

He stood to attention. 'Today?'

'Yes.'

He seemed flustered. 'Very well, sire. I'll start getting our party ready.'

I took him to one side, before looking about me. Ada was still sleeping, and the rest of the kitchen was empty of servants. I only heard some commotion in the distance as the household began to prepare for the day ahead.

'I'll go alone,' I told Edwin. 'I need to travel quickly.'

'But what of your mother, sire? And the de Caburn sisters? I hear they are to return with us to Somershill.'

It seemed that little was secret from a house full of servants. 'You must stay here and bring them all back when Mother has fully recovered.'

The idea of travelling with my mother, but without my presence, was clearly concerning him. 'I heard my lady was walking now,' he said. 'And yesterday she was singing. Everybody heard her.' Unfortunately this was true. Mother had been singing with the window open, and had attracted a crowd in the street below. Sensing an audience, Mother had sung even louder until a rotten apple was thrown through the casement and burst open on the floor. Mother had slammed the shutters and called them all philistines, but this performance had, nonetheless, demonstrated that the woman was recovering from the certain death she had been predicting.

'Is it safe for you to travel alone, sire?' asked Edwin, in some desperation.

'Yes. I'll use the Bromley road this time. It will be busy with pilgrims, now that spring is here.'

He sighed. 'Very well, sire.'

I went to my bedchamber and dressed properly for a journey, making sure I had enough money on my person. Deciding not to wake Mother with the news, for fear of some interference, I went to Eloise's chamber and knocked softly on the door. I was not relishing the next conversation, but I thought it only polite to say goodbye. However, she did not answer my knocking, and when I took the liberty of opening the door to her chamber, I found that her bed was empty.

I sought out the haughty servant in the kitchen. 'Where is your mistress?' I asked.

He shrugged. 'I don't know, my lord.'

'She's not in the house?'

'No.'

'You are sure?'

He pursed his lips. 'Yes. I saw her leave myself.'

I frowned. 'Where's she gone at this time of the morning?'

He scratched his ear and then exchanged a grin with a pretty maid to my left. 'Nobody knows, sire.'

I didn't have the time for such furtiveness. 'When will she return?' This question was met with yet another shrug. 'But I have to leave immediately.'

'Would you like me to give my mistress a message?' he asked.

I thought about this for no longer than a moment. 'No thank you. Get me a pen and ink and something to write upon,' I told him. My tone was firm and short, and he did as I requested – soon returning with a poorly cut quill, a square of dusty parchment, and a pot of lamp black ink that was so watered down I might have been writing a letter for a spy to decipher by firelight.

And then I wondered what to write to Eloise. My mind was suddenly a blank. Should this be an apology about the bird? A fond farewell? Should I be honourable and offer to write again? After all I had spent the week in her bed, even though she had called me a stupid little boy. My hand started to write such words, but I quickly crossed them out, for I didn't mean a single syllable of them. The week had been an unexpected first exploration into the pleasures of a woman's body – but now, faced with a reason to leave, I was pleased of it. I wanted to be gone from this house before Eloise returned, from wherever it was she went at this time of the morning. So I left the parchment empty of words. I gathered up my possessions and walked into the street to retrace my steps to Southwark.

I left the Cooper house as the May sun was beginning to warm the streets. I pulled up my hood and paced along the Strand towards Fleet Street, joining the early-morning crowds as they moved with urgency towards Ludgate and the markets of the city. It was then that I realised something was scampering along behind me. I speeded up, but it continued to follow me until I turned around to see my pursuer was none other than Mother's little dog, Hector. His coat was wet and sticky, and pasted in muddy clumps – but he was as pleased to see me as I was to see him. I picked him up, despite the smelliness of his fur, and let him lick my hand. Just the once.

As we fondly reacquainted ourselves, something in the distance, towards Ludgate Prison, caught my eye. A figure was approaching with a lithe and graceful gait. I knew it could be nobody else, despite the thick furs about her body. It was Eloise, the very last person I wanted to meet. I would tell you I called out for her, in order to explain my sudden departure, but instead I took the absconder's option and quickly ran up a dark alley beside St Clement's Well and hid with my back against the wall.

When I was sure she had passed, I watched her progress back along the Strand towards her home, and now realised that she was not alone. Instead she appeared to be conversing with two companions. One was an adult – most probably a man, given his style of walking – and the other was a child. But it was impossible to say more, given that they both wore long, cloaked gowns with hoods.

I should have followed them. It would have conveyed this story to a quicker end, but instead I put Hector to the floor and hurried past Saint Paul's and over London Bridge – happy to make my escape from London and reach the inn at Southwark.

The miserable widow opened the decrepit door to me. 'So you're back then,' she said, sucking at her few remaining teeth with her tongue, as if they might give up some leftover food from breakfast.

'Where's Geoffrey?' I said.

Now she gave a small snort. 'The boy?'

'Yes.'

'He disappeared. The day after you left him here.'

'What?'

'Said he was going off to see London Bridge. And that he'd be straight back.' Now she picked at a gap between her teeth with a fingernail, before running her finger around her gums. 'Never saw him again.'

I felt a rage brewing. 'But I told him to stay with the horses.' Hector broke out in a sympathetic growl.

The widow removed the crooked finger from her mouth. 'Don't blame me. I'm not the boy's nursemaid.' Then she pointed at Hector. 'He's not going to bite me, is he?'

I ignored this question. 'You should have sent me a message.'

She continued to look warily at Hector, and began to close the door. 'A message about what?'

'Geoffrey of course.' I put my foot on the threshold, so that she could not shut the door any further.

'Where would I have sent it to?' she said, looking down with some disgust at my boot. 'You didn't tell me where you were going. Just that you'd be back the next day.' She started to lick about her gums again. 'Except you weren't.'

'I sent a message here, for Geoffrey's attention. To advise him of our delay at Mistress Cooper's. Did this message not arrive?'

'It came all right. I've still got it in the kitchen.'

'Then you knew where we were staying.'

'How would I know what it said?'

I threw up my hands in frustration. 'Are you telling me you can't read?'

She wrinkled her nose. 'No. Of course I don't know how to read.' She said this as if being literate were an affliction. 'And you're just lucky that I didn't sell those horses. It's cost me a lot of time to tend to them, I can tell you. What with all my other jobs.'

'And nothing has been heard of Geoffrey since he left?'

She shook her head.

I sighed and looked to the cobwebs on the ceiling. 'I hope he's safe. Stupid boy.'

'Oh don't be concerned about him,' she said. 'I bet he got a better offer.'

'Such as?'

She pursed her thin lips. 'Well there's plenty of grand houses on the other side of the river, needing pages and grooms. A smoothly-spoken boy like him would have no trouble in securing a good position. Even as a squire.' Then she spoke as an aside. 'Though in my opinion he liked his books a little too well.'

'He should have stayed here,' I said. 'I told him not to leave this side of the river.'

Now she laughed, wrinkling her pitted nose in amusement. 'There's plenty who don't do as they're told any more, my lord.

Haven't you noticed? London is full of them.' Then she made her final attempt to shut the door, before I pushed my way inside, dog and all.

I settled my bill for the care of the horses, and told the widow to expect the rest of my party in the next day. She clasped her bony hand around the coins like a clam snapping its shell, then closed the door on me with a grumble and a sigh, as if she had been somehow cheated.

I saddled Tempest and set off for Somershill, with Hector trotting along beside me. At first he seemed peeved by this arrangement, as he was used to cushions and laps – but I noticed he soon took to life as an ordinary dog, sniffing at the many delights of the London streets and pissing on every tree and corner post.

We were soon away from Southwark, and as we reached the crest of One Tree Hill I pulled on Tempest's reins and we stopped for a short while, to look down upon London. I felt little sadness at leaving. The sky was once again as cold and white as a block of Carrara marble, whilst a layer of smoke hung over the city in a thin gauze. And through this murky haze, the great spire of Saint Paul's reached up into the sky, alongside its many smaller daughters and sons across London, each with their thin and tapering pinnacles pointing to something in the heavens. Something that I could not see. Something that I did not believe in. And then, as I looked into this sea of humanity, I wondered where Geoffrey was – hoping, with little confidence, that he was safe.

I kicked at Tempest, and slowly the houses and inns of London gave way to the hedgerows and fields of Kent, as the blossom of the may and the nodding heads of the bluebells called me back to Somershill.

Chapter Eighteen

After a day's journey, I saw the windows of my home across the low meadows, reflecting the evening light back at me like a wall of fiery beacons. I had left the road at Sevenoaks and travelled south-west across the Medway Valley towards Somershill. It was here, in these large and fertile fields, that I saw the true emptiness of England. Great flocks of corn buntings danced over neglected fields, landing and rooting around in the barley stubble – stubble that should have been ploughed back into the soil the previous autumn.

The estate at Somershill was equally empty of faces as I arrived, and I didn't see anybody until opening the door to the solar, where Clemence sat next to the fire, nursing her baby. Humbert remained in his usual corner, as motionless as a watchful owl. In fact, I could tell you that the scene was exactly as I had left it. This is one of the comforts of the countryside, I find. Little changes, no matter how long you stay away. Hector was at my heels, but soon began to circle the room at speed.

'You're home at last,' said Clemence, looking up from her baby's face.

'I came as quickly as possible.'

'What kept you in London?' She regarded Hector with some distaste. 'And where's Mother?'

'I've left her at the Coopers' house. She was taken ill.'

'But you have her dog?'

'It's quite a story.'

She frowned. 'And what about Mary and Rebecca? I thought you were bringing them with you?'

'They'll return with Mother. Once she's recovered.'

Clemence removed Henry from her breast and passed the swaddled lozenge of an infant to Humbert. Henry's face was puffed with satisfaction, and a milky bubble formed on his lips before dissolving into a long dribble.

'Where is everybody?' I asked.

Clemence rearranged her tunic and then turned to speak with me. 'Searching for John Barrow.'

I winced. 'Everybody?'

She stiffened. 'Yes, Oswald. A child murderer is on the loose. Wouldn't you expect the whole village to be searching for him?' She looked to Henry, who now rested over Humbert's immense shoulder and slept like a she-cat. 'Or don't you care about children?'

It was a ridiculous assertion, which I dismissed by pulling one of my most withering stares, though I don't believe my sister noticed. 'Is the dead infant still in the cellar?' I asked quickly.

Clemence shuddered. 'Yes. She is. Poor thing.'

'Can I see her now?'

'Don't you want some supper first? You've been travelling all day.'

I shook my head and then laid my hand upon her arm. 'Just tell me. How did Barrow escape? I left instructions for the north-west tower to be kept locked.'

She shook me off with some irritation. 'I don't know. He must have picked the lock. He's not as mad as he pretends.'

'Did the priest help him?'

She screwed up her nose at this suggestion. 'Father Luke? Why do you say that?'

'I caught him whispering with John Barrow. In the days before I left for London.'

She gave a mocking laugh. 'Well. Father Luke must be involved then. If he was discovered *whispering*.'

'I just want to know if he visited John Barrow in the days before he escaped?'

She folded her arms. 'Why? So you can blame this whole calamity on a priest?'

'No,' I said, perhaps a little too defensively.

She looked me up and down. 'This problem is of your own making, Oswald. You should have listened to the people in the village. They told you John Barrow was to blame.' She sighed. 'It's not how my father would have behaved.'

This was yet another of her taunts that no de Lacy blood flowed in my veins. 'I was trying to help Barrow, Clemence,' I said, flopping upon a bench. 'I thought he was innocent.'

Clemence ignored this statement and walked to the door. 'Come on. Let me show you the corpse. Then the child can be buried at least.'

She picked up a candle and led me down the stairs towards the cellar. 'I had to insist upon a delayed burial,' she told me, as our feet touched the cold stone steps that led into the void beneath the house. 'The baby's mother was distraught at the suggestion, and would only cooperate when I threatened her with a fine.'

'Thank you, Clemence.'

She stopped for a moment and looked at me – seemingly embarrassed at my gratitude, as if a drop of my appreciation might somehow taint her. 'Yes. Well, I know how much you like to prod around at dead bodies,' she said tartly, before carrying on again down the stairs. 'Though it's fortunate you returned today, as Gilbert has been complaining at the smell down here. He says the whole cellar is becoming infected by the foul odour and will spoil the brandy.' This sounded exactly like the sort of warning Gilbert would give. Pessimistic and impossible.

Clemence opened the heavy door of the cellar and passed me the candle, but didn't put her own foot over the threshold.

'You're not coming in?' I asked.

'No.' A shiver ran through her body. 'The child is in the corner. On a stone slab to keep cool.' She held her nose, though there was no stench, other than the musty damp that crept about this room like a thief. 'I'll wait for you upstairs, Oswald.' She then clattered up the steps in an enormous haste that brought on a fit of coughing.

I soon found the infant's body, wrapped in clean linen. Taking a deep breath, I pulled back the strips to find a small and bloated face, framed by a shock of wet and black hair. She was truly a newborn, for when I removed the linen across her stomach the stump of the cord was still attached to the knot at her belly button, already green and stinking.

I held the candle over her abdomen and looked for the signs of murder. But I saw nothing, apart from a line of dried vomit at her mouth and the scratches upon her skin where her naked body had been thrust into the thorns. Perhaps the pitiful little girl had died of exposure to the cold, since it was only early in May and the winds were still icy and harsh. A person need only put a baby outside in such weather and the infant would be dead within a few short hours. Every midwife knew to wrap a newborn in blankets and keep a fire burning so that the child could settle to the climate of the world outside his mother's womb.

Examining the body, I tried to imagine why John Barrow had done this. Why had he stolen a newly born child from the warmth of her home, stripped her naked, and impaled her upon a bush? This was not madness. It was depravity.

I wrapped up the child, not wanting to look again upon her wrinkled face, and then I slumped to the floor, with my head in my hands. But what purpose did this remorse serve? It was nothing more than self-reproach, even self-pity. I got to my feet again. I picked up the child, and made for the village.

*   *   *

I took her to the priest's house, as I wanted Father Luke to look upon her face. To see her bloated wretchedness. Just as I had. He was entangled somehow in this tale. I was sure of it.

I rapped with some force at the priest's door, though the hermit must have heard my approach, since Tempest's hooves pound at the soil like hammers. In my arms I held a sack, containing the dead child.

His servant opened the door. The toothless man who had warned me about the bird at my last visit. I pushed my way in. 'Where is your master?'

Father Luke crept out from a corner of the room. 'My lord. I didn't expect you.'

'You say that every time I see you. Should I provide a week's notice?'

He stared at me for a few moments, as if my words had made no sense. Then he folded his body into a cringing bow, before shooing his servant out of the room. 'Bring some ale and cheese for Lord Somershill. Quickly.'

'I don't want anything to eat,' I said. 'I'm here to discuss John Barrow.'

He bristled. 'Have they found the man?'

'No. Do you know where he is?'

He shook his head. 'No, sire. I do not.' He looked at me for a moment, then cast his eyes back to the floor. The man quaked. His eyelid twitched like a dowsing rod.

I opened my sack and presented him with the dead child, now bound up in her linen strips.

He recoiled. 'Sire?'

The smell of her bodily decay was evident in this hot and stuffy chamber. The odour of a carcass on the turn. I pulled back a strip of linen to reveal her face. 'You should recognise her, I think. Did you baptise her recently?'

He withdrew a little, trying to hide his eyes with a pair of delicate hands. 'Yes. Her name is Margaret Beard.'

'And yet now she's dead. Just as Catherine Tulley died. Immediately after baptism.'

His hands fell slightly. He stuttered. 'I . . . er.' He hesitated, suddenly aware he was caught at the centre of some accusation. 'It's nothing more than coincidence.' Flecks of sweat glistened on his greasy forehead. 'I baptise many infants. Most are still alive.'

'Have you baptised any others recently?'

He opened his mouth to say something, but then shut it again.

'So Catherine and Margaret were the only two infants born in the village in recent weeks?'

He drew himself up in an attempt to sound assured, but still wouldn't look me in the eye. 'Yes. That's correct.'

I passed the child to him, making sure he did not flinch from taking the body in his arms. 'She needs to be buried now,' I said. He held the child so limply, I thought he might drop her to the floor. 'Take care!' I warned him. 'Hold her properly.' He bustled away with Margaret's corpse, soon passing her over to his servant, and then telling the man to put the body outside.

I shouted through the doorway. 'No. Leave her in the house. The fox may take her!'

Father Luke returned to the room, rubbing his hands upon his clothes, as if to remove the taint of the child from his person. His movements were agitated and repetitive, so I told him to sit down and calm himself. He duly complied with my request, looking as small and pathetic in his wooden chair as a child waiting to be scolded by his tutor.

'Why were you whispering with John Barrow?' I asked him.

He now scratched the side of his face. 'When was that, sire?'

'When I found the two of you in the tower at Somershill.'

'We were praying, sire.'

I sighed. Such an excuse. 'Would praying cause such a guilty reaction upon discovery?'

'I don't know what you mean.'

I leant over him. 'Don't lie to me, Father. Or I will assume you are complicit in these murders.'

He turned his face from me, sweat now dripping from his nose. 'I had nothing to do with any murders. I only wanted to help John Barrow.'

'How? By telling him where the newly born children lived? So he would know where to find them?'

His face reddened. 'No, sire. I would never be party to such evil. I'm a man of God.'

'Then tell me what you were whispering about.' He remained silent. 'I could inform the men of the village that you were John Barrow's accomplice.' I leant once more into his face. 'Imagine how they would react to such news.'

His mouth bubbled with spittle. 'Please, sire. Don't tell them such a thing.'

'Why?'

He wiped his mouth. 'Because it isn't true.' His voice became more forceful. 'None of this is true.'

'Then tell me the truth.'

He took a breath to calm himself. 'I counselled John Barrow. No more. We only whispered because of . . . his sin.'

'What sin?'

His voice had lost its agitation and was now quiet and wearied. 'It was a Confession. I cannot say.'

I banged the back of his chair. 'Yes, you can!'

The priest flinched from me, and put his hands to his mouth. 'The man wanted to kill himself. He wanted me to help him do it.'

I leant in. 'How?'

'By bringing him a knife or a rope.' Now he looked me straight in the eye. 'But I refused. I would not assist a man to perform a mortal sin and risk eternal damnation.' Now he spoke with renewed vigour. 'You must believe me, sire.'

I stepped back a little. 'So you took him nothing?'

'Only items to improve his mood, and to allay his despair. Barrow can't read, so I brought him a paternoster, and some needlework to pass the time.'

Now I screwed up my face. 'Needlework?'

'Yes, sire. He asked for some wood and a chisel, which I would not provide. He might have used the chisel to kill himself. So, instead I took a small tapestry.'

'You fool! He used the needle to pick the lock of the door.'

The priest trembled. 'I didn't know he would do such a thing, sire. I only sought to help a man in despair. I didn't suspect he would abuse my charity.'

He began to shake uncontrollably, so I waited until his agitation had subsided. 'Do you know where Barrow is hiding?'

He shook his head and mumbled. 'No, sire. I don't.'

'Is there somewhere he mentioned.'

'I can't remember anywhere.'

I put my hand upon his shoulder. 'Think, Father. We need to find the man.'

And then he did the most extraordinary thing. He placed his left hand upon mine, and stroked my skin with his fingers. 'You are a good man, sire. He said you were.'

I pulled my hand away quickly. 'Who said that?'

He turned to me. 'Brother Peter.'

'When did you have such a discussion?'

He froze again. 'I told you before, sire. I knew him in Rochester.'

'Why would he tell you such a thing?'

He stumbled over his words. 'I don't know.'

I leant into the priest's face and once again caused him to flinch. 'I don't want to hear about him. Ever again.'

'I didn't mean to cause offence, sire,' he said, now holding his head in his hands. 'Please forgive me.'

I straightened my clothes and walked to his door. 'Make sure to bury the girl's body in the finest plot. And do not charge a fee.'

Chapter Nineteen

The infant Margaret Beard had been born to Christina Beard – a widow of the parish who lived with her one surviving daughter in a house they had only recently rented from me. The plot and cottage would have been beyond the pockets of the Beard family in 1348, but now its large rooms, virgate of land, and commuted duties were easy for them to afford – and I was glad they rented the place, since nobody else was interested.

I called at the door with a heavy heart, and when Christina Beard answered it did not lighten. The woman bowed her head, as she knew she must, but could not disguise her displeasure at seeing my face. She looked older and paler than when she had paid her entry fee to take over this property. On that occasion I remember smiles and curtsies, since the fee had been so reduced as to hardly be worth charging.

I put my foot over the threshold. 'May I come in?' She moved aside and led me into the middle hall, where a brass cauldron hung on a broche over the fire. The chamber was empty of furniture other than a wooden stool where Christina's daughter sat, counting beads on a line of leather. She was a girl of maybe fourteen, but possessed the mind of a small child. The girl smiled at me and pointed, and then made a strange, grunting sound.

Christina was embarrassed and crossly waved the girl into the inner chamber, from where she peeped at me from around the woollen blanket that covered the opening. I noted the door that had once hung in this gap was now cut into strips, ready to be burned. It seemed Mistress Beard and her daughter could afford the reduced rent at this property, but had neither the goods nor the means to live here in any comfort.

I cleared my throat. 'I'm sorry to hear of your infant's death.' The girl behind the curtain made a groan and flapped her arms, only to be rewarded with a quick reprimand from her mother.

'Get to your bed,' the woman shouted, as she approached the blanket and shooed the girl back into her hidden corner. 'Lord Somershill doesn't want to hear your squawking.'

Christina turned back to face me, though we continued to hear her daughter's strange gurgling noises. 'I'm sorry, sire. Faye can be trying when we have visitors.' Her voice was tired and despairing. 'She can't settle in this house. My daughter preferred our small cottage.'

I tried to smile. 'She must also be upset by her young sister's death.'

Christina sighed. 'Yes. We're both grieving.' Then she threw me a bitter glance. 'Though we were unable to bury Margaret, since Lady Clemence said you would want to inspect her dead body.'

'I've finished now,' I said. 'The priest will bury her tomorrow.'

'Did you find anything?' the woman asked me.

I shook my head. 'No. Not really.'

She looked at me curiously and then wiped a tear from the corner of her eye. A long silence followed, until I summoned the courage to continue. 'I need to ask you a few questions, Mistress Beard. About Margaret.'

Now she raised an eyebrow, the tear gone. 'Oh yes?'

'About the circumstances of her disappearance.'

She took a deep breath. 'If you feel it's necessary, sire.' Her tone was scathing. 'Though we all know who's guilty. John Barrow and his bird.'

'Did you see Barrow anywhere near your house?'

'Of course not! I would have raised the hue and cry.' Then she cleared her throat a little. 'Anyway, they say it is his bird that steals the child. Not he.'

I went to answer, but we were interrupted by more groaning from the chamber next door. It was now so loud and pitiful that Christina stalked back to the blanket and shouted, 'Be still, Faye! You foolish girl. Or I'll come in there and beat you into silence.' Then she turned to me with a face full of tears. Full and heavy tears this time. 'I don't mean to chastise the girl, sire. But she's so vexing at the moment.' She threw her hands up in despair. 'I just wish she would give me a little peace.'

I rose. 'I'll come back tomorrow, Mistress Beard. When you're feeling more disposed to speak to me.'

Christina wiped her eye with the corner of her tunic. 'I wouldn't bother, sire. I've nothing more to tell you.'

'But—'

She hardened her chin. 'I swaddled the child. I put her to sleep by the back door, and when I came back with the firewood, she was gone. I have no more information that could help you.'

'And where was the child found?'

'On the common pastures. Same as poor Catherine.'

'And who found her?'

She flicked her hand in front of her face. My questions appeared to be irritating her, like a bothersome fly. 'Some men from the village. Thomas Tulley told them to look there.'

'Why?'

'Because his own child was discovered there, of course.' She now looked at me with something akin to hatred in her eyes.

I looked away, to ease my discomfort. 'You can't think of anything else that would assist in my investigations?'

Her answer was a resolute no.

I left the house soon after, but as I walked down the front path poor Faye opened the shutters of her chamber and called to me, as sadly as a cow yowls for its slaughtered calf.

*   *   *

The street was empty apart from a flock of crows that pecked at the cleaved stomach of a dead rat. They rose into the air as I passed, flapping and cawing. The air was warming now that spring was stroking the world with her soft green fingers. Passing the row of cottages where the Tulleys lived, I smelt the piquant, spurge-like scent of herbs as they boiled upon Agnes Salt's hearth, the odour reminding me of my recent and unpleasant visit to the woman. There was a face at her window. It was Agnes herself, with a countenance as wary and hostile as the old bull's.

I caught Agnes's eye and went to acknowledge her, but she only slammed her shutters. And I met this reaction again and again as I walked through the village. Nobody was brave enough to confront me outwardly about John Barrow, but they made their feelings plain with their silent stares or their hastily closed doors.

Only Old Eleanor, Mother's previous lady's maid, called to me. 'Good evening to you, sire.' As ever she was sitting outside her cottage with her swollen foot resting upon a stool. Her deaf and mute grandson was twisting a gimlet into a block of wood, making a series of deep holes, for no purpose other than his own entertainment.

I bowed to the woman and would have made my usual escape, but on this occasion it seemed worth stopping. She could tell me what was happening with the search for Barrow, if nobody else would. 'Might I take some ale with you, Eleanor? I'm thirsty.'

Her face crumpled into a smile, and she struggled to her feet. 'But of course, sire. Come into my home.' She ushered me inside and pulled the boy to one side, giving him clear instructions to fetch the best ale. He looked at her lips intently and then disappeared into the side room, soon reappearing with a pewter mug.

'Your dear mother gave me this mug,' Eleanor told me proudly. 'I don't ever use it for usual guests. It only comes out for the proper family.'

I wanted to launch straight into my questions, but since I had been presented with Eleanor's best ale and mug, I felt obliged to enquire after her health. Though I soon wished I hadn't.

'My legs are still cursed with the dropsy,' she told me. 'They swell to the size of tree trunks. And the skin is so red, sire. Blistered and cracked it is. Like a side of roasted pork fat.' She lifted her skirts. 'Would you like to see it?'

I quickly held up my hand. 'Thank you, Eleanor. But no. I'm not a physician.'

She dropped her gown a little, cocked her head, and looked at me quizzically. 'But you trained under an infirmarer, didn't you? Brother Peter wasn't it?'

I had to think quickly. 'Yes. But we only treated men at the monastery. So I am woefully ignorant of the female anatomy.'

She sighed with disappointment. 'Oh. I see.'

'But couldn't you visit Agnes Salt? I hear she produces herbal tinctures. She might have a cure for your legs.'

Now Eleanor pulled a face of disgust. 'Not her.' She leant towards me conspiratorially. 'Agnes Salt doesn't know a thing about medicine, sire. She says there are no such things as the four humours. And she doesn't hold at all with leeches.' She threw up her hands. 'I ask you. What sort of healer is that?'

Her grandson interrupted us by bringing his log into the chamber and recommencing his attempts to mine a thin shaft from one side to the other. I managed, at this point, to turn the conversation in my favour. 'Is there any news yet of John Barrow?'

'Not so I've heard,' she told me. 'But what a thing to happen, sire. Another baby gone.'

'I've just been to visit Christina Beard.'

Eleanor shifted from one buttock to the other. 'Oh yes.' Then she gave an uneasy cough. 'Her.'

'Why does her name make you uneasy?'

She shifted buttocks again. 'I don't know if I should say anything, sire.' I was about to demand an answer, but this story didn't need any tipping out. 'It's God's punishment,' she told me.

'What is?'

She frowned. 'Her baby being taken. By that bird.'

I sighed. 'And why would Christina deserve such a punishment?'

She looked at me with some degree of disbelief. 'That baby was a bastard, my lord. Christina's husband has been dead well over a year. He was one of the last to die in the Plague. So he couldn't be the father, could he?'

'Who is the father then?'

Eleanor gave a knowing smile. 'That's the question, isn't it? Christina Beard has always been so godly, sire. Always warning others of their sins,' she leant towards me and whispered, 'when in truth she was bedding strangers for money.'

This story took me by surprise. 'Are you saying Christina Beard is a whore?'

'Well. She's a widow. And she's as poor as a hermit. She can barely afford to feed that simple daughter of hers.'

I knew the Beards needed money, as I had watched them burning their own doors. But I still found it hard to believe that Christina was a whore. I thought back to the girl by the stew in Southwark. The girl who had called to me in the street. She was jaded perhaps, but she was young and pretty enough to draw custom. Christina had the face of a worn-out donkey and would not have been an attractive proposition – not even to a drunk man in the dark.

'Are you certain of this story, Eleanor?'

She nodded with a gasp. 'Oh yes, sire. That's why she rented that bigger cottage from you. It's got more rooms for entertaining men, you see. And it's away from the village. Where nobody could see what the old hypocrite was up to.' Then she gave a little sigh. 'Still. At least she got the infant baptised. Though it was a bastard.'

'Did Father Luke know that the child was illegitimate?'

'Oh no. Not him.' Then she laughed. 'This new priest is such a wet rag of a boy. Don't you think?'

I coughed. 'I find him acceptable, thank you Eleanor.'

She folded her arms, disappointed I would not agree with her assessment of Father Luke. 'If you say so, my lord.'

'I do.'

I stood up to leave and she struggled to get back to her feet. I told her to stay in her chair, but she insisted on showing me to the door. As I pulled on my gloves, she whispered into my ear, 'They say he's a sodomite, sire.'

'Who is?'

'The priest.'

I stopped on the threshold. 'Who's saying such a thing?'

She hesitated. 'Just people around the village, sire. They say you shouldn't have appointed him.' I looked her straight in the eye until she looked away. 'But not me, sire. I don't say such a thing.'

'Good.'

I walked away from her cottage with some degree of irritation, feeling sullied by this conversation. And what had I learnt? A foolish piece of tittle-tattle about Christina Beard, and an allegation I had already guessed at concerning Father Luke. It served me right for talking to gossips.

As I passed Joan Bath's cottage, a wagon blocked my path. Her two sons were loading a crate of hens, a bench and a table into its tilt. I grabbed the youngest boy by the ear, though he tried to avoid me.

'What are you doing?' I asked him.

'We're moving,' he said, and then succeeded in squirming away from me like a wriggling cat.

'Where to?'

The boy ran into the cottage shouting for his mother, and soon Joan appeared at the door, wearing a thick cloak and a shawl about her face that softened its severity.

'What's happening here?' I asked her. 'You didn't inform me you were moving.'

A frown criss-crossed her forehead and tarnished her fleeting appeal. 'I tried to tell you a couple of weeks ago, but you just rode off. Though I'm sure you saw me waving at you.' Her dog growled at me from the shadows, and though she closed the door on it, I saw that the creature had grown a good deal fatter since our last meeting. 'In the end I gave notice to your reeve, Master Featherby,' she said. 'Everything has been done correctly.'

I sat down upon the bench that the boys were yet to load onto the wagon. She joined me and told her boys to disappear for a while so that we could talk privately. But now alone, we sat in silence for a long while, both awkward and tongue-tied. It was Joan who spoke first. 'I understand you're yet to raise the wages,' she said reprovingly. 'I asked Featherby.'

I sat up straight. 'I have other troubles right now, Joan.'

'I'm not the only person leaving this estate, you know. There's many of us. Particularly from Burrsfield.'

'So why are you going then?' I said. 'It's not wages. I don't pay you anything.'

She looked to her hands. 'I can't stay in Somershill, Oswald. You must understand that. I'm going to Norwich. To marry.'

I stifled a laugh. 'What?' Then I quickly changed my tone, for I could see she was offended. 'I'm sorry. I meant to whom?'

'You're surprised anybody will marry me. Is that it? Because I used to be a whore.'

'It's not that,' I lied. 'It's just that you don't need to marry, do you? You're prosperous in your own right.'

She pulled at the fingers of her gloves. 'Every woman needs to marry, Oswald. Or to have been married. If only for the sake of her children.'

'You didn't used to believe that.'

'Well I do now. Nobody will give my boys a chance in this place. In their eyes they will always be the sons of a whore. Though their real fathers walk about the village and sit with their wives in church.' Some of her old sourness came through, seeping into her words like a spoonful of lemon juice. I thought she might even spit upon the ground. Instead she composed herself and returned to her previous manner of speaking – with poise and dignity, as if she had never uttered a curse in her life.

'The man I intend to marry is old and rich. He has no children left alive after the Plague. He wants a son to inherit his land and sees I have produced a string of boys in the past.'

'And if you don't again?'

She smiled, a little hesitantly. 'I will.'

'And what of your flock of sheep?'

She pulled back her cape and tapped at a leather purse on her belt. 'I've sold them all to Master Featherby. For a good profit.'

'And is he going to rent your land as well?'

'I don't know. You'll have to ask him yourself.'

I looked at the bulging purse. 'You must take care, Joan. It's a long journey to Norwich and you're travelling with a lot of money on your person.'

'Richard is meeting me in Rochester.' It was the first and last time she mentioned his name.

'Why not come to Somershill?'

'Nobody knows me in Rochester. It's easier that way.'

I wiped my hand across my forehead and sighed. 'I wish you were staying. I have few enough friends here.'

She looked to me. 'I have to go, Oswald. There are too many bad memories in this place.' Now her face darkened and a solitary tear ran its course down her face. 'The people of this village burned my son to death. I see their faces every day as I go about my business. Every time I drive my sheep to the common pasture, I pass the patch of earth where they built the fire. I can still smell the fumes from his burning body when I open the shutters. I've tried to forget. But I can't. And now they are searching for John Barrow. Another man they believe is guilty of a crime. Only this time it's not a dog-headed man. They think he is in possession of some make-believe bird. When they find him, they will kill him.'

'I won't let that happen, Joan. Barrow will be properly tried. At court.'

She raised an eyebrow. 'Will he?'

I looked to my hands. They trembled like leaves caught in a spider's web. 'Yes.'

She took my hand in hers. Again we sat in silence.

'I was a fool to give Barrow my protection, wasn't I?' I said.

'No. That piece of kindness is to your credit.' Then she squeezed my hand. 'You did it because of Leofwin.' I nodded dolefully. She leant into my ear and whispered, 'But you must put his burning behind you.' And then she kissed my cheek. 'We both must.'

'Please don't go,' I said.

She let go of my hand and stood up. 'I have to.'

I helped to load the last few remaining items onto the wagon and we embraced, before saying goodbye. As I passed the pony's reins to her for the last time, a question occurred to me. 'Can I ask you, Joan? Do you know Christina Beard at all?'

'Mother of the dead child?'

'Yes.'

Joan tapped the pony on its hindquarters and the wagon began to move slowly away. 'Of course I know the woman. She used to call me a Jezebel.' Then a bitter smile worked its way across her lips. 'Until she produced a bastard of her own. Then she had no right to shout insults at me.'

'Do you know who the father of the baby was?'

She shook her head.

'And you never heard that she . . .' I scratched my head to think of a polite way to put this, as I didn't want to infuriate my old friend at our parting.

'Never heard what?' She cocked her head inquisitively.

I took a deep breath. 'That Christina was a whore.'

Now Joan pulled on the pony's reins and brought the animal to a firm halt. 'For the love of Saint Catherine. Who would pay to spend a night with that old kipper?' And then she laughed. Soon she could barely speak, such was her amusement.

'Well, somebody got her with child,' I said.

The boys ran around from the back of the wagon. 'What is it Mother? What's so funny?' they asked as they pulled at her gown, pleased to see their mother so happy for once.

She calmed herself down. 'Nothing for you to know about,' she told her sons, as she moved the pony off again. 'Get back behind the cart and make sure the chickens don't fall out.'

'So you have no idea who the father was?' I said, now walking quickly to keep up with her.

She shook her head. 'Why don't you ask her?'

'She wouldn't tell me.'

She smacked the reins. 'Then, dear Oswald, you have another mystery to solve.'

Chapter Twenty

I caught up with the men later that same day and joined their search for Barrow, though they showed nothing but antipathy to my presence – particularly Tulley, who refused to ride near me. Their feelings towards me only thawed when I offered to provide a meal at the house, when the light faded and we could not continue our search.

We resumed the hunt the next day, but with each successive day our party grew smaller, leading us to find nothing but the odd footprint or extinguished fire. Wherever Barrow was hiding himself, he had made a good job of it, since he was not even detected by the dogs. At the end of the second week without success, I rode back one night to Somershill to discover that Mother's party had returned from London. The unkempt carriage was being cleaned by Piers, while Edwin was seeing to the horses. But there was another, finer carriage alongside with four tall wheels and four horses. The tilt was covered with a cloth of red and gold, and the flaps were rolled up to reveal an interior arrayed with velvet cushions and a Persian rug. The carriage stood tall enough for a chest to hang easily on a ring beneath the rigid frame – just as Mother had tried to achieve with our own.

I called Piers over. 'Who does this carriage belong to?' I asked.

'Mistress Cooper, sire.'

'Eloise?' I froze on my feet. 'What's she doing here?'

It was a ridiculous question, and alarmed the boy. 'I thought she was invited,' he said nervously.

'Why?' This was even more foolish, but the boy obviously felt the need to answer. 'I don't know sire. Perhaps Mistress Cooper wants to visit the house?'

My legs suddenly felt weak and I had to quell the urge to run to the garderobe. An urge I had successfully defeated in recent months. The thought of facing Eloise terrified me, however. We had not parted on good terms, since I had fled her house without saying goodbye, or even leaving a letter. Escape at dawn had seemed a good idea at the time, but now it felt tawdry and ill-mannered.

Pulling back the hair from my face, and checking that my breath was sweet, I walked into the great hall at Somershill. And into the bear pit where this story would finally play itself out.

The long table on the raised dais had rarely seen so many women about its edges. The only man at the table was baby Henry, who was sitting upon Clemence's lap and blowing his milky bubbles. Eloise faced me, silent and unreadable. To my right were the young de Caburn sisters, squirming on their stools and desperate to free themselves from the hall and return to their haunts about the estate. I noted their fingernails were dirty, despite the grand dresses they were now wearing. Eloise had only succeeded in polishing their manners on the exterior, whereas their true characters were working their way out like the gesso beneath a gilded canvas. I was pleased to see it. In truth, I liked their spirit and pluck.

The atmosphere was awkward, the conversation stilted.

Mother turned to me with a clap of her hands. 'So, Oswald. I expect you've solved the mystery of the butcher bird by now.' Then she leant towards Eloise. 'Oswald is our great investigator, you know.'

Eloise raised an eyebrow. 'Your son is a man of surprising

talents, madam.' She licked the lard from her finger in a manner that only a few weeks ago had stirred my loins, but which now churned my stomach.

Eloise picked up a stale crust from her plate. 'Do you have any more of this bread, my lady?' she asked. 'I am quite intrigued by the . . . coarseness of its texture.' She then deliberately picked the husk of a wheat ear from her teeth and laid it beside her plate.

Mother snapped her fingers to call a servant, but it was only Gilbert who wearily shuffled in. 'Yes, my lady.'

Mother adopted her most affected tone. 'Please bring some more of this delicious country bread, Gilbert,' she said. 'Mistress Cooper is finding it a hearty fare after all that French flimflam they serve in London.' Gilbert looked awkward, as if he were about to admit that there was no further bread, but Mother dismissed him with a haughty flick of her hand.

Eloise exchanged a look of amusement with the girls and then spoke to me. 'Do tell me more about your investigation, Oswald. It sounds exciting.' Clemence bristled at Eloise's use of my Christian name.

'It's not exciting at all. Two infants have been found murdered in the village.'

Mother interrupted. 'Such terrible crimes. One wonders what will happen next.'

Eloise picked another husk from her teeth. 'I doubt you experience such wickedness as we must endure in London.'

Mother was challenged. Her hackles were raised. 'Oh but we do, Mistress Cooper. Please don't be fooled by our peaceful fields and silent woods. Last year two girls were found in these very forests with their throats cut. And then, when a boy with the face of a wolf was burned in the village, demons escaped from his head.'

Eloise raised an eyebrow. 'Is that so? Who would have guessed I was coming to such a nest of corruption. Perhaps Mary and Rebecca should return to London with me?'

Clemence gave a snort. 'I can assure you the girls will be safe here,' she said, without noticing the wink that Eloise had given to her nieces. 'Don't listen to my mother, Mistress Cooper. Somershill is nothing but a quiet backwater.'

A mischievous new current blew across Eloise's face. 'But what of this butcher bird, Lady Clemence?'

She was goading us. 'There is no butcher bird,' I said. 'Only a madman who attacks small infants.'

Eloise turned to look at me. 'Indeed?' Then she feigned a puzzled expression. 'But is this not the man to whom you gave protection?'

I cleared my throat. 'Yes. It is.'

'Have you found him yet?'

'No.'

Eloise smiled slyly and then turned to Clemence. 'You must be concerned about Henry? With such a madman on the loose?'

Clemence pulled the baby close to her. 'Not in the least, thank you Mistress Cooper. My son is guarded every hour of the day.' She waved into the corner where Humbert stood to attention. 'My servant is always present. Even when we sleep.'

Eloise raised an eyebrow. 'Even in your bedchamber, my lady?'

'Well . . . yes,' said Clemence cautiously, now aware of some trap she might be walking into.

'That must be distracting,' said Eloise, turning to look at Humbert's unblinking face. 'To have such a sizeable man watching over your sleeping face. Most women only ever share such intimacy with their husbands.'

Clemence steamed. 'It's a perfectly usual arrangement.'

Mother chimed in. 'Of course it is. I've often had a servant in my bedchamber. Even on my wedding night. My father even sent in the priest to make sure—'

I groaned. 'Thank you Mother.'

Eloise clasped her small hands together and bowed her head to my sister. 'Please forgive me, Lady Clemence. I'm sure there's not a reason in the world to worry for the safety of baby Henry.

He is such a healthy boy. And so . . . sizeable for his age, don't you think?'

Now Clemence grimaced – clearly thinking of some acid response to make, while Mary and Rebecca giggled, enjoying the sport at the expense of their hated stepmother.

Knowing this conversation could only end in outright acrimony, I quickly stood up. 'Mistress Cooper. I expect you would like a walk after the long journey from London.' I held out my hand to Eloise. 'Allow me to show you our orchards at Somershill.'

She took my hand in her own. 'Thank you, Oswald. I would be delighted.'

The cool sun of spring was warming a pale blue sky. Beneath the trees of the orchard, a number of sheep grazed at the long grass, while starlings jabbed at the soil in search of worms. In the distance a boy was trying to catch bullfinches in a long-handled net before they nibbled the setting fruit from the branches. He sat beneath the cherry tree, patiently waiting for the rosy-chested robbers to appear.

Eloise took my arm. 'How I've missed the country.'

I looked into her face. 'Really? I thought you preferred life in London.'

She shook her head. 'I was raised at Versey Castle, Oswald. The country is my true home.'

Somehow this wasn't convincing, but before I had the chance to argue, she released her arm from mine. 'Why did you leave London so suddenly?'

I had been dreading this moment since first seeing her carriage in our courtyard. 'I received news of another murder at Somershill. I was needed here.'

'Could you not have written to me?'

'I tried to, Eloise.'

'Don't you have parchment and a quill in this place?'

I couldn't think of an answer to this taunt, and a long silence followed, during which I stared into the distance, as she stared into my face. Eloise was the first to speak. 'I'm sorry for what I said to you, Oswald. When we discovered that bird. You're not a stupid boy.'

I didn't look at her. 'Those words were said with venom, Eloise. They sounded heartfelt.'

She pulled her cloak about her shoulders and shivered. 'I was upset that you wanted to destroy a bird that was precious to my nieces. And you were wrong about it attacking children, weren't you?'

I set off again, but she soon caught up with me. 'Please forgive me Oswald. I didn't mean what I said. You must believe me.'

I stopped. 'What happened to Rab then?' I asked. 'Did you have the bird killed?'

She shook her head.

'I hope the bird has not travelled here. He may not attack children, but he certainly takes lambs.'

She grasped my arm again. 'Goodness no.' She cleared her throat, seemingly a little embarrassed. 'I've told the girls that I'll find the bird a new home.'

'And will you?'

'Of course.' She looked into my eyes. The fur of her cloak framed her face and squared its length. She was so oddly and transiently handsome that it was tempting to study her features to catch each different facet of her beauty.

I must have stared too long, for it gave her the chance to take my hand. 'Do you love me, Oswald?' she said.

I quickly broke my gaze, horrified. I did not love the woman. I had simply enjoyed a week in her bed. I opened my mouth to say something, but she cut me short. 'Because I love you.' Then she suddenly grasped me about the neck. 'And I have a wonderful secret to share.'

I stiffened. 'Oswald, please. Relax,' she said. 'This will make you so happy.'

The boy with the net was staring at us, so I shouted at him to be on his way. I did not want to hear Eloise's secret. This revelation. Because I had a horrible feeling that I knew its nature.

Eloise stood upon her tiptoes to kiss my lips. 'I had to tell you this in person. A letter would not have sufficed.'

'What is it?' I said nervously, trying to back away from her.

Once again she took my hands in her own. 'I am with child, Oswald. Our child.'

I took a deep breath and tried desperately to quell the urge to run away. 'Are you sure?'

She nodded. 'I've missed my bleeding.' Then she dropped my hands and looked into my eyes. 'I thought you would be happy?'

I wanted to say yes, but the lie would just not worm its way out. Instead we stared at each other in silence, until she raised her beautiful, green eyes to look at something distant in the sky.

'Will you renounce me then, Oswald?' Tears were welling and her voice was choked. 'Both me and our child?'

I immediately swore not to renounce them both, without truly understanding what the alternative meant.

'Do you mean it?' she said.

I winced at the stinging of my lies. 'Of course.'

'Then it's settled,' she said. 'We'll marry in the next week.'

I suddenly held up my hand and found my latent voice. 'But, but . . .'

'But what?'

'It just seems so fast.'

She held both hands to her stomach. 'But your child grows in my womb, Oswald. Would you have him called a bastard?'

'Well, er no. But—'

'If we mean to marry, Oswald. Then we must act quickly.' A shadow fell across her face, and it seemed for the world as if a small maggot were growing from the corner of her eye. Looking closer I identified it as a bead of soft yellow rheum that was popping in and out of her tear duct as she spoke.

She poked a finger into my arm. 'Oswald. Are you listening to me?'

My face felt hot and my hands clammy. 'I'm sorry. What did you say?'

'Are we to marry, or not?'

I took a deep breath. 'I'm sorry, Eloise. This has come as a shock to me.'

Then she crumpled into the long grass, her red and green gown falling about her. Tears stained her cheeks.

I don't like women crying. I don't understand what it means. Mother seems to be able to shed tears at will – mewling like an infant when we can't find her dog, or even when she notices a stain upon a favourite handkerchief. Were these tears that particular sort of crying, or were they the tears of Joan Bath as she wept for her dead son? I was unable to distinguish.

'Please. Don't cry,' I said, placing my hand on her shoulder, though she continued to sob, her body now shuddering. 'I'm sorry, Eloise. It's just such unexpected news.'

'What do you think happens when you bed a woman, Oswald?' she blubbered. 'A child can be conceived. Have you never seen a boar covering the sow? Four months later the piglets are born.'

There was nothing I could say to this, for the truth was embarrassing and showed the true extent of my naivety. I'd never given the possibility of conceiving a child the slightest thought. It certainly hadn't been my intention when I crept into Eloise's warm bed.

I began to compose some platitudes in my mind in order to give myself more time to think, when the conversation took a new turn.

'I'm sorry, Oswald,' she said. 'I shouldn't have come here.'

'No, no. I'm glad you did.'

She looked up at me from her crumpled state in the grass. 'Please, Oswald. Don't lie. I understand. This is not the sort of news that a young lord wants to hear.'

'Well . . . um.' Now what was I supposed to say? She had completely unseated me.

She sighed. 'This was not what I planned either. I like you well enough, Oswald. But I do not love you. And I know you do not love me.' I went to make some sort of half-hearted protest, but she held up her hand. 'Please. Do me the honour of being honest.'

I sat down beside her. 'So what are we to do?'

She shrugged. 'I can return to London quickly. I'm sure Master Dukinfield would marry me quickly. He's asked many times. And he holds me in enough regard to accept your child as his own.'

Now I felt sick again. The thought of that great slab of boasting belly fat having anything to do with my child was nauseating. 'You can't marry him, Eloise. The man is obnoxious.'

'So what would you have me do then? Go to a nunnery? Or perhaps I could hide in my bedchamber for nine months and pretend to have a lame leg?' Now she appeared to be almost talking to herself – running through the options aloud. 'Except such news will always get out. Particularly once a child is born. And I could hardly keep that a secret. Unless I travelled to France and paid for the child to be cared for in a monastery.' Then she looked up at me again. 'I'm already called a witch. Now I will be a whore.'

'But—'

She took my hand. 'I will marry Dukinfield, Oswald. Let's not argue any longer. I have been stringing the man along enough anyhow. He deserves an answer to his constant badgering.'

And then a great gust blew into my lungs, whistled up my throat, and loosened my tongue. I don't know where it came from, but it was strong and unstoppable. 'No. Eloise. We will marry.'

'But—'

'There will be no more discussion.' I stood up and pulled her to her feet. 'I will advise Mother and Clemence immediately.'

'But you don't love me, Oswald.' I sensed a little of her

play-acting now. Perhaps she fluttered her eyelashes a little too desperately and fell into my chest a little too readily?

'I'm sure our love will grow,' I said. 'There are plenty who marry without strong feelings and are very happy.' God knows, Mother had told me often enough about such marriages.

'Thank you Oswald,' she said, with such relief in her voice. 'I will make you a good wife.'

'I know.'

She smiled, but now it was not relief that shaded her face, instead it was victory. 'And our son will be a lord,' she said. 'Lord Versey.'

I should have told Eloise, there and then, about my promise to Clemence: her son Henry would have this position, not any son of ours. I would tell you that I forgot to mention this, but, in truth, it was cowardice. For, at that moment I just could not stomach another drop of drama.

Mother was predictably horrified when I informed her of my plans to marry Eloise. 'Why on earth would you want to marry such a woman? She's as ancient as a woody taproot.' Then she held up Hector to growl in my face, as if he might be equally displeased with my choice of bride. Hector did not oblige how-ever, as the dog now preferred my company to my mother's, and would often escape her lap to follow me about the estate, digging at badger earths and barking at squirrels. Much to Mother's consternation, it seemed that her dog liked behaving like a dog.

'Eloise is not that old,' I said. 'In fact she's——' but I was unable to finish the sentence, since I did not truthfully know her age. I had never thought to ask. 'She's only twenty-eight,' I guessed.

'Twenty-eight indeed?' said Clemence, who had appeared at the door, like a fly before a storm.

'Eavesdropping again, Clemence? You might be sorry what you hear.'

She waved away my comment. 'Eloise Cooper must be thirty. At least.'

I shrugged. 'It doesn't matter to me. It's a good match.'

'Well Eloise Cooper is rich,' said Mother, now encouraging Hector to lick her face. 'I'll agree with you in that respect.' Then she gave one of her preposterous squeals. 'And we could use the Cooper house in London when we're visiting the king.' Then she frowned. 'Though we would have to appoint a new cook.'

I tried to catch Clemence's eye, so we might share a mutual amusement in Mother's pretensions, but she ignored my attempts at camaraderie and pressed on with her own agenda. 'I hope you've told Mistress Cooper that my son Henry will inherit Versey?'

I despised being needled by my sister, so I lied. 'Yes. She knows all about it.'

Clemence pulled a face. 'And she wasn't disappointed?'

'Not at all.'

'You do surprise me, Oswald. I expected Eloise Cooper to want Versey.'

'Well you're wrong,' I said with more bravado than I felt. 'She is fully aware of my promise to you. Now, can we drop the matter?'

Clemence inclined her head to me, but suddenly we heard a creak from the stairwell, causing Hector to leap from Mother's arms and run towards the door. I followed the wiry-haired creature, looked down into the dark and empty spiral staircase, but saw nothing but a flurry of dust and the backside of a small dog as he descended the stone steps. I listened for a few seconds before coming away.

Mother was now eating a hunk of rye bread that she had brought up to the solar from the breakfast table. Although it had always been Mother's rule that we only ate in the hall, she continued to flout her own decrees without the slightest whiff of hypocrisy. Her mouth was full as she spoke. 'Was it a ghost, Oswald?'

'No. Just the wind.'

'No, no.' said Mother, now waving the bread. 'I'm sure those stairs are haunted.'

Clemence laughed. 'Who by?'

Mother pursed her lips. 'Sometimes an icy hand tickles the inside of my leg as I descend.' Clemence rolled her eyes. 'Yes it does,' insisted Mother. 'It quite gooses me.'

Not knowing how to respond to this, I didn't bother.

Hector soon reappeared at the door and Mother enticed him back to her knees by dangling a crust of bread in the air. 'Is Mistress Cooper expecting a child?' she asked me, as the dog performed small leaps to reach the titbits.

The question came as a surprise, but I remained composed. 'No,' I said firmly. 'She's not.'

I needn't have worried about causing suspicion, for Clemence once again burst out laughing. 'Expecting a child? This is Oswald we are discussing, Mother. Can you imagine him lying with a woman before their wedding night? I doubt he will even manage to do the deed once they're married.'

I went to protest, but Mother spoke over me. 'Don't be so sure of that, Clemence. Look at Geoffrey of Anjou,' she said, now letting the dog lick the crumbs from her fingers. 'The boy was only thirteen years old when he married Queen Matilda. And he sired a son soon enough.'

'But he was French, Mother,' said Clemence.

Mother nodded. 'True. I suppose an early start in the marriage bed distracts them from all that awful food. So much garlic.' Then she frowned. 'But then again, they do say that garlic stirs up the passions and hardens the wood.' She clapped her hands. 'Perhaps we should get hold of some for Oswald. He could eat it daily before he marries?'

I stood up. 'Will you both be quiet! Mistress Cooper is not with child. But I'm quite sure I'll be up to the job once we're married.' Mother went to speak, but I interrupted her. 'Even without the assistance of garlic.'

'So the sap is rising then Oswald?' said Mother with the most vulgar and horrible grin. Wet bread was stuck between her teeth like the daub in a wall. 'Is that what the hurry's all about? Can't wait to get her into bed?' Mother winked at me. 'Mind you, Eloise Cooper is a handsome woman. I'll give you that.'

Clemence harrumphed. 'If you like that type of thing.'

'Shouldn't you be feeding your child?' I said, turning to my sister. 'I'm sure his screaming will begin soon.'

She crossed her arms. 'You're not worried that people say Eloise Cooper is a witch?'

Hector barked at this word, as if he had been trained to respond. Mother hushed him with a last crust.

'I'm not worried at all,' I told Clemence. 'For a start I don't believe in witches.' Hector repeated his bark, and was only silenced this time by a smack on his nose. 'And secondly, Eloise has told me the true story that spawned such a stupid tale about witchcraft. She simply nursed her poor dying daughter.'

'But didn't die herself?'

'She had suffered the cow pox as a child.'

'And?'

'It can protect a person against the pox.' I coughed. 'Everybody knows that.'

'And so can witchcraft,' said Mother, now holding Hector's mouth closed, so he couldn't bark. 'I've heard that some of them douse their breasts in bull's blood to prevent infection. Either that, or they eat the brains of a goat.'

What was the point in talking to these women? I quickly took my leave of them both, but as I descended the stone steps, Clemence caught up with me and took me by the arm. 'Wait a moment, Oswald,' she said.

I stopped. 'Why? Are there some insults you've forgotten to throw?'

Her voice had lost its harsh and carping edge, and she spoke to me in the soft tones she sometimes used with baby Henry. 'I'm just concerned about you, Oswald. Are you sure about marrying this woman? I don't like her.'

'That's because she's a de Caburn. And you're judging her by the standards of her brother.'

She shook her head, refusing to be riled by my comment. 'No. It's more than that. The woman is . . .'

'What?'

Her face hardened again. 'Just beware of her. That's all I'm saying.'

I turned away. 'There's no need.'

That evening I watched the swallows return to the stables where they nested each year in the wooden eaves. As they soared and swooped over the gardens, their pink underbellies caught the setting sun and their clicking calls cut through the air. And then, as I watched them catching the moths and flies of dusk, I caught sight of Eloise and her two nieces, their outlines hazy in the evening light. They were dancing in a circle, spinning around and around in a game that was both wild and unyielding, almost fierce in its speed. I would tell you I felt pleased to see Mary and Rebecca so happy, since they had seemed subdued since their return to Somershill, but there was an edge and an energy to their dancing that made me feel uncomfortable.

I wondered if I should join them, but knew I would not be welcome.

Instead I went to my chamber and rested. For the next day we were to make our final search of the estate. We hoped, at last, to find John Barrow.

Chapter Twenty-One

I awoke to the sound of a cold, penetrating scream that caused me to jump from my bed and throw Eloise from my arms.

She sat up, flustered and sweating, her chemise tangled about her body. 'What's happening?'

'I don't know,' I said, walking to the door and opening it to look out into the darkness of the short passage. 'But you need to get back to the solar, before they find you here.' Eloise had sneaked into my bedchamber the night before, and though I had vowed not to touch her again until our wedding, the feel of her skin and the sweetness of her lips had been too difficult to resist. There was, however, no point in hiding, as we were quickly discovered. Clemence burst into the room. Her hair was wild; the white linen of her gown was gaping. 'He's gone,' she screamed.

'Who?'

'Henry.'

She didn't even look at Eloise. Instead she ran about the room, throwing my clothes from the chair and looking under the bed. 'Is he here? Have you got him?' she screamed at me. Then she took me by the shoulders and shook me. 'Where is he?'

Eloise pulled the sheets tightly about her face.

A sickening dread gripped my stomach. 'Are you sure he's gone, Clemence?'

'Yes!' she screamed at me. 'He's been taken from his crib.'

'But what about Humbert? He always guards the boy.'

She snarled, as viciously as a rabid dog. 'The fool fell asleep. And then your ward took Henry. The viper that you invited into our home.'

I shook my head. 'No, no. It can't be John Barrow. We've searched the whole estate.'

She gripped me. 'Who was it then?' She beat her desperate hands into my chest. 'Who flew in and took him? The butcher bird?'

We ran through the estate. Every man and boy from the village. We had torches and dogs, and we scoured every cottage, barn and byre. We searched the church, the wells, the common pastures and the closes. We listened for the call of an infant or the cry of a deranged man. But we heard nothing, save the prayers of the women who still had their own babies alive, and had hidden their children away in case the murderer returned.

By evening we had found nothing, apart from a starving boy hiding out in a charcoal burner's hut, deep in the forest near Versey. Featherby dragged him to me for questioning, and as his filthy body unfurled, I saw it was Geoffrey. We had not seen each other since we parted in London.

He snivelled and shook. 'I'm so sorry, sire. I shouldn't have left the horses.'

'Why did you then?'

'I wanted to pray at Saint Paul's.' He wiped the dripping mucus from his nose. 'And I wanted to hear the lions roar at the tower.'

His face was drawn and pained, and I could hardly recognise him as the same boy. 'What happened to you, Geoffrey?'

He started to cry again. 'I fell in with some men, sire.'

'What men?'

'They said they would show me the city.' I groaned at his naivety, knowing full well how this story would end. 'They were kind to begin with,' he said. 'They took me to a tavern. And . . .'

'And then what?'

'They weren't Christian, sire,' he whispered. 'I had to escape.'

I will admit to sighing. Loudly. This was trouble heaped upon trouble. 'What were you doing in the forest Geoffrey? Why didn't you come straight back to Somershill?'

He covered his face with dirty fingers, and then began to cry. 'I thought you would be angry with me, sire.'

I placed my hand upon his trembling shoulder, feeling the bones beneath his ragged tunic. He looked no better than a beggar or an apprentice cutpurse. I sent him off to Versey and told him to stop at the kitchen to ask for some bread and frumenty. Before Geoffrey disappeared, however, I called him back. 'Have you seen anybody else in the forest?'

'Only John Barrow, sire.'

I looked to Featherby. 'John Barrow! Why didn't you tell us this before?' But then I realised that Geoffrey would have no idea about the terrible events of recent days. 'When did you see him?' I asked.

Geoffrey resumed his trembling. 'It was at dawn this morning, sire.'

'Did you speak to him?'

'No.' He suppressed a sob. 'I was hiding.'

Featherby grasped the boy and shook him like a branch full of ripe apples. 'You'd better be telling the truth, boy.'

Geoffrey broke down in tears again, which only prompted Featherby to shake the boy with yet more ferocity.

'Let him go, Featherby,' I said.

'He's not telling us everything, sire.'

'Stop it!'

Featherby dropped the boy, but pulled a face to show exactly what he thought of my judgement.

I then led Geoffrey away from the other men and leant down to speak into his ear. 'Was John Barrow carrying anything?' Geoffrey looked blank. 'An infant,' I said. 'Did he have a small baby with him?'

'No, sire. There was nobody with him.' I looked to the sky and breathed a sigh of relief, but this release was short-lived. 'He only held a large sack. It was slung over his shoulder like a sheaf of wheat.'

'Could this sack have contained a child?'

'Er . . . er . . .' Geoffrey appeared to find the question confusing. He reddened and said nothing.

'Think!'

'It's possible, sire.'

I groaned in frustration. 'Where were you, when you saw him?'

'In the glade by the charcoal kilns.'

'Which direction was he heading in?'

'Towards Burrsfield.'

We had already searched this area, but after this sighting of Barrow we would look again, so I collected together a group of men and we rode there without delay.

'Can the boy be trusted, sire?' Featherby asked, when we had slowed our speed to a trot. He had sidled up beside me, as I was bashing through the undergrowth with a long stick. The sweet chestnut and hazel was dense in this remote part of the forest and could be hiding any number of fugitives.

'Why would Geoffrey lie?' I said, without extending Featherby the courtesy of turning to face him. I'd noticed some of the bluebells were trodden down in the glade to my right. Their violet heads were turning brown, and their polished leaves were flattened in a path that led towards the deepest part of this hollow.

'Send some men to look down there,' I said.

Featherby did as I asked, but soon he was back at my side. 'Just seems very odd, don't you think?'

'What does?'

'That Geoffrey runs off from you in London, and then he turns up in this forest. Just as we're searching for baby Henry.'

Now I stopped my horse and turned to him. 'Are you suggesting that Geoffrey has something to do with this crime?'

Featherby didn't yield. Instead he drew his horse closer to mine, so that our legs touched. If it were possible to loom over a fellow rider, then this man was succeeding. 'I just find his story suspicious.'

'He's a boy, Featherby.'

'Children are capable of evil, sire.'

I looked at him and kicked my horse. 'Let's just proceed with the search, shall we?' Tempest shied and we carried on.

There were more than eighty men with me – every man and boy from Somershill. At Burrsfield I recruited yet more men to join our party. But we had over a thousand acres to search, and other than Geoffrey's sighting of Barrow, there were no other clues to guide us. We split into smaller and smaller groups, working our way through the hunting forests until I found myself completely on my own. The light was fading quickly and the forest was pulling on its cloak, ready to enter into its second world – a domain that no lord, other than darkness, could rule. I had not heard the calls of my fellow trackers for some time. An owl hooted nearby, and a large bat flitted about Tempest's head causing him to shy. My mount was also tired and irritable, but I couldn't turn for home. Henry was out here somewhere. And I had to find him. Even if he were dead.

I dismounted and tied Tempest to a tree, deciding to find somewhere to take an hour's rest. Settling upon a spot beneath a smooth-barked beech, I soon found the dry leaves disguised the damp mud beneath. I moved to another spot, but found the same again, and then realised that everywhere in this particular dell was likely to be wet and cold.

I moved about for a while until I found a small patch of moss to lie upon, but as I looked upwards into the canopy of leaves, I heard a rustling from somewhere ahead of me in the darkness.

Tempest snorted and pawed at the ground. He also sensed a presence nearby.

'Who's there?' I said, getting to my feet and cautiously taking my knife from its sheath. My breath was steaming in the cool air, and the large bat once again flitted about our heads. Something was watching me from the shadows, but it was not a fox, nor even a wolf. I could be sure of that. It was a man – his fleeting shape briefly appearing and then disappearing between the branches of the undergrowth.

'Show yourself,' I said, trying to steady my faltering voice.

Tempest reared and broke loose from his tether as I readied myself for the fight. The shadow advanced – and then, as he came closer I knew him immediately. I went to call out his name, but it was too late. A hard and heavy object hit my head, and the world receded to utter blackness.

Chapter Twenty-Two

I woke in a room that was familiar, though I had not been past its doors since the previous summer, when Walter de Caburn's dirty servant John Slow had opened its horrors to me with an iron key. It was the small chamber in the south tower at Versey Castle. The room de Caburn liked to use for winter sport.

My arms and legs were tied, and I was lying on the floor. My clothes had been removed, apart from my braies. A cold air whipped against my legs and chest, but this was the least of my troubles, for my head ached acutely at the temple, where the weapon, most probably a rock, had been smashed against my skull. As my eyes became accustomed to the dim light of a candle, I realised there were other people in the room.

I wanted to shout out, but instead vomited down the front of my chest, heaving until there was nothing to spit out but green bile. Then I squirmed desperately to escape, but the ropes about my arms and legs were tied too tightly. During this episode, my captors kept to the shadows of the room, only creeping out when my energy left me. It was Humbert who came forward first, followed by my sister.

The bitter taste of vomit still stung at the back of my throat. 'What are you doing, Clemence?' Then I began to cough and couldn't stop.

She ignored my question and bade Humbert bring me a cup of

water. The stupid boy held the cup to my lips and then tipped it so quickly into my throat as to cause another spasm of coughing.

Clemence swept the cup away and leant into my face. 'What have you done with my child, little brother?'

'I don't know what you mean, Clemence. Let me go.'

'You and that whore have taken him, haven't you?'

'What?'

She laughed scornfully; her face was knotted with anger. 'Don't lie to me. I know what you're doing. I have her as well.'

'Eloise? Where is she?'

'In the dungeon. Where she belongs.'

I tried to slow my breathing. 'Listen to me, Clemence. Eloise and I have nothing to do with Henry's disappearance.'

'But everything to gain from it.'

'What are you talking about?'

'Your wife wants Versey for her own children.' I went to answer this, but she pressed her foot against my face. 'I know she carries a child, little brother. Don't insult me with your lies.'

'How do you know?'

'Because she told me.'

I squirmed again. 'Did you hurt her?' I shouted now. 'Tell me you didn't hurt her.'

Clemence stepped back a little. 'I didn't have to. She confessed immediately. In fact, I would say she even boasted about her child.'

I coughed again. My mouth was dry and tasted metallic. No longer of bile, but now of blood. 'Eloise doesn't know about my promise to you, Clemence. She would have no reason to harm Henry. She thinks our children will inherit Versey.' I paused. 'Unless you told her otherwise?'

Now Clemence leant into my face. Her breath was hot. 'I know what's going on, little brother. Don't think me foolish. It's *you* that wants Versey for your sons.'

'For the love of Christ, Clemence,' I said, now struggling

against my bindings. 'I didn't even want Somershill. Remember? I offered to go back to the monastery.'

She grasped what she could of my face in her small hand. 'Where is he? What have you done with Henry?' Now she rasped, 'If you've killed him, then you will die very slowly.'

My throat was dry and bleeding. 'I haven't touched your baby. I would never do such a thing.'

Clemence released her grip. 'I don't believe you.' She then beckoned for Humbert to come forward. 'The Judas chair first, I think,' she said, pointing to the large chair adorned with polished spikes.

'No, please Clemence,' I begged. 'You're wrong.'

'Let's see, shall we? I'm told most people will speak when the spikes cut.'

I trembled. 'You wouldn't torture me, Clemence. You're not so cruel.'

She laughed. Pointing at the knee splitter that sat in the corner, rusting and repugnant. 'Don't underestimate me. I might use that, as well.'

'You know I would never harm Henry.'

'Do I?'

'Of course you do, Clemence.'

She shrugged. 'What do I know about you, Oswald? Or should I call you Thomas Starvecrow, because that's your true name, isn't it? The son of a poor village girl and a drunken priest. A thieving cuckoo.' She leant into my face. 'A wolf that walks with the lambs of this family. He has not a spoonful of de Lacy blood in his body. So why should I trust anything that he has to say?'

'Please let me go, Clemence. Please.'

She had no sympathy. 'Then tell me where Henry is.'

I began to feel light-headed again. The knock against my skull had been so forceful that I was losing consciousness again. 'I don't know.'

'You do know. But if you won't tell me, then your whore will.

She's next in here. Though I hoped you might admit to your sins and spare her.'

'Don't touch her.' My eyesight clouded over. 'You leave her alone.'

Then the blackness washed through me again – the room diminished from a coloured and shifting fantasy to an empty void, as I slipped away into darkness.

Unconsciousness is a catalepsy unlike sleep. It does not water and feed a resting mind with dreams and notions, instead it is a noth- ingness that robs a person of time and perspective. As if you have been dead and then resurrected.

In reviving, I found myself upon the cold, stone floor of a chamber that was completely devoid of light. At first the still and velvety black terrified me, and I wondered if I were indeed dead, or whether this was some type of purgatory? An eternity of oblivion, with nobody but myself for company. My first thought was desperation – but then, as my senses came back to life, I realised that I still lived and that this was the dungeon at Versey. I recognised the dank and muddy smell of the place.

My head and jaws ached, but, touching them cautiously, I found that nothing was broken, though my scalp felt slimy and hot. I tasted my fingertips and found them to be covered in the metallic and salty mixture of blood and sweat.

Slowly my eyes adjusted to the light, and I was able to make out the rutted stone of the walls and the iron bands across the door. A thin strip of light made its way into the room from beneath this entrance, but it was grey and weak and gave only the slightest illumination to the chamber. Slumped against the damp wall I began to cry. There was nobody here to see me, so I did not bother to hide my tears.

Then I heard a noise in the darkest corner of the room. It was neither a scratching nor a rustle, so it couldn't be the rats that often ran about this place. A shape moved slowly in the shadows.

'Is somebody there?' I said. 'Is that you Eloise?'

My answer was merely a heavy breath and the whisper of cloth against cloth. But this was not Eloise. That much I could tell.

I edged further into my own corner. 'Who is it?' I said. Still my companion kept to the shadows, dark and silent.

'Stay where you are then,' I said. 'I don't care.' And I didn't care. My head ached as badly as it had ever done in my whole life, and I had neither the energy nor inclination to play guessing games with the fellow occupant of this cell. I fell back against the wall and clutched my poor, throbbing head.

The breathing came again. Then a small voice. 'It's me, Oswald.'

I groaned. 'No. It can't be.' Was this an illusion? An evil fantasy invented by my aching brain? But no, the words were real enough – for then a face appeared in the gloom, though it did not match the voice I knew so well. It was disfigured and scarred, with a complexion so pink and stretched it might have been a skinned rabbit. Eyelids pulled tautly over two slits, and swollen lips that surrounded a lopsided mouth.

'I thought you were dead,' I said.

The face tried to smile at me, though its skin would not oblige. 'No Oswald. I live.' He shuffled forward and took my hands in his own. Hands that were still human. 'Clemence tried to kill me a second time. But I still live.'

I pulled away. 'What are you doing here, Brother?'

Peter cocked his head to look at me through the strange holes in his face. 'Aren't you pleased to see me, Oswald?'

I didn't answer.

'Does my appearance revolt you?'

'No,' I lied.

'This is Clemence's doing.' He held up his hands to his face and cupped it in a fan of fingers. 'She threw boiling water upon my face. Don't you remember?'

'She only acted in defence.'

'I wouldn't have hurt you, Oswald.' He attempted to frown. 'You're my son.'

'Don't say that.'

'But it's true.'

'You merely provided the seed to give me life.'

His face relaxed a little. 'Ever the pedant, Oswald.' Then he tried to laugh, though his lips struggled to accommodate the movement, and he had to keep licking their distorted edges to stop the pale skin from cracking. 'I'm glad to see you've not changed.'

'Why are you here?' I said.

'The priest betrayed me to Clemence.' He coughed. It was a hoarse and rasping sound. 'Feeble little Judas.'

'Father Luke?'

He nodded. 'I've been staying with him. He's kept me hidden in his tithe barn.'

'Why?'

'I wanted to watch over you.'

'I meant *why* did the priest let you stay in his barn?'

He coughed again and now cleared his throat. 'He didn't mind.'

'I don't believe you.' I shifted further into the corner. 'Why would he risk doing that for you? Was it intimidation? Or bribery perhaps?'

Peter sighed. 'Father Luke is a sodomite. I discovered him and his young friend in the crypt at Rochester. Not a story he would like told about the parish.'

'So you threatened him.' And now I did laugh, despite the shooting pain in my temple. 'You haven't changed, have you? Still steeped in evil.'

Peter shuffled forward and grasped my arm. 'Keep your voice down, Oswald. They might be listening to us.' He pointed to the door, but the line of light remained perfectly still, giving no indication that a person was lurking on the other side. Now he whispered, 'They've put us in the same cell, so they might hear what we say. To implicate us in the disappearance of the child.'

'I have nothing to hide Brother Peter.' I hesitated and looked to his melted face. 'Do you?' But the ridged skin and the taut redness of his countenance gave nothing away.

I went to say more, but a pain shot through my head, causing me to gasp.

'Did Clemence torture you?' Peter asked.

'No. But her servant hit me.' I pointed to my temple. 'Here.'

'Let me help you, Oswald.'

I backed against the wall once again. 'Keep away from me.'

He felt about his tunic.

'Do you have some Madeira in there, Peter?' I said bitterly. 'Or brandy? You always have something about your person to drink, don't you?'

Peter looked up at me, now with a small flask in his hand. 'I rarely drink these days.'

I laughed. 'I doubt that.'

He held the flask to my face. 'Drink it. The spirit will soothe your pain.' I turned away and refused, which only caused him to thrust the flask at me with more insistence. 'Go on Oswald. Drink it all. I don't need it any more.'

I pushed the flask away. 'Another lie, Brother?'

'It's the truth.'

'You want me to believe that you no longer drink? It was the only thing that kept you alive.'

Now Peter grasped my arm again and tried to take my hand. 'No, Oswald. It was not the wine that kept me alive. It was you. My son.'

I would not listen to such declarations, so I pushed him roughly away. He rolled into a ball and then wept so freely that I suddenly felt guilty for my rudeness and hostility.

'What do you want from me, Peter?' I said.

He mumbled something into the cowl of his habit.

'Speak up. I can't hear you.'

He looked up at me, and somewhere behind this scarred mask I saw the Brother Peter of old, his face kind and wise. 'I only want forgiveness, Oswald.' A tear formed in the deep slit to one side of his nose. An eye looked out at me, red and familiar.

I reached out and took his flask of brandy. It was weakness, but as the warm fluid slipped down my bruised throat, I felt grateful for Peter's presence in the cell. 'Where have you been for all these months?' I asked him, when the spirit had taken its effect. 'I thought you were dead.'

'I hid myself away in a remote cottage for many weeks. There are many such abandoned homes since the Plague. It was not difficult to find.'

'What did you eat?'

He smiled, turning a corner of his mouth upward with some difficulty. 'Oh Oswald. Not all of us were born with supper on the table. I learnt to hunt and scavenge as a child. It's a skill I've never lost.'

I was irritated by this gibe. 'Don't scorn me, Brother. You put me in this position, so don't criticise me for growing up as a nobleman.'

He nodded. 'Very well, Oswald. Please accept my apology.'

I paused a moment. 'I went to Thomas Starvecrow's grave and dug up his coffin.'

'I know you did,' said Peter. Then he chuckled, as if any of this was funny. 'Clemence told me. When she was tightening the screw.' He cast a glance at me. 'Oh yes. She might not have tortured you, but she tortured me.'

I ignored this. Was it true? Was it a lie? Who could tell any more? 'Why was the coffin empty, Brother?' I said. 'You told me the infant had died. But I found nothing inside. Nothing but a wooden effigy.'

Peter sighed. 'You should have left the coffin alone, Oswald. Sometimes it is better not to know these things.'

'Not for me.'

He smiled. 'No. You're a good boy. A truth seeker.'

'So tell me the truth then.'

He ran his fingers through his hair. 'Your true mother believed the infant was dead. He would not be roused, not even for nursing. I took his body to the church to bury him, but then the child revived. At first I thought it was the death rattle, but his lungs filled again with air and he began to cry.'

'What did you do with him?' A lump began to form in my throat.

Peter puffed out his lips. 'I'd met a travelling knife grinder and his wife. Their boy had recently died, so they took him. And called him after their own dead baby.'

'Why didn't you just take him back to the cottage? Where my mother could have nursed him?'

He stumbled over his words. 'I don't know.' He hesitated. 'I can't explain it.' Then he picked at the mole on his neck. A short tag of skin that he had always twisted when he was nervous. It was one small part of his face and neck that had not been scarred by Clemence's boiling water. 'I should have taken the boy back. You're right.'

'Yes. You should have.'

He stared at the dark floor and sighed. 'But then——' He stopped, and would not finish the sentence.

'But then I would not have become Lord Somershill. Is that what you were going to say?'

'No.'

This was a half-hearted rebuttal. 'If you had returned the boy, then I would not have become Oswald de Lacy. The position you so desperately wanted for me.'

Peter opened his mouth to answer this accusation. I knew what he planned to say. That I should be grateful for this act. That I should be happy to be known as Oswald de Lacy when my true name was Thomas Starvecrow. That I should be thankful for his intervention in my fate. But he knew what my reaction would be, so he wisely kept his mouth shut.

'What name did the knife grinder give to the boy?' I said.

Peter shrugged. 'I can't remember. It was so long ago.'

'Did you ever see the boy again? Or enquire after his well-being?'

'No. The family were travellers. Our paths never crossed.'

I raised my eyebrows. 'How convenient.'

Peter dropped his shoulders and sighed. 'I asked for forgiveness, Oswald. Not sarcasm.' Then he pulled the hair back from his face, revealing an ear that was as bulbous as a lobe of bracket fungus. 'I can't reverse what happened. But you must believe me when I say I'm sorry.'

'Are you?'

He looked at me with such solemnity. 'Yes, Oswald,' he said. 'I am. Truly.'

I can tell you this much. At that moment I did forgive Peter. For all his lies and deceit, I wanted to believe him. I had missed his company and his guidance. I had been lonely without him. For that moment I thought our story was done. That his repentance gave me reason to accept this confession and pardon his sins. That we were reconciled. Father and son. Son and father.

But our story was not a completed circle. Instead it was as unfinished as a wheel with no felloes or metal bandings. It was deficient, broken and could never be mended.

The pain from my temple now seared into the side of my face, stabbing and cruel. I held my jaw and groaned, and before I could think better of my actions, I laid my head onto Peter's lap and let him stroke the sweating hair on my head.

'Were you struck with a rock?' he asked me as his fingers lightly touched the dents in my forehead.

'Yes,' I groaned turning my head to look up at his face. His nostrils misshapen and stretched unnaturally against the skin of his cheeks. 'Clemence has lost her child, Peter. And she thinks I'm responsible.'

He shook his head gently. 'Clemence lacks the courage and conviction to harm you any further. I'm sure of it.'

I shrugged his hand from my head. 'She's stronger than you think. And desperate to find Henry. She'll do anything.' I allowed Peter's finger to return to my scalp. 'I can't blame her,' I sighed, as his hands lulled me towards a welcome peace. 'Henry is her only child. You should understand that more than anybody.'

Peter's voice was low and melodic, as soothing as a nursemaid trying to settle a fractious baby. 'Don't worry about her child, Oswald.'

I closed my eyes. 'But I do, Peter. I want to find him.'

'Shh. It's not your concern. Try to sleep.'

The pain continued to radiate about my jaw, but its peaks were weakening. 'What if Henry is dead? Taken by a lunatic. The man I had sheltered.'

Peter placed his hand on my cheek. 'Henry de Caburn is nothing to you, dear Oswald. Though it's typical of your kindness that you should care about him.'

'He's my nephew, Peter. Of course I care.'

I turned my head again, but he pushed me gently back to his lap. 'Close your eyes. Rest.' He stroked my hair so rhythmically that I did very nearly fall into a deep slumber, and perhaps he thought I was already sleeping, for then he whispered softly, 'Don't concern yourself with Henry de Caburn. Think about the future of your own child instead. The child already conceived and growing in the womb of Mistress Cooper.'

I opened my eyes sharply. 'What did you say?'

Peter blustered some words that caused me to sit up.

'How did you know that Eloise was with child?' I said. 'It's a secret.'

Once again he tried to say something, but the words made no sense.

'Do you know Eloise Cooper?' I said.

He pulled at the mole on his neck. 'No, no. I don't.'

I tried to scrutinise his face, but he had turned away into the shadows. 'What made you mention a child?'

'I don't know.' Then he stuttered. 'I must have guessed.'

'I don't believe you.'

He smoothed his habit and now looked straight at me, his face as snake-like as an adder's. 'It's no secret that you're to marry.'

'No.'

'So it's obvious, isn't it?'

'Not to me.'

'I merely guessed about the baby.'

When I went to protest, he held up his hand to my face. 'It's not unknown for a man to bed his wife before the wedding day, Oswald.' Then he tried to force a laugh. 'Goodness me. Many brides are with child as they make their vows. I should know. I've performed enough ceremonies.' Then he laughed again, though it was an ugly, grating sound. 'Some brides are so heavy they might even give birth in the church porch.'

I studied his face a while. It is difficult to judge emotion in a stretch of mutated and distorted skin, but behind this mask, his eyes were unable to hide their secrets from me. 'You're guilty, Peter. I know it.'

'What are you talking about?'

'Henry's abduction.'

'But I've been locked in here for more than a week, Oswald. How could I be involved in his disappearance?'

Suddenly my pain was forgotten and I ran over to the door of the cell and shouted for Clemence. My sister arrived so quickly that she must indeed have been in the passageway outside, trying to eavesdrop on our conversation, just as Brother Peter had warned. 'What is it, Oswald,' she said. 'Are you ready to confess?'

I rattled the door. 'Let me out, Clemence. Please. I know how to find Henry.'

A key turned in the lock, and Humbert's solemn face peered through the narrow gap – his hand firmly upon the door in case I should try to push past.

I didn't see Clemence, but only heard her voice. Thin and desperate. 'Where is he, little brother? Tell me, or I shall lock you in the head crusher and screw down the cap until your skull breaks.'

'I need to see Eloise.'

The door opened a little further and now the light of a candle crept into the cell and illuminated a pathway across the filthy floor to the back wall. Clemence's face peered around the door and grimaced. 'Why do you need to see her?'

'She knows where the child is.'

'I'm not falling for your little trick to escape.' The door shut again, but I managed to put my foot into its path and stop it from closing completely. 'Please, Clemence. Just listen to me. We don't have long.'

The pressure on the door relaxed and I was able to push it open far enough to look into my sister's eyes. She had been crying. 'Why should I trust you?' she said.

I pushed my arm past Humbert's chest and grabbed a handful of Clemence's gown. 'Just take me to Eloise,' I said, pulling at the cloth. 'There isn't time to argue.'

Still she just looked at me.

'I'm begging you Clemence.'

The door opened and I was led away.

I did not turn to look back at Brother Peter, though he called my name.

Chapter Twenty-Three

Eloise was imprisoned in a cell that was every bit as dank as my own, located at the end of another tunnel beneath Versey. I had rarely ventured down into this maze, being less taken with dungeons than the previous Lord Versey, Walter de Caburn – a man who had spent nearly as much time down in these fetid chambers as he did above ground, particularly in the winter, when it was too wet to hunt. A normal nobleman might spend the colder months attending to his custumnals and ledgers. He might use his spare time for reading a rare manuscript or the learning of Syriac. If he were really bored, he might even sharpen his sword or whittle out some useless thing from a piece of wood. But it takes a particular type of individual to list torture and dungeons amongst their favoured diversions. I shuddered as we passed along the damp tunnel, imagining what horrors these walls had absorbed, digested, and then expelled as their green and spongy slime.

Before the door to Eloise's cell was opened, I whispered to Clemence, 'You must leave me alone with her.'

Clemence stiffened. 'Why?'

'She might not reveal the truth if you're in the room.'

Clemence exchanged a look with Humbert. Maybe she could read the strange impassive expression upon his lumpen face, for I could not. She turned to me. 'Very well, Oswald. You have a

short time alone.' Then she pinched my cheek. Hard. In just the
way she had done when we were children. 'Don't try any tricks.
I'll be waiting outside.'

I found Eloise in the corner of the cell with her back against the
wall. Clemence had given me a candle so I might look upon
Eloise's face, but thus far it had only illuminated the foul conditions of the windowless chamber. Filthy straw lay across the stone
floor, strewn with rat droppings and small bones. The place smelt
as putrid as the River Fleet.

Eloise greeted me with relief. 'Oswald. Thank God. Are we to
be freed?' She put out her hand so I might help her to her feet,
but I didn't move. Instead I held the candle to her face. Even in
this dark cell the woman was handsome. The flame reflected in
her green eyes and picked out the Cupid's bow of her top lip.

'Tell me what you've done with Henry,' I said. 'Then you may
leave.'

Now her face lost its beauty. 'What?'

'Just tell me, Eloise. I know you're in league with Brother
Peter.'

Her eye twitched. 'I don't know what you mean?'

'It was Peter who led the girls to London, wasn't it? Who else
could have carried that enormous eagle?'

She turned her head away from me. 'They ran away from your
cruel sister.' Then she held her hands about her body. 'And now
we see what the bitch is capable of.'

'He led the girls to London, so that I would follow. I felt his
eyes on my back as soon as I crossed London Bridge. He was even
the leper in the alley, wasn't he? Saving us from cutpurses.'

'I don't know what you're talking about.'

'Was it also Peter's idea that you seduce me?'

She gave a small laugh. 'You think so much of yourself.'

I dismissed this gibe. 'You thought our child would inherit
Versey, didn't you?'

She looked back at me and put her hands to her belly. 'Our child should inherit Versey. It's his birthright.'

'But then you discovered that I'd promised Versey to baby Henry.'

Her eye twitched again. 'No.' She was surprisingly poor at lying. 'I knew nothing of that. Not until your odious sister informed me, as she threw me into this cell.' Then she huffed, 'Though it sounds like a foolish promise to me.'

'No. I think you knew before. Mary or Rebecca told you,' I said, thinking back to Mother's ghost in the stairwell. 'They were eavesdropping.'

Eloise looked back to the shadows, so I knew I was right. 'Tell me where Henry is,' I said, 'and then you may get out of here.'

'I don't know where he is,' she spat. 'How dare you accuse me of such a crime? I was in your bed the whole of the night that Henry was taken. How could I have abducted a baby?'

'You and Peter had an accomplice.'

'We did not.'

'It's John Barrow, isn't it?'

Now her eye twitched a third time. 'John Barrow?' Then she clasped her hands together in a show of astonishment. 'Oh yes. I remember. The madman you sheltered.' Now she laughed. 'But then he escaped.' She fixed me with a stare – cold and accusing. 'It is very cowardly to blame me for your own mistakes.'

I seized her small wrist and squeezed it. 'Just tell me where Barrow has taken the baby.'

She tried to wriggle free, but I tightened my grip. 'Leave me alone,' she hissed.

'Tell me where they are.'

'No!' She struggled again. 'I mean, I don't know.'

I dropped her hand and ran to the door of the cell, calling for Clemence. The door was swung open immediately and Clemence faced me with her arms folded. 'Well,' she said. 'Has she told you?'

'No.'

Clemence's face dropped.

'But she's confirmed my suspicions.'

'What use is that?'

I took a deep breath, for this was a gamble. And I am not a person who often plays the fates. 'Give me one hour, Clemence. That's all I ask.' I made sure Eloise could hear every word.

Clemence's arms remained folded. 'And then what?'

'If I've not discovered Henry by that time, you may do what you please with Eloise.'

My eyes met Clemence's. I could see both panic and indecision. The moment seemed to drag. 'Even though she carries your child?'

I attempted the coldest of shrugs. I think it was convincing.

'Very well, little brother,' she said, after a long pause. 'You have one hour.' Then Clemence took my arm. 'But remember this. You'd better find him. Because this whore will receive no mercy from me.'

I shook my sister away. 'You may torture her to death. For all I care.'

At these words Eloise scrambled to her feet. 'Oswald. What are you doing?'

I didn't turn to look at her, for she might have seen the fear in my face.

'Please, Oswald,' she begged. 'I don't know anything.'

I stepped out of the cell, let the door close behind me, and then walked the length of the tunnel. I moved with the tremulous steps of a man into a dark cave, holding his breath with the fear of meeting a wolf, or of falling into a hidden hole. I thought my gamble had failed, but finally, as I reached the steps at the other end of the tunnel, my ploy paid off.

In the distance Eloise screamed my name. 'Oswald!'

I stopped, but didn't answer.

'Oswald!' she screeched again.

'What is it?' I shouted back along the tunnel. My words echoed from the walls.

'Go to the watermill. By the River Guise.'

Clemence let me take my own horse, though she insisted that Humbert join me.

'I had nothing to do with Henry's disappearance,' I told her as she watched me saddle Tempest. 'Now do you believe me?'

She wouldn't meet my gaze. 'Just bring back my child, Oswald.'

'I just hope he's still there.'

'What do you mean?'

'Their accomplice may have moved Henry, Clemence.' I didn't like to introduce the possibility that Henry might already be dead. Though I think my sister understood this prospect as well as I.

'Their accomplice?' she said, pulling at her ear.

'They couldn't have abducted Henry themselves. You had Brother Peter in chains at the time of Henry's disappearance. And Eloise was with me all that night.'

She pulled a face. 'Who is it, then?'

I took a deep breath and then cleared my throat. 'I believe it's John Barrow.'

She sighed. 'You've been such a fool, Oswald. Such a fool.'

I kicked my spurs into Tempest's flanks, moving away across the field before Clemence had a chance to ask me any more questions. Humbert followed astride a horse big enough to pull a felled tree from the forest, its hooves digging up the soil like the coulter blade of a plough.

As we crossed the field, Clemence shouted after us. 'Be quick. Find my child.'

We rode through the wet fields of the Versey estate. This upland terrain was of little use for farming, other than as pasture for cattle and sheep – but before the Plague the villagers had stead-fastly attempted to grow their barley and wheat upon its clay soils. And where a villager grows a cereal crop, a lord must build a mill – or face the prospect of his subjects grinding flour with their own quern stones and therefore not paying their banalities.

The mill on the Guise was abandoned, now that the Versey estate was dedicated almost exclusively to livestock. Any rye, wheat or barley grown in these fields was ground at the mill in Somershill, leaving this old watermill to stand on its lonely bank, with its decaying paddles doing nothing more than picking up the detritus of the river and spinning it over and over in the water.

We approached the river through the woodland, with the heady scent of the first elderflower in the air. When we could see the mill in the distance, we tied our horses to a tree and then made our way slowly towards the building, making sure to creep forward in the undergrowth, not wishing to alert a soul to our presence.

As we stepped through the cow parsley, our attention shifted from the mill towards a small clearing, where a clamour of rooks was pecking at something in the grass. Now Humbert gave a small gasp, for we could see that the birds were squabbling over carrion – squawking and flapping their wings as they fought over a lump of bloodied flesh.

I tried to hold Humbert back, so I might reach this ugly sight first, but the boy had the strength of Heracles, running towards the birds and scattering them into the air. When I caught up with him, I looked down to see a corpse that was stinking and red. Its eyes had been hollowed out by the birds, and its ribcage was open to the air, strings of flesh still clinging miserably onto bone. The rooks skulked menacingly in nearby trees, squawking with indignation at this interruption to their feast. Their beady eyes regarded us cruelly. Their oily feathers caught the sun like polished wood. But it was not the corpse of a child they had been scavenging. Instead it was the remains of a spring lamb – small and rotted. Humbert muttered something that I took to be a prayer, as I put my head in my hands and heaved a heavy sigh of relief.

We headed back towards the watermill, and above the babble of the river and the churning of the old paddles, we heard something. We stopped and looked at each other with relief, even delight, for at last we were nearing our quarry – this was the faint cry of a baby. It was not the insistent and demanding screams that we usually associated with Henry however – instead it was the thin and helpless call of an infant who has nearly given up on life.

I whispered to Humbert. 'It must be him. He's still alive.'

Once again, my cumbersome companion set off at a pace, but this time I held him back successfully, though it was as difficult as stopping a flighty ox at the plough.

'What are you doing? Leave me alone,' he said, nearly causing me to drop his tunic in shock. The boy had spoken a whole sentence.

'We mustn't just run in there, Humbert.' He eyed me with suspicion. 'We need to see who is also in there with Henry first.'

'You said it was John Barrow.'

'Even more reason to choose our moment. The man's a lunatic. We don't want to alarm him, or he might hurt Henry.'

The logic of my argument appeared to roll about Humbert's face like a marble in a bowl, waiting for somewhere to stop, and I could only be thankful when he agreed to use caution, since I could not have held the enormous boy back a moment longer.

The mill on the Guise is sited in such a lonely place, with its back towards the forest and its face towards a river that moves quickly through this dreary place towards the lower reaches of its path, where its waters lap gently at the bulrushes of Kent until they are eventually pushed out to sea.

We crept through nettles and dock, but Humbert was no creeper and sneaker, and threatened to give us away with each step forward. With some difficulty I persuaded him to stay by the oak trees situated a few yards from the mill, arguing that he could watch my every move forward from this vantage point. When he still seemed unsure about this plan, I warned him that Clemence would not be forgiving if he scuppered our chance of saving Henry. It seemed that this caution, if nothing else, was enough to secure his cooperation.

There was a single window in the mill, next to a door that was shut fast. There was no glass in this window, nor even a wooden shutter – instead a length of ragged cloth hung behind its bars. I crept forward as stealthily as a hunting cat and reached the sill without making a single sound. I could now hear Henry crying again, and at first I wondered if the child had been left alone in this abandoned place? This hope was soon frustrated when I heard footsteps across the boards of the floor within the building.

Waiting until the sun passed behind a cloud, I peered very slowly around the edge of the window to look inside the mill. Lifting back a corner of the ragged cloth, I could see little through the gloom, other than the outline of a person in the corner of the chamber – a person who sat with their back to me, with a swaddled baby lying next to them on the floor. It was impossible to see their identity, for they wore a brown cloak with a raised hood. But, just as it had been quickly obvious that the rooks were not picking over the bones of baby Henry, I knew immediately that this was not John Barrow. It was a boy.

And then a memory tugged at me – from the morning I had left London. In the early mists I had seen Eloise and two hooded companions walking away from me along the Strand. The larger man was Brother Peter – of this I was now sure. But who was the third? It had been a small person. As small as a boy.

A mind will work at speed at times such as these – as if an elixir has been poured into the head, bestowing the fleeting powers to slot each piece of the puzzle together. My mind alighted from nowhere onto Geoffrey – and suddenly I knew the boy was the third person we hunted. His disappearance in London and then his reappearance near Versey was not a coincidence. He was the boy I had seen with Peter and Eloise in that milky-misted London morning. When we had discovered Geoffrey hiding out in the forest, he had even tried to point us towards Barrow. A heavy feeling sank its way down into my stomach, for Geoffrey was yet another person in whom I had put my confidence, for it only to be betrayed. Featherby had been right not to trust him.

What could have persuaded the boy to do this? The answer was simple enough. He had abducted the child for money.

I would tell you I crept into the mill and grabbed the boy before he had a chance to escape, but my actions were foolish and naïve. I simply called out Geoffrey's name. The boy was startled and quickly picked up the infant. He then climbed the wooden ladder inside the building to reach the upper storey of the mill.

I turned to Humbert, who still watched me from the trees, motioning for him to head around the other side of the mill, in case there were an alternative exit. Pushing at the closed door, I entered a chamber with a ceiling so low that I was forced to bend my head. The place smelt stale – of damp wood and mildewy grain. Looking up, there were large gaps in the planks of the ceiling. As the wood creaked, I could see Geoffrey's feet above me.

I climbed the ladder cautiously to see the hooded boy next to the bare window that overlooked the giant waterwheel. Baby Henry mewled in his arms. Opposite me, Humbert peered through a hole in the wall, where a great patch of wood had been pulled away and stolen. As we watched Geoffrey, the great wheel still churned through the river, mindlessly obeying the force of the water.

I spoke softly. 'Give the child back, Geoffrey.'

Humbert stepped through the gap in the wall. I climbed the final rung of the ladder. We were closing in.

Or so we thought.

Now the boy thrust Henry through the window, letting his

shawl drop and his pink legs dangle precariously over the great paddles of the wheel. The hood fell from Geoffrey's face. 'Come any closer and I'll drop him.'

But this was not Geoffrey Hayward. This was another child altogether.

I froze. 'Mary?'

She looked at me defiantly, though there was a beading of sweat across her forehead.

'What are you doing?' I said. 'Henry's your brother.'

Mary reddened. 'No he's not. I hate him.' She shook the baby and he squealed.

From the corner of my eye I could see that Humbert was preparing to leap forward. His hands were tightened into fists. Terrified that such a move would only cause Mary to drop the baby into the paddles of the wheel, I edged forward to look upon the girl's pale and pained face. 'Don't do this,' I said. My voice was soft. I did not want to alarm Mary, for the baby would not survive the long drop from the window onto the wheel. If the giant wooden paddles did not break his tiny back, then the icy water of the river would certainly end his short life.

She trembled, and her grip on the baby seemed to falter. 'Stay away from me.'

'This wasn't your idea, was it?'

'Go away!'

'It was Eloise's, wasn't it? And Brother Peter's. You don't really want to harm Henry, do you?'

'I'll drop him,' she screamed. 'He won't live.'

A whistle came from the corner of the room, and I turned my attention to the shadows, where I saw Becky crouching in the shadows. Next to her, on its rotten perch, sat the large, hooded bird that I had last seen in London.

'Becky,' I said, 'tell your sister to let Henry go.'

Becky only backed away further into the corner, as if she wanted the walls to consume her. Her face was stained with tears.

The bird gave another rasping whistle and began to dance from foot to foot.

I took a further step forward. 'Mary, please. Don't do this. You're a kind and merciful girl.' I pointed to the bird. 'You rescued Rab from your father, didn't you? Why would you want to harm a small and innocent child?'

A tear had formed in her eye. 'This boy has stolen everything from me and Becky.'

'You don't mean that, Mary. Those are somebody else's words.'

She dangled the baby further out into the cold air. He squirmed and kicked, as if he knew this was the end of his life. 'My father was Lord Versey too,' she said.

'Just give Henry back to me, Mary. This is not the way to solve your grievances.'

'Go away!'

'Your brother deserves to live.' I kept my eyes firmly upon hers. 'He's just a baby.'

Her face was now coated in tears.

'You can learn to love Henry,' I said, edging forward another step. 'I know you can. Despite what your Aunt Eloise says.'

'Keep away from me,' she said, but her voice was losing its bristle.

Another step. 'Just give Henry to me, and we can forget this ever happened.' I held out my hands.

'I hate him,' she said, though now she held the baby a little closer to her body.

'Please, Mary.'

'I can't.' Her bottom lip quivered and her eye twitched. 'I promised.'

'You don't need to keep such a promise.' Another step.

'Yes I do,' she blubbered.

'Let me take him.' I was so close now. Her eyes were locked into mine.

'I can't,' she whispered.

'Just let me have him. Nobody will be angry. We love you.'

Her face dissolved into tears. She thrust the baby at me, and then ran into the corner to seek solace with her sister – but Becky would not touch her.

After Henry had suckled at his mother's breast for more than an hour, he fell asleep, and Humbert was able to carry him away to his crib.

'Don't take your eyes from him,' said Clemence as Humbert left the room. This was a redundant piece of advice, since I don't believe Humbert would even have contemplated blinking.

Clemence readjusted her tunic, and then looked to me.

'You should have believed me,' I said.

She took a long slurp of ale to quench the raging thirst that was always kindled by feeding her son. 'Surely you understand why I suspected you?'

I gave a snort and shook my head. 'No, Clemence. I don't.'

She frowned. 'You had a lot to gain from the death of Henry,' she repeated, as if this were an accepted truth.

'Except that I'm your brother and I'm not a murderer.'

Her face reddened, and I would say she was embarrassed. Ashamed even. 'Yes, Oswald. You are my brother. Even if we don't share the same parents.' She looked to the floor. 'And I am truly sorry for doubting you.'

She held out her hand to me, but I would not take it. Instead I felt my temple, where Humbert's stone had cut my skin. 'You've inflicted a good wound.'

She tried to smile, but it was awkward. 'Women like a man with a battle-scarred face.'

'Would you have tortured me, Clemence?'

She looked to the floor again. 'My baby had disappeared. I was desperate.'

'So, that's a yes?'

'No,' she said firmly.

We watched the fire for a while, before I summoned the energy for our next discussion. 'You must be merciful to Mary,' I said. 'She's just a child herself.'

My sister shuddered. 'A child who abducted and then tried to murder my son.'

'She was indoctrinated, Clemence. By her own aunt, and a priest. She wouldn't have hurt Henry. I'm sure of it.'

Clemence pursed her lips. 'Don't ask me to forgive the girl, because I won't.'

I sighed. 'Couldn't you try? She is your stepdaughter.'

'No.'

She poured me some ale and served it to me. The act was symbolic, as she had never done so before. Then she sat next to me on the bench. 'So we have not one butcher bird, but two. Eloise Cooper and Brother Peter.'

I rubbed my hands through my hair and felt at the scabs on my scalp. 'I don't think they had anything to do with the murders of the other infants.'

'You still suspect John Barrow?'

I nodded.

She raised an eyebrow sceptically. 'Are you sure the earlier murders were not part of their plan? Make us believe a madman is hunting for newborn babies, so that they could disguise their own crime against Henry?'

'Peter wouldn't kill two small children, Clemence.'

She stood up. 'Of course not. Instead he would persuade an eleven-year-old girl to do his work. The man is a veritable saint.'

I sighed. For this *saint* was my father. His blood ran in my veins. Could his cruel nature be bred into my bones? My eyes returned to the fire, where the flames licked at the wood, forming a miniature palace beneath the trivet of oak. When I was a child I used to look into such blazing chambers and imagine I could see into a different world, where tiny people lived among the burning embers and soaring flames. Sometimes I fancied I could see their beds and their chairs. Even their horses and cows.

The flames had entranced me, and I must have been falling to sleep, for Clemence touched my arm. 'Go to bed, Oswald. You're exhausted.' I stood up and left the room, but she called me back. 'Thank you, brother. You saved Henry's life.'

The dungeons beneath the castle still held Eloise Cooper and Brother Peter – and though it was tempting for me to ride away and leave their punishment to my sister Clemence, it would have been the coward's option. Before I went to bed I sought out Slow, the dirty servant who slept by the fire, and told him to take some supper to Eloise, for, regardless of her crimes, the woman still carried my child. I resolved to speak to them both the next morning. The events of the past day had indeed been exhausting – Clemence was correct. But as I tried to sleep that night, the sobs of Mary de Caburn kept me awake. The girl crouched in the corner of the solar and kept her guilty face hidden from the world.

The following morning, after a quick breakfast, I descended to the dungeons to carry out the unpleasant task of questioning Eloise and Peter. Clemence insisted upon coming with me, but for once, I was pleased of her company and support.

When the door to Eloise's cell was opened, an unpleasant fug emerged from the chamber. Eloise was standing in the corner, and though she was tired and dirty, she attempted to hold herself with some dignity. Once I might have been impressed by her composure, but now her self-control repulsed me.

Seeing my face at the door, she appealed to me. 'Oswald. For Christ's sakes. Get me out of here.'

'You think you deserve to be freed?'

She cursed under her breath. 'It was just a joke.' She gave a shrill laugh and then pointed to Clemence. 'We just wanted to give this vicious old bitch a scare. Imagine her as your stepmother. No wonder the poor girls ran away to London.'

'Stop lying Eloise,' I said.

She waved her hand at me. 'What will you do then? Keep me here for ever and starve me to death?'

Clemence butted in. 'That would be a suitable punishment for you.'

Eloise held her stomach. 'Just give me some food. I beg of you.' She looked to me pleadingly. 'Oswald. Have mercy. I'm carrying your child and I've had nothing to eat since this woman locked me in here.'

'I sent down some pottage last night with John Slow.'

She snorted. 'Well it never reached this cell.'

Clemence spun around to me. 'You sent her food?'

'For the sake of the child.'

Clemence dissolved into laughter. 'That old tale. Surely you don't believe she's truly expecting your child, Oswald?'

I will admit this thought had crossed my mind at first, but there was already a change to Eloise's body, even though her confinement was only in its first stages. I was hardly likely, however, to describe the fullness of Eloise's breasts to my sister. 'Of course she's with child,' I said. 'A physician has confirmed it.'

Eloise looked to me gratefully, mistaking this lie as a gesture of support.

Clemence laughed again. 'I would wager the child is not even yours, Oswald. This siren would lure any sailor onto the rocks.'

Now it was Eloise's turn to laugh. 'Says you! The woman who passes off that fat little bastard as the son of my brother.'

Clemence's hands balled into fists. 'What do you mean by that?'

'Anybody can see that Henry is the son of your manservant. What is the stupid boy's name?' She looked to the ceiling. 'Oh yes, Humbert.'

'How dare you?'

Eloise's eyes glinted. 'Did you think we hadn't noticed? Sister.'

'Be quiet!'

'My brother was murdered only days after your wedding. Not time enough to get you with child. So you asked your faithful clod to do the job.'

'I did not!'

'Of course you did. The fool is always in your bedchamber. Better watch out he doesn't father any more de Caburns. Because you can't attribute *them* to my dead brother.'

This last comment was enough to provoke a fight. Soon the two women rolled about the filthy straw and dust of the room like two street urchins fighting over a pie crust.

I separated them at length.

But only once I had enjoyed the performance.

We left Eloise in the cell, for want of knowing how to punish her. But there was one person who could stand in a court and be sentenced. If not for the abduction and planned murder of baby Henry, then for three murders the previous summer.

As we walked along the long and shadowy tunnel towards the cell at the other end of the castle, the faint smell of pottage began to meet our noses. Clemence turned to me, the candle illuminating her tangled hair and scratched cheeks. 'I think your supper for Eloise ended up in the stomach of the wrong prisoner.'

I thought of Slow's doleful face and his look of confusion as I had told him to take a bowl of soup to the dungeon the previous night. It seemed he had delivered the food to Brother Peter, rather than to Eloise.

As we reached the gloomy brown door at the end of the corridor, I called through the grate. 'Peter. Stand aside.'

No answer came from within.

I looked to Clemence. 'Just open it,' she said. 'This will be a short interview. We only need to tell him that we will be writing to the royal judge and hope to shortly see him hanging by his neck.'

A wave of nausea swept through me. For despite all of Peter's sins, I did not want to watch his body struggling and writhing against death, knowing of its inevitability. But when we opened the door and shone the candle into the room, there was no Peter to be seen. Instead, a crooked and naked crab-like man sidled across the floor nervously his bandy legs like a pair of arch braces.

I recognised him immediately. 'Slow? What are you doing here? Where's Brother Peter?'

The man fell to the floor and crawled his way towards me like a grovelling dog. 'I gave him the pottage like you said, sire. But he tricked me.'

I held my head in my hands. 'No. Please.'

'He stole my clothes. And then he ran away.'

'Why didn't you shout?'

He cringed again, as if I might hit him – which, in all honesty, I felt inclined to do. 'I did, sire. But nobody can hear a sound from down here. Lord Versey made sure of it.'

Clemence spun out of the room, and screamed the length of the tunnel.

We sent out dogs, men and horses. But nothing was found of Peter.

Not even a footprint.

Chapter Twenty-Four

You might wonder that I could forgive my sister – a woman who had ordered her servant to assault me and who had then threatened to torture me. But I have seen the lengths to which a parent will go, for the sake of their own child. My own father had killed three people to protect my position as Lord Somershill. I condemn this, without hesitation. But I am, at least, able to comprehend his motivations.

It seemed that this sentiment, this need to protect one's own offspring, also ran in my blood, for I was not prepared to dispense the punishment to Eloise that Clemence felt she deserved. Instead I wanted to broker a truce with the woman. And why? Because Eloise was carrying my child. My own little piece of eternity.

Eloise spent only the one further night in the cell, before she was released into the anteroom to the great hall, where a guard stood at her door.

'Are you feeling any better?' I asked, passing her a plate of morning bread. Her face was wan, and there were dark lines below her eyes. She was dressed in the same clothes and sat on the edge of the wooden truckle bed, as if she were about to leave.

She pushed the plate away. 'When will you send a clean gown? This one is filthy.'

'When I receive some answers to my questions.' I had tried this same conversation the previous night, only to be soundly ignored.

Today she seemed a little more cooperative. 'What is it you want to know?' she asked, with a small sigh of boredom. She drummed her fingers upon her thighs.

'How did you meet Brother Peter?'

She looked to the arrow slit in the wall, allowing a sharp breeze to blow the hair from her face. In this light, her face looked old. 'He found me in London.'

'He just knocked at your door, did he?' I said. 'And your servant admitted him? A scarred man in a dirty cloak?'

She moved her gaze to meet mine. 'No. Peter approached me by letter, if you must know. He told me that Mary and Becky were being ill-treated by Clemence. I agreed to meet him, in order to discuss the matter.'

'Was it your suggestion they run away to London?'

She frowned. 'Of course not. When I met Brother Peter, I merely expressed my shock at hearing the news. I did not expect him to bring the girls to me.'

'So Brother Peter led them to London. Thank you for confirming that much.'

She winced, angry with herself. 'I believe he met the girls by chance, when they reached the city.'

'Don't lie to me, Eloise. The two girls did not travel from Somershill to London on their own. Not even dressed as boys.'

'They are clever children, Oswald. Don't underestimate them.'

'But they couldn't have carried Rab all the way, could they? The bird is too heavy.'

She stopped drumming her fingers and now played with her hair. 'If you must know, the whole thing was the priest's idea. He wanted to cause trouble for Clemence.' Eloise got to her feet and walked to the wall, poking her hand out through the arrow slit and letting it move about in the air outside. 'Look at what your sister did to his face with her pan of boiling water. The priest will spend the rest of his life hiding in the shadows. Your mother even thought he was a leper.'

'Do you know *why* Clemence threw boiling water over Peter?' I asked.

Eloise pulled her hand back and turned to look at me. 'No. He wouldn't tell me.' She hesitated. 'But you were there when it happened, I believe. So why are you asking me?'

I shrugged to disguise my relief. It seemed Brother Peter had kept my true identity a secret from Eloise. It was something to be grateful for, at least.

'Why did you go along with Peter's plan, Eloise?'

She hesitated. 'Versey, of course.' I was surprised at her honesty and must have let my mouth fall open. 'Oh don't be so shocked, Oswald. I wanted to live in a castle at last. A house made of stone. Not some great wooden barn, which every noblewoman may laugh at. And you need a wife and an heir, Oswald. So where is the evil in this plan?'

Now I had to stifle a laugh of incredulity. 'You induced a young girl, your own niece, to abduct a baby. That seems evil enough to me.'

She waved her hand in irritation. 'I only made a foolish suggestion, Oswald. I didn't expect Mary to act upon it.'

'I don't believe you.'

She sat back upon the bed and placed her hands demurely in her lap. 'I assumed our child would inherit Versey, so the news that you'd promised the estate to Henry came as a shock to me, Oswald. You must see that.' Then she twisted her head from side to side and stretched her neck. 'It was cowardly of you not to tell me yourself. I had to hear about your promise from Mary.'

'So she was eavesdropping? As I suspected.'

Eloise sniffed a little, seemingly embarrassed by her next statement. 'When Mary told me the story, I did wish the boy harm. I don't deny that.' She then laughed. 'But I didn't mean my words. They were said in a moment of fury.' She looked at me again, her eyes green and penetrating. 'I didn't command Mary to abduct the boy. Neither did your disfigured priest. In fact, I'm horrified that the girl did such a thing.'

What was I to believe? Who was I to trust?

I looked Eloise over. 'Are you with child? Truly?'

She placed a hand upon her stomach. 'Yes. Of course I am.'

'But he or she will not inherit Versey. You understand that.'

She looked to the ceiling and gave a bitter sigh. 'Yes.'

A week later I set out for Somershill with Eloise, having decided that we would marry – whether Eloise liked it or not. Our child would not be a bastard. The de Caburn sisters accompanied us to Somershill, since they could not stay at Versey Castle – not after Henry's abduction. With Brother Peter's disappearance, Clemence now had guards at Henry's crib, so I feared that Mary, despite her sincere remorse, would be blamed for every sneeze or cough the child suffered. And had Mary accidentally tarried near his room, she might even have been stabbed with a pike. No. It was better for all concerned that I removed the girls from Clemence's company.

As our band travelled home, I noticed that the oaks of the forest were finally sprouting their leaves – a yellow green that was as vivid as the body of a grasshopper. Summer was here at last. Every so often, I looked back to see Mary and Becky, stopping the wagon so that they might fuss over the box containing their decrepit fea-thered friend. I had yet to decide the fate of Rab.

Our silent progress was interrupted when we saw a horse and cart in the distance. Recognising the rider upon the horse to be Father Luke, I galloped ahead to speak with him.

He greeted me by looking over my shoulder. 'Is Lady Clemence with you?' His face betrayed a certain terror that I might say yes.

'No. Luckily for you, she isn't. But she's told me you confessed to sheltering Brother Peter.' Father Luke's mouth fell open. 'I suppose that's why you kept mentioning the man to me?'

The priest put his fingers to his cheek, and I noted that his face was now completely covered with the spots and scabs of an anxious adolescent. 'Yes, sire.' Then he whispered some words to himself that failed to reach my ears.

'Peter threatened to reveal a secret about you. Is that correct?'

The young priest nodded his head. 'It was a mistake, my lord. A sin of which I have repented.'

'Which sin is that then? Harbouring a felon? Or being a sodomite?'

He simply looked at me with one of his long, confused stares and I didn't press him for an answer. Frankly I didn't care what he had done in the crypts at Rochester.

'Where are you going now?' I asked. 'We are a long way from Somershill.'

The question was simple enough, but Father Luke was unable to answer. His stumbling hesitation raised my suspicions. 'What's in your cart?'

'Nothing,' he stammered.

'Then you won't mind if I look?' I pulled at the cloth that covered the contents of the cart, but he grasped it away from me, as if I were trying to steal it from a market stall. 'It's a dead body, sire. I don't think you should look.'

'Whose dead body?'

'Just a person who needs burying at St Giles. You wouldn't know him.' His pony began to shift about, unhappy at the tension in the reins.

'I'll look anyway,' I said. 'I may know his face.'

The priest began to panic. 'Please, sire. Don't look. Please. It will upset you.'

'Get out of my way,' I told him, now pulling the cloth away. A familiar face looked back at me from within the cart – though his skin was bloated and his dead eyes stared glassily into space. 'John Barrow?'

The priest let go of the reins and put his head in his hands. 'Yes. I found him in the forest. Hanging from a tree.'

My stomach churned. 'Who killed him?'

Father Luke trembled. 'Nobody, sire. He killed himself.'

'Are you sure?'

'Yes,' he said with the deepest of sighs. 'He told me repeatedly that he meant to do it. He even took his own rope.' I remembered Geoffrey's description of the sack that Barrow had carried. The bag I once suspected of holding the body of baby Henry. 'I tried to stop him,' said the priest. 'But he wouldn't listen. He believed he had released the butcher bird.'

'Did he confess to you? Did he admit to killing Catherine Tulley and Margaret Beard?'

The priest began to pick at the scabs on his face. 'Yes, sire.' He sighed. 'But mostly Barrow spoke in riddles, so I can't be certain of his guilt.' Then he looked me straight in the eye. 'Can you?'

How to answer his question? Barrow had been at large when both the children were murdered. He was a madman with his own warped motivations. He had even confessed his crimes to a priest. So, why wouldn't I be certain? A wake of buzzards circled above us, their feathers splayed at the ends of their wings like outstretched fingers. I watched them soar and swoop above the treetops, watching for prey in the open spaces below. In the distance, Eloise was staring at me with her arms crossed.

'What will you do with his body?' I asked.

'I can't bury him in the churchyard. Suicide is a mortal sin. But there is some land in the glebe field that I've set aside for such burials.' Then he gave a sharp intake of breath. 'You won't tell the bishop, will you?' He seemed flustered again. 'He would insist the body is decapitated and hung in the village.' He gulped and reddened. His large Adam's apple moved up and down in his neck. 'The church says such a disgraceful end deters others from trying to take their own lives. But I don't believe that. And I would hate to see his body mutilated.' He looked back into the wagon. 'His sin was madness.'

Perhaps I should have objected to this burial? Why should

Barrow have received any favours, even in death? But I said nothing. For, in truth, at that moment I wanted this whole affair buried along with Barrow's corpse. I turned my horse to rejoin my party when a thought crossed my mind. 'I need you to perform my marriage ceremony,' I told Father Luke.

The colour had returned to his cheeks. 'Indeed. When?'

I had given this matter little thought, but did not want to give that impression. 'The day after tomorrow,' I announced.

His hand trembled. 'So soon?' His words were hesitant. 'But what about the betrothal ceremony? It should be carried out forty days before the marriage.'

I stared at him. 'You performed it already, Father Luke. Remember? It was done privately. A few weeks ago. Just Mistress Cooper and myself were present.'

The priest frowned. His face a picture of confusion. 'But . . . er. No, no. I don't think I did.'

'Yes you did.'

'Are you sure, sire?' He didn't seem to take my meaning at all. 'I don't remember it.'

'Perhaps then I should speak to the bishop regarding your memory?' I pointed to the body of Barrow in the cart. 'And any other matters which might interest him.'

His face twisted into a grimace, but then relaxed, as he finally understood me. Sometimes our priest displayed the mental capacity of a mouse moth, running into a flame. 'Of course. I see.' He scratched his balding head. 'Yes. The betrothal ceremony. I do remember now.'

'Thank you.'

'And the marriage is the day after tomorrow?'

I groaned, fearing I might have to write it down for him. 'Yes Father Luke. Exactly as I said.'

As we returned to Somershill, I noted that the apple trees brimmed with setting fruits, but the fields were empty of people.

Two more homes had been abandoned in the village – their doors removed and their roofs stripped of thatch. Somebody was on the roof cutting out the beams, but when we passed, they shot into the shadows. Soon these same materials would adorn another person's home – petty thieving was becoming a constant problem on the estate. I didn't have the time to accost this particular thief, so we rode on towards the house, to be met by Gilbert's unwelcoming face and his usual complaint that he hadn't been warned of our arrival. Eloise, who had barely spoken a word since we left Versey, told my truculent valet to shut his mouth.

I found Mother in the solar with her feet in a basin of steaming water. I held my nose, for the stink about the room was appalling. She tried to stand up, but the bowl was slippery and she nearly lost her balance.

'Stay where you are, Mother,' I said, kissing her quickly upon the top of her head.

She caught my hand. 'Dearest Oswald. You're home. And I hear you saved our poor little Henry from the claws of the butcher bird.' Her eyes were wild with childish excitement.

I had persuaded Clemence and Humbert to keep quiet about Henry's discovery, arguing it would be unfair to brand Mary as the child's abductor. She was still such a young girl herself. Clemence had agreed to my request with great reluctance, and Humbert was unlikely to say anything to anybody. Instead we told everybody that Henry had been found in the forest – though this was a poor story to quench the thirst of the village for drama, especially as the episode entailed the discovery of a missing child. So, in place of my mundane explanation for Henry's reappearance, the villagers had simply invented their own tale. I featured strongly in this new version, but so, unfortunately, did the butcher bird. And no matter how many times I denied the bird's existence, it was now said that I had wrestled baby Henry from the claws of this creature, while the monster lifted me into the sky with the intention of taking us both to its eyrie.

I looked to Mother. 'No. The true story is much less interesting. We found Henry in some bushes.'

Mother waved her hands. 'Oh stop it, Oswald. Why must you always be so modest? You are the family's great investigator. Everybody knows that.'

She stood up and suddenly the stink of the steaming basin reached my nose. 'What is that smell?'

'Just a tincture that I added to my footbath.'

'Tincture of what? It smells like something brewed up from the charnel house.'

'Come along Oswald. You know yourself that the worst-smelling medicines are the most effective. I'm not sure Master de—' Then she stopped herself. 'I bought it from a travelling physician.'

I felt my anger ignite. 'Is de Waart here?' I said. 'I told you to keep him away from this family.'

She removed her feet from the water and placed them upon some clean linen. 'Now listen to me, Oswald. The skin on my legs has been terribly dry. I even bled all over the sheets after scratching at them.' Then she gave a great sigh. 'And you haven't been here to help me.'

Our discussion was interrupted as Eloise entered, her face sharing my disgust at the stink. Not that Mother noticed this reaction. She clapped her hands. 'Mistress Cooper. Dear Oswald here doesn't believe in the efficacy of foul-smelling tinctures. What do you say?'

Eloise bowed her head to Mother. 'I would say it depends upon the physician who has prepared the herbs, my lady.'

Mother clapped her hands a second time. 'I agree. But Oswald doesn't care for my physician. Though I've found him myself to be entirely trustworthy.'

'Except for nearly killing Clemence after she gave birth,' I said.

Mother held her hand to her ear and feigned deafness. 'I can't hear what you're saying Oswald. Stop mumbling.'

I went to repeat my words, when Eloise interrupted, 'Is your physician in the house, my lady?'

Mother looked to me warily. 'He might be,' she said, believing herself to sound vague. 'I'm not at all sure.'

'Perhaps he would call upon me?' said Eloise. 'I'm feeling a little melancholic.'

It was my turn to interrupt. 'You don't want to see this man, Eloise. I can assure you. He will do nothing to improve your mood.'

She turned to me, her eyes hateful. 'I've also been nauseous, Oswald. As well you know.'

'I don't care if you vomit all day. You are not consulting with Roger de Waart.'

Now she bristled with indignation. 'Indeed?'

'Indeed.'

A silence followed that was only broken when Mother let out the most offensive burp. She then rubbed her stomach. 'There, you see. The tincture has worked perfectly.'

'I thought the tincture was a cure for dry skin?'

Now Mother laughed. 'This cure is both for cold and warm ailments, Oswald. Which is the wonder of de Waart's medicine. He rarely treats one imbalance. Not when he can treat two at the same time.' She turned to Eloise and whispered, 'It's far easier on the purse.'

Thankfully we were prevented from continuing this mindless conversation by a knock at the door. Featherby entered, stooping to cross the threshold — a foolish affectation since the door was perfectly tall enough to accommodate his height.

Featherby had not called upon me at a favourable time. I was both tired after my journey from Versey, and irritated to discover that de Waart was lurking somewhere about the house. 'What is it?' I said.

The man stepped forward and came so close to Eloise that she cursed him and told him to get away from her with his farmyard stink. How she smelt Featherby over the scent of Mother's foot basin was hard to imagine.

Featherby withdrew to a courteous distance and bowed. 'I'm sorry to trouble you, sire. I saw you were home and needed to speak with you urgently.'

'What about?'

He shifted awkwardly on his feet. 'Farm business.'

Mother swept up Eloise by the arm and pushed her towards the door. 'Come along, Mistress Cooper. Let us leave these men to discuss their affairs.'

Eloise stiffened at this suggestion, but let herself be thrust out of the room nonetheless. When the door was shut, Featherby resumed his advance on my person, causing me to retreat to the fire. 'So what is this urgent business?' I asked him,

'I've lost too many men, sire. It's just as I warned you. There's no chance I can finish the sowing.'

'But—'

'Last week Gideon Hoad moved out. Said he was moving upcountry. But I've heard he's heading out to the marsh.'

'Romney Marsh? What would he go there for?'

Featherby ignored this question. 'And now Thomas Tulley says he's going as well.'

'Well he can't. He's not free to leave this estate.'

'But Tulley's been causing a lot of trouble, sire. Might be best to let him go.'

I suddenly longed for a drink. Gilbert hadn't brought me any ale since I'd arrived home, and now my tongue stuck to the roof of my mouth. 'What's your point, Featherby?' I said with irritation. 'First you tell me that you don't have enough men. Then you say you want one of them to go.'

Featherby cleared his throat. 'I can't say it any plainer than this, sire. I can't manage any more. The men who remain won't work for the wages you pay them. The ones who've gone will never come back.'

My head ached. 'I'm not raising the wages, Featherby. I told you that before.'

He advanced. 'Well I'm asking you, one last time, to reconsider.'

'I can't.'

He sucked his teeth. 'You can't?'

My temper was stretched to the tension of a hide on a frame. The journey. My thirst. The stink of de Waart's tincture. 'I mean, I won't.'

The churl raised an eyebrow at me. He even folded his arms.

'Just get out of here, Featherby,' I said.

He paused and then bowed. 'Very well, sire. But you should know this. I'm thinking of leaving myself.'

I steered him to the door. 'Then good riddance to you.'

I slipped between the cool and smooth sheets of Rennes linen and closed my eyes. In the peace of this chamber my troubles hid amongst the embroidered creatures in the tapestries upon the walls at the end of the bed. I was not even bothered by the mouse that scuttled across the floor, nor the spider that spun its web in the corner. I shut my eyes instead upon the dark world inside my head, where all the ghouls and goblins of my real life were reduced to shadows. In their place I dreamt of my pleasures. Geometry. Astronomy. Latin and Syriac. But this only made me more melancholic, for I couldn't remember the last time I had studied a book – other than the grubby manuscripts that were still hidden beneath my mattress. When I thought of geometry, I could barely remember the most simple of formulas. And my Latin vocabulary was as rusted as the nails in our old portcullis.

Then a shadow formed into a shape in my mind. It split into two shapes that drifted and flitted, before forming themselves into the bodies of two small babies. Catherine Tulley and Margaret Beard. And then it split again. And now a new shadow formed. He was the smallest and the hardest to see, but I knew him immediately. This infant was my unborn son. I stretched out to touch him, but he vanished.

Then, at last, sleep found me and I did not wake until late the next morning when my slumber was interrupted by a shriek. Mother ran into my room and grasped me by the shoulders.

My head was thick and my eyes were crusted. 'What are you doing?' I groaned. 'What's wrong now?'

'Come quickly, Oswald. Mistress Cooper is bleeding to death.' She shook me to emphasise her point. 'There's blood every-where.' Then she pulled a face. 'It has ruined my new feather mattress.'

I pulled a tunic quickly over my head and followed Mother into the ladies' bedchamber, where Eloise lay across the bed in a white linen gown that was stained with red. She looked up at me plain-tively, her face cold and white.

I ran to take her hand, which was limp and sweating. 'What's happening?' I asked her.

She indicated that she wanted me to draw closer. I obliged, and when my ear was by her mouth she whispered, 'Get me a bucket, Oswald.'

'Why?'

'I'm losing the child.'

I felt faint. 'No, no. You can't be.'

'I am.'

Mother pulled me away. 'What's she saying to you about a bucket?'

'You're not supposed to be listening,' I snapped.

'I only heard the part about the bucket, Oswald. I wasn't lis-tening when she mentioned losing the child.'

It took me a moment to focus. The room was too warm and smelt of blood. 'Just get a bucket,' I said.

Mother frowned. 'That won't cure the problem.'

'It's too late for a cure, Mother!'

Mother crossed herself at these words, and staggered with

some dramatic effect to a bench at the other side of the chamber. 'Shall I ask Master de Waart to return?'

'What do you mean? Has he seen Eloise already?'

She crossed herself again. 'She was nauseous, Oswald. And melancholic.'

I looked about the bed and found a large clay mug. Inside, leaves and flowers swilled about a mucky brown brew that smelt foul and bitter. 'What is this?' I asked, thrusting the mug under Mother's nose. 'Is this one of de Waart's cures?'

'Yes,' she stammered. 'I think it is.'

'What's in it? Cow dung? Bird shit?'

Mother pushed back her hair. 'Of course not. Mistress Cooper asked for some herbs.'

'Which herbs?'

She waved her hand at me. 'I can't remember, Oswald.'

'Try.'

'She said they would help to settle her digestion.' Mother mopped at the corner of her eye. 'Her constitution is far too dry and hot, Oswald. It is no wonder she feels nauseous. If I was her, I would—'

I grasped the foolish woman by the arm and shook her. 'God's bones Mother. Which herbs did she ask for?'

'I believe it was Parsley and Mint.' She sighed and looked into the distance. 'Or was it Penny Royal and Tansy?'

Eloise slipped off the bed and was now leaning against the wall with her arms upstretched. 'Where's the bucket?' she wheezed, as I tried to lay a comforting hand upon her back. 'Get me the bucket.'

'I'll go and get it,' I said.

Her face was twisted with pain and she was panting like a thirsty dog. A pool of blood was forming at her feet. She pulled up her gown and squatted upon the floor, causing Mother to flee the room with her hand in front of her mouth.

In truth I was tempted to do the same, for Eloise was now

groaning and writhing, and any words of sympathy were met with a scowl or even a screamed curse.

'What did de Waart give you?' I asked, when she relaxed for a few moments.

She resumed her pose against the wall. 'What do you mean?'

'He's poisoned you, Eloise.'

She placed one hand on her back and wailed as a great clot of blood slipped greasily down her leg and onto the floor. I wanted to be sick. But instead I collected a sheet from the bed and wrapped up the bloody mess without looking too closely. For I knew what the soaking sheet contained. It was the essence of a small and barely formed life. The child I had seen in the shadows.

Thankfully Gilbert arrived with a bucket, for Eloise continued to bleed. It seemed as if the flow would never stop, though I tried to stem it with the sheets from the bed. I called for Ada, and she brought some woollen blankets and some linen swaddling of Henry's that Clemence had left behind.

Eventually the torrent of her bleeding began to ease, and Eloise lay down upon the bed and slept. I looked upon her face, which was both beautiful and serene, and my feelings became confused all over again. I had never loved Eloise, but I had been in her thrall. It could only have been a bewitchment, but as I watched her sleep, I began to wonder if it might grow into more.

But these thoughts were delusions. Born out of my youth and sentimentality.

I kept a vigil at Eloise's bedside, and when she woke and asked for beer, it was I who held the pewter cup to her mouth.

'Are you feeling better?' I asked, tipping the warm beer onto her cracked lips. I had asked Ada to bring the best ale, which was both strong and dark.

She grunted a response. I took her to be slightly delirious.

I picked up her small hand from where it lay on the bed sheet and stroked it. 'I'll make de Waart pay for this. But we will have other children. We're both young enough.'

Her eyes opened at this.

'I think we should still marry, Eloise. Despite what's happened.'

She gave a small laugh, which soon dissolved into a cough. 'But what if I disagree?'

'Do you?'

She took her hand away and turned away from me.

'We'll speak about this when you're recovered,' I said.

'No we won't.' She yawned. 'There's nothing to say. The child is gone. There's no reason for the marriage.'

I put my hand on her shoulder. 'Rest, Eloise. You're exhausted.'

But this attempt at compassion only seemed to inflame her, for rather than close her eyes, she summoned the courage to sit up. 'What would be the point in marrying you, Oswald?'

I hesitated. 'It was just a suggestion.'

'A poor one.' She thumped the bed. 'I wanted our child to inherit Versey.'

'Versey has an heir already. Henry de Caburn.'

She poked her finger into my arm. 'That boy is not the son of my dead brother. You know that. He's a bastard conceived by your sister and her manservant.'

I went to protest, but suddenly she seemed so deflated that I lifted the pewter cup to her lips instead. I dismissed her bitter words about Henry as a consequence of her sorrow. 'Have another sip, Eloise. It will revive your spirits.'

She pushed the cup away. 'Tell my servants to prepare my carriage. I'll be leaving in the morning.'

'Don't be foolish, Eloise. You've just lost a child.'

Now she sighed. 'Oh Oswald. You are so naïve. I did not lose this child.'

'What do you mean?'

'I expelled it.'

'What?'

She pointed to the concoction in the clay mug. 'What do you think's in there? A tonic for melancholia?'

I stuttered. 'I . . . I don't know.'

'It's a brew of herbs. To expel a child before the quickening.'

'I don't understand.'

She rolled her eyes. 'I don't want to marry you, Oswald. And I don't want your child. Can I make it any plainer?'

I sank onto the bench.'

'Don't be sentimental. This is the practical solution to our problem. You will not give me Versey. And I would not make you happy.'

'You killed our child.'

'Not a child, Oswald. Look into that sheet and you'll see what it was. Just a clot of blood and flesh. Nothing more.'

I put my hands to my mouth. I will admit to feeling sick. 'No. I don't agree.'

She leant over and tried to touch me. 'Listen. I'll tell you the truth of this matter.'

I pushed her away. 'Keep away from me. You're evil.'

'You don't know what you're talking about.'

I wanted to cry. 'Yes I do. It was a child. A son. I saw him in a dream.'

She grabbed my hands in her own, and would not let go. 'You must see things from a woman's point of view for once.' She squeezed my hand tighter. She spoke into my face, with passion and urgency. A ball of spittle hit my skin. 'We are traded in this world. Sold to old men who we don't care to marry. Handed over as easily as a cage of chickens in Cheapside market.'

'That's not true.'

'It is, Oswald. We have so little control over our lives. So do not deny us this. To sometimes choose who we bring into this world and who we don't.'

I wanted to say something, but my mouth was dry.

She regarded me for a while and then settled back down in the bed. 'I would not have been a good wife for you, Oswald. Soon you will be pleased of this.'

'No I won't.'

She only smirked, but as I watched Eloise leave the next day, the pleasure came sooner than I had expected.

I bumped into Mother as she descended the stone steps from the solar. In her hand she held a clay mug and was sniffing gingerly at its contents. Her small dog Hector was jumping up at her dress as if the mug might conceal a titbit or treat. Since I had left Somershill to search for Henry, Mother had reclaimed Hector as her fawning pet, and equally he had forsaken his life as a dog.

Immediately recognising the crude brown vessel Mother held as the mug containing Eloise's herbal concoction, I tried to take it from her. 'What are you doing with that?' I said.

She pulled the mug away from me and protected it beneath the folds of her gown. 'It smells foul, so I thought I might rub it into my feet. They say Tansy dissolves calluses.'

'Amongst other things,' I said bitterly.

She frowned. 'What was that?'

'Just give it to me, Mother.'

She placed the mug beneath the folds of her gown. 'But these herbs are difficult to find, Oswald. This shouldn't go to waste.'

I grabbed the mug before she had a chance to object further. 'Find de Waart. I'm sure he has some more he could sell you.'

She reddened. 'I think he's left Somershill.'

I marched away. 'I hope so. For his own sake.'

Mother pursued me, with Hector now barking at my heels – thinking that I was making off with his pot of treats. I kept ahead of them both until they caught up with me by the moat. Mother was panting. 'I'm sorry about Eloise,' she said.

I threatened Hector with my foot and then poured the vile concoction into the moat, where the slop of sodden flower heads and sludgy leaves soon dissolved into the other foul soup of filth and kitchen waste. Even Hector was reluctant to descend the slippery banks to investigate further.

Mother touched my cheek with her scaly hand. 'It's better that Eloise ridded herself of the child.'

I grasped her hand. 'You knew what she was doing?'

She pulled her fingers away with surprising vigour. 'I suspected her. Yes.'

'Why didn't you tell me?'

She picked up Hector and wiped the spittle from about his mouth. 'Mistress Cooper didn't want the child. So who was I to stop her?'

'But it's . . .'

She kissed Hector's head. 'It's what? Evil? Barbaric?'

'Yes.'

She whispered into my ear. 'This is a cruel world for women, Oswald. Sometimes herbs are all we have left.'

I looked back at Mother, and suddenly I knew.

Chapter Twenty-Five

I arrived at the Long Ditch just in time. There was a cart outside the cottage, one end loaded with a cauldron, a bench, and a rolled mattress, the other jammed with a collection of stone bottles, leather pouches, and glass vials containing some herb or root. The familiar mewls and moans of Mary Tulley's three infants cut through the air from the neighbouring cottage. The eldest boy was complaining that he was hungry, only to be ejected through the door for his troubles. He looked at me, stuck out his tongue and then crawled around to the back of the cottage, looking scrawnier and paler than the last time I had seen him. His feet were black and his tunic was perforated with holes.

Agnes looked up as I crossed her threshold. 'Sire?'

'Where are you going, Mistress Salt?'

'To visit my sister.'

'With all your belongings?'

'She's a widow and needs help with her children.'

'Then bring them here. You're not free to move from this estate.'

She smiled, revealing the pink of her gums. 'Sire. You must be thirsty. Let me fetch you some mead.'

'No thank you. The last time I drank your mead, it nearly poisoned me.'

'It can be strong, sire. For a young man.' She stepped around the embers of the fire and tried to fix me with her eyes. So large and blue, like two pale orbs.

'Sit down,' I told her.

She inclined her head. 'I don't have a stool. It's on the wagon.'

'Then sit on the floor.'

She hesitated. And then, with a show of reluctance, she dropped to the dusty floor and took some time to find a comfortable position. Once she had settled, I made sure to keep behind her and prop the door open.

'What's on your mind, sire?' she asked me. 'You seem agitated.'

'The murders of two infants, Mistress Salt.'

She raised an eyebrow. 'Yes. Poor Catherine and Margaret. Killed by that lunatic, John Barrow.' She twisted her neck to look at me. 'And his bird.'

'Stay where you are,' I said.

'I'm only stretching my back, sire.'

'Stay still. And don't look at me.'

She smiled and turned back to face the wall. 'Are you sure you wouldn't care for some mead, sire? I'm sure it would settle your nerves.'

'So you can poison me for good this time?' I approached the back of her head and whispered into her ear. 'Because you're good at that, aren't you?'

She didn't answer.

I stepped back and once more kept my distance. Outside the door, a pigeon was pecking at something in the mud, its head bobbing methodically at the soil like a hammer. 'Did you suggest poisoning the babies to Christina Beard and Mary Tulley? Or did they ask you to do it?'

Agnes stiffened but said nothing.

'Except Margaret wasn't Christina's baby, was she?' I said.

Agnes gave a shudder, but then quickly composed herself. She still remained silent.

'The baby was the child of her simpleton daughter, wasn't she?' Agnes shuddered again. 'Christina couldn't keep such a child in her house. A bastard. Not with her devotion to the Holy Father.'

'You don't understand,' said Agnes. 'This has nothing to do with the church.'

'Then explain it to me.'

She simply laughed and refused to answer. The door blew shut, leaving the room to fill with its stuffy scent. Sweet and strange odours that had worked their way into the walls from the years that Agnes had dried herbs and flowers from the rafters. I went back to the door and once again propped it open, frightened that I might be overcome by some miasma.

'Let's talk about Mary Tulley,' I said.

'There's nothing to say.'

'She didn't need another mouth to feed, did she? Poor Mary. With three sons already in her house. One still clinging to her breast. And a husband who makes trouble wherever he goes.'

Again silence.

'She requested a quick and painless death for the child, didn't she? She just wanted the baby to go to sleep and never wake up. Mary's not a cruel woman.'

Agnes turned around to look at me, her eyes bright against the dark of the chamber. I held her head and pushed it back to face the wall. Once again I leant over and whispered into her ear. 'Did you tell yourself you were helping them, Mistress Salt?'

'What would you know?' she spat.

A voice came from the door. 'Don't blame Agnes. Please, sire.' It was Mary Tulley. Her face was sweating and bloodless.

'Don't say anything, Mary,' said Agnes. 'This fool has no evidence against us.'

'Both infants smelt of vomit,' I said.

'Babies always stink of vomit, my lord.' Then she sneered. 'Not that you'd know much on that subject.'

'This was not the milky posset a baby usually brings up,' I said. 'This had the acrid smell of a poisoning. Was it wolfsbane?'

Mary yelped at my words and held her hands to her mouth, causing Agnes to leap up and run to her neighbour. 'Be still Mary,' she said, stroking the other woman's head tenderly. 'Catherine didn't suffer. She just went to sleep. This vomit was nothing more than a residue that must have slipped from her mouth. She felt no pain.'

'You admit it then?' They both looked to me, as if they had forgotten I was in the cottage.

Mary trembled. 'Please don't tell Thomas, sire. Please. He would never forgive me.'

I backed away. 'You'll both face a royal judge at the Hundreds court. Of course your husband will be told.'

Mary suddenly screamed and threw herself to the floor. 'Please, sire. Please. Don't tell the constable. What will happen to my children if I hang? Thomas can't look after them.'

Instead of staying to comfort her friend, Agnes now pushed her face into mine. There was no option but to look into her eyes, though they were no longer bright and compelling. Instead they were dark and full of hatred. 'You would sentence Mary's whole family to death, would you? The three boys that she already has.'

I tried to shove Agnes away, but the scrawny woman was strong. 'She murdered an infant,' I said. 'With your help.'

'And so did Eloise Cooper,' said Agnes. 'Will you report her to the constable as well?'

I stepped back. 'What do you know about that?'

She laughed again, like a whinnying horse. 'Where do you think your mother's physician obtains his herbs? De Waart comes to me.'

'To you?'

'Yes! I knew why he was asking for those particular plants.'

I felt empty and nauseated. 'Get away from me,' I said, though

Agnes remained exactly where she was – so close that I could see the warp and weft of her tunic.

'What do you think drives a woman to kill her own child?' she whispered to me.

'Evil.'

She poked her finger into my arm. 'Shall I tell you? It's hunger and poverty. The type that is everywhere about this pathetic estate. Your estate.'

'That's no excuse for what you've done.'

'Most women just starve their infants in such circumstances. Did you know that? They just leave them in a corner to die. But that's a long and painful death, wouldn't you agree?'

Now I really felt sick.

'Mary and Christina brought their babies to me instead. Will you condemn them for such an act of kindness?'

'I don't call murder a kindness. You poisoned two infants and left them in a bush. You wanted people to believe they had been killed by some sort of bird. You wanted them to blame John Barrow.'

She locked her eyes onto mine, and this time I was unable to look away. 'Barrow was going to kill himself sooner or later. I felt no guilt. He came to me often enough for deadly poison.' Then she laughed. 'Though I wouldn't help him.'

'Why not? You would kill two babies, but not a grown man?'

'He was a madman. I could not trust him to keep his mouth shut before he died.'

'Whereas an infant can tell nobody?'

She turned away from me. 'You have no understanding of our lives. In your great house. With your servants, and your kitchens full of food. You cannot see that a butcher bird haunts this place.'

'What are you talking about?'

She sneered at me. 'It is a creature that feeds upon the weak and vulnerable. But it has no wings and it cannot fly.'

'Shut up.'

'It is a cruel and wicked thing. With gold and land. But it will not share these gifts from God. Instead it keeps its men as slaves. Slaves that it will not free from bondage. It lets them starve.'

I felt her breath upon my face. It was icy cold and so caustic I could taste its bile in the back of my throat. 'Get away from me,' I said.

'Mary and I are not murderers, sire. It is you. You who drove these women to kill their babies.'

I cringed away from her. 'No. That's not true. I didn't.'

'But you did. There is a butcher bird in Somershill. You.'

I galloped home, and after lying in my bed and staring at my canopy for many hours, I searched out Featherby.

He opened the door of his cottage to me with a self-satisfied face. 'Yes, sire? Come to beg me to stay on the estate, have you?'

I ignored this remark. 'I've decided to raise the men's wages,' I told him.

He was taken aback by my words. 'I see. But I thought—'

I straightened my gown. 'I've listened to your arguments, Featherby. About losing men to other estates. And I'm convinced we must act. Regardless of the Statute.'

He poked his tongue about his cheeks. 'I thought you wouldn't break the law.'

'I've changed my mind.'

He frowned. 'If you're sure.'

I cleared my throat. 'We'll record the men's wages at the lawful level in the ledgers, but secretly we'll pay them more. That way, our accounts will be in order when Hatcher visits.'

Featherby raised his eyebrow. 'It's a risk, of course. If the men talk.'

I stepped towards Featherby and made myself as tall as I was able. I would tell you I even loomed over the man. 'Then make sure they don't.'

Epilogue

Two months later I was throwing a ball about the orchard with Mary and Becky, when Clemence's carriage came into view across the field.

Mary dropped the ball like a stinging beetle. 'I didn't know my stepmother was visiting,' she said, clasping my hand. Becky bolted into the distance and climbed a tree.

'Neither did I,' I told Mary.

The girl began to cry. 'She hates me.'

'No, she doesn't,' I said.

Her lip trembled. 'She'll never forgive me.'

Unfortunately this was difficult to deny.

I sent both girls to the ladies' bedchamber and told them to change into fitted gowns and surcoats. In recent weeks I had allowed them to roam about Somershill in their simple woollen tunics, so that they could climb walls and run around in the fields. This privilege had restored some of their former happiness, and at times they seemed like the children of old. But I did not want my sister to see them in their rough clothes. I could not stand to hear her words of disapproval.

Once Clemence was seated at my chair in the solar, I tentatively asked the reason for this unexpected visit. 'Can't a sister visit her brother?' she said.

'Of course. I'm pleased to see you.' Baby Henry bounced upon her knee, as fat as a suckling pig. At her shoulder, Humbert stared into space, never more than a few feet from his mistress.

'Where's Mother?' she asked.

'She's gone on a pilgrimage to Canterbury. To thank God for the return of Henry.'

Clemence smiled at me. At least I took it to be friendly, for the line between a smile and a sneer from Clemence was only the breadth of a hair. 'It's not God we should thank for Henry's return.' She leant forward and squeezed my knee. 'It's you.'

I coloured a little. It was rare to receive a compliment from my sister. Then I instinctively touched the scars on my forehead – the holes that had been marked in my skin by Humbert's attack.

Clemence noticed this and looked sheepish. 'It's healed well.'

'I think the skin will scar.'

Her face now soured a little. 'Have the grace to accept my apology, Oswald,' she said, a little crossly.

Gilbert shuffled into the room with a tankard of ale, which he handed to Clemence as uncouthly as if she were a farmhand. He was, no doubt, as irritated as ever by the lack of notice he had received regarding guests.

'I see our valet remains as bad-tempered as a boar pig,' said Clemence, when the man had lumbered back out of the chamber.

'He's been complaining of toothache. And the girls wear him out.'

Clemence looked to Humbert. 'Oh yes. My stepdaughters. How are the child-snatchers?'

'Don't say that, Clemence. Mary's sorry for what she did.'

She raised her eyebrows. 'Really?'

'Have the grace to accept an apology, Clemence.'

She looked at me and smiled. Her complexion was recovering some of its colour, now Henry was being weaned onto solid food. I would say she was fresh-faced, even handsome.

'You think I should just forget what happened?' she said. 'That my stepdaughters abducted my son and tried to drop him onto a waterwheel?'

'No, Clemence,' I sighed. 'But you should try to forgive them.'

She smacked her lips and took a deep breath. 'Very well.' Then she clapped her hands. 'Please call for Mary. I wish to speak with her.'

I eyed her suspiciously. 'Why?'

Clemence wriggled in her chair. 'To offer forgiveness, of course.'

I left the chamber to find Mary myself, rather than call for a servant to do the job, since I knew the girl would not want to attend an interview with her stepmother. In the end, Mary only agreed to come into the solar if I promised to hold her hand.

Clemence gave a curt smile as we entered. 'Good day to you, Mary. Are you and your sister well?'

Mary curtsied, though her hand trembled in mine. 'Yes, Stepmother. Thank you.'

Clemence left a long and deliberate silence. 'Would you like to see your brother, Mary?' she said at last, indicating that Mary was allowed to approach the baby in her arms.

Mary froze, but I pushed her forward gently. 'Don't be frightened,' I whispered.

She edged forward with her eyes to the floor until she reached Henry, and when she looked upon his face it seemed she was about to burst into tears.

Clemence stood up quickly and thrust the baby into Mary's arms, before the girl had the opportunity to cry. 'I'd like you to take Henry for a walk in the orchard, Mary.'

Mary's eye twitched. A strand of blonde hair was stuck to the skin of her lip, and though she tried to say something, not a word came out.

'Go on,' said Clemence. 'Hurry up. I need to speak to your uncle.' The girl held tightly onto the baby and walked to the door.

'Be sure not to drop him, Mary,' warned Clemence. 'And keep his shawl about his chest. Henry feels the cold.'

With Mary gone, I grasped Clemence and kissed her. 'Thank you, sister. This will make Mary very happy.'

She scowled. 'Maybe.' Then she turned to Humbert, who had remained at her shoulder. 'Follow that girl every moment,' she told the boy. 'Don't let her out of your sight.'

I went to object, but Clemence put a finger on my lips. 'Let me deal with this on my own terms, Oswald. Henry is my child.'

Once we were alone, Clemence stood up and walked to the squint, where she watched Humbert follow Mary out of the great hall below. She smiled. 'Humbert is so very fond of Henry.' Her tone was sweet and gentle.

'Yes,' I said.

She spun on her heel and fixed me with a glare. 'So you believe the story then, do you?' Her dark eyes flashed.

'What story's that?' I lied.

'Come on Oswald. The story that I lay with Humbert. To conceive a child after my husband was murdered.'

'No,' I said, though my tone was less than convincing.

'But you think that Henry looks like Humbert, don't you?'

I scratched at my cheek. 'I hadn't really thought about it, Clemence.' I was lying again.

'Don't take me for a fool, Oswald!'

I stood up to leave. 'I think you should return to Versey after a meal, Clemence.'

'What?'

'This is my house. And I don't care to be spoken to in such a manner.'

'This is not your house.'

'Yes it is!' I opened the door to show her out. 'This is Somershill. And I am Lord Somershill. So you will not speak to me again in that tone.'

'But—'

'You have Versey, Clemence. And your son will have Versey. I made that promise to you. So, let me tell you this. I don't care who Henry's father is.' I ushered her to the door. 'Come on. Time to take a rest, I think. Your temper needs sweetening.'

She pushed me away. 'Close the door, Oswald.'

'No.'

She sighed. 'Please, Oswald. I apologise. I didn't come here to argue with you.'

'Then what is your purpose?'

'I wanted to talk to you about Humbert.'

'As I just said, Clemence, I don't care if Humbert is Henry's father. That is entirely your own business.'

She shut the door herself, and looked about the room to make sure we were completely alone. 'Please listen to me, Oswald. This is your business. It's important to both of us.' I had rarely seen Clemence so animated.

My interest was piqued.

'Henry does look like Humbert,' she whispered. 'That can't be denied. But there is a good reason for it.'

'What reason is that?'

She remained silent.

'Is he the child's father?'

She shook her head. 'No.'

'Then the similarity is a coincidence.'

She shook her head again. 'No. It's not.' She hesitated. 'They are related.'

I frowned. 'What?'

'Please come away from the door, and I'll tell you. We must talk quietly.'

We sat together on the bench by the window that Mother used to insist we both squeezed onto as children. For the most part Clemence had appeared to hate me in those days. But sometimes, when my older brothers, William and Richard, had pinched my ear or stolen my shoes, she would secretly donate me a sugarplum to make amends. If they had locked me in the cellar, then Clemence was the one to let me out. If they beat me, she was the one to chase them away. But I was never allowed to be her friend, no matter how often I tried to slip my hand into hers. I was not even allowed to thank her with a kiss, for risk of receiving an even harder pinch than my brothers had dispensed.

'I questioned Peter about Thomas Starvecrow's coffin. When I had him imprisoned in the dungeon,' she told me. 'The child was not dead after all.'

'I know. Peter gave the infant to a travelling knife grinder,' I said.

Clemence seemed surprised by this. 'So you asked him as well?'

'You imprisoned us both in a cell. Remember? Of course I asked him.'

'Did he tell you the name of the knife grinder?'

'No. He said he couldn't remember.'

'And you believed him?' Her eyes darted about my face.

'I had other matters on my mind, Clemence. Henry had just been taken. Your manservant had just assaulted me with a rock.'

She waved this point away. 'I made Peter give me a name.'

'You tortured him?'

She touched her hand to mine, and didn't answer this accusation. 'I found the knife grinder, Oswald. Only last week. Nineteen years later.'

'And the boy? What happened to him?'

'He was dumped back at Somershill when he was seven years old. Left in the hay barn, because they considered him stupid and too expensive to feed.'

I took a deep breath. 'Humbert.'

'Yes. The true Oswald de Lacy. The true Lord Somershill.'

'And he is Henry's uncle. A blood relative.'

She nodded. 'Which explains their resemblance.'

'Does Humbert know any of this?'

She shook her head. 'No.'

I saw my whole world dissolving onto the floor, like a doom painting being washed from the lime plaster of the church. 'We should tell him, Clemence. Perhaps he already suspects?'

Now she laughed at me. 'Of course he doesn't.'

'But he's not as simple as they say.' I thought back to the day when I had overheard the boy's lullaby.

'Humbert is kind. He is brave. But he couldn't be Lord Somershill. You know that.'

'Do I?'

She squeezed my hand. 'I haven't always treated you kindly, have I?'

This show of affection was making me suspicious. 'No.'

'Listen to me, Oswald. You are more of a brother to me than Richard and William ever were.'

I couldn't help but frown. 'Do you mean that?'

She squeezed my hand again. 'In these last months you have saved my life. You then saved the life of my child. I've seen true nobility in you, brother.' Now she whispered into my ear. 'It is not blood that makes a lord. Oswald. It is heart.'

We sat in silence and listened to Humbert's sweet singing from the garden.

Historical Note

In the late 1340s the pandemic, now known as the Black Death, swept westwards across Europe from the Mongolian Steppes – reaching the south coast of England in 1348. For the next two years this plague killed an estimated half of the population, causing fear, panic and despair as it spread across the country. In those years the Plague was seen as a retribution from God. A punishment for sinners. People understood it was contagious, but had no idea about the link between the disease and the rat population. This link was only properly understood in the late nineteenth century, when the bacillus yersinia pestis was identified – a bacteria carried in the digestory tract of infected rat fleas.

In the years of the Black Death the Plague took two main forms: the Bubonic Plague, which infects the lymphatic system of the victim via a flea bite, causing boil-like buboes to form in the groin and armpits; and the Pneumonic Plague, when the bacillus enters the body via the respiratory system. It is now believed that it was the Pneumonic Plague, rather than the Bubonic Plague, that was responsible for such a high mortality rate. The pneumonic form was easily spread, rather like flu, via coughing and close contact. It progressed quickly through a population that lived in cramped conditions and didn't properly understand sanitation. The pneumonic form of the Plague was always fatal.

The effect on society of losing one half of the population was immense. After the many months of misery and despair, the survivors of this nightmare found the world to be a different place. Particularly the poorest people in society – the families living in the rural estates and farms of England.

England had been ruled by Norman-style feudalism since the invasion of 1066. The land was divided into estates or manors, which were owned ultimately by the Crown or by the Church; but which, at a practical level, were controlled by a lord or a monastery.

There were two types of labourers in these manors – the free and the unfree. The 'unfree' or 'villeins' were bound to the estate and had many aspects of their lives controlled – such as who they could marry and where they could live. They rented land in return for providing labour in the lord's fields. The 'free' were tenants on the estate. They also rented land from the lord, but didn't suffer the same restrictions on their movement and conduct. These tenants were often expected to work in the lord's fields as part of their tenancy agreement – but they were paid for their work. I should say the above is a rather simplistic explanation of feudalism – it was a complex and varied arrangement. For example there were tenants who provided labour for free as part of their tenancy, and a villein might be paid for his or her labour, at the lord's discretion. But, broadly speaking, this definition held true.

The Black Death put a great fist into the face of feudalism, however. The lords of England were suddenly, and very chronically, short of labour. In some rural communities, as the population was reduced by nearly seventy per cent, there simply were not enough men and women left to work the land, and slowly the labour market became subject to supply and demand, in a way it had never previously been. Put plainly, workers were able to demand higher wages.

The Plague had provided the lowest classes of people with a

new advantage. It gave them a new confidence, a new voice. Not only were they demanding to be paid more, they were also asking for freedom from villeinage. Left with fields that needed harvesting, and livestock that needed tending – the lords and abbots of England were suddenly forced to acquiesce to these demands or risk losing their workforce to a nearby lord who would.

This new boldness amongst the lower orders led to concerns at the highest levels in society. The villeins and tenants no longer appeared to accept their place in the world. It should be said here that the medieval mindset split people into three distinct groups – those who fought, those who prayed and those who worked. But suddenly those who 'worked' were no longer happy to do as they were told. They were causing trouble. Some were disobedient, some were agitators. It was soon clear that something had to be done . . .

In the summer of 1349, the King, Edward III, wrote to the Sheriff of Kent. His letter formed the 'Ordinance of Labourers', instructing the Sheriff of Kent to ensure that agricultural workers were not to be paid any higher daily rates than they had received before the Plague in 1346. This ruling was endorsed by Parliament in 1351, to form the Statute of Labourers. It will come as no surprise that this law was highly unpopular with the peasants of England. They resisted it vigorously, and eventually the Statute proved ineffectual. Despite the best efforts of the nobility, the Statute was difficult to police – the balance of power ultimately lay with the workers.

Not everybody was a winner in these post-Plague years, however. True enough, many survivors inherited property and goods they had never dreamt of possessing. And for those whose status was 'free', it was possible to find better paid work outside of your estate of birth. It was also, briefly, a time of opportunity for women, as they were now able to take over tenancies from the dead males of their family, and manage their own affairs in a way that had previously been denied them. On the other hand, those villeins who remained 'unfree' were not always able to capitalise on these new opportunities. The harvests of 1350 and 1351 were very poor, due to bad weather conditions, resulting in very high food prices, particularly for grain. For these people, the very poorest in society, the post-Plague years were often difficult and sometimes ruinous.

Glossary

Banalities

All wheat on the estate was required to be ground at the lord's mill. The banality was the fee, paid to the lord, for use of this mill, and usually took the form of a percentage of the wheat ground.

Braies

The medieval version of underpants for men. A loose under-garment – usually made from a length of linen that was wound about the legs and bottom and then tied at the waist with a belt.

Constable

The constable reported crimes to the bailiff at the Hundreds Court.

Cottar

The poorest class of villein. A person with very little land, usually only the curtilage of their own cottage.

Custumnal / Custumal

A document that outlined the customary agreements and arrange-ments between a lord and his villeins and tenants. It might include duties that were required about the estate, such as the cutting of hedges; and duties that were required on the lord's demesne fields, such as number of days labour expected at harvest.

Dais

A raised platform at the end of the dining hall/great hall. Usually furnished with a table and benches, it was reserved for people of high status within the household.

Demesne

The fields on the manor estate that were reserved for the lord's personal use and profit. Local villeins would work this land in return for the ability to rent their own plots. Tenants were often expected to work in the demesne, although they received wages for their labour.

Hue and Cry

If a dead body was found under suspicious or unnatural circumstances, every man in the village was required to join a noisy search party to alert the local neighbourhood to the murder, and to flush out the culprit.

Humours

Harking back to the teachings of Galen in antiquity, the human body was said to be ruled by four humours, or bodily fluids, which needed to be kept in balance. Yellow bile, phlegm, black bile, and blood. The balance of your humours ruled both your health and your disposition. So, for example, an excess of black bile caused a person to become melancholic.

Hundreds Court
A court that dealt with serious crime, or cases that could not be tried by the manorial court. This court was presided over by the sheriff, unless the case involved murder – in which instance a royal judge was summoned.

Infirmarer
The infirmarer managed the infirmary at the monastery, where the sick and elderly of the community were cared for. The position was a prestigious post, and the infirmarer was usually trained in basic surgery and medicine.

Indulgences
Taking the form of a letter or receipt, an indulgence was an award for the remission of sin. It was earned by prayer and good deeds, but increasingly in the later Middle Ages through a money donation.

Kirtle
A tunic-like garment, usually made of wool.

Lay Brother / Lay Monk
A monk of lesser status than the ordained members of the monastery. The lay brothers undertook much of the heavy agricultural and domestic work for the community.

Manorial court
This court was overseen by the lord of the manor. It usually dealt only with minor issues restricted to the manor itself, such as disagreements between tenants, or infringements of the lord's rights.

Pottage
A type of soup often made with dried peas, grains, and sometimes meat or fish.

Purlieu
A deforested area on the edge of hunting forests, still subject to forest law – especially with respect to hunting.

Reeve
An officer of the estate, responsible to the lord for organising and overseeing agricultural work on the demesne fields. A position of status within the community.

Royal Judge
Royal judges, from the court of the king's bench, were responsible for justice with regards to serious criminal cases. Travelling to each county approximately twice a year, they tried the criminal cases, which had been referred to them by the sheriff.

Scullion
A servant employed to perform the most menial tasks, such as cleaning the spits or building the fires.

Sheriff
The position held the ultimate responsibility to the king for law and order in a shire. Literally the 'shire reeve', he had the power to arrest, imprison, hold trials, and organise juries, but not the power to try and sentence a suspect for a murder.

Solar

A room set apart from the rest of the household for use of the lord's family. This room usually had a large window, giving rise to the idea that it was named after the sun. However, the word may also have derived from the French word 'seul', which means to be alone.

Surcoat

A tunic or outer coat.

Tenant

A person who rented farmland from a lord, but who received payment for working on the demesne. The status of the tenant was as a free man, meaning he and his family could leave the estate without the permission of the lord.

Villein

Villeins worked the lord's lands, but were not usually waged. Typically they worked for three days a week, with extra services required at certain times of the year such as at harvest. In return for their labour they were able to rent land from the lord. Their status was unfree, meaning the lord had a great deal of control over their lives.

Virgate

A unit of land, roughly thirty acres in size.

Yeoman

A richer tenant farmer, who had the means to rent larger areas of land, and could afford to employ both servants and farmhands. They often acted as officers for the manor, such as the reeve or

constable, giving their family greater status. Often more prosperous than the lord himself, in the wake of the Black Death they
were known to take over the management of whole estates in
return for paying fixed rent.

Acknowledgements

This novel has been the stereotypical 'difficult' second book – so I would like to thank the following people for helping me to navigate through to the finish.

Firstly my wonderful editor Nick Sayers, for his wisdom, patience and insight. To my assistant editor Laura Macdougall, for her boundless energy, support and guidance. Of course my agent Gordon Wise, for his enduring belief in my writing, and to my friends at Curtis Brown Creative. If I hadn't attended their novel-writing course in 2012, then I wouldn't now have two published novels.

My biggest debt of gratitude, however, goes to my family and in particular my husband Paul. At the book launch of my first novel *Plague Land*, I described him as the patron saint of writers' partners. He continues to prove himself worthy of this accolade. He is endlessly supportive, he is my first trusted reader and he is amazingly tolerant of my strange work patterns. Thank you Paul.